# A Passion
# Denied

**Other books by Julie Lessman**

The Daughters of Boston series
*A Passion Most Pure*
*A Passion Redeemed*

THE DAUGHTERS *of* BOSTON · 3

# A PASSION DENIED

## JULIE LESSMAN

## Revell

a division of Baker Publishing Group
Grand Rapids, Michigan

Published by Revell
a division of Baker Publishing Group
P.O. Box 6287, Grand Rapids, MI 49516-6287
www.revellbooks.com

Printed in the United States of America

Library of Congress Cataloging-in-Publication Data
Lessman, Julie, 1950–
    A passion denied / Julie Lessman.
        p.    cm. — (The daughters of Boston ; bk. 3)
    ISBN 978-0-8007-3213-4 (pbk.)
    1. Irish American families—Fiction. 2. Sisters—Fiction. E. Boston (Mass.)—
Fiction. 4. United States—History—1913–1921—Fiction. I. Title.
PS3612.E8189P36  2009
813′.6—dc22                                                                2009000246

Scripture is taken from the following versions:

The King James Version of the Bible.

The *Holy Bible*, New Living Translation, copyright © 1996. Used by permission of Tyndale House Publishers, Inc., Wheaton, Illinois 60189. All rights reserved.

To the love of my life, Keith Lessman—
the true definition of God doing
"exceedingly abundantly" more than I think,
hope, or pray—
every day with you is better than the last.

O Lord my God, how great you are!
You are robed with honor and with majesty . . .
You make the clouds your chariot; you ride upon the
    wings of the wind.
The winds are your messengers; flames of fire are your
    servants.

Psalm 104:1–4 NLT

# 1

BOSTON, MASSACHUSETTS, SPRING 1922

*Oh, to be a calculating woman!* Elizabeth O'Connor sighed. She dodged her way down the bustling sidewalk of Boston's thriving business district, wishing she were more like her sister, Charity. She chewed on her lip. Regrettably, she wasn't—a definite character flaw at the moment. And one that would have to change.

She sidestepped a rickety wood wagon heaped high with the *Boston Herald*, hot off the presses. The freckle-faced boy hauling it muttered an apology before disappearing into a sea of pin-striped suits, short skirts, and bobbed hair. On his heels, a young mother ambled along, cooing to a wide-eyed baby in a stroller. The baby's soft chuckle floated by, and the sound buoyed Elizabeth's spirits. Spring in the city! Despite the whiff of gasoline and tobacco drifting in the unseasonably warm breeze, she sensed that the promise of love was in the air. Her heart fluttered. And maybe, just maybe, a little spring fever would do the trick!

She pressed her nose to the window of McGuire & Brady Printing Company and peered inside. John Morrison Brady was bent over a press with a screwdriver in his hand, his lean, muscled body poised for battle. Her chin hardened, and her smile faded. That man suffered from a terminal illness that would be the death of their relationship: *friendship*. Elizabeth straightened her shoulders. And the worst kind of friendship at that—the big-brother kind.

She touched a hand to the wavy shingle haircut her friend Millie had talked her into. "It's all the rage, Lizzzzzie Lou," Millie had insisted, the sound of Lizzie's name buzzing on her tongue in Millie's typical busy-bee manner. A self-proclaimed modern woman, Millie had convinced Elizabeth "Beth" O'Connor to change her name to Lizzie over a year ago—to add excitement to her life, she'd said. And now, in the throes of radical 1920s fashion, Lizzie's best friend had also convinced her that the chestnut tresses trailing her back simply had to go. The result was a short, fashionable bob, newly shorn just yesterday. Softly waved, it fell to just below her ear, showing off her heart-shaped face and slender neck to good advantage. Or so Millie had said. She squinted at her reflection in the window. She did look older, more sophisticated, she supposed. And it certainly seemed as if she had turned a few more heads at the bookstore where she worked. She took a deep breath and opened the door, spurred on by the tinkling bell overhead. *Now to turn the right one . . .*

Her brother-in-law, Collin, looked up from his desk where he tallied invoices for printing jobs just completed. A slow grin spread across his handsome face before he let out a low whistle, causing a pleasant wash of heat to seep into her cheeks. "Sweet saints above, Lizzie, is that really you? What are you trying to do? Break a few hearts?"

Her gaze flicked to the back room where Brady lay on a flat wooden dolly beneath their Bullock web-fed press. She studied his long legs sprawled and splattered with ink, then looked back at Collin with a shaky smile. "Nope, only one. But I suspect it's forged in steel."

Collin chuckled and glanced over his shoulder, stretching muscular arms overhead. "Yep, I'd say so, but I admire your tenacity. You might say you're the little sister he never had. But I suspect that pretty new hairdo and stylish outfit could go a long way in changing his mind."

She grinned and planted a kiss on his cheek. "Thanks, Collin. One can only hope." She tugged on her lavender, low-waisted dress, then smoothed out its scalloped layers with sweaty palms. "And pray, I suppose, since it is Brady we're dealing with here."

Collin stood and draped an arm around her shoulders. He lowered his voice and gave her a squeeze. "He'll wake up one of these days, Lizzie. I just hope it's not too late. You're too pretty to be waiting around. And he's a slow one, you know."

She sighed and leaned against him, staring at Brady with longing in her eyes. "Now there's a news flash for you."

Collin laughed and gave her a gentle prod toward the back room. "Show him no mercy, Lizzie."

She nodded and made her way to the rear of the shop, her pulse tripping faster than the tap-tap-tapping of Brady's trusty screwdriver. She stopped at the foot of the press and sucked in a deep swallow of air. "I have a notion, John Brady, that whenever you want to get away from the world, you disappear under that silly machine."

A deep-throated chuckle floated up between the rotors of the press. He rolled out, flat on his back. The smile froze on his face. "Beth? What'd ya do to your hair?"

Heat flooded her cheeks. "I had it bobbed. Do you like it?"

He sat up and rubbed his jaw with the side of his hand, screwdriver angled as if he were playing a violin. "Yeah . . . it's pretty, I guess. In a newfangled sort of way."

She twirled around to give him the full effect, her smile brimming with hope. "Well, I am a modern woman, in case you haven't noticed."

He lumbered to his feet. His tall frame unfolded to eliminate everything else in her view. He squinted and scrunched his nose, causing smudges of ink to wrinkle across his tanned cheek. "Mmmm . . . makes you look old."

"I *am* old, Brady, a fact you refuse to acknowledge. Almost eighteen, remember?"

He chuckled. "Seventeen, Beth, and I'll give you the half."

He turned and ambled to the sink to wash his hands. His husky laugh lingered in the air. She stared at the work shirt spanning his back and barely noticed the ink stains for the broad shoulders and hard muscles cording his arms.

He dried his hands on a towel and turned to lean against the counter. The corners of his mouth flickered as if a grin wanted to break free. "You'll always be a little girl to me, little buddy, especially with your wide eyes and those roses in your cheeks. I suspect I'll feel that way when you're long gone and married, with a houseful of little girls all your own. That's just the way it is with big brothers."

She notched her powdered chin in the air. "You're not my brother, John Brady, and no amount of touting will make it so." She propped hands to her waist and gave him a ruby red pout. "And I'm not a little girl. I'm a woman . . . with feelings—"

"Beth, we've been over this before." He slacked a hip and ran a calloused hand over his face. His brown eyes softened with compassion. "I see you as my little sister, nothing more. These 'feelings' you think you have for me—"

"*Know* I have for you! I know it, even if you don't." Her chest rose and fell with indignation.

He groaned. "All right, these feelings you *know* you have for me . . . I've known you since you were thirteen, Elizabeth, and I've been a mentor in your faith since fourteen. It's natural for you to think you have feelings—"

She stomped her foot. "Know, Brady, I know! And if you weren't so socially inept and totally blind—"

He rose to his full six-foot-three height, making her five foot seven seem almost petite. The chiseled line of his jaw hardened with the motion. "Come on, Beth, totally blind?"

His gaze flicked into the next room as if he were worried Collin was listening.

Tears threatened and she wanted to bolt, but she fought it off. This was too important. Fueled by frustration long dormant, she slapped her leather clutch onto the table and strode forward. She jabbed a finger into his hard-muscled chest. "Yes, blind, you baboon! And don't be looking to see what Collin thinks, because he knows it too. Honestly, Brady, as far as the Bible, you're head and shoulders above anyone I know. But when it comes to seeing what God may have for you right in front of your ink-stained nose, you don't have a clue." She dropped a trembling hand to her quivering stomach. *Oh my, where had that come from?*

He stood, mouth gaping. A spray of red mottled his neck. "Beth, what's gotten into you?"

She faltered back, shocked at the thoughts and feelings whirling in her brain. With a rush of adrenaline, she crossed her arms and stared him down, energized by her newfound anger. "You've gotten into me, John Brady, and I want to know straight out why you refuse to acknowledge me as a woman? Am I not pretty enough? Smart enough? Mature enough?"

The ruddiness in his neck traveled to his ears. He took a commanding stride toward her and latched a hand on her arm. With a firm grip, he pushed her into a chair at the table and squatted beside her. "Beth, stop this! I'm close to thirty, which is way too old for you. You're young and beautiful and smart, and more mature than most girls . . . women . . . I've met. You're going to make some lucky man a wonderful wife."

She stared at his handsome face, the contrast of gentle eyes and hard-sculpted features making her heart bleed. Wisps of cinnamon-colored hair curled up at the back of his neck, softening the hard line of his jaw, which was already shadowed by afternoon growth. She swallowed hard, the taste of dread pasty in her throat. "Just not you," she whispered.

A muscle flinched in his cheek. He smothered her hands

between his large, calloused ones. "I love you, you know that—"

She looked away, unable to bear the empathy in his eyes. "But you're not attracted to me—"

As soft as a child's kiss, he lifted her chin with his finger, urging her eyes to his. "Of course I'm attracted to you—your gentle spirit, your thirst for God, your innocence—it draws me to want to protect you and care for you—as a friend and a brother."

*Brother*. The sound of that hateful word stiffened her spine. She jerked her hand free and angled her chin. "But not as a woman, is that it? Someone you can take in your arms and kiss and make love to?"

Blood gorged his cheeks as he stood up. A rare hint of anger sparked in his eyes, and satisfaction flooded her soul. So he wasn't pure stone. Good! At least she could arouse his temper, if nothing else.

"So help me, if you spent a fraction of the time reading the Bible as you do those silly romance novels, we wouldn't be having this problem."

She jumped up with tears stinging her eyes. "And if you took your nose out of your Bible long enough to see that God has a plan for your life other than smearing yourself with ink, you might see that you *are* the problem." With a gasping sob, she snatched her purse from the table and rammed it hard against his chest, pushing him out of the way. She turned toward the door.

He stumbled back, then grabbed her arm. "Beth, wait! We need to pray about this . . ."

She flung his hand away. Humiliation and anger broiled her cheeks. "No, you pray about it. It seems to be the only thing you know how to do. And while you're at it, pray that he heals that stupid streak inside of you . . . and in me, too, for loving you like I do." She bolted for the door, ignoring Collin's gaping stare.

"Beth—" Pain echoed in Brady's voice.

She whirled around, hand fisted on the knob. "And one more prayer, Brady, if you don't mind. Pray that I hate you, will you? Shouldn't be too hard, I don't think. You make it so easy."

The door slammed closed, rattling the glass.

Brady blinked at Collin. "What just happened?"

Collin let out a low whistle and arched a brow. "Don't look now, ol' buddy, but I think you're back in the Great War. What'd ya say to set her off like that? I've never seen Lizzie lose her temper before."

Brady exhaled and dropped into his desk chair. He mauled his face with his hand. "Beth. Her name is Beth, Collin, and I didn't say anything I haven't said before."

"She's been Lizzie for over a year. It's what her friends call her and her family most of the time. You're the only holdout—in more ways than one."

Brady glanced up, his eyes burning with fatigue. "And what's that supposed to mean?"

"It means she's not thirteen anymore, she's a grown woman. You're the only one who still treats her like a kid."

"Don't start with this, please," Brady groaned. "I'm way too tired."

Collin sighed and shuffled to the rack over the door to snatch his keys. "So is Lizzie. Tired of being in love with someone who treats her like a little sister. She wants more. How long are you going to ignore it?"

Brady dropped his head in his hand to shield his eyes. "I haven't ignored it. I've been praying it would go away."

"Burying your head in the sand—or in your prayers—won't work, ol' buddy. You taught me that."

The truth congealed in Brady's stomach along with the cold oatmeal he'd eaten for lunch. "I know," he whispered.

Collin stared for a moment, then wandered over to Brady's desk. He sat down on an old proof sheet and crossed his arms.

"Look, I've tried not to butt in where Lizzie is concerned, but it's kind of hard right now. And to be honest with you, I'm worried."

"You don't need to worry about Beth."

Collin sighed and rubbed the back of his neck. "It's not Beth I'm talking about."

"Well, don't worry about me, either, because first thing Monday, I'm going to sit her down and explain once and for all why we can't be more than friends."

Collin's gaze narrowed. "And why is that, exactly? Because you're not attracted to her?"

Heat blistered Brady's cheeks.

Collin stared, then broke into a grin. "You are, aren't you?"

"Knock it off, Collin."

Collin chuckled. "No, Brady, I won't 'knock it off.' Everybody in this family knows how Lizzie feels about you, but nobody really knows how you feel about her. Until now."

Brady jumped up and headed to the back room, heat stinging his neck. "I'm going home."

"You're in love with my sister-in-law, aren't you?" Collin hopped up and followed. "Why don't you just admit it?"

Brady spun around. "I love Beth, but not in that way."

Collin hesitated and his smile faded. He cocked his head. "I know you won't lie, so I'm asking you one more time. Are you attracted to Lizzie?"

"I don't have to answer that."

"No, but I'm asking as a friend—to both you and Lizzie. Are you?"

Brady stared, his heart pounding in his chest like the rotors of the Bullock pounding behind them. His voice was barely a whisper. "Yes."

"I knew it! That's great news. So, what's the problem?"

"Because I can't love her that way."

Collin frowned. "Why not? I don't understand. You're a man and she's a woman—"

"No!" Brady shocked himself with the vehemence in his tone. "She's like a sister to me. I could never—*would never*—think of Beth that way."

Collin blinked. "Calm down, ol' buddy. Lizzie is not your sister no matter how much you see it that way. I can't help but think there's more to this, John, something you're not telling me. What is it? Why are you holding back?"

Nausea curdled in Brady's stomach. He fought back a shudder. "Nothing, Collin. Nothing I care to go into."

Collin stared long and hard. He finally sighed and jingled the keys in his pocket. "Okay, I'll leave it be. For now. But I can't leave Lizzie be. She's in love with you, my friend, and if you don't intend to return that love, then you better do something about it. Now."

Brady braced a hand against the doorframe while fear added to the mix in his gut. "I know."

"That means cutting her loose. No more Bible study or private prayer time or lunchtime chats. Every minute you spend with that girl is only leading her on."

Brady closed his eyes. "Yeah."

Collin gripped an arm around Brady's shoulder. "I love you, John. You're the brother I never had and the best friend I've ever known. It tears me up when I think you're not happy. I know how much Lizzie means to you. And I'm here, if you need me."

"I know. I appreciate that."

Collin cuffed him on the shoulder and headed for the door. "See you tomorrow."

Brady looked up. "Collin?"

"Yeah?"

"Don't tell Faith . . . or anyone . . . how I feel about Beth, okay?"

Collin stared, his lips poised as if to argue. He released a weighty sigh. "Okay, old buddy, not a word. Have a good night."

Brady nodded, then swallowed hard. *Yeah, as if that's possible.*

❦ ❦

Strangers were gawking, but she didn't care. She bolted down the crowded sidewalk like a madwoman, tears streaming her cheeks and her chest heaving with hurt. Curious gazes followed as she tore down Henry Street where the farmer's market was in full sway. Patrons swarmed wooden stands heaped high with oranges and lemons freshly plucked and shipped from Florida groves. Stern-eyed ladies rifled through leaf lettuce while apron-clad vendors hovered and hawked their wares. Lizzie ignored them all, racing past and almost tumbling as she hurdled a crate of potatoes in her path.

"Miss, are you okay . . ."

Lizzie heard the concern in the shopkeeper's voice, but she dared not acknowledge his kindness. It would surely unleash the broken sob that lodged in her throat. Right now all she wanted to do was to crawl into a dark corner of St. Stephen's Church and cry. She sniffed. That and spit into John Brady's eye.

She flew up the church's marble steps and tugged at the heavy oak doors. The hallowed darkness inside strained her eyes as she adjusted to its dim light. She scanned the pews to make sure she was alone. With a shuddering heave, she made her way to the right alcove at the front and sank into her favorite row in the back corner. She set her clutch purse aside and lay down on her back, stretched out like she used to when she was a child, in search of her own little world where she could read and dream and pray. Recess in grade school had always been filled with giggles and games of Red Rover and girls flirting with boys who didn't know they existed. But at times, when the pull of a favorite book or a longing for romance would strike, she would steal away, unbeknownst to the nuns. It was here, in this shadowed church, lit only by the soft glow of flickering candles and sunlight shafting through stained-glass windows, that she would finally connect with God.

She'd lie on the polished wood bench and look up, squinting to imagine that Jesus was lying down too, on a bench in the balcony across the way, ready to chat. At times, she could almost see his white gown through the marble balustrade as he listened to her. She always felt close to him there, amidst the lingering scent of incense and lemon oil. As if they were best friends. And they were. Their brief encounters always filled her with peace, often providing a much-needed balm to her young soul.

With a weary sigh, she closed her eyes and allowed her thoughts to stray to Brady as they so often did. In her frequent daydreams, she found herself comparing him to heroes she idolized in favorite books. Her lips curved into a sad smile. Without question, John Brady was her Mr. Darcy, possessing all the exasperating prejudice of Jane Austen's hero in *Pride & Prejudice*. At least he was when it came to her, she thought with a twist of her lips. Too blinded by his own stubborn perceptions to see what everyone else so clearly saw—that his "little buddy" was destined to be his very own "Lizzie."

She stared now, lost in a faraway look that blurred the flame of the sanctuary light as it glittered in its scarlet holder. "Why, God? Why can't he love me? I know he cares—I can see it in his eyes and feel it in his touch. And I love him too—you know I do. But he gives me nothing."

She peeked up at the balcony. "He's a man after your own heart, God, which has me wondering if you're as stubborn as he. I surely hope so, because I'm going to need help in matching wits with him. And if you don't mind my saying so, when it comes to stubborn, this man is one of your finest creations. But if we belong together—loving each other while loving you—then you've got to open his eyes to the truth. And if I've missed it all these years and not heard your still, quiet voice, then please, *please*, set me free from his hold."

She closed her eyes and settled in once again, her focus intent on the prayer at hand. All at once the heavy oak door squealed open, emitting a shaft of light that filtered in from the vestibule. The sound of hurried footsteps echoed through the cavernous building and then stopped. A broken sob pierced the darkness. Lizzie's eyes popped open and she stiffened in the pew. *What in the world?*

Pitiful heaves rose to the rafters as Lizzie sat up and scanned the dark church. Nothing . . . except the painful sound of someone's grief. With a tightening in her chest, she rose and followed the sound of the weeping. Her eyes widened as she discovered its source in the very last pew. "Ellie? Is that you? Oh, honey, what's wrong?"

A sprite of a girl lay collapsed in the pew, her ragged overalls torn and tattered. Wisps of carrot-red hair escaped from stubby braids, lending a halo effect that reminded Lizzie of a fuzzy spider monkey. Her slight shoulders shuddered with every heartbreaking heave, but at the sound of Lizzie's voice, she jolted upright. She blinked in shock, enormous hazel eyes glossy with tears.

"Lizzie! I-I thought I was a-alone." She sniffed and swiped at her nose with the sleeve of her blouse. With a lift of her chin, she squinted up, forcing a million tiny freckles to scrunch in a frown. "And nothing's wrong."

Lizzie folded her arms and arched a brow. "It's a sin to lie, Eleanor Walsh, and well you know it. And in a church, no less."

The faintest hint of a smile flickered at the edges of the girl's mouth. "So I'll duck in the confessional on the way out. Betcha God will barely notice."

"He notices everything, Ellie, especially when one of his favorite little girls is making such a ruckus in his house." Lizzie nudged her over and sat down. "What's wrong?"

"Aw, Lizzie, you wouldn't understand."

"Mmm . . . maybe. Maybe not. But you won't know till you tell me, now will you?"

Ellie glanced up, her face skewed in thought. She took a deep breath and settled back against the pew, expelling a long, heavy sigh. "I beat up Brian Kincaid."

Lizzie leaned forward in shock. "What? That big, hulking boy from the seventh grade? Sweet Mother of Job, how? *Why?*"

"Because he's a snot-nosed bully, that's why. So I walloped him."

"Good heavens, Ellie, he's a foot taller than you!"

A grin parted the nine-year-old's lips, revealing a flash of teeth. "Not anymore. I thrashed him down to size just like I do my brothers when they fire me up. That'll teach him to call me names."

Lizzie bit back a smile. "What kind of names?"

She jutted her lip and folded her arms, squinting hard at the pew in front of her. "Calls me an 'it.' Says I'm not a girl." She looked away, but not before Lizzie caught the quiver of her chin. "A 'freak of nature'." Her voice wavered the slightest bit before it hardened. "'Ellie Smellie, the circus sideshow.'"

Hot wetness sprang to Lizzie's eyes and fury burned in her throat. She grabbed Ellie in a ferocious hug. "Bald-faced lies, all of it! You're a beautiful girl, Eleanor Walsh. And Brian Kincaid is nothing but a bully who is appropriately named—Lyin' Brian."

Ellie pulled away, clearly avoiding Lizzie's eyes for the tears in her own. She sniffed several times. "No, Lizzie, he's right. I'll never be a girl—at least not a pretty one like you." Her small frame shivered as she looked away. "Ain't nobody to teach me since Ma up and died—" Her voice cracked before she continued. "And even if there was, Pop barely makes enough to feed me and the boys. He sure can't buy me no fancy dresses."

Lizzie's heart squeezed in her chest as she studied the frail little girl whose mother died three years prior, giving birth to her fifth son. Since then, Ellie had become one of the Southie neighborhood's scrappiest tomboys, weathering her fair share of cruel teasing and fights. Lizzie chewed on her lip in deep thought. "Ellie, my sister Katie is a few years older than you, and I'll just bet we can come up with some clothes that don't fit her anymore if you don't mind hand-me-downs."

Ellie flicked the strap of her threadbare overalls. "Mind hand-me-downs? Gosh, Lizzie, I'd be naked as a jaybird if it wasn't for my older brothers." Her jaw leveled up a full inch. "But I don't aim to take no charity."

"No, not charity. I was thinking more along the lines of earning it. Do you like to read?"

"Nope. Got no money for books either."

Lizzie smiled. "You don't need money for these books. I'm talking about helping me—at Bookends, the bookstore where I work. You know, story time on Saturdays?"

One pale strawberry brow angled high. "Ain't that for kids?"

"Yes, but I could use your help with setting up and cleaning up." Lizzie's eyes narrowed as she gave Ellie a tight-lipped smile. "And there are one or two little troublemakers who I bet you could keep in line with a withering glance."

A grin sprouted on Ellie's face. "Boys, I hope—they're my specialty. With a houseful of brothers, I'm real good with boy troublemakers."

Lizzie stood to her feet with a chuckle. "Are there any other kind?"

"Nope. Least not for me." She squinted up. "I'll bet you never have trouble with boys, do ya, Lizzie, pretty as you are?"

Brady's handsome face invaded her thoughts. Her jaw stiffened. "Don't be too sure, Ellie. Boys can be troublemakers at any age, trust me."

Ellie rose to her feet and shoved her hands deep in her pockets. "Yeah, especially brothers." She gave Lizzie a curious look. "You got a brother that gives you trouble, Lizzie?"

Brother. The very word grated on Lizzie's nerves. She wrapped an arm around Ellie's shoulder. "Yeah, I do, Ellie, but

I have every intention of taking care of it. Just like I'm going to teach you to take care of bullies like Brian Kincaid."

Ellie looked up. "How?"

"Well, for starters, if you'll work story time with me for the next four Saturdays, I will pay you back by taking you home to try on all of Katie's hand-me-downs. And then, if you want, I can cut your hair and show you how to fix it. What do you say?"

"Gosh, Lizzie, that would be swell!" She paused, her smile suddenly fading.

Lizzie's brows dipped. "What?"

"Well, what if it doesn't work? I mean, what if everybody still thinks I'm an 'it'?"

"They won't, trust me."

A glimmer of wetness shone in Ellie's eyes. "But what if I'm too much like a boy to ever learn to be a girl?"

Lizzie bent and gently cupped Ellie's face in her hands. "You'll learn, Ellie, because this is too important. And when something is that important, you do whatever it takes."

A smile trembled on Ellie's lips as she threw her arms around Lizzie's waist. "Gosh, Lizzie, you sound just like my momma before she—" She pulled away and straightened her shoulders, then swiped her eyes with the back of her hand. "I gotta go, but I'll see you on Saturday, okay?"

Lizzie blinked to clear the moisture from her own eyes. "Saturday, ten o'clock. Don't be late or I'll send Lyin' Brian to hunt you down."

Ellie nodded and grinned before bolting out the door, once again leaving the sanctuary in a state of peaceful calm. With a heavy sigh, Lizzie made her way back to her pew and lay down. With no effort at all, her thoughts returned to Brady.

*Whatever it takes.*

At the thought of her advice to Ellie, a smiled flitted on her lips. She lay there awhile longer to drink in the peace and the strength of God's house, and then sat up and squared her shoulders, finally rising to her feet. She smoothed out her skirt and lifted her chin. Resolve kindled in her bones. An air of stubbornness settled in, shivering her spine like the cool air currents that whistled through the domed ceiling of the drafty church. "Okay, God, I plan to take my own advice and do whatever it takes. Mr. John Brady is no longer dealing with 'his little sister.' He's dealing with a woman in love." Lizzie plucked her clutch purse from the pew and marched to the door with renewed purpose. "It's said that 'hell hath no fury like a woman scorned,'" she mused. "Ha!" Her lips clamped into a tight line. "Just wait till he sees a woman ignored."

Brady buried his fists in his pockets and hung his head, barreling toward his apartment on Rumpole Street with one driving purpose: to be alone. His thoughts couldn't be farther away from the pretty spring evening in his bustling Southie neighborhood than if he were safely locked behind his apartment door. Any other night, he would have enjoyed taking his time, stopping to chat with a neighbor, or been easily coerced into a game of stickball with a rowdy group of kids. He would have enjoyed the faint haze of green in the trees as new buds burgeoned forth, washing the landscape with a soft watercolor effect. But for once, the rich scent of freshly hewn mulch as neighbors readied their gardens, and the shrieks of children at play and birds in song, failed to coax a smile to his lips.

No, not tonight. Tonight his thoughts were elsewhere. Mired in a place where the innocent laughter of children and the peace of a wholesome neighborhood were as foreign as an ice storm on a balmy spring day. Brady shivered inside in spite of the sixty-degree temperatures. He quickened his pace when he neared his three-story brick brownstone. Flanked by graceful federal pillars and forsythia heavy with yellow blooms, it welcomed him home, tonight more than usual. He hurried up steps lined with crocus and littered with the occasional pressed-steel toy truck and cap-gun cannon. He sucked in a deep breath and grasped the steel knob of the glass-paned door with rigid purpose, seeking nothing but solitude.

"Hi ya, Brady, what's your hurry?"

Brady hunched his shoulders and moaned inwardly. He turned slowly, a poor attempt at a smile on his lips. "Hi ya, Cluny. Enjoying the weather?"

Fourteen-year-old Cluny McGee looked all of ten years old as he grinned, a spray of wild freckles lost in a layer of dirt on his delicate face. The cuffs of his pants were still several inches too short, and his ill-fitting shirt strained at the buttons despite a spindly chest. He slapped a strand of white-blond thatch out of his twinkling blue eyes. "Yeah, gives me spring fever for all the pretty girls."

Brady forced a grimace into a smile. "This time of year will do that. Well, enjoy." He yanked the door open, desperate to escape to the haven of his home.

"Wait! You goin' to the gym tonight? I thought maybe we could box a match or two." Cluny flexed his muscles. "Gotta shape up for the ladies, you know."

Brady hesitated. He glanced at Cluny, not missing the hopefulness in his eyes. He managed a smile. "Too tired, Cluny. How 'bout tomorrow?"

The boy grinned, exposing a smile that could melt stone. "Sure thing, Brady. Same time as usual?"

Brady nodded and waved, exhaling as the door closed behind him. He mounted the steps with trepidation, hoping to make it to the next landing as quietly as possible. This was one night he needed to be alone, to fall on his knees before God and seek his peace.

A door squealed open. So much for peace.

"Brady, you're home!"

He stopped on the steps and smiled at his eleven-year-old neighbor. "Esther, why aren't you outside with your friends?"

She giggled and ducked her head, then flipped a long, thick braid the color of molasses over her shoulder. "Because I baked cookies. Your favorite kind—gingerbread. Wait here."

She darted off, leaving the door ajar, then returned with a plate of cookies, still warm. The delicious smell filled the tiny foyer, evoking noises from his stomach. She giggled and held them up. Her proud look warmed his heart. He tweaked her braid and smiled, then hoisted the cookies with one hand. "You're going to spoil me, Esther Mullen. What's the occasion this time?"

"For lending me the books, of course. I'm almost finished with the last one."

He tucked the cookies under one arm and shifted a hip. "Which was your favorite?"

She scrunched her nose in thought. "*Jane Eyre*, I think, although I love *Pride & Prejudice* too. I'm almost done. Do you have any more?"

"Tons. You just knock on my door whenever you need a new batch, okay?"

She smiled shyly. "Thanks, Brady."

He chucked a finger under her chin. "And thanks for the cookies, Ess. You're going to make a wonderful wife the way you bake like you do."

A sweet haze of pink dotted her cheeks, and she nodded. "Good night, Brady."

"G'night, Esther."

The door closed and Brady sighed. *Forgive me, Lord, for being so grumpy. And thank you for small blessings like Esther and Cluny.*

He trudged the last few steps to his door and fished the key from his pocket. He caught a whiff of gingerbread and smiled, unlocking the door and prodding it closed with his shoe. He put the plate of cookies on the table and sampled one as he made his way to the kitchen cupboard. He reached for a glass, then opened the icebox to pull out the milk. He poured it and frowned, suddenly remembering the scene with Beth. His gut curdled like the two-week-old milk in the glass. Brady sighed and leaned against the counter.

*Why, Lord?* She was the only good and decent thing in his life. His love for her was deep and genuine and, yes—through the grace of God—pure. He wanted to protect her and nurture her and always be there for her. Why did he have to give her up?

Brady poured the sour milk into the sink and rinsed it out. He absently washed the glass as he struggled with his thoughts. He traipsed to the sofa and collapsed, dropping his head back and closing his eyes.

He knew why.

*As far as the east is from the west, so far hath he removed our transgressions from us.*

A bitter smile twisted his lips. If only he could forget as easily as God. Remove his own shame as far as the east is from the west. Instead, it burned inside him like an eternal fire, singeing any hope of beauty and innocence. Any hope of Beth.

Brady hunched on the couch and put his head in his hands. "Help me, Lord. I'm sick with grief over what I have to do. I love Beth more than my own life. Help me to give her up, to let her go. Give me the grace to do it. To see it through. I pray that you will help her understand. And bring a godly man who will love her like she deserves to be loved."

A heaviness settled on him like the cloying heat of his tiny apartment. He rose and crossed to the window to lift the sash and let in what little breeze he could. He inhaled the fresh evening air, heartened by the scented promise of rain. He grasped his leather Bible from the mahogany desk and settled back into the couch. He began to read and felt the gentle wind of God blowing through his mind with every anointed word.

As always, peace flooded his soul. He exhaled. *Thank you, God.* His eyes lifted to roam his tiny apartment, grateful for the oasis it offered. Though sparse in décor, it exuded a definite masculine air that made him feel comfortable. Heavy but simple wood pieces were arranged in a practical manner. His antique mahogany desk, a gift from his Aunt Amelia in New York, was laden with books wedged between brass bookends from his father. On its polished surface, there was just enough room for a simple wood and brass lamp in the shape of a sailing vessel. His eyes scanned across the dark burgundy sofa on which he sat, moving on to admire the framed prints of ships hung on the walls throughout the room. Their nautical feel always seemed to soothe him. He closed his eyes and pictured the blue of the ocean as he sailed across it in his mind. Sailing, free and easy as a bird, the wind in his face. Not moored to a past . . . nor a future.

Brady expelled a breath and opened his eyes to the imposing chestnut bookcase across the room. He had made it himself. Its shelves were lined with the rich hues of literature that helped to sate the inevitable loneliness that surfaced from time to time.

He suddenly thought of Beth and her love of reading, and his earlier malaise returned with a vengeance. He stared at his collection of leather-bound books. Her hands had touched every volume on his shelves, cradled them in her lap, fingered each page with care. He had bought them all for her, to satisfy her craving for literature.

He laid his hand on the worn pages of his Bible and closed his eyes, remembering his arrival in Boston almost fours years ago. He hadn't known a soul but Collin, but the O'Connors had quickly drawn him into the warmth and security of their family. He had fallen in love with all of them, completely in awe of the closeness they shared, a reaction only heightened by his own bleak childhood. Beth had been thirteen then, almost fourteen, a shy and fragile little girl with soft violet eyes and a gentle nature. She had taken to him at once, enamored with his own love of literature and God. Seeking him out, making him feel special.

Brady dropped his head back against the couch. She was the little sister he'd longed for. The one feminine touch in his life that would never become corrupt. All he had wanted was to protect her, nurture her, love her in the purest sense of the word. It was never meant to be more.

Not for her. And certainly not for him.

With a heavy expulsion of air, he closed his eyes, as if by doing so, he could shut out the feelings that had begun to surface over the last few months. When had the seeds of attraction been sown? At what precise moment had the tilt of her smile begun to trigger his pulse? Fear tightened his stomach. When had she ceased being a little girl? He opened his eyes with new resolve and cemented his lips into a hard line. It didn't matter. He was her friend and mentor, a devoted big brother who wanted nothing but the best for her.

And he was definitely not it.

An urgent knock at the door shook him from his thoughts, and he lunged to his feet. He opened it to the sound of weeping. His neighbor across the hall stood on his threshold, her face streaked with tears. Strands of brown hair fluttered free from a disheveled bun as she stared up at him, her dark eyes pleading. "Oh, Brady, you're home! Can you help me, please?"

Brady's gut tightened. "Pete again?"

She nodded and clutched her arms around her middle, her body shuddering.

"*Ei-leen!* Where the devil are ya?" Pete's slurred tone rumbled from the bowels of the dark apartment, bringing with it a whiff of stale whiskey.

Brady stared at the bruise on her cheek and rested a hand on her shoulder. "Are you okay? Did he hurt you—"

She shook her head, then wiped her face with her sleeve. "No, I just got home. All he had time for was one quick whack across my face. I thank God you're here to stop him. You always seem to have a way with Pete when he gets like this."

Brady pulled her into his apartment. "I'll talk to him, Eileen, but I want you to stay here. I thought he'd given up the bottle. What set him off this time?"

"*Ei . . . leen!* So help me . . ."

She shivered. "He was home before me, so I'm guessing he lost his job again. Oh, Brady, I'm so scared! What are we going to do?"

Brady wrapped an arm around her shoulder and led her to his kitchen. He gave her a quick squeeze. "Same thing as always, Eileen, we pray. God always turns it around, doesn't he?"

She nodded and sniffed.

"There's coffee in my cupboard. Make a pot, will you? Double strength. I'll go in and talk to Pete, and you bring it in when it's ready, okay?"

She nodded and then threw her arms around Brady's middle. Her voice broke. "Oh, Brady, you're a gift from God, ye are! Sometimes I think you're an angel instead of a man."

Heat scalded the back of his neck. He patted her shoulder. "No, Eileen, I'm just a man who's found the grace of God." He steered her toward the cupboard, then headed for the door. He turned and gave her a reassuring smile. "Prayer and coffee, in that order, okay?"

A smile trembled on her lips and she nodded. He closed the door behind him.

"*Ei . . . leen!* I'm gonna blister you . . ."

Brady strode into Eileen and Pete's apartment and drew in a deep breath for the task ahead. *An angel instead of a man.* His lips quirked into a sour smile. That would certainly be nice. Especially at a moment like this. His jaw tightened. *As if I could qualify.*

Angels didn't have his past.

## 2

Lizzie pushed through the swinging kitchen door, and it slammed against the wall with a loud *thwack*. Their golden retriever, Blarney, lumbered up with a fierce bark and trotted over to lick her hand. Lizzie absently patted his head, then blinked at her older sisters, Faith and Charity, seated at the wooden table in their mother's large but cozy kitchen. Both sisters stared in shock, hands stilled on the potatoes they were peeling.

"What are you two doing here?" Lizzie asked, scanning the floral-papered room for some sign of their mother. She noted the freshly baked loaves of wheat bread on the counter and two lattice-top pies, their golden crusts bubbled over with peaches her mother had canned last summer. She took a sniff, and the heavenly smell of pot roast watered her mouth. "Where's Mother? And Faith, why aren't you at work?"

"One question at a time, Lizzie. Mother had a doctor's appointment, and Charity volunteered to take care of Katie, who—thank you, God—happens to be taking a nap at the moment. I wasn't feeling well, so Father brought me home from work on his lunch hour, and I took a nap too. Now, suppose you tell us why you're rattling the door off its hinges?"

"I hate him." Lizzie dropped into the nearest chair and plunked her elbow on the table, chin propped in her hand. She closed her eyes to ward off threatening tears.

"Who?" Charity asked, dropping her peeled potato into a cast-iron pot. She wiped her hand on the stained dishtowel draped over her shoulder and absently rubbed her pregnant belly.

"Who do you think? The most stubborn man alive."

Charity angled a brow and shifted in the chair with a groan. "That would be my husband, Lizzie, and I'm pretty sure you're not talking about him."

Faith chuckled and jumped up to close the kitchen window. "Knowing Mitch Dennehy, I'll vouch for that. But trust me, Collin isn't far behind. Brrr . . . I'm chilly. Anyone for tea?"

Charity sat up straight to massage her back. A wicked grin surfaced on her lips. "Must be men in general," she muttered, "compounded by Irish descent, no doubt." She loosened the top two buttons of her blouse and began to fan herself with a well-worn copy of *Harper's Bazaar*. Golden strands of honey blond hair quivered in the breeze. "I can't believe you closed that window. Sweet saints above, it feels like the devil's kitchen in here."

"Sorry, sis, but if you weren't almost four months pregnant, you'd have goose bumps like me. Lizzie, you want tea?"

"Go ahead and brew it. She looks like she could use it." Charity stopped fanning to lean in and give Lizzie the eye. "So what's Brady done to you now?"

Lizzie sighed. Her anger faded into hurt. "Nothing—and that's the problem. I thought with this new hairdo and turning eighteen this year, he'd start to take notice. You know, see me as a woman? But he hasn't. And this afternoon, he made it pretty clear I'll never be anything more than his little sister."

Faith turned at the stove. "He told you that?"

Lizzie hopped up to get some cups from the cupboard, her anger refueling once again. "Yes. Says he's too old for me."

Charity huffed and commenced fanning. "Too old? That's ridiculous. Mitch is almost sixteen years older than me, and he's not too old." Her brows dipped into a frown. "Although, come to think of it, he can get rather crotchety at times."

Faith grinned and returned to the table. She grabbed a potato and sat down. "That's not age. The man was born that way."

Lizzie sighed and clunked three china cups and saucers on the table before sagging into a chair. "All I know is that Brady is a mule, through and through. I know he cares for me—I can see it in his eyes, hear it in his voice, but what good does it do?" She groaned and flicked at one of the cups and watched it teeter in its saucer. "Why did God let me fall in love with a man who obviously doesn't want me?"

Her sisters exchanged glances. Faith gently touched Lizzie's arm. "Well, as much as I'd like to pop Brady right now, maybe we need to take the high road. Might be that he just needs time to get used to the idea that you're all grown up. You have been his little sister for almost four years now, a constant shadow underfoot. All of a sudden his gangly little protégé has blossomed into a beautiful butterfly. That would take some getting used to for any man, much less a man like John Brady."

Lizzie frowned and looked up. "What do you mean 'a man like John Brady'?"

"Well, he's not exactly a womanizer. Collin says he's never even dated a woman in all the years he's known him."

"But he was engaged before the war, he told me so. So he must like women." Lizzie bit her lip.

"Oh, trust me, John Brady likes women," Charity said. She slapped the magazine on the table and closed her eyes to reach and knead the muscles at the small of her back. She released a low groan of ecstasy when she hit the right spot.

Faith and Lizzie stared. "And how, exactly, do you know that?" Faith demanded.

Charity's eyes blinked opened. "Because he kissed me once, that's how. And trust me, it was the kiss of a man who likes women . . . and then some."

Faith gaped. "Dear Lord, Charity Dennehy, who *haven't* you kissed?"

Charity's lips pressed tight. "I'm not the same woman I was then, all right? My past is my past. Besides, one kiss with Brady convinced me that there's a passion inside that man bordering on wildfire out of control. Believe me, if it hadn't been for Mitch returning when he did, I might very well be Mrs. John Brady right now."

"Oh, Charity, I would have hated you!" Lizzie shivered and slumped further into the chair.

Faith blinked. "I didn't know that. Why didn't I know that?"

"I don't tell you everything," Charity said.

"Yes, you do. At least since you came to your senses and started talking to me again."

Charity's blue eyes squinted in thought. "Yeah, I guess I do. But maybe I didn't mention it because that was the week Mitch showed up and forced me to marry him."

Faith rolled her eyes. "Oh, yeah, I remember when he put *that* gun to your head."

"I can't believe Brady kissed you!" Lizzie blurted out, relief and jealousy squaring off in her brain.

Charity reached for Lizzie's hand. "Only once, and I only mention it now because it showed me that Brady really does need a woman in his life. A woman like you."

Lizzie closed her eyes and imagined what it would be like to have John Brady's lips tasting hers. Better than all the romance she'd ever read, she was sure. "Was it wonderful?" she whispered.

Charity chuckled. "Yes, but let's not get off track. My point is that Brady is a normal, red-blooded American male, yet for some mysterious reason, he refuses to pursue a romantic relationship."

Faith squeezed Lizzie's shoulder. "It's true, Lizzie. All I know is, according to Collin, women come in the shop all the time trying to catch Brady's eye, but apparently he has no interest in spending time with any of them."

Charity planted her arms firmly on the table and leaned in. "Only you, Lizzie. He only spends time with you."

Lizzie blinked and then grinned. "I know. Three times a week at lunch, and we don't always study the Bible or pray. Sometimes we just talk." She sighed. "What am I going to do? I'm so in love with the man, I'm sick."

The teakettle whistled and Faith bounced up to get it. She poured the steaming liquid into each of the three cups, then returned the kettle to the stove. The sweet scent of jasmine billowed into the cool air as she placed three spoons and cream on the table. "Well . . . maybe our Brady needs a little jolt . . ."

"A jolt?" Lizzie sat up.

Faith grinned and glanced at Charity. "Wouldn't you say, Charity? Something to make him more . . . attentive?"

Charity chuckled. "Goodness, I'm ashamed I didn't think of it myself. Heaven help me, this pregnancy must be dulling my manipulative skills."

Faith stirred some cream in her cup and took a sip. "Well, hopefully not too much, because I'm counting on you to teach our Lizzie a few feminine wiles."

"And you'll cover the prayer department?"

Faith laughed. "What else?" She cocked a brow at Lizzie. "But I'll only be praying for you and Brady to get together if it's what God has in mind, all right?"

Lizzie pouted. "And what do you think I've been doing the last four years? Knitting? I've asked God over and over again to take Brady out of my heart if it's not right, but my feelings have only grown. Why do you think I've turned down every boy who's ever asked me out? If God hadn't intended Brady for me, wouldn't I have known it by now?"

Faith smiled and patted her hand. "Seems like it. All right, then it's settled. Charity will handle the romance, and I'll handle the prayer." She gave Charity a playful smirk. "Because obviously I've never had *her* abilities with men."

"I don't remember you doing too badly," Charity said with a grimace. She turned toward Lizzie, her brows bunched deep in thought. "Well, let's see. You'll need privacy, of course, and you can't get that at the shop, not with Collin there."

"Collin's not always there at lunch when Brady and I have Bible study. Sometimes he runs deliveries." Lizzie drowned her tea with a hefty dose of cream.

Charity shook her head. "No, you need someplace romantic, someplace where you and he can be alone, without his Bible to hide behind." She scrunched her face. "Is he coming to dinner on Saturday?"

Faith grinned. "He is if I get Collin to ask him."

"Good! That's perfect." Charity waggled her brows. Her tone was thick with conspiracy.

"Perfect for what?" Lizzie guzzled her tea.

"For seduction, of course."

"What?" The tea pooled in Lizzie's throat while the cup trembled in her hand. "You want me to *seduce* Brady?"

"No, nothing that sinister. Just enough to get him thinking about you as a woman instead of a little sister."

Lizzie's cup clattered to her saucer. She glanced at Faith. "And you're in agreement with this?"

Faith sighed and crossed her arms on the table. "Well, I'm not going to argue with the master. Besides, for what it's worth, I've always had a sense that you and Brady fit together, like it was meant to be somehow. But ultimately, it's God's decision, not ours." Her serious tone lightened with a lift of her brows. "Which means, little sister, that *if* it is what God wants, then John Brady needs a fire lit under him in a big way. And let's face it—there's nobody who knows how to do that better than Charity. I say we try—providing it's innocent enough."

Lizzie's pulse picked up pace as she blinked at Faith, then at Charity. "Okay, if you think I can do it. But just being close to Brady makes me so nervous, I don't know if I'll be any good."

Charity chuckled and rubbed her stomach. "Oh, you'll be good, if I have anything to say about it."

"But what if Brady doesn't respond? Maybe he isn't attracted to me."

Charity's eyes narrowed. "Do you think he is?"

A blush heated Lizzie's cheeks. "Sometimes. Every now and then I get this warm, funny feeling when he looks into my eyes. But he always jumps up and starts doing something right away or grabs his Bible, so I can't really be sure."

"Sounds sure enough to me. What do you think, sis?" Charity grinned at Faith.

Faith smiled and leaned back in her chair. "I'd say Brady's in a heap of trouble."

"So, what do I do?" Lizzie giggled nervously and propped her chin in her hands.

Charity took a deep breath. "Well, first we get him to come to dinner Saturday night. Faith will take care of that with Collin. Then, we'll scour your closet for your prettiest dress, and I'll help you get ready. The works—makeup, perfume, attitude. After dinner, you'll tell Brady that you have a problem you need to discuss, something that's got you really upset."

"You mean, like him?" Lizzie asked with a wry smile.

"No, not him. But close. A problem with another man. Maybe that Weston boy who's always calling."

"Tom? But, what kind of problem?" Lizzie was losing her nerve.

Charity's lips skewed in thought. "Didn't you say Tom tried to kiss you at Millie's party?"

"Well, yes, but that was last year."

Charity arched a brow. "Brady doesn't have to know that. As long as it's true, you can tell Brady that you're thinking of going out with Tom, but you're not sure how to handle him if he gets fresh."

Lizzie's eyes widened. "But I'm not thinking of dating Tom. I don't want to be with anyone but Brady."

Charity huffed an impatient sigh. "We know that and you know that, but Brady doesn't know that, or at least he won't if you play your cards right. Do you like Tom at all?"

Lizzie thought about the boy who had hounded her since freshman year. Tom Weston—smart, ambitious, good-looking, yes, but far from perfect. She sighed. Or at least far from Brady. "He'd be okay, I guess, if I wasn't in love with you know who."

"Good! Then that's the card we'll play. I'm not proud of some of the shenanigans I pulled with Mitch, but a little healthy competition never hurt any man."

"So you want me to date Tom Weston?" Lizzie's voice cracked.

Charity tilted her head. "Maybe. That can be a backup plan if Plan A doesn't work."

"And what exactly is Plan A again?" Lizzie chewed on her thumbnail.

"After dinner, tell him you need to talk about a problem and get him outside on the swing. Make sure you snuggle close so he can smell your perfume. And for goodness' sake, lean your head against his chest. That should fan any embers if they're there."

Lizzie gulped and put a hand to her cheek to cool the heat that surged. "What about my embers? The man turns me to putty."

"Forget your embers, Lizzie, this is war! The battle of the sexes, as age-old as the Garden of Eden. Do you want Brady or not?" Charity stared her down.

Lizzie nodded and bit her lip.

"Then you have to be tough and focus on the end result—getting Brady to admit he's in love with you."

"But how do I do that?"

Charity pursed her lips in a satisfied smile. "With the most deadly weapon in a woman's arsenal."

Both Faith and Lizzie stopped breathing. They leaned forward. "And what's that?" Lizzie whispered.

Charity paused, her tone hushed with reverence. "The kiss."

Lizzie's mouth dropped open, and Faith chuckled. "Almost four months pregnant, and she doesn't miss a beat. I'm glad I had God in my life when you and I were butting heads over men."

Charity pretended to scowl. "Yes, I remember, but now he's in my life too, so we're even."

"You want me to kiss Brady?" Lizzie's voice was little more than a squeak.

"Only as a last resort if he doesn't kiss you. Call it Plan B."

"But, how . . . ?"

Charity studied her sister, her lips skewed in thought. "Well, it would certainly help if you could cry. Can you cry on demand?"

Lizzie blinked. "I've never tried. But why do I have to cry?"

"Because it weakens their defenses. I suggest you practice in your room. If you have trouble, try putting something irritating in your eyes like a cracker crumb or anything like that. Once your eyes begin to water, just think about how much you love Brady and how awful it would be if he didn't love you back. Then, voilà! Cry yourself a river."

"God help us." Faith shook her head and settled back in the chair. "Amazing. Absolutely amazing."

Charity grinned. "Thank you." She turned back to Lizzie. "So, with cracker crumbs handy in your pocket, you sit on the swing with Brady in the moonlight. Tell him since you know there is no hope for a relationship with him, you feel you need to focus on other men. Tell him the truth—that Tom

Weston has repeatedly asked you out for two years and you're considering dating him, but that you're afraid. Get weepy on him. Explain that Tom cornered you and kissed you at a party and that he has a bit of a reputation."

Lizzie blushed. "How do you know Tom has a reputation?"

"He was one of the most popular boys in your high school, was he not?"

Lizzie nodded.

Charity hefted her chin. "He's got a reputation, trust me. Besides, I've seen him once or twice. The way Tom Weston looks, I suspect women make it very easy for him."

"Charity!" It was Faith's turn to blush.

"Well, it's true, Faith, and you know it. Collin was the same way, and so was Mitch for that matter. Too good-looking for their own good." She grinned. "And ours."

Faith sighed. "I suppose so. It's the grace of God that he got ahold of both of them."

"Thanks to you. In case I never told you before, I'm forever indebted."

Faith smiled.

Charity turned her attention back to Lizzie. "So, after you start crying and he starts comforting you, press in close and start to sob against his chest, keeping in mind that your future with this man depends on this. And then slowly—very slowly—lift your face to his and ask him what you should do. Make sure you keep your lips parted ever so slightly, maybe even biting on the edge of your lip. Like this . . ." Charity demonstrated with face lifted. "Then start praying your heart out that he kisses you."

"But what if he doesn't?" Lizzie's voice edged toward alarm.

"Then you simply switch to Plan B. You kiss him."

"Oh no, I don't think I can do that—"

"Oh yes, you can. You're my sister, aren't you? There must

be at least a trace of the vamp in you. I couldn't possibly have gotten it all."

Faith's lips squirmed. "I wouldn't bet on it."

"Well, even so, you're a woman. And a beautiful one at that. It's about time you acquire these skills. You'll need them even more after you're married."

"I take exception to that. I don't need them," Faith said.

Charity gave her a telling look. "And I suppose you don't use your flashing green eyes and feisty temper to bully Collin into your way of thinking whenever he plays the mule?"

Faith blushed. "At least it's not fake tears brought about by cracker crumbs."

"Tears or temper, every woman has her means of turning her husband's head. It's the ebb and flow of romantic relationship, ladies. Besides, it keeps the men we love on their toes and the relationship a thrill a minute."

Faith shook her head and laughed. "I suppose."

"But I still don't know if I can do it," Lizzie whispered.

Charity pointed a threatening finger into Lizzie's face. "You have to. You don't have a choice. A kiss is the only thing that will haunt him until he admits he's in love."

"But what if he pushes me away?"

"He won't."

"But how do you know?"

"Because one kiss told me that when it comes to women, that man is a powder keg waiting to blow. Everyone sees Brady as this wall of iron, and so did I. I don't know how to explain it, but that one kiss convinced me otherwise. If you ask me, I think that's the reason he feels so safe with you as a little girl, a little sister. I have a suspicion he can't handle anything more than that. Something tells me his desire is so strong, it scares him. Wouldn't surprise me if that's the reason he's steered clear of women altogether. I don't think the man trusts himself."

Lizzie's pulse pounded in her brain. "That's it, Charity, I just know it! I always thought that Brady's intensity, his passion, came from this bottomless wellspring of love for God, and it does, I know. But lately, well lately, I've been feeling something else. Like a slow-burning fire underneath it all, something white-hot way down deep that's been drawing me. Brady says I've been reading too many romance novels, but I tell you, I feel like I can sense it . . . I can sense his . . ." She blushed to the roots of her hair, then lowered her voice to a bare whisper. "His passion for me."

Charity began fanning herself. "Whew, Lizzie, I don't think that's your imagination. Brady does have a fire inside, and I believe you're the one who's going to tap it. Goodness, this conversation makes me want to spend some quality time with my husband."

Faith chuckled. "Can't wait to go home, eh? I would think that would be the last thing on the mind of a woman in your condition."

"That's what I thought too," Charity groaned, "but it's just the opposite. The bigger my stomach, the more I seem to need Mitch's love."

Lizzie clasped her hands together. "Really, Charity? That's so romantic!"

Charity's lips twisted into a wry smile. "You think everything is romantic, Lizzie. I might agree with Brady on that one. Even so, I just wish Mitch felt the way you do."

"You mean he doesn't?" Faith rose to dump the peeled potatoes into a pot of water on the stove. She lit the fire beneath it, then glanced over her shoulder.

"Nope. Oh, I know the man is crazy in love with me all right, but I don't think he's attracted to me anymore." Charity lumbered to her feet and pressed her hands to the small of her back, issuing a low moan. "Not that I blame him. Kinda hard to make love to a baby whale."

"Charity, stop that!" Faith scolded, her cheeks burnished with apparent discomfort at the topic. "First of all, you're more beautiful now than you've ever been, and that's saying something. But . . . well, I'm not sure Mitch would like it if he knew you were discussing your love life with us."

Charity lifted her chin, and wetness sparked in her eyes. "I have to, Faith. You and Lizzie are my sisters, and I have to tell somebody. I'm too embarrassed to talk to Mother, and Emma's my friend, but she's so busy running our store since Mitch doesn't want me working, that I don't want to bother her. But it's killing me inside. All of my confidence, my womanhood, has always been based on men's reactions to my looks. Now when I seem to need affirmation most, my own husband has no interest . . ."

The whites of Faith's eyes expanded in shock. "None?"

Charity sniffed and plopped back into the chair. "Well, almost none. He's always too tired or doesn't come to bed till after I'm asleep. And even when I do wait up, he kisses me on the forehead, snuggles, and mutters how exhausted he is." Charity swiped at a renegade potato peel and popped it in her mouth. "I just wish he knew that I need his love now more than ever."

"So tell him. It's not like you to hold things back," Faith said.

Lizzie reached across to touch Charity's arm. "Mitch would want to know how you feel. The man's crazy about you. Anybody can see it."

Charity shook her head. "No, I don't want his love out of pity. I want him to want me. Like before."

Lizzie smiled and folded her hands neatly on the table. "Well, why don't you take some of your own advice? And then we can work on our 'projects' together?"

Charity blinked. The light went on in her eyes and she sat straight up, causing her tummy to jut in defiance. She released a little-girl giggle that brought a pretty blush to her cheeks. "Oh my goodness! See, I told you this pregnancy was dulling my brain. Seduction! Saints preserve us, why didn't I think of it first?"

Lizzie laughed and grabbed both of her sisters' hands, so

grateful for them in her life. "So what do you say we pray about it, then go to work?" She grinned at Faith. "Anything you need to pray about in the romance department?"

Faith chuckled and snatched Charity's magazine off the table. She began fanning her cheeks, which were bright pink. "Yes, but on the opposite side of the bed, I'm afraid. I need Collin to let me get some decent sleep. I have a feeling he's trying to go head-to-head with Mitch in the baby department."

Charity swooned. "Oh, that I could be plagued with such a problem!"

"Okay, ladies, then let's put our prayers to the task at hand." Lizzie grinned, feeling better than she had in weeks. "Faith, you're on." She squeezed her sisters' hands and closed her eyes.

Charity tugged on her arm. "Wait a minute. Before we pray, I want to make sure you're clear on one thing. The most important thing is that you get that kiss—one way or the other. Understand?"

Lizzie nodded, her heart thumping in her chest.

"Good. So I've given my expertise, now Faith can give you hers. Ready?"

Faith grinned. "Finally—a battleground I feel comfortable with!" She closed her eyes. "Lord God, we thank you for our husbands . . . and potential husband in Brady. Help us to be the wives you want us to be. Give Mitch an overwhelming attraction for Charity, especially now when she needs it most. Give Charity wisdom in this situation, and please turn it around. And as far as Collin goes, Lord, I think he wants a baby really badly. We both do. So I'm putting that in your hands too. Psalm 113:9 says that you 'make the barren woman abide in the house as a joyful mother of children.' That's what I'm asking, Lord. For me, Charity, and Lizzie. And speaking of Lizzie, we only want what you want. So if Brady's not right for her, please heal her heart and bring the right man into her life. But if Brady is being stiff-necked and blind to the woman you have for him in Lizzie, we're asking that you open his eyes. And if there are other barriers in the way, knock 'em down, Lord, like a tunnel of dominoes. Give Lizzie wisdom and patience in the process . . . and Brady a swift kick in the behind. Amen."

Faith opened her eyes and grinned. "Get ready to say goodbye to Big Brother Brady, Lizzie. Something deep down inside tells me that man is history."

∼§ §∼

"Lizzie O'Connor, it's about time! God knows I've done everything I can to drag you into the modern era." Millie sighed. "Including changing that goody-goody name of yours into something more hotsy-totsy. You're lucky to have sisters like Faith and Charity. Meg wouldn't do that for me."

Lizzie grinned at her best friend, then turned to fiddle with the display of bestsellers in the window of the Bookends bookstore. She stood back to assess with a critical eye. "That's because you don't need any help, Millie. Frank already thinks of you as a woman."

Millie's throaty giggle brought a hint of warmth to Lizzie's cheeks, confirming Lizzie's statement, and then some. Millie tossed her head back in a saucy display of modern womanism and patted her boyish bob. Her square cut and short bangs were as scandalous as her scarlet lips and pencil-thin brows. She fluttered mascara-smudged lashes in a provocative way. "I'll say he does, Lizzie, and if you'd just follow my advice, Brady would think the same of you."

Lizzie gave her a lopsided smile. "I'm afraid Brady would think I'd lost my mind. He's more of an old-fashioned type of man, Millie, and I don't mind. To a point. But like my sisters say, Brady needs a jolt, and I fully intend to give it to him."

"Attagirl, you'll have that man carrying a torch for you in no time. Why, half the men who come in this shop have a crush on you. Brady must be half blind or way more religious than you say. What did your sisters say to do?"

Lizzie grinned and carried a hefty stack of bestsellers to a nearby table. She shot a quick glance at the front desk where Mr. Harvey was assisting a customer. Millie trotted behind, sporting a considerably smaller pile of books in her arms. Lizzie peeked up at her friend beneath sweeping lashes bereft of mascara. She blushed. "They said I have to get him to kiss me."

Millie whooped, and Mr. Harvey looked up with a frown. It was Millie's turn to blush, rare color flooding her powdered cheeks. Her demeanor sobered considerably as she quickly helped Lizzie arrange the books into an attractive display. "That had to be Charity's idea. That woman is a regular Mata Hari."

Lizzie lowered her eyes, aware of Mr. Harvey's intense scrutiny. She bit back a smile and focused hard on the task at hand. "Yes, it's always been a talent of hers, it seems. So between Faith's prayers and Charity's skill with men, I hope I can turn Brady's head." She sighed and straightened the price placard in front of the books. "But I don't know if I can do it. Just the thought of kissing that man leaves me weak in the knees."

Millie chuckled and put the finishing touches on the display by fanning out several books in front of the exhibit. "You can do it. Just pretend it's a scene in a play like you did last year in drama class. You were wonderful, as I recall. A real live wire." She grinned. "Unlike the way you actually live your life."

"Thanks a lot."

Millie chanced a peek at Mr. Harvey to make sure he was still occupied with a customer. "But I have high hopes for you, Lizzie O'Connor. On the outside you're this shy, demure little thing, but on the inside there's all this passion and drama just itching to get out. Just like story time with the kids—you fairly sizzle with excitement and stimulation. Unfortunately, when it comes to men, you're a real sad case." She wiggled her brows and grinned. "Almost eighteen and never been kissed."

Lizzie propped her hands on her hips. "Have to! Must I remind you that Tom Weston cornered me on the back staircase at your party last year?"

Millie folded her arms and arched a brow. "Did you kiss him back?"

"No, of course not."

"Then you haven't been kissed. And for the love of Mike, I still don't know how anyone could not kiss Tom Weston back. That man is the bee's knees. Is he still calling?"

Lizzie wandered to the back of the store to set up for story hour, with Millie close on her heels. She sighed as thoughts of Tom Weston dampened her mood. "Every month, like clockwork. Charity calls him Plan C."

"Sometimes I think you're a bit balmy. If Tom Weston looked at me, I'd say, 'Frank who?'" Millie stopped in her tracks, her eyes as wide as her gaping mouth. "What do you mean 'Plan C'?"

Lizzie bent over to arrange a number of small, brightly colored chairs into a perfectly formed semicircle. "If Plan A doesn't work."

Millie nodded and plucked several books off a shelf. She held them up. "Which one? Fairy tale or adventure? Oh, I see. Plan A being the kiss? What's Plan B?"

Lizzie puckered her brows and studied the books, then snatched the fairy tale. "Kissing him, instead. But I'm hoping and praying there won't be a need for a Plan B *or* C." The bell over the door jangled and she looked up, smiling at several children and mothers who entered the shop. She glanced at her watch. "Goodness, they're coming in early today. Could be a crowd."

Millie rolled her eyes. "Correction. Will be a crowd. Children and men—you have an uncanny knack for drawing them both, including Tom Weston. All, that is, except John Morrison Brady. I'd hold on to Plan C, Lizzie, if I were you. I think you're going to need it."

Lizzie scowled. "Maybe not."

Millie chuckled and headed for the front of the store, shooting a wicked grin over her shoulder. "Fairy tales, my friend. You read them so well. And live them even better."

## 3

Sweet saints in heaven, surely the scores of romantic novels she'd read should have prepared her for this! Lizzie made her way down the stairs with all the confidence of a woman with a wart on her nose. Instead of the happily-ever-after glow of a love-struck heroine, she was stuck with sweaty palms and a tiny belch bubbling in her chest—not attractive features for a woman who hoped to sweep a man off his feet. A man far more adept than she at giving love the brush.

The belch threatened, and she stifled it with a shaky hand to her mouth. Maybe she couldn't do this. After all, she was merely Beth O'Connor, the shy and quiet bookworm of the family. Not Charity with her seductive charm or even Faith with her spitfire spunk that seemed to draw Collin like a moth to flame.

She stopped for a split second at the foot of the stairs and sucked in a deep breath, fully aware of Charity's hand pressed firmly at the small of her back. No, she *could* do this! Charity was right. Sweet Beth was gone, and dangerous Lizzie was here to stay, hopefully to threaten John Brady's emotional health considerably.

And thanks to Millie and Charity, she did *look* different, she supposed. And she was starting to feel different too. Apparently years of timid longing had finally erupted into flashing eyes and a backbone of steel. A smile flickered on her lips at the thought of Brady's face when she had lost her temper at the shop. In all the years she'd known him, she'd barely ever raised her voice above a whisper. She'd been too in awe. But whether Brady knew it or not, he was no longer dealing with that same shy little girl. She was a modern woman now, in love and tired of waiting for him to notice. She hoisted her chin, determined to take on the challenge.

Lizzie forged through the kitchen door and stopped cold. Warmth braised her cheeks at her family's response: Mitch gaped. Collin and her brother Sean whistled. Faith and her mother gasped. And Katie's ecstatic shriek rounded out the reception.

"Lizzie, you're gorgeous!" ten-year-old Katie gushed.

Charity prodded Lizzie from behind. "Thank you, Katie. She does clean up nicely, doesn't she?"

Faith bounded up from the table to give Lizzie a squeeze. "Saints alive, Lizzie, look at you!" She pulled away and grinned at Charity. "You did it. Had my doubts that you could make her any prettier than she already is, but obviously I underestimated you. *Again!*"

Mitch leaned back against the counter and chuckled, ginger ale in hand. "A fatal error, I've learned."

Charity arched a brow in his direction. "Took you long enough."

He fixed her with a smoldering gaze while slowly sipping his drink, the passion in his eyes clearly undaunted by a year and a half of marriage. His eyes flicked back to Lizzie. "Katie's right. You do look gorgeous."

"Thanks. I just hope Brady thinks so."

Charity sauntered over to Mitch's side. He hooked her waist and kissed the top of her head. She grinned at Collin. "So, what's the verdict? You think your partner will notice?"

Collin shook his head and sank back in his chair. The soft glow from the brass chandelier overhead accentuated the slow grin that traveled his lips. He slashed an X in the middle box of a game of Tic-Tac-Toe he was playing with Katie. "I think the poor guy will never know what hit him, Lizzie. You're beautiful."

Lizzie bit her lip and whirled around to diffuse the nervousness she felt, causing the handkerchief-style hem of her blue silk dress to flare just a touch. Charity had insisted that she wear the matching T-strap heels that Millie had talked her into buying. They lent at least two inches to her already long-legged height, making her feel a bit more "womanly" than she was used to. When she'd said as much to Charity, her sister had winked and told her if she wanted to convince Brady she was a woman, she would have to "think sultry." Lizzie drew in a deep breath, careful not to press her sweaty palms to the stylish dropped-waist, which had easily glided over her slim hips. Out of the corner of her eye, she glanced nervously at her mother, a bit self-conscious about the hint of cleavage afforded by the pretty scoop neck of her dress. "What do you think, Mother?"

Marcy O'Connor put a hand to her mouth, barely obscuring the smile on her lips. "I'd say you're definitely grown up, and if Brady doesn't realize that soon, he's going to be too late."

"It would serve him right," Charity said, burrowing deeper into Mitch's hold. "But we're going to try and spare him that pain, aren't we, Lizzie?"

"I just hope I can remember everything you taught me."

Mitch pulled back to eye his wife. "And just exactly what are you teaching her?"

"How to win his heart." Charity said with a secret smile.

He hiked a brow. "Like you won mine?"

"It worked, didn't it?" She broke free and hurried to take the pot of steaming potatoes out of her mother's hands.

Mitch stared her down. "Yeah, but I didn't like it. Scheming is no way to win a man's heart."

"Oh really?" Charity grinned and rubbed her swollen belly. "Well, suppose you tell that to your unborn child who wouldn't be here without it."

A hint of a smile played on his mouth. "Even so, you shouldn't be involved. This is between Lizzie and Brady."

Lizzie looked up from the icebox with a pitcher of milk in her hands. "But that's just it, Mitch. Brady refuses to see me as anything but his little sister. And I love him. What am I supposed to do? Forget him? Even though I know deep down we were meant for each other?"

Charity turned at the sink and gave Mitch a pointed look. "Sound familiar?"

"I say forget him, Lizzie. Boys are saps." Katie began tapping on the piece of paper, intent on beating Collin at a new game of Connect-the-Dots.

"Hey, who you calling 'saps'?" Collin shot her a narrow look. "I don't see any females playing word games with you. Besides, you're only ten. What do you know?"

"Eleven in a few weeks. And enough to know I'll never let some sap boy steal my heart like Lizzie has, even if it is Brady."

"You'll eat those words someday, Katie Rose," Collin said, tweaking the long, blond pigtail trailing her shoulder.

Katie scrunched a freckled nose. "Everybody knows you can't eat words."

"Oh yes you can," Charity said. "Ask Mitch."

Faith chuckled. "Oooo, good one!" She grinned at her brother-in-law. "Tasted a little bitter, did they now, Mr. Dennehy?"

Mitch grinned as he seared Charity with a heated look. "Not as bitter as those my wife will be tasting after we get home."

"Oh, I just love a good fight!" Charity notched her chin, blue eyes twinkling. "Especially the part where we make up."

Mitch shook his head and laughed. "God help me, I married a vixen."

Sean chuckled as he reached for a glass from the cupboard and poured himself some milk. "Well, I'm no expert, sis, but I agree with Mitch. Why scheme to get Brady's attention when other guys are lining up for a chance with you? Besides, Brady's obviously not looking for anything more. As far as I can tell, he seems pretty content the way things are."

Charity tossed her head and commenced with mashing the potatoes. She grunted with each thrust in the pot. "Only because he's too stubborn to know when he's not happy. If women didn't use their God-given feminine wiles, most men would spend their lives alone and miserable"—she looked up at her brother and smiled—"like you."

Milk sputtered from Sean's mouth in a near choke. "Hey, I'm not miserable, and neither is Brady."

"Well, just for the record," Faith said, hoisting the roast from the oven, "Brady isn't happy. He needs a woman like Lizzie."

Collin reached to snatch a piece of meat. "Who says Brady's not happy?"

Faith whirled around, her eyes as wide as the hole Collin had just put in the roast. "Why you did, last night, remember? You wanted to pray for Brady because he wasn't happy."

A pink haze colored the back of Collin's neck. He gulped the meat down in one large swallow and tried to cover with an innocent grin. "What I meant was, Little Bit, that he's obviously not as happy as we are." He leaned in to nuzzle her neck before snatching more roast.

"Don't you dare try to bamboozle me, Collin McGuire! You've told me more than once that you wished Brady would find a woman he could love because he wasn't happy. Well, Lizzie's a woman he could love."

Charity bludgeoned the potatoes for good measure. "Well, I love Brady like a brother and you all know that. But if Lizzie's the one God has for him, then we intend to do everything in our power to make it happen." She smirked at her husband. "Whether Brady likes it or not."

"Well, I can tell you right now, he won't like it, will he, Mitch?" Collin asked with a wad of roast in his mouth.

Mitch drained his ginger ale and set the glass down. He

leaned back against the counter and folded his arms. "Nope. And neither do I. But that won't stop 'em. You should know that by now." He glanced at his mother-in-law. "How does Patrick feel about this? Is he comfortable with all the female plotting going on around here?"

Marcy hefted a tray of biscuits from the oven. Wisps of blond hair, loose from a pretty chignon, feathered the neck of her pink percale housedress. She placed the tray on hot pads and wiped her hands along the contour of her slim, high-belted waist. "I'm afraid Patrick's been a bit preoccupied with business at the *Herald* to be fully aware of what these three have been up to. You know how busy he's been since taking the editor position." She sent a tired smile in Mitch's direction. "But I suspect he'd side with you men, being the stubborn Irishman he is."

"Speaking of Father, why isn't he home yet? It's Saturday, for pity's sake. I thought he intended to go in for just a few hours." Faith pulled a carving knife from the drawer and handed it to Collin with a quick kiss. "Here, earn your keep by carving the roast."

Marcy glanced at the clock. "He did, but you know how that goes." She lifted her chin and hardened her tone. "But he did promise to be home by dinner, which I fully intend to put on the table in ten minutes, Patrick or no."

Lizzie and her sisters exchanged glances. "We can wait, Mother, really. Brady's not here yet, either." Lizzie hesitated. "Are you . . . feeling okay?"

Marcy sighed. "Yes, I'm just tired. I think I'll run upstairs for a moment and freshen up, if you girls don't mind. Hopefully your father will be home by the time I'm done."

"You do that, Mother." Lizzie gave her mother a hug. "We'll get dinner on the table."

"Thanks, Lizzie."

Marcy left and Lizzie frowned. "You think everything's okay? She seemed quiet."

Faith sighed. "She did at that, but then she has been cooking all day, which is enough to wear anybody out. And I know she doesn't like it when Father works on Saturdays."

The doorbell rang. Lizzie startled and slapped a hand to her chest. "It's Brady. I'll get it."

Charity clamped a hand on her sister's arm. "Oh no you don't. For the last four years, you've run for that door every time Brady's come to dinner. Not tonight." She gave Sean a pointed look. "Mind letting him in, Sean? Lizzie's busy."

"Unbelievable," Mitch said, shaking his head.

"Yeah, she's busy all right—spinning a web," Sean said with a tease in his tone.

Lizzie blinked. "But I'm not busy."

"Oh yes you are. Sean, stall Brady at the door a few moments, will you? Lizzie needs to make a quick phone call to Peter Henly."

"Peter Henly? Why on earth am I calling him?"

Charity parked a hand on her hip. "Because if you hope to have a prayer of turning Brady's head, you'll have to incite his interest with a bit of jealousy. And Peter called earlier about a homework assignment, so we may as well take advantage. When Brady walks through that door, I want you talking to Peter in your most hushed but charming tones, understand?"

Collin paused with knife in hand. The expression of shock on his face mirrored Mitch's. "A *prayer* of turning Brady's head? You don't really think God is going to sanction this . . . this female trickery, do you? Are you crazy?"

Faith looped an arm around Lizzie's waist and shot her husband a mischievous grin. "Maybe a little crazy, but if it's meant to be, then Brady will be crazy too—about our very own Lizzie. Care to join us?" She wriggled her brows.

Collin chuckled and turned to slice the roast clean through. "Nope, you go right ahead, Little Bit, but leave me out of it. The name's Collin McGuire, not Benedict Arnold."

Patrick listened to the table chatter with half an ear, barely tasting the pie he methodically shoveled from plate to mouth. His favorite, he suddenly noticed—coconut cream. The realization unleashed a burst of pleasure to his taste buds and a sudden swell of gratitude for his wife. He glanced at her, but she seemed as preoccupied as he, absently pushing at the uneaten cream filling on her plate as she hunted for pastry, the only part she liked.

He smiled and touched a hand to her arm. "Thank you, Marcy, for making my favorite. I know how you can't abide coconut, and it's a special treat after the week I've had."

She startled the slightest bit and stared up at him, the blue of her eyes wide with an innocence that never failed to draw him in. Suddenly his focus stilled to only her. Collin's laughter and Charity's droll comments and Katie and Steven sparring over whose turn it was to do dishes—all faded away as he searched his wife's face. Seldom did she seem as tired as she did tonight, rare lines of fatigue more pronounced despite the soft glow of candles flickering across her features. He thought he saw a glaze of wetness in her eyes, and his stomach tightened.

"You're welcome, Patrick. I know how hard you've been working, so I wanted to make something special." Her eyes flitted back to her plate. She patted his hand, which was still draped on her arm. "Will you need to do this much longer . . . working on Saturdays?"

His concern for her evaporated at the mention of work. He sighed and pushed his plate away with a frown. "I don't see any way around it. At least not for the foreseeable future. I could work seven days a week and not put a dent in it, it seems."

"Patrick . . ." Her voice was so low he had to strain to hear it.

"Yes, darlin'?"

"I . . . we . . . we need to—"

"Father, it's Steven's turn for dishes and he won't do it!" Katie's high-pitched shriek rattled his senses.

"Father, no! We traded last week because she had play practice, and now she's trying to weasel out of her turn."

Patrick ignored the viselike grip of tension at the back of his neck and slowly rose to his feet, his conversation with Marcy forgotten. His eyes flicked from the sober face of his fourteen-year-old son to the bulldog stare of his ten-year-old daughter. He suddenly had an overwhelming urge to demoralize someone—anyone—in a game of chess. He jagged a brow in Katie's direction. "Katie Rose, did you trade dishes with Steven last week?"

Katie blinked, and Patrick could almost hear the wheels turning behind those batting blue eyes. "Yes, Daddy, but—"

He pushed his chair in with enough force to shimmy the table and quiver the candles. The family's chatter died to a hush. "No yes-buts, Katie Rose. You'll do the dishes this week without another word or you'll be doing them a lot longer than that."

"But, Daddy—"

Patrick shot her a look that sealed her lips. "*Two* weeks and not another word. Or would you care to make it three?"

She blinked, the mulish line of her jaw matching his. "Does 'no' count?"

Patrick stared her down, battling the urge to smile. "You're a handful, Katie Rose, and God knows if I don't keep you in line at the tender age of ten, some poor man will shoot me later." His gaze traveled the table. "Anybody up for blatant humiliation? I intend to vent every frustration from work in a ruthless game of chess."

Collin chuckled. "Then I'd say Mitch is your man. He's got the same bleary-eyed look of blood in his eyes as you. Something to do with the *Herald*, I suppose." Collin draped an arm around Brady's shoulder. "And this *is* Brady's first dinner here in a while, so common courtesy says he's off the hook."

Patrick squinted at Mitch. "It does make perfect sense, I suppose, although I hate to debase my best editor."

Mitch grinned, stood, and pushed in his chair. "Debase away. I'm married to your daughter. I have no pride left whatsoever."

Patrick winked at Charity and headed to the parlor with restrained vengeance flowing in his veins. "Then let the carnage begin," he muttered, allowing Mitch to lead the way.

Patrick's laughter, which echoed from the foyer, sounded almost predatory. Brady elbowed Collin as he rose to his feet. "Close call. I'm not up to a beating tonight. All I want to do is sink into the sofa and bury myself in the newspaper." He glanced at Marcy. "Mrs. O'Connor, dinner was wonderful. I wouldn't know what a home-cooked meal was if I didn't come here."

Marcy's smile seemed tired. "You're more than welcome, Brady. We love having you, you know that. And you can come every night of the week, if you like. Not just when Collin's here, you know."

He returned her smile, then sensed that Beth was watching him. Heat stung the back of his neck. "Thank you, Mrs. O'Connor, but I work late a lot. I never know when your son-in-law is gonna overload us. You may not know this, but he has a problem saying no."

"Hmmm, I'll vouch for that." Faith grinned and stacked dishes on the table.

Collin arched a brow. "And what's that supposed to mean?"

She gave him a quick peck on the lips. "Nothing, my love, except you could do with a little restraint from time to time. You don't have to be so driven in everything you do."

He pulled her close and nestled his lips at the crook of her neck, causing her to giggle. "I'm not driven in everything I do, Little Bit. Just work and—" His tease faded off into a kiss that lasted several seconds.

Brady nudged his shoulder. "Let the woman breathe, will ya, Collin? I'm going to the parlor." He ambled into the next room and snatched the newspaper from the sofa before settling into his favorite spot on the far edge of the worn paisley couch.

"By the way, did Mrs. Tabor get a hold of you last week?" Collin strolled in behind him. He wrestled a section of the paper from Brady's lap before he plopped on the other side. "Said she wanted to thank you for designing the program for her ladies' auxiliary. Hate to tell ya, ol' buddy, but I think she's gunning for ya. Says you have a real . . . let's see, what did she call it? 'A real flair for design.'" He grinned. "I'm guessing she's got a flair for design herself—involving you and her unmarried daughter."

Brady chuckled and adjusted the newspaper in his lap, refusing to give Collin the satisfaction of a glance. He rattled the page and scanned the headlines. "She did. And she does. Invited me to dinner next week."

"I swear, you could eat out every night of the week if you had a mind to. You going?"

Brady grunted and turned the page. "Nope. Can't afford the indigestion."

"Gotta be better than loneliness."

Brady shot him a one-sided smile. "That was your problem, Collin, not mine. I don't need a woman to make me happy."

Collin laughed. "No, I guess not. I gotta give it to you, though. You're a stronger man than me, that's for sure. Before Faith, I couldn't say no to save my soul. And here you are, a flesh-and-blood male with enough females batting their eyes to cause a stiff breeze, and temptation is not even a word in your vocabulary. I'd like to know how you do it. I'd market it and make a small fortune."

Brady grinned and snapped his paper back up. "It's called willpower, ol' buddy, something you knew almost nothing about before Faith. While I, on the other hand, have perfected it to a fine art, steeled by the grace of God and the power of prayer."

"Brady, can we talk?"

He glanced up, and the taste of his words soured in his mouth. His hands began to sweat, adhering to the newspaper. Beth stared down at him with violet-hued eyes fringed with sooty lashes that seemed longer from this angle. He glanced at Collin out of the corner of his eye, then shoved the paper aside. He rose to his feet and swallowed the dread that cleaved to his throat. "Sure, Beth, where?"

She nodded toward the porch, then clutched her arms around her waist in that little-girl way she had when she was nervous. Only this time, the motion produced a slight swell of her breasts, revealing a hint of a cleft at the low-scooped dress. "It's pretty out. Can we sit on the swing?"

"Sure, but you'll need something warm, little buddy. It's chilly." He averted his gaze, determined to ignore both the heat crawling up his neck and Collin's annoying grin. He licked his dry lips and strode straight for the coat rack, plucking his jacket off with way too much force. He searched for Beth's warm coat, but found only her thin wrap.

He held it while she slipped it on. She smiled over her shoulder. "Thanks, Brady."

He opened the front door and waited patiently, pretending his heart wasn't hammering triple time in his chest. *Fine. We need to talk anyway. The sooner, the better.*

The porch was dark except for a soft wash of moonlight that cast distorted shadows as he leaned against the railing. He crossed his arms and waited while she settled on the swing with a soft swish of her skirt. She patted the seat beside her. "Why don't you sit here? This could take awhile, and I want you to be comfortable."

*Comfortable?* With her scent as clean as lilacs in rain and her burgeoning body obscuring the little girl he once knew? He sucked in a full breath and stood up straight, shoving his hands deep into the pockets of his trousers. Exhaling, he positioned himself on the far right of the swing, determined to ignore the wood of the beveled handle as it sliced into his waist. He shifted to face her and draped an arm along the back of the swing. "So, what's on your mind, little buddy?"

She bit her lip and scooted close enough that he could feel her body shivering. "Do you mind if we snuggle? It's colder than I thought."

He stared straight ahead, lips clamped tight as the heat of her body singed his. It set his nerves on edge, but she seemed nervous too—from the tug of her teeth against her lower lip to the clutch of her hands as they fidgeted in her lap. His arm—which had been resting comfortably on the back of the swing—suddenly felt like hardwood lumber. With almost painful motion, it hovered over her shoulder for eternal seconds before finally drawing her close. *For pity's sake, this is Beth and she's cold. Settle down, Brady, and just get through this.*

"What's on your mind, Beth?"

She sighed and burrowed into his arms, causing the scent of her hair to invade his senses. It triggered an unwelcome warmth, despite the coolness of the night. But at least she was warm, he reasoned, noting her shivers had stopped. He closed his eyes and ground his jaw. *While mine are just beginning.*

Her voice was soft and low. "I'm sorry for losing my temper the other day, but I . . . well, I guess I've been struggling with my feelings for you."

Tension stiffened his hold. "Beth, these feelings you're having, they've got to stop."

"I know, Brady," she whispered. "I finally understand."

He drew in a breath and glanced down at her. "You do?"

She looked up with a soulful expression. "Yes, I do. It doesn't change the attraction I have for you or the love I feel inside." She blinked several times, as if to clear the gloss of wetness from her eyes. His gut twisted. "But I finally realize I need to move on . . . I don't want to lose your friendship."

The tightness in his chest suddenly released like an audible sigh. *Thank you, God, we can still be friends!* He exhaled the weight of the world from his shoulders and scooped her into an overwhelming hug of relief. "Oh, Beth, I'm so grateful you understand. I love you too, and I'll always be there for you, the best friend you've ever had."

She returned a tremulous hug. The sound of her words rumbled against his chest. "That's good, Brady, because I could use the advice of a friend."

"Anything, little buddy!" He leaned back against the swing and tucked her safely under his arm. She was his sweet little Beth once again, flooding his soul with joy. "What kind of advice do you need?"

"About men. Actually, one in particular."

His joy fizzled faster than warm foam on week-old root beer.

She glanced up with wide, innocent eyes, a stark contrast to the jealous surprise churning in his gut. "There's this boy—his name is Tom Weston—and he's asked me out, on and off, for over two years now. And lately, well, . . . it seems he won't take no for an answer."

He blinked. Men have been asking her out? For two years? His Beth?

He sat up, desperate to convey a composure he didn't feel. "Well, Elizabeth, you're almost eighteen, I suppose it's time . . . time to find the man that God has for you. Do you . . . like him?"

She sighed. "Well, he's certainly attractive and hardworking. He's worked two jobs as long as I've known him and plans to go to law school after he graduates college next spring."

The jealousy rose in his throat like bile. "So, you're . . . attracted to him, then?"

"Well, I wasn't initially because I had hoped you and I . . ." Her voice faded. She took a deep breath. "But I think now . . .

now that I know you and I can only be friends, well, I think maybe I could be attracted to him."

"Does he go to church?"

Her soft chuckle floated in the air. "Well, if you mean is he as spiritual as you, no, he's not. But he's from a good family who go to church regularly, and I think in time—"

"Is he a gentleman?"

Lizzie felt herself blush to the tips of her shingled hair. She bit her lip and turned away, slipping her hand into the pocket of her jacket. With trembling fingers, she pinched the cracker she'd hidden there and swiped crumbs into both of her eyes.

"Beth?"

She didn't answer. She was too busy blinking.

He reached for her chin and gently tugged her gaze to his. He was suddenly the consummate big brother, concern etched in his handsome face. "Answer me. Is he a gentleman?"

The crumbs were masterful as they welled in her eyes. "I'm . . . n-not sure."

"What do you mean you're not sure? Has he given you cause to think otherwise?"

"Well, he . . . he kissed me once."

Disapproval darkened Brady's features. "Did you encourage him?"

Her lips parted in shock. "No! I promise you I didn't. He c-cornered me."

"So, he's not a gentleman?"

Her eyes went wide. "I don't know . . . maybe . . . but probably not."

She began to shake, not sure if it was her nerves or the drumming of Brady's fingers hard on the wood. He eyed her through narrowed lids. "Well, he doesn't sound like the type of young man you need. I suggest you forget about him and look elsewhere."

She blinked. "What?"

"You wanted my advice as a friend, and I'm giving it. Forget him."

A rare rush of indignation flared in her cheeks. "I wanted your advice on how to ward off his advances, Brady, not if I should date him. I've already decided on that."

"You can't date some clown with one thing on his mind."

Crackers and fury forced hot tears from her eyes. He didn't want her, but no one else could either? She rose to her feet. "How dare you, John Brady? I have no choice! My heart is breaking because of you, and if it takes Tom Weston to get over you, then so be it."

He jumped up. "Beth, forgive me, please, and don't cry. We can pray about this—"

Disbelief paralyzed her for a painful second. "No! You leave me be. I don't want any more of your prayers—"

His hand gripped her. "Beth, please, sit with me? Can't we just talk and work this out?"

She relented, allowing him to tug her back to the swing, where the feel of his powerful arms only enflamed the longing in her soul. He bundled her against his shoulder, and the clean, pure scent of musk soap taunted her senses.

"Beth, you're so special to me," he whispered. "I never want to hurt you." He kissed the top of her head, and she could smell a trace of the peppermint he kept for children at the shop. A sharp ache pierced her heart. He was her Brady, good and strong and kind . . . but he would never really belong to her. Not the way she yearned in her heart—as a husband, a man, *a lover*. The thought all but crushed her, and she collapsed against his chest in painful weeping.

"Beth, don't cry, please. I love you . . ."

She felt his lips in her hair, and her anguish surged. She jerked away. "No, don't lie to me, Brady! You don't love me—"

He groaned and embraced her. "I do love you, little buddy, more than anyone in this world." With grief in his eyes, he searched her swollen face. He caressed her wet cheeks with gentle hands. "You mean everything to me," he whispered. He bent to press a light kiss to her forehead.

Shallow breaths rose from her throat at the warmth of his lips against her skin. Her body stilled. *"A kiss is the only thing that will haunt him until he admits he's in love."*

She lifted her gaze, taking great care to impart a slow sweep of lashes.

"Beth, are we okay?" He ducked his head to search her eyes, then brushed her hair back from her face. A smile shadowed his lips. "Still friends?"

*Friends.* A deadly plague only a kiss could cure. Resolve stiffened her spine. "Sure, Brady . . . friends."

He smiled and tucked a finger under her chin. "That's my girl. Now what do you say we pray about some of these things?"

He leaned close with another quick kiss to her brow, and in a desperate beat of her heart, she lunged, uniting her mouth with his. She felt the shock of her action in the jolt of his body, and she gripped him close to deepen the kiss. Waves of warmth shuddered through her at the taste of him, and the essence of peppermint was sweet in her mouth.

"No!" He wrenched back from her hold with disbelief in his eyes.

Too late. She had never felt like this before. Years of seeking romance from flat parchment pages had not prepared her for this. This rush, this desire . . . her body suddenly alive, and every nerve pulsing with need. All shyness melted away in the heat of her longing, and she pounced again, merging her mouth with his. *John Brady, I love you!*

A fraction of a second became eons as she awaited his rejection. His body was stiff with shock, but no resistance came. And in a sharp catch of her breath, he drew her to him with such force that she gasped, the sound silenced by the weight of his mouth against hers. He groaned and cupped the back of her head as if to delve into her soul, a man possessed. His lips broke free to wander her throat, and shivers of heat coursed through her veins. In ragged harmony, their shallow breathing billowed into the night while his arms possessed her, molding her body to his.

"Oh, Brady, I'm so in love with you," she whispered.

Her words severed his hold as neatly as the blade of a guillotine. He staggered to his feet, and icy cold replaced the warmth of his arms. She opened her eyes and saw pain in his. She grabbed his arm. "Brady, can't you see? You love me too . . . not as a friend or a sister, but as a woman."

"God help me, Beth, I can't love you that way." He stared like a zombie, chest heaving with jagged breaths that swirled into the cool night air, drifting away—just like her dreams.

She reached for his hand, but he pulled it away. She blinked. "You just did, John. Nothing can convince me otherwise. You love me . . . and you want me . . . just like I want you. Why can't you admit it?"

His tone was rough with emotion. "Because it's wrong, Elizabeth. You're a little sister to me, nothing more."

She rose, along with her ire. "I see. And that's how you kiss a sister?"

Blood gorged his cheeks. His shoulders straightened as he stood stiff and tall. An uncommon show of anger glinted in his dark eyes. "I regret what happened tonight, and I apologize. Please give my thanks to your mother and my goodbyes to your family." He moved toward the stairs.

"Brady, wait!" She latched onto his arm while tears pooled in her eyes. "You can't leave like this. Not now. I opened my heart to you . . . and you took it when you gave me that kiss."

The anger in his eyes faded to pain. "I know, Beth. Forgive me. It won't happen again." His back was rigid as he strode down the steps.

She ran after him. "No! Don't leave—please! Friends don't leave when you need them the most."

He stopped, hand poised on the gate, and the coolness of his manner was totally foreign. He turned with a look of agony she had never seen.

"No, Beth, they don't."

And without another word, he unlocked the gate and hurried away. Fading quickly—just like her hope—into the darkest of nights.

# 4

Lizzie shivered and wept on the swing until all that was left was a wet blotch on her face, swollen eyes, and a broken heart she hoped no one would see. She squared her shoulders and rose to head inside, determined to present a calm demeanor. She quietly opened the front door and carefully shut it again. With a lift of her chin, she hurried to the stairs, desperate to escape notice.

"Lizzie? Where's Brady?" Charity stood on the bottom step, her swollen belly effectively blocking her way. She blinked in surprise, one hand on her stomach and the other bracing her back as she studied Lizzie with concern. "He didn't leave already, did he?"

Lizzie nodded and blinked hard to ward off more tears. "Will you please tell everyone that he said goodbye and I said good night? I don't feel well. I'm going to bed."

Charity touched her arm. "Faith and I will be right up."

She sniffed and nodded again, then continued up.

Charity watched her sister ascend the stairs and released a heavy sigh. She rubbed at the soreness in her back and peeked in the parlor where Mitch was playing chess with Patrick.

Faith looked up from unbraiding Katie's hair while Marcy dozed in her chair by the hearth. "What's wrong?" she mouthed, and Charity lightly shook her head before forcing a bright smile.

"Brady said to give his goodbyes to everyone, and Beth said good night. She was tired, so she went on up to bed. Faith, why don't you and I go tuck her in?"

"Brady left? So soon?" Collin glanced up with a frown.

"No doubt exhausted from working with you," Faith teased.

"Or fed up with deceit," Mitch muttered.

Charity gave her husband a thin smile. "Father, I suggest you teach Mitch a few lessons in strategy."

Patrick looked up with a chuckle. "I'll be happy to educate the boy for ya, darlin'."

Mitch studied the board. "No, thanks, I live with the master."

Charity stuck out her tongue and turned toward the stairs while Faith hurried after her.

"What happened?" Faith whispered.

"I know nothing except that Lizzie's been crying her heart out. So help me, if John Brady hurt her again . . ." Charity mounted the steps with a groan.

Faith clasped an arm around Charity's waist to help shore up her strength. "Don't worry, we'll get to the bottom of this. Brady would never hurt Lizzie on purpose. There must be a reason. We just need to find out what it is."

"Oh, there's a reason all right, and I for one intend to get to the bottom of it. If marriage has done one thing, it's made me most proficient at dealing with stubborn men."

Faith chuckled and knocked on Lizzie's door before gently turning the knob. "A natural outcome, I think. Lizzie? Can we come in?"

A low, broken moan drifted from the bed where Lizzie lay prostrate on her pillow, still clad in her dress.

Her sisters hurried to her side. "Are you okay?"

"No, I'm n-not okay. I've l-lost him f-forever."

Faith crouched by her side. "What do you mean, you've lost him?"

Charity lowered herself to the bed with a grunt. "For pity's sake, you can't lose him, Lizzie, the man is crazy about you. Did you kiss him?"

"Yes." Lizzie sniffed and raised up on her elbow.

Charity squinted. "And?"

"I d-did everything you said—sat close on the swing, batted my eyes, and cried enough cracker tears for a whole box of Saltines. But nothing worked. So, yes, I was forced to resort to Plan B."

Faith stood to her feet. "Oh my goodness, Lizzie, you actually kissed him?"

"Twice," she muttered. She maneuvered on the bed to sit cross-legged. Her chin began to quiver. "It was the most wonderful thing I've ever felt . . ." Her voice trailed into a sob.

Faith and Charity exchanged grins.

"Yes, we know," Charity said, "but this is no time to start blubbering. Just give us the cold, hard facts. Did he kiss you back?"

Warmth surged to Lizzie's cheeks at the memory, and she put her hands to her hot face. She closed her eyes. "Kiss me? No, it was more like he devoured me!"

Charity giggled and tried to tuck a foot under her skirt, to no avail. "See? Didn't I tell you he was a powder keg waiting to blow? Why on earth are you crying? You should be celebrating."

Lizzie opened her eyes and sniffed. "Because he said it would never happen again. Said he can't love me that way."

Faith scrunched her nose. "Why not?"

"He said it was wrong. That I was a little sister to him and nothing more."

Charity grunted. "Hogwash. No man kisses a sister like that."

"Exactly. And when I pointed that out, he became colder and angrier than I've ever seen. Then he said goodbye and just stalked away."

Charity's brows dipped. "Did you try and stop him?"

"Of course! I ran after him, sobbing my heart out, but he just kept going, as if he didn't even care. I even tried guilt as a last resort, telling him that friends don't leave when you need them the most."

"Good girl. Did it work?" Charity leaned in, her shapely brows arched in expectation.

"No, and that's the worst part." Lizzie closed her eyes, seeing Brady's look of pain once again. "He said, 'No, they don't,' and then left, just like that." Her eyelids fluttered open to a fresh wash of tears. "Don't you see? It's over. He doesn't even want to be my friend."

"That's ridiculous. There must be some reason why he's acting like this, something he's hiding." Faith paced the room with a glint in her eyes.

Charity pressed a hand to Lizzie's arm and sat up straight on the bed. "Wait! That's it. I remember now." She squeezed her eyes shut as if to conjure the memory. "He told me once, after we kissed that time, that I wasn't ready . . . and that he wasn't ready, either. He said he had things . . . things from his past." Her eyelids flipped open. "He said I deserved more, and I remember being shocked when he said it. I mean, what more could a woman want than a man like Brady? Faith's right— he's hiding something, something so awful from his past that he won't even let himself look at a woman, let alone fall in love with one."

Lizzie sat up and wiped the tears from her eyes. "But how do we find out? I don't think he'll talk to me, especially now."

"Oh, we'll find out all right, trust me." She waved a hand toward Faith, who helped her to her feet with a grunt. Charity groaned from the effort and rubbed the small of her back. "First thing tomorrow morning, before church, I am going to pay a long overdue visit to my good friend, John Brady."

Lizzie's eyes grew wide. "What are you going to say?"

"I don't know," Charity said with a lift of her chin, "but I know it will be good. Good enough to rattle his cage and give him something to think about. And you know why?"

Lizzie blinked and Faith smiled.

"No, why?" Lizzie asked in a hush.

"Because you two will be praying, that's why. John Brady may have the willpower of ten men in fighting against flesh and blood. But it was John Brady himself who taught me that a man hasn't been born who can fight against prayer and win." She reached for both of her sisters' hands and smiled. "Shall we prove him right?"

～ ～

One of the dim bulbs dangling over Tucker's Bakery flickered and caught Brady's eye as he hurried down Connover Street. It barely illuminated the large, crudely scripted sign that hung in the window, obscuring the last word. To him it looked like "Fresh Homemade Dread."

How appropriate. That's exactly how he felt—his gut weighted down with a rock-solid loaf of dread. Not to mention pain. His lips twisted into a bitter smile. "The bread of adversity," he reflected, recalling his reading from Isaiah 30 that morning. He exhaled his frustration with a noisy breath that swirled into the air as he scaled the steps of his apartment, hands buried in his pockets and shoulders hunched. Noting the lights peeking through the Venetian shades in his landlady's apartment, he quickly glanced through the glass-paned front to make sure the hallway was clear. He turned the heavy knob with the utmost care, desperate to avoid making a noise. It was only nine o'clock, after all, still early enough for a neighbor or two to poke out a head and engage in a chat.

He dug his key from his pocket and carefully inserted it into the lock, then released a sigh of relief when he escaped inside. The door quietly clicked behind him, and he sagged against the wood and dropped his head in his hands. A dull headache was beginning at the base of his head. All at once frustration surged, and he ripped his coat off and hurtled it across the room. It narrowly missed his nautical lamp and landed in a heap on the floor.

"Gosh, Gram would tan my hide if I did that."

Brady's muscles jerked. He squinted in the dark. "Cluny? What the devil are you doing here?" He grappled to turn on a small lamp by the door, then whirled around to see Cluny McGee bundled in a blanket on his sofa. His grimy face revealed blue eyes still groggy from sleep. "How in blazes did you get in?"

"Mrs. Cox has a key." A flash of white teeth gleamed in the dark as Cluny scratched his skinny chest with a touch of bravado. Brady could swear he saw him wink. "I told her she was pretty."

"Why?"

"Because ladies like that—"

"No, I mean *why are you here*?"

Cluny appeared hurt. "Gosh, Brady, you said I could spend the night sometime, if it was okay with Gram, so here I be."

Brady charged across the room and yanked Cluny's covers clean off. The small-framed boy was dressed in the same dirty clothes he'd worn earlier in the week. And the smell confirmed it. "Well, not tonight; you're going home."

"Cain't."

"What do you mean, you can't?"

Cluny pulled the covers back up in a show of modesty. "I mean, I cain't. Gram's gone home to see her sister—Arkansas. She's sick something awful."

Brady grabbed a wiry arm and pulled the boy to his feet. "Your mother, then."

Dirt and freckles merged into one as Cluny scowled. "Shoot, Brady, she ran off with another no-good boyfriend last month. Don't ya remember?"

The headache began to throb at the top of his skull. His

nerves felt like they were twitching under his skin. Brady swore under his breath and slacked a hip. "Isn't there anybody else you can stay with tonight? A neighbor, a friend?"

Cluny squinted. "I thought you told me I shouldn't cuss? And come on, Brady, you know you're the only real friend I have."

Brady forced his frustration out with a loud blast of air. "I wasn't cussing, Cluny, I was muttering."

Cluny arched his pale brows and folded his arms, going on thirty rather than fourteen. "Same thing, far as I can tell."

Brady groaned and scrubbed his hands over his face, finally relenting with a thin smile. "Okay, Cluny, you're right. I was cussing and I'm sorry. It's just that tonight has been the worst night of my life, and God knows this is not the best time for you to be here."

Cluny's brows pinched in thought as he peered up through narrowed eyes. "And maybe it is, Brady, ever think of that? Maybe God 'knows' you'd be needin' a real good friend tonight. Ya know, somebody to take your mind off things?"

Brady's eyes burned as he turned away, blinking hard to dispel the wetness. He bent to pick up the blanket. "Well, get your carcass down the hall and into the tub then, because there's no way you're sleeping in my bed until you're squeaky clean."

"I ain't taking your bed. I'll sleep on the couch."

"No, you're sleeping in the bed or out in the hall, take your pick. I'll take the sofa." Brady headed to the bathroom and tossed the cover in the hamper, then leaned in to turn the faucet of his claw-foot tub.

Cluny followed and propped against the door. He scratched his stomach with a wide yawn. "Why? I don't want to cause you no trouble."

Brady studied the slight boy with a hitch in his heart. He was certain that the Southie neighborhood had never produced a more neglected—or dirtier—street urchin in all of Boston. "Because you're a guest . . . and a good friend."

Cluny beamed, even through all the dirt. "Thanks, Brady. We won't be any trouble, I promise."

The blood in Brady's veins slowed to a crawl. "We?"

Cluny provided an ample show of teeth that reminded Brady he probably hadn't seen a toothbrush anytime lately. "Miss Hercules and me."

Brady pushed a hand to his forehead and closed his eyes. *Lord, no!* He'd forgotten about Miss Hercules. "Where is she?" he whispered, opening his eyes once again, even though he wasn't quite ready to face the truth.

Cluny grinned from ear to dirty ear. "In your bedroom." He banged on the doorframe. A deafening bark shook the walls of the flat.

Brady groaned and slowly opened his bedroom door. Miss Hercules lay, in all her matted glory, like the Queen of Sheba. She lifted her head and barked, dominating his nice, clean bed with muddied paws and panting tongue, as only an English sheepdog can.

"Gee whiz, Brady, there was so much ruckus in the hall every time somebody would be a-comin' or a-goin', that ol' Miss Hercules would keep trottin' to the door and barkin' like a fiend." Cluny leaned close and winked, as if man to man. "I need my beauty sleep for the ladies, ya know. After all, it's you and me, Brady. We got a lot of hearts to break, if you know what I mean."

Brady hung his head. A faint smile touched his lips despite the sick feeling in his gut. Yeah, he knew. He was already well on his way.

෴

Charity flipped a strand of long, golden hair over her shoulder and nervously dabbed a hint of lilac water behind each ear. Nibbling on her lip, she applied the scent to her throat, then lowered her robe enough to reveal the deep cleft of her new, satin nightgown. She exhaled the breath she'd been holding and smiled into the mirror with her best come-hither look. "Feel like a back rub, darling?"

Her lips skewed into a wry grin as she let the robe drop to the floor, unveiling a protruding belly. Her grin faded into a sigh. "Or maybe a really firm pillow for your head?"

"Charity! Are you coming? You know I can't sleep without you."

"I'm coming, I'm coming!" And, yes, she knew. She straightened her shoulders and smiled into the mirror. "And tonight, Mr. Dennehy, I am not going to sleep without you." She braced a hand to her back and squatted in an attempt to pick up the robe without success. With a frustrated grunt, she flipped it with her toe and launched it on the chair.

"Charity!"

"Coming!" She doused the bathroom light and hurried into their darkened bedroom, pausing to adjust her eyes. She scanned the room for their golden retriever Runt, who lay sprawled in the middle of the floor. With a flick of her toe, she quickly massaged his ear. "Good night, big guy," she whispered and slipped into her side of the bed. A shaft of moonlight illuminated her husband's six-foot-four frame stretched out with eyes closed and chest bare. Her pulse picked up as she eased under the covers and nestled as close as her stomach would allow. "I'm here, for heaven's sake. Did you remember to lock the doors?"

"Yes, ma'am."

"Put the milk bottles out?"

"Yes, dear."

She snuggled closer and stroked playful fingers across the blond coiled hair on his chest. "Love your wife?"

She could feel his smile in the dark. He looped a powerful arm around her shoulders to draw her close, then stopped. His hand started feeling the back—or lack thereof—of her new nightgown. His eyes flipped open. "What the devil have you got on, and where's your nightgown—the warm, flannel one?"

She giggled and pulled back so he could enjoy the view from the front. She saw his hard-chiseled chin drop a full inch. She preened like a peacock when a lump bobbed in his throat. "Do you like it? Lizzie's friend Millie says it's all the rage in lingerie."

"How in the devil would Millie know?" Mitch rasped, eyes trained on her full breasts as they strained against the sheer fabric. He sucked in a ragged breath and exhaled slowly. "Yes, I like it. Too blasted much, I like it. Turn around," he growled, "so we can spoon and I can get some sleep. I'm exhausted."

Her chin notched the slightest degree, and he knew he was in trouble. "Oh no, you're not going to sleep—not yet." With a mischievous smile, she casually flicked the silk strap of her gown. It slithered off her shoulder. "I'm warning you—don't make me seduce you, Mitch Dennehy, I'm way out of practice."

He could feel the blood heating in his veins and forced his gaze to her face. *Bad move.* Her lush, full lips were moist and parted, waiting for his kiss.

He vaulted from the bed, desperate for a glass of water—cold, *cold* water.

"Where are you going?"

"I'm thirsty."

"At this exact moment?" Charity's voice raised several octaves.

He bolted for the bathroom, closed the door, and bent over the basin with a groan. He flicked the spigot on to splash cold water in his face, then leaned heavily against the sink, eyes tightly closed.

The door flew open with a loud crack. His head jerked up, and light flooded the room, blinding his eyes. "Are you seeing another woman, Mitch Dennehy?"

"What?" His mind reeled. He blinked to adjust to the light, staring at his beautiful wife as if she were speaking a foreign language. That incredible negligee was heaving with every breath she took, and her blue eyes were swimming with tears.

"There was a time when you couldn't keep your hands off of me," she sobbed, "a time when you thought I was pretty."

His heart clutched in his chest, and he quickly scooped her up in his arms. "God help me, Charity, there's not a woman alive who can hold a candle to you, even pregnant. No woman has ever turned my head like you, and no woman ever will. I love you, little girl, don't you know that by now?"

She sniffed in his arms and looked up, melting his heart. "Lately I wonder. You never seem to want to hold me or kiss me anymore."

He exhaled and pulled her against his chest, pressing his lips to her hair. "I've just been exhausted, you know that. The paper has been a madhouse—just look at the hours your father's been keeping." He gave her a tender kiss on the lips. "I promise, in another three to four months, things should slow down and—"

"Three to four months!" She jerked free from his arms. New tears welled in her eyes. "But that will be after I have the baby! That proves it—you think I'm hideously fat. You're not attracted to me."

He sensed another crying jag coming and gripped her arms. "Listen to me—do you think it's easy keeping my hands off of you?" He tugged her back to soothe her with a slow, rocking motion. "I'm crazy about you, but I just think it would be better if we waited—"

"Waited?" She pushed him away with a hard slap to his chest. "Until when—I shrivel up and die?"

His gaze strayed to her full breasts, and his lips quirked into a smile. "Not likely, little girl." He lifted her up in his arms like she weighed nothing at all and gently laid her on their bed, then crawled in alongside and snuggled close. "Charity, listen to me, please. I have been exhausted lately, it's true, but there's another reason I think . . . well, that we need to wait." He hesitated, reluctant to say too much. "I . . . I would rather not be intimate right now. I worry about the baby."

She bolted up in bed and wiped the tears from her eyes. "The baby? What do you mean?"

He stroked her belly with the full palm of his hand. A sense of awe filled his soul followed by a rush of love for the woman before him and the child she carried. Just as quickly, another image flashed in his mind, of a swollen belly writhing in pain and a bed drenched in blood. Mitch fought off a sting of tears. "I just don't want to take any chances, that's all. I love you both too much."

Charity feathered his raspy jaw with kisses. "But nothing will happen, except you'll make the mother of your child a very happy woman." She pulled back to search his eyes. "Mitch, I've spent my whole life drawing my confidence from how I look and whether or not men were attracted to me. I know it's not right, but that's a hard thing to break. And although this baby means the world to me, I can't help but feel unattractive, especially when the man I love avoids me like the plague."

"Charity—"

She held his face in her hands. "No, Mitch, listen to me, please. I need your love tonight. I need to feel your arms around me, your love, your passion. And you need me too, desperately. Besides, Dr. Wilson says it's perfectly safe for the baby."

He sat up in the bed. Heat singed the back of his neck. "You asked him about this?"

"I most certainly did. When my husband goes from ravaging me on a nightly basis to near narcolepsy, I had to do something. It's safe, Mitch, I promise. We're not going to hurt the baby."

She rose to her knees to press a kiss to his forehead. He was pretty sure that the painful proximity of her breasts was no accident. Heat rolled through him.

With a low groan, he tugged her close, his breath hot against the soft swell of her breasts. "God help me, you little brat, there's no fighting you, is there?" He laid her back on her side and devoured her mouth with his, the heat of her kiss driving all caution from his mind. With a hungry sweep of his hand, he caressed her body, desperate for more. "I love you, Charity, body and soul."

Her soft laugh tickled his cheek as she pressed in close. "Mmm . . . body and soul. Now we're talking."

Saints alive, she may never sleep again! Lizzie adjusted the pillow beneath her head for the twentieth time—for all the good it would do. She was fairly certain she was destined for a sleepless night, seesawing between the sweet, warm ecstasy of Brady's kiss and the cold, hard reality of his sudden departure. Dear Lord, she was doomed! Here she was, more in love with the man than ever before, and now farther away than she ever thought she'd be. It wasn't fair. Why had she ever fallen in love with him?

*Ridiculous question.* From the moment she had laid eyes on him, he'd been her Prince Charming, straight out of the pages of a fairy-tale romance. A tall, gentle soul with quiet good looks and a heart of gold. Where other suitors were riddled with imperfection, John Brady was the perfect man—a tower of strength and a fortress of conviction. A knight in shining armor. A man with an unquenchable fire that bespoke a true passion for God. Lizzie swallowed hard. And another passion, apparently, tucked away where no one could see. Warmth seeped through her bones, and her breathing shallowed. A passion she had tasted for herself, tonight in his arms. Confirming once and for all that John Brady's air of indifference was only a facade.

She closed her eyes to relive the memory. As a young girl, a kiss in a novel had been sweet, but this—this was what she had longed for, dreamed of since she'd been small, a love-struck little girl swept into the world of happily ever after. Her lips parted to expel a quivering breath. And tonight she had experienced it for the very first time—her very own Prince Charming, his mouth on hers—warm, possessive, and hungry. Heat pulsed through her, and her eyes flipped open. Oh, she needed to stop! Her thoughts were treading on dangerous ground.

*Lord, forgive me, but I love him! I want him as a husband as well as a friend. Don't let him turn me away, please.* Tomorrow would tell. Charity had vowed to talk to him. She bit her lip and curled on her side, then closed her eyes and began to pray.

A soft knock sounded before the door squeaked open. Her father entered the room, and she watched as his shadowy form leaned over Katie to bestow a good-night kiss. He turned and moved toward her, and the familiar smell of musk soap and pipe tobacco gladdened her heart. She smiled up in the dark.

"Why are you up so late, Father?"

His low laugh vibrated against her forehead as he kissed her good night. "I had some papers from the *Herald* to go over, but I could ask you the same thing, darlin'." He sank down on her bed and stroked a hand to her cheek. "Rumor has it a devious plot was afoot between you and your sisters. Care to talk about it?"

"It was completely innocent, really. You see, Charity had this idea—"

Patrick chuckled. "I'm guessing if the idea belonged to Charity, it was anything but innocent."

"Well, maybe, but Faith thought it would be okay, and we prayed about it first."

He lifted a brow. "A prayerful plot . . . I see. And did it work?"

She chewed on her lip, and her father gave her a wry smile. "Spare me the details, darlin', and just tell me one thing. Are you okay? You disappeared awfully quickly after dinner, without even a kiss for your tired, old father. That's not like you, Lizzie."

"I'm sorry, Father. I just haven't been myself lately."

He studied her for a long moment, then kissed her forehead again. "I know, darlin', and it's been worrying me. I love you, Lizzie. From the moment you could read a book, you've always been my shy bookworm, in love with the idea of being in love. But I believe God has the real thing waiting for you, down the road a wee bit. But you just have to be patient and understand . . . it might not be Brady."

She nodded her head, and a single tear sailed down her cheek. "I know, Father. Pray for me, will you?"

He reached to gently brush the tear from her face and then scooped her into a deep hug. "I already do, darlin', and I've no plans to stop." He rose to his feet. "I love you, Lizzie, you're my girl. Now get some sleep, you hear?"

Her father's calming scent lingered long after his footsteps faded from the room. She finally turned on her side with a groan. "Sleep," she muttered to herself, then punched her pillow with a final thrust. "Easier said than done."

⌇ ⌇

Patrick jolted awake, his toothbrush still foaming in his mouth. Sweet mercy from above, how could a man fall asleep on his feet while brushing his teeth? He spit in the sink and rinsed, quite certain he had never been this tired.

With a yawn that almost hurt, he lumbered down the hall to his room, vaguely aware that he hadn't even kissed Marcy good night. He crawled into bed like a man dragging himself onto a lifeboat, desperate to collapse and drift away. The warmth of Marcy's body drew him close, and he sank hard against her side, her familiar scent relaxing him further. He looped an arm around her waist and exhaled, giving himself over to blissful sleep.

Marcy rolled away, and he jolted awake with a grunt. Half numb, he butted in close once more, almost asleep when she did it again. Comprehension suddenly prickled like icy sleet pelting against bare, frigid skin. His eyes popped open in shock, and his breathing quickened. She had barely spoken through dinner and then had fallen asleep by the fire after. God help him, had he forgotten her birthday? Their anniversary? He pinched his brow and tried to think. No, nothing like that. Could she be angry because he'd forgotten to kiss her good night?

He released a weary breath and sidled close to her back, hooking a firm arm to her waist. She tried to wriggle free, but he held her securely, his mouth against her ear. "And what have I done now, darlin', to incur your wrath?"

"Let me go," she hissed, and he clutched her more tightly. When she couldn't break loose, she tried kicking his leg. Pain seared through his shin, and he groaned. All exhaustion washed away in a rush of angry adrenaline. His breathing was heavy as he arched over her. "Marcy, what in blue blazes have I done now?"

He half expected to see sparks in the dark, shooting from her eyes. She squirmed beneath his grip. "Don't you dare act like you don't know."

He groaned. "If I knew, I wouldn't be doing it, now would I? Forgive me, but I'm rather partial to my sleep."

She jerked free and shoved him away. "Well, sleep all you want—on your own side of the bed, but don't expect to cozy up against me. You want cozy, Patrick O'Connor? Why don't you throw your sore leg over a stack of the *Boston Herald*?" She shot over to the far side of the bed, teetering on the edge. The bed quivered with her silent weeping.

Patrick hung his head. "Marcy, listen to me, please. We're two editors down right now, what with Logan in the hospital and Schyer out of town, and we can barely keep up. Even Mitch has been pulling extra hours."

She spun around, her face wet with fury. "Not like you! Three and four times a week you're late for dinner, working on Saturdays and always bringing work home. For pity's sake, Patrick, you're the editor, the one in charge: You can do what you want."

He reached for her hand. She jerked it away. "I don't want to work all these hours, darlin'," he whispered, "but somebody has to."

"No, they don't! Ben never worked these hours when he was editor, and as his assistant, neither did you. Sometimes I think you're married to the *Herald* instead of to me."

"Marcy, darlin'—"

"Don't you 'darlin'' me. Something's got to change, Patrick, or the sleep you're so 'partial' to will be taking place in a very cold bed, indeed."

His chin hardened. "Don't threaten me, Marcy. I don't like it."

"No? Well, I don't like having a husband who's never home, nor one who only uses a bed for one thing—his precious sleep!"

Heat stung his neck. He lowered his head, ashamed at the truth of her statement. He couldn't remember the last time he had really held her in his arms, kissed her like he meant it, wanted her like he used to . . .

With grief in his heart, he reached out and gently pulled her to him, and this time she didn't fight. "Marcy, forgive me. I, well . . . work has been so demanding, I lose track . . . of everything." He cupped her face with his hands and kissed her gently, slowly, taking his time to enjoy her. "I love you, Marcy, more than I can express, and I'll work on it, I promise. You're my world, darlin', I don't want it to grow cold."

He felt her arms succumb and twine around his back. With a low groan, he kissed her again, deepening it until her passion matched his own.

She kissed him back with a vengeance and then pulled away.

"Patrick, I'm not over this yet," she whispered, "not completely. But I do love you . . . so much it hurts."

He sighed and held her close, tucking his head into the curve of her neck. "I know, darlin'. God knows I don't always deserve it. But I do know."

# 5

Brady shifted on the sofa and then flipped to stare at the ceiling for the umpteenth time. He glanced at his watch in the moonlight and groaned—4:40 a.m. He tried closing his eyes once again. The scene with Beth on the swing reeled in his brain like a silent movie. His eyes blinked open, dazed and staring, just like they'd been all night, always accompanied by a throb of heat, and always with a siege of guilt.

He sat up on the couch and shifted his bare feet to the floor, dropping his head in his hands. His heart was racing and his hands were sweating, and his body buzzed with a desire he thought he'd long since conquered. God knows he hadn't asked for this. Had, in fact, done everything in his power to avoid it. But the beast had been unleashed the moment Beth's mouth had singed his. He licked his dry lips, and the taste of fear pasted his throat. *God help me*, he prayed, all the while craving the touch of her body against his. Shame burned along with the heat of desire, and he shivered involuntarily, fingers trembling as they sifted through his hair. *God forgive me*.

He jumped up and began pacing the room. He was desperate to block the thoughts from his mind: the touch of her skin, the taste of her mouth.

All at once, he sagged to his knees with a painful groan and buried his head in his hands. "Strengthen me, Lord, I beg you. Infuse me with your grace to do your will and not my own.

You said the spirit is willing, but the flesh is weak. Oh, God, you know me so well—I need your strength, *please*, for I am so weak."

*God is faithful, who will not suffer you to be tempted above that ye are able; but will with the temptation also make a way to escape, that ye may be able to bear it.*

The air stilled in his lungs. God's Word, so warm and familiar, drifted in his mind like a soft, calming breeze that gentled his soul. His breathing slowed and his runaway pulse returned to a normal rhythm. He drew in a deep breath and sat back on his heels, eyes still closed. "Thank you, Lord, for your peace, your strength. You have never failed me, not once. Please help me to never fail you."

Something wet and akin to sandpaper slurped across his cheek, and Brady opened his eyes. A sleepy Miss Hercules, still damp from her bath, delivered another soggy kiss. The smell of wet dog rose to his nostrils, a timely reminder of God's intervention in his life. He lassoed the sheepdog around the neck and smiled, planting a kiss of his own on the tip of her cold, wet nose. "You smell to high heaven, you know that, girl? But since it's 'high heaven' that sent Cluny and you, I guess I won't complain."

Miss Hercules grunted and plopped on the floor with a loud thump, finally slumping against the sofa to sleep. Brady carefully stepped over the bulk of her body and crawled onto the sofa with a tired groan, having little choice but to follow her lead.

The obnoxious thumping in his brain reminded him of hangovers from rowdier days. *Bam, bam, bam*—like someone pounding his skull with a padded two-by-four. Brady tried to open his eyes, but the effort was too great. It was all he could do to lift himself from the makeshift pillow beneath his throbbing head.

*Bam, bam, bam. Woof, woof, woof.* Brady moaned and flailed a hand over the side of the couch in an effort to calm Miss Hercules, who staggered up, as sleep-drugged as he. "Lie down, girl, and go back to sleep. I can't move yet." With a sleepy growl, Miss Hercules plunked against the couch, jarring Brady's senses.

Brady massaged his eyelids, crusty with sleep, until he was able to peel them open. He blinked several times before he realized the noisy pounding had come from his front door rather than his head. With a painful grunt, he tried to rise from the couch, only to stumble over Miss Hercules, who had wasted no time rejoining the ranks of the dead.

*Boom, boom, boom!* The knocks were more insistent now, and Brady stubbed his toe as he scrambled for the door. A swear word he hadn't uttered in years leapt from his lips, causing heat to shoot up the back of his neck. Breathing hard, he unflipped the lock and hurled the door wide, gritting his teeth against the pain.

"Sweet mother of Job, is this what you look like every morning?"

Brady blinked. The motion produced a nagging ache between his eyes. "Charity. What the devil are you doing here?"

"Well, nice to see you too." She maneuvered her stomach to saunter into his flat, then took off her coat and tossed it on a hook by the door. She flashed a smile so bright, it hurt his eyes.

He massaged his temple with his fingers. "Sorry, I have the most awful headache."

"Mmmm . . . restless night?"

He eyed her through narrowed lids and flipped the door closed. "Very."

Miss Hercules chose that moment to rise from the dead and amble over. She sniffed the calf-length hem of Charity's blue cotton shift. Charity spun around with a startled squeak, lurching a protective hand over her stomach.

"Dear Lord, it's a horse!" She sniffed and wrinkled her nose. "Oh my, and it smells like one too."

Brady's laugh was followed by a moan. He kneaded the bridge of his nose as he shuffled back to the sofa. "Her name is Miss Hercules, and she belongs to a friend of mine." He sat on the edge of the seat. "What are you doing here?"

She patted Miss Hercules on the head, then smelled her hand and scowled. "Oooo . . . mind if I wash my hands?"

He nodded toward the bathroom down the hall, then sank back with a yawn.

She returned a few moments later and settled on the other end of the couch. "Goodness, I must have slept through that tornado last night . . . or did it just touch down in your bathroom?"

"Don't make me smile, it hurts."

"Sorry, it's just that I've never seen you—or your things—in such disarray." She hesitated. "You're not hung over, are you?"

That got his attention. He opened one eye to glare, and it was well worth the pain. "You know better than that. I haven't touched the stuff since I was seventeen."

"Sorry, but it was a natural assumption, you know, with the headache and all." She leaned in. "Shouldn't you take some aspirin or at least eat something? Want me to make you some coffee? Mine has got to be better than the sludge you make at the shop."

He managed a smile. "Collin railroaded me into buying a newfangled dripolator at the shop, I'll have you know. But, no thanks, all I really need is a few hours of decent sleep."

"But it's almost nine! Aren't you going to church?"

Brady groaned and glanced out the window. "No, it can't be that late. My head's barely hit the pillow."

Charity gave him a ghost of a smile. "So . . . what exactly kept you tossing and turning all night, Mr. Brady? Miss Hercules? A nasty tornado? Or my sister?"

Brady scowled. "Knock it off, Charity. I'm not in the mood."

She grinned and jumped up. "Tell me where the aspirin is, my friend. Your disposition needs it something awful."

"Second shelf, next to the stove."

She bustled into the kitchen, humming under her breath. He heard the cabinet open and close, followed by running tap water. Her smile was positively annoying as she handed him the glass. He grabbed it and palmed the aspirin, giving her a hard stare while he swallowed.

"There, that's better, isn't it? Now, how 'bout some coffee?"

"I don't want to talk about it, Charity."

She hurried back to the kitchen. "No, but I do. And so does Lizzie. You can't keep avoiding it, Brady. My sister's in love with you."

He exhaled his defeat. "So I've been told."

She clattered around in the kitchen for a while, making a racket he was sure would wake Cluny. Before long, the aroma of coffee reminded him he was not only tired but hungry as well. She reappeared and handed him a glass of juice and a plate of buttered toast. "Here, eat. You look like the devil, and you're acting like it too."

Resigned to his fate, he took the glass from her hand and gulped it. He set it down and snatched a piece of toast, then began to munch. He stared straight ahead.

She put the plate on the sofa table and sat, searing his profile. "So . . . what are you going to do about it?"

He swiped another piece of toast and chomped hard. "None of your business."

"It is too. I love you, and I love Lizzie. And God knows when it comes to making a move, John Brady, even Sam Adams' statue on Washington Street moves faster than you."

He sighed and wiped the crumbs from his mouth. "There are no moves to make. Lizzie is like a sister to me."

"That's not what I heard."

"What?"

"I heard you kissed her. And pretty intensely, from the sound of it."

Blood shot to his face. "She told you that?"

"Yes, Brady, she did. Right after she cried herself silly. So, I repeat, at the risk of becoming a nag—what are you going do about it?"

He slumped on the sofa. "I don't know," he whispered.

"What do you mean, you don't know? You love her, don't you?"

He didn't answer.

"Brady, this is me, Charity, the one you hammered on that lying was wrong. Tell me the truth. Do you love Lizzie?"

"Yes, you know I do, as a sister—"

"No, Brady, I'm not talking about that kind of love. I'm talking about the kind of love where she makes you warm inside, tingly. You know, where you want her, like a man wants a woman?"

"I don't have to answer that." He avoided her eyes.

A soft, weary breath escaped into the air. "No, Brady, but the way you kissed her did. It told Lizzie loud and clear that you're attracted to her."

His head snapped up. "Don't say that. It's not true!"

She arched a brow.

"All right, it is true," he muttered, "but it can't be. You don't understand, Charity, I can't act on it."

She folded her arms on top of her stomach and assessed him through slitted eyes. "And why is that, exactly? You have a sudden hankering to be a priest?"

His laugh was hollow. "God help me, don't I wish."

"Well, something's holding you back, and Lizzie has a right to know. She told me you were engaged once, but your fiancée broke it off during the war. Does that have anything to do with it? Are you afraid?"

"No."

Charity was losing her patience. "Well, what, then? So help me, Brady, Mitch wasted two years of our lives pretending he wasn't in love with me. I don't want to see Lizzie go through the same thing."

Brady met her gaze. "She won't."

"She already is." Charity shimmied back into the deep cushion of the sofa, arms folded, as if to settle in for a while. Her lips flattened into a mulish press. "I'm not leaving this room, John Brady, until you tell me the truth. What's stopping you from loving my sister? Spill it—now! What deep, dark secret are you hiding?"

He lunged up from the sofa and started pacing, sidestepping Miss Hercules, who sprawled on the floor in a limp mass of fur. He finally stopped, his back to her. "I can't love her, Charity . . . because I'm weak."

"What do you mean, 'weak'?"

He breathed in deeply and exhaled. "I mean I have a problem . . . or at least I had a problem." He turned to face her with shame in his eyes. "Last night, when Beth kissed me, I was shocked at first. But then, I couldn't stop myself . . . I wanted to run, but . . . she was like a drug in my system, a craving I couldn't fight. I wanted more."

Charity's brows crinkled as she leaned forward. "Of course you did. You're in love with her. That's natural."

He groaned and raked his fingers through his hair. "No, it's not. Not for me. You don't understand . . . it's like I can't stop. Even last night, I couldn't sleep because I couldn't get it out of my mind, the thoughts, the desire . . ." He started pacing again.

"So get married—quickly—like Mitch and I did."

He paused, his muscles sagging from lack of sleep. "No, it's more than that."

"What, then?"

He looked away, unwilling for her to see the fear in his eyes.

"My love for Beth . . . it just feels wrong to me. Kissing her—even thinking about kissing her—feels dirty somehow, sinful. And she deserves more."

"For the millionth time, Brady, Lizzie is not your sister."

"No, no she's not, but every time I look at her, I see that gangly thirteen-year-old with wide, innocent eyes, and I . . . I can't help it, my mind sees her that way."

"But not your body."

He hung his head. "No." He finally looked up with grief in his eyes and a warning in his tone. "But I can't go there, Charity, don't push me. It can never happen."

"We can pray about it—"

"No! I've prayed about it enough, and this is the answer I've been given."

"The answer? Or the excuse?"

A muscle flickered in his cheek. "It doesn't matter. The decision's been made."

"And I suppose Lizzie doesn't have a say?"

He steeled his jaw. "No."

"I see." Charity exhaled a heavy breath, then strained to rise to her feet. "You're going to lose her, you know."

He flinched. "I know."

She marched to the door and snatched her coat off the hook, then jerked it open without a look back. "I never thought I would say this, John Brady, but just for the record, you're a fool."

She slammed the door behind her and he blinked, moving to the sofa in a trance. He slumped hard into the cool leather seat and put his head in his hands.

Yeah, he knew that too.

Brady took deadly aim. The basketball sailed through the air and into the basket with a hard whoosh, giving him a profound sense of satisfaction. He rolled his neck and grinned at Father Mac, who was sweating profusely despite being in remarkably good shape for a forty-three-year-old priest. Brady palmed the ball and tucked it under one arm while swiping at his face with the other. This was one way to release pent-up frustration and energy, he supposed. As long as he wasn't excommunicated.

Father Mac doubled over, hands on his knees, huffing like he needed last rites. "It might behoove ya to show a little mercy, you know. God doesn't take too kindly to trouncing the clergy."

"Sorry, Father, fresh out of mercy today," Brady said with an off-center smile. He extended his arm and thrust the ball with a quick flick of his wrist. It sloped into the basket with a neat, clean whish.

Father Mac pried a finger around his collar and coughed, his face flushed after a grueling game of one on one in the blazing sun. He made his way to the rectory door with as much dignity as possible, given a strained muscle and a black clerical shirt soaked with sweat. "Well, I suggest you start practicing it, John. You're going to need it yourself when some young whelp wipes the court up with you. You want an iced tea?" He turned, brow lifted. "I'm exercising mercy, mind you."

Brady smiled and followed him inside. He sat at the table in the cozy black and white kitchen that Mrs. Clary kept in spic-and-span shape, and instantly felt at home. Maybe because he'd spent many a night here, debating theological study with Father Matthew McHugh, a man who was more a friend than an associate pastor. Brady had taken to Father Mac immediately when he'd attended St. Stephen's with Collin almost four years ago. Raised without religion, Brady's conversion to Christ and subsequent hunger for the Bible had taken place in his late teens. It seemed his extensive knowledge of God's Word had proved to be a competent match for Father Mac, who reveled in sparring with Brady over any and everything Bible related. When Brady had decided to convert, Father Mac had taken him under his wing, and in very little time, the two men had forged a deep respect for each other, as well as a close friendship.

Brady studied him now as he poured the tea, wondering if perhaps his own fate wasn't meant to follow a similar path. Matt, as Father Mac had insisted he call him, seemed an unlikely match for the priesthood. His boundless energy, even at forty-three, sometimes put Brady to shame, making the fifteen years between them almost nonexistent. At six foot, he was an impressive cut of a man, with the stocky build of hardened muscle and dark hair sifted with gray. He had a warm smile and an easy personality laced with dry wit, and certainly appeared to be attractive to women, or at least Charity had told him so. But he'd chosen to serve God instead, and that single fact held great fascination for Brady.

Father Mac hunched his shoulders several times, obviously working out some kinks before setting the tea on the table. He strolled over to smell a fresh-baked pecan pie on the counter, then shot Brady a narrow look. "Now this would be true mercy on your heartless soul after the royal shellacking you gave me. Allow me to demonstrate turning the other cheek, if you will. You starve me of dignity, and I feed you with mercy." He reached for utensils from the drawer and two saucers from the cupboard, then proceeded to cut them each a piece. He set the plates on the table and dropped into a chair with a groan of relief and a twinkle in his eye. "So what were you trying to vent out there? A vendetta against Collin? What's he done now?"

Brady reached for the tea and upended half the glass before answering. "Nope, Collin doesn't frustrate me most of the time. He's family." He dug into the warm pie with a faint frown. "You could say he's the brother I never had."

"Well, something lit your fire today. Normally you don't resort to such blatant humiliation."

Brady glanced up and grinned. "Sorry, Matt. I figured if anybody could handle it, you could. Collin tends to get grouchy when I whip him at sports, and I sure couldn't take it out on Cluny."

"No, no, I'm glad. It's rather handy, actually. You annihilate and repent, and I absorb and absolve. Nice and neat." He hunkered down to tackle the pie. "So, what is bothering you, John?"

"What makes you think something's bothering me? Maybe you're just lousy at basketball. Ever think of that?"

"No, I can't say that thought ever crossed my mind, at least not until today." He nodded at Brady's pie, which he'd inhaled in three rapid-fire gulps. "Maybe it's the way you're bolting down that dessert or even the annoying twitch in your leg, which hasn't stopped teetering the table since you sat down, despite an hour of near-maniacal exercise. Either way, something's on your mind." He swallowed some tea and set the glass down with a pronounced thud. "But, you're in luck, my friend. I just happen to be in the business of listening when people have something to unload. Take advantage."

Brady sighed and pushed his plate away. The notion had appeal, but he didn't want to think about his feelings for Beth, much less talk about them to Matt. Still, he was curious about something. He reached for his fork and began twiddling it on the plate. "What made you want to be a priest?"

Matt eyed him as he chewed. His dark hair fluttered in a gentle breeze that billowed through Mrs. Clary's black and white chintz curtains. It filled the room with the smell of fresh-mown grass and honeysuckle. "You mean over and above the great food, clean house, and dazzling wardrobe?" He rose to pour them both more tea. "I'd have to say my parents. Sometimes I think they had thirteen kids just to better their odds at getting a priest in the family. We all thought it was going to be my older brother, Ralph, but he ended up quitting and becoming a teacher. About broke their hearts."

"So you saved the day?"

He sat back down, then leaned in the chair and smiled, his eyes taking on a faraway look. "You might say that. I went with a couple of girls, almost married one, but couldn't shake the feeling that I was on the wrong path. I had this fire inside, you know? I suddenly realized it wasn't for her." He looked up and grinned. "Or maybe I should qualify that. I had a fire for her all right, but it was pretty much physical. In my head and my heart, I was being pulled in another direction. So I prayed about it and wrestled with it for a while, then finally decided I had a calling."

"Do you like it?" Brady squinted up at him.

Matt laughed. "What's not to like? All the comforts of home and no nagging. But, yeah, I'm content. It feels good devoting your life to God . . . to helping people. Why, you interested?"

It was Brady's turn to laugh. "I doubt I'd qualify. Too many skeletons in my closet and a past that even Harry Houdini couldn't escape."

Matt angled a brow. "Yeah, well, that's the beauty of faith in God. Forgiveness is a great fringe benefit." He paused to notch out another forkful of pie. "But while we're on the subject of major life decisions, suppose you tell me why you've never married."

That took him by surprise. Heat chafed the back of his neck. "Never met the right girl, I suppose."

"Hard to do, I guess, when you avoid them like the plague."

Brady glanced up. "Did Collin—"

"Yeah, he did. On more than one occasion. He worries about you, John. Thinks you're lonely."

Irritability twitched under his skin. "And that coming from a man who once couldn't sleep alone if his life depended on it." Brady glanced up. "Sorry, Father. His morals have obviously changed for the better, but he's still got this thing about being alone. Trust me, I'm no Collin."

"Obviously. Before the war, his reputation with women was

the meat of many a prayer. Especially his mother's." Father Mac paused, rubbing his thumb along the bottom of his glass. "Do you like women, Brady?"

The heat from the back of his neck bled into his face. "What?"

"Do you like women? Are you attracted to them?"

Brady stared. "What the devil kind of question is that?"

"An honest one." Father Mac leaned both elbows on the table, his eyes suddenly serious. "And perhaps a necessary one."

"What?" He couldn't get the words out fast enough. "Yes, of course I like women." He thought of Beth, and blood surged to his cheeks. "I just don't choose to act on it, that's all."

"Why?"

His jaw dropped. "Why? You're a priest and you want to know *why*?"

"It's not a sin to spend time with a woman, John."

Brady rose abruptly to fetch the tea from the counter. He jerked the pitcher over his glass, unleashing a deluge of liquid onto the table. He ground his jaw and filled Matt's glass before swiping a dishrag from the sink. "I never said it was. I spend plenty of time with women—Beth O'Connor, for one, not to mention her sisters."

A faint smile creased Father Mac's lips. He took a sip of tea, observing Brady over the rim of his glass. "Ah yes, Elizabeth O'Connor. A beautiful girl. Collin says you like her."

The dishrag hung limp in his hand, not unlike his jaw at the moment. "You might as well absolve me right now, Matt, because I'm gonna hurt Collin real bad tomorrow morning."

Father Mac let loose with a low chuckle, then swallowed some tea. "Do you?"

Brady arched the dishrag into the sink as precisely as a ball into a net. "Sure. She's the little sister I never had. I love her. Want the best for her. Period."

"And you're not it, I suppose? The best, I mean?"

Brady forced a smile and dropped into the chair. "No, definitely not."

"Even if you're attracted to her?"

Brady shoved his empty plate away. "Okay, that settles it. Collin's a dead man. Look, Matt, I've told Collin, I've told Beth, and now I'm telling you. Beth O'Connor is one of the most special people I've ever met. But she's nothing more than a sister to me, plain and simple. I have no romantic designs on her whatsoever, nor any woman. Not because I don't like them, but because I don't need to marry one to be happy. Unlike Collin." He guzzled the rest of his tea, then pushed his glass back with a grin he hoped would soften the strain of his words. "Besides, I think I may have a calling."

Matt didn't smile. "Yeah, I think you do. And something tells me you're running away from it."

Brady blinked, then stood to his feet, his jaw suddenly tight. "Look, Matt, my personal life is my business. I have enough problems keeping Collin out of it. Don't start with me, please. I value your friendship way too much."

Matt nodded and rose, his eyes meeting Brady's. "And I, yours. Forgive me for stepping over the line, John. But like Collin, I'm only guilty of caring."

Brady swabbed his face with the palm of his hand. "I know, Matt, and I'm grateful. And maybe sometime down the road, we can talk. Just not now."

Father Mac smiled and carried the dirty dishes to the sink. He turned and fixed a challenging eye on Brady, softened by a glint of humor. "That's fine, John, for now. You can stop me from probing, but you can't stop me from praying. About this . . . or our next game of basketball. Be warned. I plan to win if it takes a chain of novenas to do it."

A grin traveled Brady's lips, chasing all tension away. He swiped his basketball from the counter and strolled to the door, sparing one final look at his friend. "Thanks for the game and the pie, Father. And God be with you. You're gonna need it."

Collin sauntered into the bedroom with a damp towel over his shoulder and that look in his eye. His chestnut hair was slicked back and dark from his bath. "Tired?" he asked.

*Tired? At 11:00 o'clock on a Sunday night, after a hectic day?* Faith glanced up from her book to give him her full attention and felt the same catch in her chest every time her husband entered a room. It was almost two and half years since they'd taken their vows, and yet he never failed to draw her gaze or quicken her pulse. She took in the sculpted curve of his muscled arms and the hard, lean chest that tapered into pajama bottoms slung low on his hips, and still couldn't believe it. Collin McGuire, the gleam of longing in so many girls' eyes, was all hers. She took a quick breath, enjoying the warmth he stirred within.

Her smile was mysterious. "Not too."

His gray eyes twinkled as he ambled over and carefully took the book from her hands and placed it on the nightstand. He tossed his towel over a chair. "Good to hear," he whispered before turning out the light and slipping under the covers. His skin was still damp from the bath, and she could smell the clean scent of his soap. He immediately pulled her close and ran his hand down the curve of her flannel nightgown. Her pulse was pounding when his mouth found hers, teasing her lips with a gentle tug of his teeth.

"Are you doing this because you want me or a baby?" she whispered.

His low laughter rumbled against her throat. "A baby. You're just a tempting excuse."

She giggled and tried to bat him away, but he only tugged her closer with a dangerous glint in his eye. "You best love me like you should, Mrs. McGuire, or I'll be asking Father McCovey or Father McHugh to pay you a visit."

"Oh, and you'll be trying to get the Church on your side, will you?"

He grinned. "I will at that. I'll be needing a son to carry on my name, so I suggest you comply, or else . . ."

She teased the curve of his full lip with her finger. "Or else what?"

He laid her back on the bed and buried his head in the crook of her neck. She felt the vibration of his wayward chuckle. "You'll be giving your notice at the *Herald* from sheer fatigue, Little Bit, and make no mistake." His mouth found her lips again and took their time. She moaned and he slowly pulled away. He studied her through hooded eyes. "Maybe you should anyway."

She smiled. "Should what?"

His smoldering gaze seemed intent on hypnotizing her. "Give your notice."

"What?"

He leaned to press his mouth to her ear, pausing to feather her earlobe with his tongue. His words were warm and low. "Come on, Faith, we don't need the money. I provide a good living. Wouldn't it be nice not to go to work for once, just stay home like Charity? Spend more time with your mother and sisters?"

The sweet warmth of his breath suddenly blew cold in her ear. She stilled, measuring her words. "Charity works. She has the store."

"Which Emma now runs since Mitch put his foot down."

"She still does the books—"

"From home, when he lets her, which isn't all that often." Collin silenced all further protest with a kiss.

She pushed him away. "That's it, isn't it?"

"What?"

"You want me to stay home like Charity, be pregnant like Charity, and all for one reason—you're competing with Mitch!"

Collin scowled. "You're out of your mind. I could care less about Dennehy. I've wanted you to quit way before he came on the scene."

Heat flooded her cheeks that had nothing to do with her husband's touch. She shoved him away and jumped from the bed, bare feet in ready stance. Her eyes burned with anger as she swiped at the wild strands of hair tumbling down the front of her gown. "So we're back to that, are we? You wouldn't let up before we were married, and now I suppose that's why you hound me every night too—some diabolical plan to get me pregnant so I'll be forced to quit my job."

Collin sat up in the bed, his eyes glazed with shock. "*Hound* you? That's what you call it? Well, forgive me for disturbing your beauty sleep—I'll make sure you get plenty in the future. And while we're on the subject of 'diabolical,' I suppose you think you and your sisters' cold, calculated manipulation of Brady's emotions would be sanctioned by the Pope."

She slapped her hands on her hips and leaned in with fire in her eyes. "It's for his own good, and you know it."

"Yeah, that's why he tore out of here faster than you fall asleep when I'm in the mood."

Faith caught her breath, stunned at his attack. With a grunt, she snatched a pillow and pelted it at his face. "*In the mood?* You're never *out* of the mood, you drooling baboon. As far as I'm concerned, you only have one mood in that one-track mind of yours, and it isn't to sleep. You want a baby so badly? Well, be my guest—cozy up on the couch and dream of one!"

Collin leapt up and jabbed the pillow under his arm. He jerked a cover from the bed. "With pleasure. I suggest you get yourself another blanket from wherever the devil you keep them. You'll be needing it." He charged from the room and slammed the door hard, rattling the hinges and stealing her wind.

She dropped to the bed and put her head in her hands, too dazed to understand what had just happened. Tears stung her eyes. *Oh, Collin!*

She bounded up and started for the door.

*He wants you to quit the job you love.*

She stopped, allowing pride to steel her heart.

*He knows you love it, but he doesn't care. His pride is at stake. To be equal with Mitch.*

Renewed fury flared, and she marched to the closet and yanked a quilt off the shelf before hurrying back to their bed, her lips stiff with defiance. She snapped the blanket in the air with a hard pop, then laid it over the bed and crawled in, chilled to the bone.

*Pride goeth before destruction, and a haughty spirit before a fall.*

Faith curled on her side and jabbed her pillow hard. "Well then, Lord, maybe you should tell *him* that! After all, it's his stubborn pride that's causing all this." She huffed out a sigh and closed her eyes, still seething from Collin's remarks.

*Be ye angry, and sin not . . .*

Faith rolled on her back and stared at the ceiling with a moan. "But it's *so* hard! I never knew it was going to be this hard. Forgiving Charity was one thing. Submitting to a pigheaded Irishman when he's completely wrong is more than I bargained for." She blew out a blast of air and balled her pillow under her head. "Oh, all right. I'll apologize in the morning—"

*Let not the sun go down upon your wrath.*

She gritted her teeth and squeezed her eyes tight, pretending the thought had never come. No! She was not about to give in tonight. Let him stew. She turned over with a grunt and tried to get comfortable. She *would* sleep tonight, she vowed, and deal with her husband in the morning.

Twenty minutes later, she eyed the clock with a groan. She shot up in the dark and glared at the ceiling. "All right, okay, you win! I'll do it your way, but only because I need my sleep. And you have to help me, because I really, *really* don't want to do this right now. But I will—and only for you." She sighed and got out of bed, her anger slowly dissipating. She tiptoed to the door and put her hand on the knob. All at once, her sorrow chilled her more than the cool drafts in the room. She hung her head and put a hand to her eyes, sagging against the door.

"Oh, God, what was I thinking? I'm so sorry for hurting my husband, for not respecting him as you've commanded me to do. I love him, Lord, and I let my foolish pride push him away. Please forgive me."

She drew in a clean breath, opened the door, and padded down the hall to the parlor. Collin was sprawled on his back across their gold brocade sofa, one leg stiff on the arm and the other dangling off the front. Faith chewed her lip and pressed a hand to her chest. *Oh my, he couldn't possibly be comfortable!* She spotted the cover bunched in a wad across his midsection and shivered. With his hair mussed, eyelids closed, and spiky lashes way too long for a man, he looked like such a little boy. His soft breathing filled the room, causing his smooth chest to rise and fall. Her heart ached with a rush of love.

She leaned to gently shake him. "Collin, come to bed."

He groaned in his sleep and turned, causing the blanket to slither to the floor. A heavy snort gurgled out before he finally sank into the back curve of the sofa. Her lips tilted into a soft smile. She swore the man could sleep on an ottoman if he had to. She picked the blanket up and carefully laid it over him, then pressed a kiss to his cheek. "Good night, my love. I'm sorry for hurting you. And tomorrow night . . . I'll show you how much."

6

Collin was muttering under his breath when the front door of the shop opened and closed. He ignored it, irritated by the annoying jangling of the bell, as he continued filling the Silex dripolator with cold water. He scooped ground coffee into the upper chamber none too gently, forcing a measure of the precious granules to skitter all over the counter. He mumbled under his breath and gave the "on" button a belligerent swipe, then glared at the clock on the wall. Six a.m. *It's too blasted early for this.*

"Whoa, take it easy, buddy, we just spent a fortune for that silly thing." Brady's tone took on a hint of jest. "Treat it like you treat Faith—gentle and coaxing, till you get what you need."

"Shut up, Brady." Collin pushed past his partner to storm into the front room. He dropped into his chair with a loud squeak and shoved a neat pile of invoices out of his way. They fanned across his desk like a deck of cards, several fluttering right off the edge. Collin swore again and snatched at the hefty pile of orders heaped high in his in-basket.

Brady quietly retrieved the stray papers from the floor and stacked them with the others, far from Collin's reach. He perched on the edge and eyed his friend with deep concern. "So . . . why are you here at this ridiculous hour and what made you wake up on the wrong side of the bed?"

Collin grunted and started scanning the orders, never seeing a word. He finally flung them in the direction of the invoices and leaned back to heave his legs up on the desk. He exhaled a tight breath and put his hand to his eyes. "Couch."

"Pardon?"

"It was a blasted couch, not a bed, and it was the blasted woman in the bed who's responsible for me getting up on the wrong side."

Brady crossed his arms and whistled. "No kidding? Faith threw you out of her bed? I don't believe it. What'd you do?"

Collin burned him with a look. "*Our* bed, Brady, not hers. And I didn't do anything but try to make love to the woman."

Brady squinted. "That's it? And she let you go to bed angry? On the couch?"

"Yeah, she did." Collin's boot pushed at a lone sheet of paper and sent it sailing to the floor. "Feels like I slept on this blasted desk. First glimmer of dawn, I hightailed it out of there while she snoozed away like a princess in a warm, cozy bed." He poked a finger hard against his chest. "My bed! She even had the nerve to accuse me of competing with Mitch. Blast it all, Brady, it's been over two years and there's still no sign of a baby! I know that if I could just get her to slow down and quit her job—"

"Wait, you didn't tell her that, did you?"

Collin shifted in the chair. Muscles tightened in his jaw. "Yeah, I did, so what?"

"Come on, Collin, you know how much Faith loves her job. Why would you do that? You don't remember all the fights you had when you were engaged?"

"Yeah, I remember, and I've laid low for a long time now. But I want a son, Brady, and nothing's happening. And apparently if I leave it up to her, it never will."

"How 'bout leaving it up to God?"

Collin's eyes narrowed. "I'm just doing my part, like she should be doing hers. But all she does is act like I'm some wanton letch with one thing on my mind."

Brady smiled. "Well, aren't you?"

Collin scowled. "No! I just want a family—like Patrick and Marcy. Is that so awful?"

"No, but you've got time for that. You're only twenty-seven, and Faith's only twenty-four. It'll happen, Collin. Just pray about it, trust God, and love your wife."

Collin sighed and massaged the bridge of his nose. "Yeah, well, for your information, I have been praying about it and I do trust God. But I have to tell ya, she's made the last one pretty tough." He looked up, hurt. "Do you know that she actually called me a 'drooling baboon'?"

Brady grinned. "She always has been a stickler for the truth."

"It's not just that, Brady, it's the fact that she doesn't seem to want me as much I want her." Collin folded his arms and frowned, a bit chastened. "It kind of hurts the ol' ego, you know? I've never had a problem like this in the past. Before I married Faith, women couldn't seem to keep their hands off me."

"Yeah, well, Faith is your wife, not a woman hoping to win you with favors. Besides, she may have a point. You're obsessed with having a family, and maybe even a bit jealous of Mitch. Add that to a man who's always had a pretty overactive drive, and I think you may be out of balance. Give her some space. Love her without the agenda."

"Yeah, I'll give her space, all right. Plenty of space. Enough to cut down on my drooling, anyway." He flashed an evil grin. "And maybe step up hers."

Brady cocked a brow. "Games, Collin? Sounds like you're nursing a grudge."

Collin's laugh was wicked as he jumped up to get coffee. "Speaking of 'games' and 'grudges,' ol' buddy, what the devil happened to you the other night? Why'd you take off?"

The tables were suddenly turned, and Brady didn't like it

one bit. He steeled his jaw and followed Collin to the back. Reaching for his work apron, he tied it with a hard jerk, then headed for the press.

Collin's hand gripped his shoulder. "Oh no you don't, John, you're not going to disappear under that machine, at least not yet. I just spilled my guts, and now it's your turn. Here's your coffee, ol' buddy, park it awhile." Collin set Brady's cup on the table and pulled out a chair. He grabbed another and straddled it. The set of his mouth was a clear indication he wouldn't take no for an answer.

Brady heaved a weary sigh and sat. He fisted the hot cup and gulped it, ignoring the burning sensation searing his throat.

Collin gritted his teeth. "Oooow! Doesn't that burn?"

Brady nodded and closed his eyes. The beginning of a headache pulsed in his brain. He reached up to massage his forehead. When he opened his eyes again, Collin looked worried.

"What happened, John? I'm guessing the plan backfired?"

"The plan?"

"To get you and Lizzie together. Charity cooked it up . . . *and* my saintly wife."

Brady took a deep breath and exhaled. "I should have known. That's not like Beth."

"Maybe it is. That girl is crazy in love with you. She'd do anything to turn your head."

"So I've learned." Brady took another hefty swig of coffee. This time he barely noticed the burn. "She kissed me."

A smile tugged at Collin's lips. "No kidding? Our Lizzie?"

Brady stared him down. "It can't happen, Collin. I refuse to get involved with her."

"You're already 'involved' with her. Didn't you like it?"

"Yeah, I liked it. Lost a whole night of sleep because I liked it. If it wasn't the attraction driving me crazy, it was the guilt. I can't handle it."

"Guilt? Over what?"

Brady leaned in, his eyes burning more than the coffee.

"For thinking of her that way, for going too far in my mind, for the sick feeling I get. I know she's not my sister, Collin, but I can't help it—I feel . . . ashamed. I can't afford to hurt her, and I can't afford to hurt God." He looked up, feeling like a man on the edge. "And I will, Collin, I will . . . if it continues. I know my own failings."

Collin blinked and his mouth slacked open. "So that's why you don't go near women? You're afraid? Of the thoughts? That you won't stop?"

Brady sagged into the chair and looked away. "I have a troubled past. I don't react like a normal man. If I were to give in to Beth, or any other woman, it . . . it would control me, take me down." He closed his eyes and swallowed hard. "Like it did before, a long, long time ago. I won't go there again, Collin, not even for Beth."

"John, God has delivered you from your past. He wants you to be happy—in every way. Marriage can do that. Marriage to Lizzie."

"No! I told you before, it's wrong."

Collin paused, then shifted in his seat, his voice slow and measured. "There's nothing wrong about it, Brady . . . except in your own mind. What happened to you, anyway? Way back when? Something's got a hold of you, my friend, and it scares me."

"God help me, it scares *me*! So much I can't even think about Beth that way without shame."

Collin placed a hand on Brady's arm. "John, talk to me. Tell me what happened. We can pray about it."

He shook his head. "No, I don't want to talk about it—ever. Just pray for me, please, that God gives me the grace to get through this."

Collin stared for a long moment, then released a quiet breath. "All right, John, I'll pray—that you can face your past and give it to God. It's the only way you can be happy."

With a weary nod, Brady looked up. "I have to avoid her. Will you help me?"

Collin looked down at his hands and sighed. "Sure. What do you want me to do?"

"Will you give this to her?" He retrieved a letter from his coat pocket and laid it on the table.

"A letter's not going to keep her away, you know."

"I know, but if I'm never here when she comes around, it might."

Collin picked the letter up and jostled it in his hand. "What if she comes at lunchtime, like usual?"

"Then I won't be here—you will. From now on, I'll take the noon deliveries."

Collin peered up beneath slitted eyes. "You got it all worked out, don't you? But are you so sure you're doing the right thing?"

"Yeah, I'm sure." He moved to the press and sank to the floor, disappearing on the dolly beneath. He stared at the underbelly of the press and closed his eyes, seeing only Beth's face. *The right thing. For Beth . . . and for me.*

⋗ ⋖

"Soooo . . . give me all the details! I'm dying to know. How was it?" Millie pounced on Lizzie like a toad on a fly, steering her toward the back room of Bookends the moment she entered the store. Millie's eyes, smudged with gray shadow and black eyeliner, blinked wide in anticipation as she pursed her cupid's-bow mouth. "Tell me the truth—did you finally let him kiss you?"

Lizzie arched her brows. "Give me a moment to breathe, will you, Millie? I just stepped through the door."

"I'll bet Tom Weston didn't give you a moment to breathe, did he?"

"*Millie!*"

"Well, did he? Every girl I know is carrying a torch for him but you. Unless, of course, he managed to change your mind." Millie wiggled her pencil-thin brows.

Lizzie put a cool hand to her hot cheek. "Stop! You're embarrassing me."

Millie laughed and grabbed Lizzie's arm. She hauled her to the back and down the hall with as much propriety as she could with Mr. Harvey glaring after them. She pushed her into a chair at the table in the rear of the store where a scarred wood counter was stacked high with boxes and books. She sat down beside her, almost breathless. "Come on, Lizzie, we've got fifteen minutes before the store opens, so level with me. Did Tom Weston kiss you?"

Lizzie felt a burn in her cheeks. "Yes."

"Did you kiss him back?"

"I suppose."

Millie grinned. "And were you a pushover?"

"Absolutely not!" Lizzie jolted up in the chair. "You know how I feel about that."

"Yeah, but that was before he kissed you." She buffed her nails on her drop-waist sweater, then peeked up beneath thick lashes. "So, give! Was it wonderful?"

Wonderful? Lizzie sighed and reflected on the night before, when she'd sat on the porch swing with Tom Weston. It had been their fifth time out together and the fifth time he had tried to kiss her. But last night had been the very first time she let him, at least without objection, and the first time she ever really kissed him back.

She thought about him now, and her pulse quickened just a tad. He had the look of an athlete, with sandy hair and hazel eyes, his muscular body casual and confident as he'd lounged against the corner of the swing. She could still see his faint smile as he'd toyed with her hair, fondling it between his fingers as she'd chatted away. All at once, his hand moved to trace the curve of her neck, and then the line of her jaw, finally silencing her lips with the tips of his fingers. She remembered how they'd felt warm to the touch, like the feeling he was beginning to stir inside her. He whispered her name and slowly bent to kiss her, and her mouth had parted in surprise at the heat he triggered. With a low groan, he'd pulled her close and deepened the kiss, reminding her of that night with Brady. At the thought, the warmth that had seeped into her body suddenly turned cold, and she'd pushed him away. "Tom, I need to go in."

He clutched her close. "Lizzie, please, don't go. I care about you."

She stood to her feet, desperate to get away. "Thank you for a lovely evening, but I do need to go."

"Can I see you Saturday?"

She had stared, seeing only Brady's face, feeling his kiss.

"It was, wasn't it?"

Lizzie blinked. "What?"

Millie shook her arm. "His kiss! The way you've been staring off into space, it must have been pretty keen. So, when are you going to see him again?"

"Saturday."

"Oh, Lizzie, I swear, you are one of the luckiest girls alive."

A slight pout settled on Lizzie's lips. "How come I don't feel like it?"

"Because you're probably still mooning over John Brady. You need to forget him, and Tom Weston is the perfect man to help you do that."

Lizzie's ire rose. "No, there's only one 'perfect' man, Millie, and his name is John Brady. There's not another like him— honest, moral, decent." A spark of anger tinged her tone.

A quiet sigh drifted from Millie's lips. "No man is that perfect, Lizzie, except maybe those in the fairy tales you read to the kids. It's time you face up to that and get on with your life. Besides, it's been over a month since you've even seen him. And his letter made it perfectly clear he wanted to be left alone."

Her lip jutted. "But I miss him."

"If you'd just give Tom a chance, he'd remedy that in no time."

Lizzie sighed, her tone resigned. She patted her friend's arm.

"Sorry, Millie, for snapping at you like that. And I will give Tom a chance, I promise. But in the meantime, I miss Brady a lot—as a friend."

Millie folded her arms and arched her brows. Her scarlet lips pursed in doubt. "A friend?"

"Yes, a friend. Nothing more. If the man doesn't want me, I'm certainly not going to throw myself at him again. I just miss talking to him, that's all, and praying with him." Lizzie released a weary breath and lumbered to her feet. "I guess we better clock in. I'm surprised Mr. Harvey hasn't dispatched a search party by now."

"So, what are you going to do?" Millie asked.

Lizzie took her cloche hat off and hung it on a hook by the door. "I'm going to work."

"No, I mean about Brady. Your friendship. What are you going to do about that?"

Lizzie stole a quick glance in the oval mirror hanging by the door. She patted her shingled bob, then shot Millie a pursed smile that indicated trouble would be brewing on the horizon for Mr. John Brady. "Like I said—I'm going to work." She cocked a brow. "On getting him back."

ᵔᵕᵔ ᵔᵕᵔ

"So . . . why are we here again?"

Brady peered at Cluny out of the corner of his eye and prayed for patience. "Because it's Easter and we were invited."

"You couldn't say no?" Cluny stared up at him with a scowl on his freckled face, which for once was as clean and glowing as a baby's behind . . . or Cluny's, for that matter. Gram had been missing in action for over a month now, with no word as to when she might return. Brady had altered the boy's life considerably in that short time: clean clothes, clean body, clean dog. He glanced at the slight fourteen-year-old in his starched cotton shirt, all neatly tucked into plaid knickers that came just below the knee. Argyle knee socks and brand-new leather shoes completed the ensemble, causing Brady to feel a sense of pride. Along with a secret wish that Gram would stay put for a while.

He smiled and pressed a firm hand to Cluny's back as they ascended the steps to the O'Connors' front porch. "Sorry, bud. Collin brought out the big guns. He had his mother-in-law call."

Cluny gave Brady a half-lidded glare. "Wimp."

Brady fought a smile and pressed the doorbell. No doubt about it, the little brat had a way with the truth.

Cluny snorted. "I don't wanna be here and neither do you."

Brady sighed and clutched Cluny by the scruff of the neck. "No, I don't. But we're going to make the best of it because that's what civilized people do."

"What's 'civilized' mean?"

Brady thought of seeing Beth for the first time in over a month and sucked in a deep breath. "It means doing what you don't want because it's the right thing to do."

"Braaaady!" The door swung as wide as Katie's grin as she looked up with twinkling blue eyes. "Don't you like us anymore? We haven't seen you in forever!" Her gaze drifted to Cluny, and her little nose scrunched up. "What's this?"

Brady looked down at Cluny to make sure he wasn't scowling, but he needn't have bothered. A grin had sprouted on Cluny's face. Brady's jaw dropped when he saw him wink. "The name's Cluny McGee, you pretty little thing, and don't be forgettin' it."

Katie stared, blue eyes gaping along with her mouth. Her lips snapped shut, pinching into a hard line. "Sorry, my memory's short. Like you. You can sit at the kids' table. In the kitchen."

Cluny arched an almost invisible brow. "With you?"

Her eyes narrowed. "Not on your life. Let Collin suffer. He's the one who invited you."

"Your loss," he said with a nonchalant air. His grin turned

cocky as he sidled past Katie into the house, hands buried in the deep pockets of his knickers. Katie had him by half a head, but at the moment, Cluny towered way over her.

She blinked, then glanced up at Brady as if he had just brought a mud-soaked Miss Hercules home for dinner. "Tell me you're not related—please."

Brady laughed and gently tugged on a blond curl trailing her shoulder. He leaned close. "Be nice. He's practically an orphan."

She sniffed and closed the door. "I can see why."

"Hey, I thought you fell in somewhere, ol' buddy." Collin strolled into the foyer and glanced at his watch. "You're cuttin' it awfully close. Marcy's putting the food on the table now." He eyed Brady up and down—from his charcoal woolen vest and red geometric tie, to his gray seersucker slacks—then let out a low whistle. "Haven't seen you look this good since . . . well, I don't believe I ever have. I'd be hard-pressed to find a smudge of ink anywhere."

Brady shot him a patient look. "Settle down, Collin, it's Easter." He nodded his head at Cluny and rolled the sleeves of his white long-sleeved shirt. "I've got an example to set."

"So I see." Collin extended a hand. "Hey, Cluny, my man, put it there. I do believe you may turn some heads in those glad rags, don't you think, Katie Rose?"

"So you sit with him." Katie said and strolled from the room.

Cluny squinted up at Collin. "A bit uppity for a girl, ain't she though? She shor don't show much respect for elders."

"Well, Cluny, if you want my opinion," Collin said with a conspiratorial smile, "I'm convinced Katie Rose is a sixty-five-year-old woman in a ten-year-old body. And as far as respect for one's elders goes, don't take it to heart. Trust me, she doesn't show much respect to anybody, me included." He grinned and lowered his voice to a whisper. "But she sure is a whole lot of fun when you ruffle her feathers."

Cluny's grin spanned the whole of his face. "Is she now?" He turned and strutted after her, reminding Brady so much of a banty rooster that he shook his head and laughed.

Collin slung a loose arm over Brady's shoulder, eyeing him tentatively. "So, you okay with this?"

Brady gave him a sideways glance. "Would it matter? Seems to be your self-ordained mission in life to keep me from loneliness. Especially on holidays."

Collin chuckled and led him toward the dining room. "Have to, ol' buddy. You don't know how."

"Brady! Sweet saints, man, we've missed seeing you." Patrick O'Connor shook Brady's hand with a solid grip and genuine enthusiasm. He ran a hand through dark cropped hair salted with gray and nodded toward Collin, his gray eyes twinkling. "Glad to see my son-in-law is finally pulling his own weight so you can have a day off."

Brady laughed. "Yeah, well, I had to take over deliveries because we were losing money. Too much gift for the gab."

Collin flicked the back of Brady's head. Patrick's husky laughter filled the room where a whirl of activity was taking place. Steven and Katie were sparring over who would sit on the end while Cluny attempted to referee. At the head of the table sat their blind, elderly neighbor, Mrs. Gerson, sipping a cup of tea with a contented smile on her face. Sean chatted with Emma, Charity's best friend from Dublin, while he poured homemade cider into Marcy's wine glasses, now bereft of wine due to prohibition. Mitch held the kitchen door open for Marcy, who bustled in with a platter of sliced ham glazed with pineapple and honey. Blarney trotted close behind with a hopeful look in his eyes, while Faith followed with a steaming bowl of scalloped potatoes. The table was set in grand O'Connor style, sporting crisp, white linens, glowing candles, and a crystal vase of Easter lilies scenting the air. Brady took a quiet breath, allowing the memory to embed in his mind with a quiet joy he'd seldom known. The warmth of this family seeped into his bones like the warm honey on the ham, reminding him just how much he had missed them.

"Goodness, Brady, you're a sight for sore eyes!" Marcy hurried over to give him a hug.

Faith grinned as she assessed him head to toe. She leaned close. "Mind taking Collin shopping sometime? He could use a little help."

Collin latched a firm hand to the back of her neck. "Is that a complaint?"

She giggled and scrunched her shoulders. "You weren't supposed to hear that."

"You do look wonderful, Brady." Beth stood in the doorway with a basket of biscuits in her arms and a shy smile on her lips.

The smile on Brady's face solidified like the warm wax cooling at the base of Marcy's candlesticks. He stared, the hands in his pockets suddenly feeling like dead weights. She looked different, as if a month had changed everything. Her chestnut hair glimmered with highlights from the crystal chandelier overhead, giving her a soft shimmer that matched the sparkle in her near-violet eyes. Her new haircut seemed to transform her from a little girl to a woman, its short gleaming waves framing her heart-shaped face like a priceless work of art. She seemed so much older, so much more assured. Her once lanky and spindly body was still slight, yet now willowy and rounded with gentle curves that bespoke a transformation he had denied far too long. He fought back a hard swallow. *God help me, when did she become a woman?*

"Thanks, Beth. You look pretty too."

A blush stole into her cheeks, and she quickly set the rolls on the table as Charity bounded through the door with a platter of deviled eggs in her hands. She stopped midway to drop her jaw. "Save my soul, is that you standing there, John Brady, or are you on loan from *Vanity Fair*?"

A lazy smile traveled his lips. "If you came to visit once in a while, you'd know that I wear more than ink and an apron."

She set the dish on the table with a groan, then hurried over to give him a tight hug. She shot an accusing glance at Mitch. "You can blame it on the lord of the manor there. He's curtailed my activities considerably in the last month."

Mitch smiled and propped against the kitchen door with arms folded. "It's for your own good, and you know it."

"So you keep telling me. And who's this?" She massaged her stomach and quirked a brow in Cluny's direction.

"Sorry, everyone. This is Cluny McGee. He's bunking with me while his gram is out of town." Brady palmed the top of Cluny's head and smiled at Charity. "He and Miss Hercules belong to each other."

"How old are you, anyway? And who is Miss Hercules?" Katie's tone was belligerent at best.

Cluny's chest expanded as he rose up on his heels, his grin as daunting as the gleam in his eye. He stared Katie down. "Fourteen, going on fifteen. You?"

Her chin rose to meet his. "Eleven next month and very mature."

He winked. "Well, good for you. Miss Hercules is my dog, and Brady says she's an English sheepdog. All I know is, she's pert near bigger than me."

"Oh, now there's an impossible feat."

"Katie Rose, I suggest you mind your tongue, or you'll be eating in your room." Patrick shot her a look of warning. "Apologize—now!"

"Sorry."

Cluny beamed. "Howdy, everyone. Much obliged for the invite."

"Well, you're more than welcome, Cluny. Any friend of Brady's is a friend of ours." Marcy placed the last of the vegetables on the table with a sigh. "Katie and Steven, Cluny will be your guest in the kitchen. Be nice. Sean's agreed to join you since this table only seats ten."

Katie's face bleached white. "But Collin already volunteered to sit in the kitchen so I could sit with the adults."

"Railroaded into it is more like it, Katie Rose, but no one can accuse me of being a welsher. Marcy, I'll sit with Brady and Cluny in the kitchen, as long as we get to fill our plates before Sean and Mitch."

Sean groaned. "That's worse than sitting at the kids' table."

Collin grinned and draped an arm over Brady's shoulder. "Yeah, we know."

"Mother, I'll take the fourth seat in the kitchen."

Brady's gut tightened at the sound of Beth's voice. Collin gave him a sideways glance and slapped him on the back. "No need, Lizzie. Faith will sit with us, won't you, Little Bit?"

"Of course I will. That way I can make sure the pies don't get eaten before their time."

Collin appeared wounded. "I'm hurt. You act like I don't have any willpower."

She reached up to kiss him lightly on the cheek. "Yep."

"Well, let's eat before the food gets cold. Patrick, will you say the blessing, please?" Marcy moved to her husband's side, and he pulled her close. "Yes, darlin', I will." His gaze drifted around the table before he bowed his head and closed his eyes, wearing the look of a contented man. His words rang through the room, reverent and low and wavering with emotion, thanking God for sending his Son. His praise resonated deep and rich in Brady's heart, extolling God's goodness and boundless mercy.

Brady stole a glance at Beth, totally relieved she would not be gracing his table tonight. He closed his eyes and released a sigh of assent. Yes, God's boundless mercy. And then some.

❦

Lizzie's absorption in dominoes was little more than pretense. She studied the mound of tiles in the center of the table with great deliberation, keenly aware of John Brady's every move. He sat across the room in his usual spot on the sofa, long legs sprawled with a paper in his lap, but his interest in news seemed to match hers in dominoes.

He leaned forward with one arm draped across the paper and grinned at Mitch, who sat on the other side of the sofa like a matching bookend, paper in lap and a smile on his face. Brady jerked a thumb at Collin, who straddled a needlepoint chair next to the couch, and their laughter rang out at something he said. Lizzie absently fingered a number of tiles, her interest far from the strategy of dominoes.

"For pity's sake, Lizzie, you're picking a tile, not a man to marry. Just do it."

Lizzie jolted back to the game and snatched a domino. "Hold your horses, Katie, I was just thinking."

"Yeah, and not about dominoes, I'll bet. Probably moonin' over Tom Weston."

"Katie, just make your selection and leave Lizzie alone." Steven leaned back in his chair and studied his tiles.

With a grunt, Katie plucked a wood rectangle from the pile. "Well, he's coming soon, isn't he?"

"So what?" Lizzie eyed the clock on the mantel. Seven forty-five. She bit her lip and peeked across the room. Tom was coming at eight, and she still hadn't talked to Brady yet. Alone.

"So you're preoccupied, and this is a game to the death." Katie's eyes narrowed when she looked at Cluny. "Right, Steven?"

"Oh!" Lizzie's pulse sped up when Brady stood to his feet and tossed the paper aside. He strolled from the parlor in the direction of the bathroom. Lizzie jumped up. "Sorry, Katie, and you're right. I am preoccupied. Why don't you all start another game without me?"

She darted away faster than Katie could object, and hurried to the bathroom. She bit her lip and paced outside the door, rubbing her sweaty hands on her blue pleated skirt. She heard the faucet running and flattened to the side of the wall. The door opened, and her heart stopped.

"Brady?"

He turned.

"Can we talk?"

The look on his face was not a good sign. Head cocked, brows furrowed, and lips skewed so tight, they triggered a nerve flickering above the hard line of his jaw. He propped a hand casually against the wall, but his tension was obvious from the stiff muscles ribbing his arm. "You mean like last time?"

Heat flooded her cheeks. She angled her chin in defiance. "No. You've made yourself perfectly clear, both in your letter and how you've shut me out of your life."

He didn't blink. "What do you want, Beth?"

"I want to talk. About our friendship . . . about getting it back."

He just stared, his eyes as cold as that night he'd left.

She shivered and looked away, fidgeting with her fingers. "You never gave me the chance . . . . to apologize, to tell you how sorry I am that I—" she swallowed the lump in her throat— "did what I did."

"You ruined what we had, Beth."

Tears welled in her eyes. "I know, I'm sorry."

"So am I." He turned away.

She gripped his arm. "You have to forgive me, Brady. You, of all people, have always taught me that."

He stopped and stared at her hand, which still clutched his arm. He exhaled hard. "I'm working on it, Beth, but you have no idea the damage you did."

She removed her hand to swipe at her eyes. "Yes, John, I do. I lost the best friend I ever had, the mentor for my soul, and the only human being I've ever really cherished, outside of my family." A sob broke loose from her throat, and she stifled it with quivering fingers. "I miss you, and I need you.

As a friend. To talk with, to pray with." Her voice softened to a near whisper. "I give you my word."

He studied her through slitted eyes while a nerve still flickered in his cheek. He drew in a hard breath and blew it out again. "All right, Beth, your word. Friendship. And not a mention of anything else."

She nodded. Her breath was thick in her throat.

He sighed and turned away, suddenly looking very tired.

She fought to keep the buoyancy from her tone. "Monday, then? As usual? We were going to study Psalms, remember?" Her tension eased when the hardness faded from his face.

"Yeah, I remember. Sounds good."

She smiled, feeling as if a mountain of guilt had just slid off her shoulders. The doorbell rang and she hurried to answer it, flashing a smile over her shoulder. "You won't regret it, Brady, I promise."

He already did. He watched as she opened the door, and an unexpected jolt of jealousy seared through his gut. A tall, good-looking kid stood on the front porch with a box of candy in his hand and a goofy grin on his face. She held the screen door while he grazed her cheek with a kiss.

Brady's jaw felt like rock as he reentered the parlor. "Cluny? It's time to go."

Cluny looked up. "Cain't, Brady. I'm winnin'."

Brady scowled and retrieved his paper from the couch. He folded it up and laid it on the table. "I've got an early day tomorrow, bud. You best wrap it up."

Groaning, Cluny pushed in his tiles.

"What's the rush?" Collin said. "Sit down and relax. Work will keep."

He remained standing. "Sorry, Collin, I'm whipped."

"I know the feeling." Mitch stifled a yawn and turned the page of his paper.

"Hey, Tom, Happy Easter." Patrick and Sean looked up

from their chess game while the boy made the rounds in the room.

Collin leaned close. "You're scowling, Brady. It's not like you. Besides, you were the one who told Lizzie to get on with her life."

"Tom, would you like a piece of pie?"

"That sounds wonderful, Mrs. O'Connor, thank you."

"Lizzie, take him into the kitchen and cut him a piece, will you?"

Brady clutched Cluny by the back of the neck. "Mr. and Mrs. O'Connor, thank you so much for a wonderful Easter, but I'm afraid we have to head home."

Charity struggled to rise up on the love seat. "But you said you would play whist after they finished dominoes."

Brady managed a tired smile. "Sorry, Charity, I'll have to take a rain check."

She plopped back down on her pillow. "Killjoy."

Faith hugged him good night, followed by Marcy. "Thanks for coming, Brady. Cluny, you bring him back, you hear?"

Cluny shot a smirk in Katie's direction, obviously ignoring her nasty look. "Yes, ma'am, count on it."

Brady steered him quickly to the door, then waved a hand in the air. "Good night, everyone. Happy Easter, and thank you. See you tomorrow, Collin." He ushered Cluny out the front door with a sigh of relief.

"Gee whiz, Brady, what's your all-fire hurry? I was having a good time."

"Sorry, bud, but all of a sudden I got real tired."

"Yeah, I noticed. Right after Lizzie's boyfriend showed up."

"What?"

"You're jealous."

Brady stopped dead in his tracks. "*What?*"

Cluny peered up. "Come on, Brady, I may be little for my age, but I'm not a kid. I heard you and Charity talking that time. Lizzie's under your skin in a big way."

Brady started walking fast.

Cluny ran to keep up with him. "You told Charity you had a 'problem.' What'd ya mean by that?"

Brady groaned and picked up pace. "You're too young, Cluny, and I'm way too tired."

"Are ya sick?"

"In a matter of speaking."

Cluny halted, his voice suddenly cracking. "You gonna die?"

Brady stopped and turned. His heart clutched at the stricken look on Cluny's face. He took a step toward the boy and laid a hand on his shoulder. "No, Cluny, I'm not gonna die. I'm afraid you're stuck with me."

Cluny shot into his arms with a fierce hold around his waist, his head pressed hard against Brady's vest. "Don't leave me, Brady. You're the only true friend I've ever had."

Tears stung Brady's eyes as he bent to clutch the slight boy in his arms. "I'm not going anywhere, Cluny, and I'm honored to be your friend."

Cluny sniffed and pulled away, wiping his eyes with his sleeve. "I hope Gram stays away a long, long time."

Brady hooked an arm around Cluny's shoulder and headed down the street, his jealousy over Beth strangely forgotten. Suddenly he felt like a lucky man. "Yeah, me too, Cluny," he whispered, "me too."

## 7

Faith reached for her favorite flannel nightgown from the hook on the door and stopped. Her hand hovered over its high-necked collar for several seconds, then strayed to a satin gown that peeked from behind—the one she'd worn during their honeymoon. She touched the silky pale green material and smiled at the memory. She hadn't worn it for long.

Nor since.

She snatched her usual gown from the hook and lifted the satin one off before tossing the other back. She held it up in the mirror and posed, tilting her head to full advantage. Her lips twisted into a wry smile. *Heaven help me, I'm reduced to Charity.*

She sighed and unbuttoned her blouse. What else could she do? Since the night of their fight, Collin seemed to be a different man. At least in the bedroom. Oh, he still stole kisses throughout the day and lavished her with love, but when the lights went out, it seemed that his interest did too. Her lips pressed into a determined line. And it was starting to wear on her nerves.

From the moment she had married the man, he hadn't left her alone. Almost night after night, his appetite never seemed to wane, whether from desire for her or a baby, she wasn't always sure. But now, sleep actually had more of his attention than she, and she was shocked to realize how much she missed him. The glint in his eye after he showered, the glide of his hand on her leg, the playful dominance of his kisses—had all been missing for weeks now, since the night of the fight. Other than an occasion or two when she had approached him, their love life had come to a screeching halt. She smiled into the mirror.

*Until now.*

She pushed the lacy straps of her camisole off her shoulders and let it drop to the floor. Lifting the satin gown over her head, she shimmied it on. The smooth material spilled over her breasts in a lustrous sheen, revealing gentle curves that mounded softly above its low, scooped neck. She reached up and pulled the pins from her hair. Her auburn waves tumbled over her shoulders the way Collin loved. With a hint of a smile, she reached for the perfume he'd given her for Christmas and dabbed a bit behind each ear. She suddenly thought of Charity and grinned, boldly touching the fragrance to the deep V of her breasts. Drawing in a long breath, she opened the bathroom door and flipped the light off before padding to their room.

Collin lay sprawled on top of the covers on his side of the bed, arm cocked on the pillow and head propped. A wayward thatch of dark hair fell over his forehead, almost into his eyes, the way it always did when he was focused. He appeared absorbed in the Bible Mrs. Gerson had given them for their wedding, and never looked up. As usual, he wore his striped flannel pajama bottoms without the shirt, revealing a lean, hard chest bereft of hair and sculpted with muscles. He turned a page with a bulge of his bicep, clear evidence of nights at the gym with Brady.

"Collin?"

He looked up with a casual glance, but the lump in his throat gave him dead away. She feigned innocence. "Are you going in early tomorrow?"

His gaze seared her nightgown. He cleared his throat and turned a page. "No, why?"

She smiled and approached him, feeling a lot like Charity as she bent to give him a quick kiss. She noted the smoky look in his eyes as he took in the swell of her breasts, and she felt almost giddy. She had him!

"No special reason, really. I just thought we'd sleep in a bit and I could make you breakfast before I leave."

She moved around the bed with almost an indifferent air, enjoying his gaze as she slipped under the sheets.

"Sounds wonderful," he said before turning back on his side. "Mind if I read a bit?"

She stared in shock at his hard-muscled back. *Read?* He wanted to read? She certainly had no desire to go head-to-head with the Word of God, but sweet sanctity of marriage, *he wanted to read??*

"Not at all," she lied as sweetly as she could, certain his back would scar if looks could singe. She stared hard at the ceiling and fumed, lips pursed and an annoying tic in her eye. What in the blazes was his problem, anyway? Wasn't he attracted to her anymore? She fought back a wave of hurt and closed her eyes, forcing herself to think. No, a man like Collin didn't lose interest overnight; he was too needy. Not unless . . . Her eyes flipped open. Unless he wanted to teach her a lesson. Pay her back. Her jaw dropped. Dear Lord, he was playing games? She peered at his back out of the corner of her eye and clamped her lips tight. All right, McGuire, two could play as well as one. She ground her jaw and tried to focus. What in the devil would Charity do?

Suddenly it came to her as if her sister had just whispered in her ear. With a jut of her chin, she turned on her side and snuggled close, pressing her breasts against the cool skin of his back. He jolted a bit, and she hooked an arm over his hips. "Mind if I snuggle while you read? I'm cold."

"No," he said, and she smiled at the strain in his voice.

She idly moved her palm across the hard surface of his stomach, occasionally sinking into the smooth slope of his navel.

He grabbed her hand. "Faith, I'm trying to read."

"Oh. Sorry."

He grunted and she grinned, molding her body closer to his. She waited.

One minute. He turned a page. Two minutes. Another. Three minutes. The book slammed shut. He put it on the nightstand and turned out the light. Expelling a heavy breath, he shoved his covers down with the heels of his feet and slithered in. He yanked them back and settled in with hands folded on his stomach. "Good night."

She neatly slid an arm around his waist. "Good night, Collin. I love you."

He grunted.

She settled in too, making sure her arm rested across his chest as she snuggled. She sighed and sidled in close, breathing slowly, evenly, in the rhythm of sleep.

This time the wait was less than three minutes.

With a frustrated growl, he flipped her on her back and descended with a low groan. "Blast you, woman, what the devil are you trying to do to me?"

She blinked. "What do you mean?"

His hands devoured her as they traveled the length of her satin gown. "Don't you dare play games with me, Faith McGuire, you know good and well what I mean. For pity's sake, satin instead of flannel? A gown that barely covers your—" He kissed her hard, taking her breath away. His mouth wandered to the lobe of her ear before he pulled away. "And perfume? Sweet saints, you're wearing perfume to bed?"

She grinned in the dark. "Guess it proves two can play."

He blinked. His breathing was heavy as he stared, thick arms propped over her. "What do you mean, two can play? Play what?"

"Your game. You know, pretending you're too tired? That you're not interested? Making me pay for hurting your pride? Well, the jig is up, and I win."

A slow smile eased across his lips. "You think so, do you? And what do you win?"

She slipped one satin strap off her shoulder, then started on the other. "The affections of the man of my dreams and the love of my life."

His grin was dangerous. "Looks like I'm forced to concede . . . at least round one." He pressed his mouth to the bare curve of her shoulder and trailed his lips to the V of her gown. His husky chuckle vibrated against her chest. "But only because I'm a good loser."

A shiver of heat traveled through her at his touch, and his breath was hot against her skin. She closed her eyes and uttered a soft moan, losing herself in the joy of his embrace.

*And, oh my, wouldn't Charity be proud?*

Collin strolled in at nine with a whistle on his lips and a gleam in his eye. He rolled up the sleeves of his starched, blue work shirt and reached for an apron, giving Brady a smile brighter than the sunlight streaming through the window. "And the top of the morning to you, ol' buddy," Collin shouted, raising his voice so Brady could hear.

Brady looked up from the noisy press, which was spitting out programs for Miss Ramona's dance recital about as slowly as Miss Ramona was at taking a hint. The seventy-year-old dance teacher was convinced Brady was the perfect match for her granddaughter. Brady scowled and hollered back. "For you, maybe—I've been here since six. What kept you? Or maybe I shouldn't ask."

Collin chuckled and tied his apron as he sauntered into the back room. He slacked a hip against the counter and picked up one of the programs. "I suppose you're invited to this one too?"

A tight smile appeared on Brady's lips. "Yep. Just call me

a glutton for the arts. So, I assume from the annoying grin on your face that you cleared the air with Faith?"

"In a manner of speaking." Collin poured himself a cup of three-hour-old coffee and turned to prop against the counter, enjoying the familiar cadence of the hum and clacking of paper against platen. "You know, Brady, you may be on to something."

Brady hiked a brow as he fed more paper into the Craftsman hand-fed press. "What are you talking about?"

"Restraint."

Brady swiped the side of his face with the back of his hand. He now had a matched set of ink smudges on both sides of his cheeks. "What?"

"It about killed me, but I stayed away from Faith to teach her a lesson, and let's just say it was well worth the wait." He took a sip of his coffee and closed his eyes. "Satin nightgown, lots of perfume, and enough fire to heat a—"

Brady held up a hand. "I'm happy for you, Collin, truly, but spare me the details, please."

Collin sighed and took another sip. "I gotta tell ya, Brady, deep down I always worried marriage might be a bit too tame for me, you know? No longer being on the prowl? But thanks to a little restraint on my part, the thrill of the hunt is alive and well in my very own bedroom. You're a genius, ol' buddy."

Brady's jaw sagged low. "You're certifiably crazy, you know that?"

Collin stood and took another sip. "Yeah, I do. Crazy about a certain redhead who I am determined will always want me as much as I want her. Enough jawing. I need to get to work."

"Collin?"

He turned. "Yeah?"

"You're back on deliveries."

Collin squinted. "That's gonna break a lot of hearts, you know, Miss Ramona's included. Why?"

Brady rubbed his jaw, then looked away. "Beth's coming by for Bible study."

"Is she now?" Collin stared for several seconds, then lifted his chin. "Ya think you can handle that? I mean you didn't do too well with the boyfriend last night."

Brady's eyes met his. "Yeah, I think I can. Have to. Don't have a choice."

"Or you do, but you won't take it." Collin released a weighty breath. "Okay, ol' buddy, but I gotta tell you it makes me nervous. Not about Lizzie 'cause she seems to be moving forward in a relationship with Tom. I'm worried about you, my friend."

Brady nodded and reached for a clean rag. "Don't be. As long as I'm praying about it, I'm going to be fine. Hey, do I have ink on my face?"

Collin grinned and headed for the front room. "Yes, you do. *Always.*"

❦ ❧

Lizzie kept her head down, walking fast to the corner of Stuart and Tremont. She stopped at the street sign and looked up, wishing her hands didn't sweat when she was nervous. She wiped them on her green plaid skirt and sucked in a breath thick with sea air, gasoline, and the noontime staple of fish and chips. She adjusted her navy sweater over her white shirtwaist and straightened her shoulders, notebook pressed hard to her chest. She continued down Tremont through the maze of people and fixed her eyes on a small blue and white sign swaying in the breeze. McGuire and Brady Printing Company. Her lips flattened. The bane of her existence.

She stopped a store away to peek into the glass, checking her appearance for the umpteenth time. She exhaled a noisy breath. How silly! What did it matter anyway? One man thought she was beautiful, and the other didn't care. But then friends didn't focus on things like that, she supposed. A lesson she would have to learn. She caught a glimpse of Brady's broad back as she entered the shop. He hefted a box, and his work shirt strained over a span of hard muscles. She sighed. A hard lesson to learn. But then he would be a good teacher, no doubt.

He turned at the sound of the bell and smiled, sending her pulse into overtime. "Hi, Brady. Can't be working too hard. No ink on your face."

He grinned and waved her into the back room. "It's amazing what a little soap and water can do. How's school?"

He was carrying on as if they'd never stopped, wiping off her chair, pulling it out, reaching for his well-worn Bible off the crowded shelf. She settled into the chair he offered and folded her hands on top of her notebook. "Good. Only one more month till it's over, then Mr. Harvey said I could work full-time. He needs the help."

He nodded and headed to the sink to make a fresh pot of coffee. "That's wonderful, Beth. You drinking coffee yet? Or do you want me to make you some tea?"

She watched as he cocked a hip against the counter, filling the coffee machine with cold water. She suddenly thought of the night on the porch when that same hip had been pressed against hers. Heat whooshed into her cheeks.

He turned around and arched a brow. "You okay?"

She yanked her sweater off. "Yes, just a bit warm, I think. There's no doubt that spring is definitely here. Coffee will be fine, thank you."

"Yeah, it gets hot in here with all the machines." He opened the back door to allow cool air in through the screen, then ambled back to plop into his favorite cane-back chair. "We said Psalms, right?" He didn't look up as he flipped through his Bible.

"Yes, my favorite." She bit her lip. "Brady?"

"Mmmm?"

"Thank you."

He looked up. "For what?"

"For being my friend."

He smiled and leaned back in his chair, his eyes never leaving her face. "It's my pleasure." He hesitated while his jaw ground the slightest bit. "How's Tom working out?"

The heat in her cheeks returned, much to her annoyance. She hefted her chin. "Good. He seems to care for me, although I don't really know why."

"Don't put yourself down, Beth. You're a beautiful woman. Is he . . . being respectful?"

She blinked. *He'd called her a woman!* She quickly opened her notebook and picked up her pen. "Yes, he is. At least, so far."

"Good. Let's get started." He rested his arms on the table and began to read, the sound of his low voice like balm to her soul.

"'Blessed is the man that walketh not in the counsel of the ungodly, nor standeth in the way of sinners, nor sitteth in the seat of the scornful. But his delight is in the law of the Lord; and in his law doth he meditate day and night.'"

He leaned back in his chair and released a heavy breath, his face calm. "That's a good place to start. Delighting in the law of the Lord, day and night. Not an easy thing to do, mind you, but a good place to start. And apparently important enough for God to put it in the first paragraph of the very first psalm. I think—"

The sound of bells clanging over the front door broke their concentration, causing both to look up. Brady rose from his chair and moved toward the front room. "Can I help you?"

Beth bent forward to peek at a young woman about her own age, timidly clutching her purse in her hands. She resembled a tall Mary Pickford, with soft blond waves covering her head to just below her ears. Her face had a childlike air of innocence as she stared at Brady with wide, blue eyes.

He stepped forward with a smile. "How can I help you, miss?"

Her mouth opened as if to speak, but nothing came out for

several seconds. She took a deep breath and a step forward. "I'm
. . . actually looking for work and was wondering if you might
have anything available." She finally smiled, and it chased the
shyness from her face. "I'm excellent at bookkeeping."

Brady scratched the back of his head. "Well, I'm sorry,
ma'am, but my partner and I do all our own bookkeeping.
We're growing, but we're still a pretty small shop, so we don't
expect to be hiring anytime soon."

The smile on her face faded into the lost look she'd worn
before. "Certainly, I understand. Thank you."

She turned to go, and Lizzie jumped up from her chair.
"Wait! I know where they are hiring."

The girl turned, her eyes lighting on Lizzie with a look of surprise. "Why . . . that would be wonderful, miss, thank you."

Lizzie pushed gently past Brady to extend her hand. "My
name is Lizzie O'Connor, and I work at a bookstore called
Bookends over on Dormer Street. Are you familiar with it?"

The girl blinked and reached for Lizzie's hand. She quickly
shook it, then pulled hers away, allowing it to flutter to the
base of her throat. "No . . . no, I'm not. My name is Mary
. . . Carpenter . . . and I'm afraid I just arrived in Boston this
afternoon."

"Well, my manager, Mr. Harvey, is actually looking for someone to help with his bookkeeping. I don't know what it pays,
but—"

"That doesn't matter right now. I just really need a job." She
sounded breathless.

Lizzie smiled and spun around. "Brady, would you mind
terribly if we cut our study short today? I'd like to walk Mary
over to Bookends before I head back to school."

He smiled. "No, I don't mind. That's real nice of you. Mary,
my name is John Brady, and we were just having Bible study
in the back room. If you would ever like to join us, you're
welcome. We meet at noon on Monday, Wednesday, and Friday."

Mary stared, apparently speechless once again.

Lizzie took her arm and steered her to the door. "Come on, Mary, Brady probably needs to get back to the presses anyway." She gave him a playful smirk. "There's way too little ink on his face for a good morning's work."

❧ ❧

"So help me, Patrick, if you don't do something about Hennessy, I will." Mitch stood over Patrick's desk, palms flattened till his knuckles were white from the strain. There was a dangerous-looking vein throbbing along the line of his temple.

Patrick looked up at his son-in-law and had the sudden urge to take an aspirin. He sank back in his chair and released a weary breath. "So, what's the problem this time?"

Mitch started pacing the room, all the while dragging his fingers through the short, cropped curls on his head. He had been a godsend when Patrick had hired him over a year and a half ago, hands-down the best editor he had ever seen. That is, up until three months ago when he started acting more like a caged animal than an assistant editor. Mitch stopped dead in front of Patrick's desk and leaned in, his imposing six-foot-four frame looming like a dark shadow. "He's worthless, Patrick, incapable of handling the most simplistic assignment. He doesn't belong at a newspaper, and we both know it."

Patrick opened the third drawer of his desk and reached for a bottle of aspirin. He took two and tossed them to the back of his throat, followed by a quick gulp of cold coffee. "Mitch, we've been over this before. He's Hennessy's grandson, which makes him untouchable. You just can't fire the grandson of the owner."

"Oh yeah? Watch me."

"Don't make me pull rank on you, son. Leave Hennessy alone. Assign Logan to keep tabs on him, and you stay out of it. You hear me?"

Mitch looked away, and Patrick could see the cords of strain in his neck as he took several deep breaths. His massive shoulders finally sagged. "All right, Patrick, we'll do it your way, but I want to go on record right now that he shouldn't be anywhere within five hundred feet of the *Herald*."

Patrick chuckled. "So noted."

Mitch started to leave, and Patrick leaned forward. "Mitch?"

He stopped at the door, hand on the knob and head cocked to the side. "What?"

"We need to talk."

"What about?" Mitch turned and gave him a one-sided smile. "Firing Hennessy?"

Patrick laughed and pointed to the chair. "No, we're done with Hennessy. Close the door and sit down."

Mitch shut the door a little too hard and dropped in a chair. "What's on your mind?"

"I'm worried about you."

"What? Why?"

Patrick ran a hand through his hair and exhaled. "Because you're not yourself. Something's wrong when the best editor I've ever had starts falling to pieces over some rich-boy pantywaist. What's going on, Mitch? Are you and Charity okay?"

"Yes, of course we're okay. Don't we seem okay?"

"Well, now that you bring it up, no, you don't. It seems like you've turned into a powder keg at work these last few months. And Charity, well, lately I've noticed you two sniping at one another now and then."

Mitch groaned and bent forward, elbows on his knees. He rubbed his face with his hands. "We're fine, Patrick."

"No, you're not. Something's eating at you, and apparently it's not only affecting your work, it's affecting your marriage."

With a heavy sigh, Mitch slumped back in the chair. "This is not an easy subject to discuss."

"Try me."

Mitch studied him through lidded eyes, as if wondering if he should even bother. He finally sighed and began rubbing the side of his head. "When Marcy was pregnant, in her later months, did you . . . ever worry that you might . . . you know, hurt her or the baby?"

Patrick shifted in his chair. "Do you mean when we—"

"Yes—that's what I mean. Did you? I mean, worry?"

"No."

"Not even the first time?"

Patrick frowned and leaned on a fist, trying to remember. "Not that I recall."

"Did you . . . refrain in her later months?"

Patrick chuckled. "No, Marcy wouldn't let me."

Mitch moved to the edge of the chair and clutched the desk. "She wouldn't?"

"Nope, at least not when she was pregnant with Faith—I recall that most distinctly. I remember being shocked because she seemed . . . so much more . . . interested."

Mitch shot to his feet. "Yes! That's Charity too. She won't leave me alone, and all I'm trying to do is protect her and the baby."

Patrick laughed. "From what? You can't hurt them, trust me."

"I wish I could, Patrick. But I've seen otherwise."

"What? When?"

Mitch fanned a hand through his hair and began to pace. "My mother, when I was ten. She . . . was seven months pregnant and . . . lost the baby. The brother I never had."

"Mitch, I'm sorry. But you think she lost it because your father—"

He stopped pacing to give Patrick a cold stare. "Not my father. He died the year before. One of my mother's many acquaintances."

"Even so, I can't believe—"

"He was there all night, Patrick, and I heard them, more

than once. He was gone by the time I woke up. Gone by the time she started bleeding."

"Dear God . . ."

"And now I have a wife who needs my love more than ever, and I cringe at the thought. Every time—every single time—I see my mother writhing in pain, a pale ghost in a pool of blood."

"Sweet mercy . . . did she—"

"No, she survived, thank God."

"Mitch, I'm sorry."

"Me too, Patrick. But now you understand the strain I've been under."

"Does Charity know . . . about what happened to your mother?"

"No, I didn't want to alarm her in any way."

Patrick scratched the back of his head. "Well, I suggest you tell her the truth."

"And scare her?"

"Knowing my daughter the way I do, I doubt it will scare her, but it certainly might relieve her own personal fears. She probably thinks you're not attracted to her anymore."

Mitch propped his hands on the back of the chair and laughed. "Yes, she does, as a matter of fact. As if that were even possible."

"It might work in your favor, you know. She would suddenly understand your hesitation and might be more willing to negotiate."

Mitch chuckled and shook his head. "Negotiate? With Charity? I thought you said you knew your daughter."

Patrick eased back in his chair and grinned. "Trust me, I do. I married her mother."

Lizzie hummed to herself as she flung her sweater on the

coatrack in the back room of Bookends. She quickly surveyed her lipstick in the mirror, then poked her head into the tiny office off the hall. Mary sat stiff and straight at a scarred wooden desk piled high with papers and a typewriter. She was chewing on the nail of her thumb. Lizzie flashed an encouraging smile. "All settled in?"

"I think so . . . me *and* the mouse."

"Ooops. Forgot to tell you about that, but you'll get used to it. Try to think of him as the pet you never had."

Mary smiled. "You headed back to school so quickly after dropping me off this afternoon that I never really got a chance to thank you for referring me. I'm very grateful, Lizzie. I think I'm going to like it here."

Lizzie glanced at the clock in the back room, then ambled in to sit down. "You're welcome. I knew he'd hired you on the spot when we walked through the door. So tell me how your first three hours have been? I've got a few moments before I'm officially on."

"Okay."

"You said you just got into town. Where from?"

Her smile seemed tentative. "New York."

"Wow, New York! I've heard it's fabulous. Why'd you leave?"

She glanced away, focusing on a movie poster hanging on the wall—Rudolph Valentino from *The Sheik*. All at once the soft innocence of her blue eyes seemed shadowed with tragedy. "Let's just say I was involved with the wrong man."

"Oh, Mary, I'm sorry. I didn't mean to pry."

"No, it's okay. The love has been gone for a long time now. And he finally gave me a reason to leave."

"Do you know anyone in Boston? Relatives, friends?"

She smiled. "I know you. But no, no relatives here, or friends, for that matter. But I'm hoping you and I can be close, Lizzie. How old are you, anyway?"

"Almost eighteen. And you?"

"Twenty-one, but some days I feel a lot older." For a moment she seemed lost in a stare, then blinked it away and gave Lizzie a wry smile. "Kind of like my life is passing me by, before I've had any fun."

Lizzie chuckled. "You want fun? Have you met Millie yet?"

A twinkle lit Mary's eyes. "Oh yes. She says you and she are good friends."

"Since the first grade. She's a little crazy, but sometimes I think I could do with a bit more of that." Lizzie tilted her head. "Millie likes to go to the dance pavilion at Revere Beach, if you'd like to join us sometime."

Mary smiled and reached for her pen. She absently rolled it between her fingers, her gaze following the motion. "I would like that a lot. But if you don't mind, what I would like even more is to join you and Brady for Bible study." Her hand stilled on the pen. "Is he your boyfriend?"

Lizzie shook her head and laughed, the sound of it hollow. "No, no, he's not. Not that I wouldn't want him to be because . . . well, Brady is really something special. But I'm afraid he'll never be anyone's boyfriend. He's more interested in God than women. Besides, I'm seeing someone else right now."

"Oh, I just thought . . . well, you two seemed pretty close."

"Oh, we are. I've known him since I was thirteen, when he became my brother-in-law's business partner. Brady and I, well . . . we love each other a lot . . ." Lizzie swallowed the lump in her throat. "Just not that way." She jumped up from the chair, suddenly anxious to get to work. "I better go or Mr. Harvey will be looking for me. It's been nice getting to know you, Mary. And it will be even nicer having you join Brady and me for our Bible study. Which day are you coming?"

Mary blinked. Hesitation softened her tone. "Well, I was hoping to come all three, if that's all right with you."

Lizzie swallowed her disappointment and gave her a perky smile. "Great! You know where his shop is, so I guess we'll see you Wednesday at noon. He's a great teacher. He has this amazing way of opening your eyes to God. You won't be sorry."

Mary's smile relaxed, and her eyes took on a faraway look. "No, Lizzie . . . I don't think I will be."

❦ ❦

Mary was a godsend. Brady listened to their chatter as he poured the coffee and silently thanked God for making this so easy. Mary Carpenter had joined them for the last month, providing a much-needed emotional buffer between Beth and him. At least for him, he thought to himself as he set their cups on the table. He sank into his chair and took a sip of his coffee, noting how much more at ease Mary seemed than the first time they'd met. He wasn't sure why, but something told him she was a very pretty woman with a not-so-pretty past. Occasionally over the last few weeks, the natural innocence of her face seemed to take on a tragic air, as if she carried burdens no one could see. From the moment Brady had laid eyes on her, he sensed in his spirit she was a soul in desperate need of healing. He gulped his hot coffee and scowled. But then, who wasn't? He certainly qualified.

"Burn your tongue?" Mary smiled at him as she blew on her coffee.

"What?"

"You were scowling. I figure it was either that large gulp of hot coffee you took or the problem Lizzie's having with Tom."

Brady smiled and took a more manageable sip, studying her over the rim of his cup. "Sorry. Wasn't listening."

Lizzie arched a brow. "Brady! You're supposed to be my spiritual mentor, and you're not even listening to what I'm saying?"

He gave Lizzie a lidded stare. "I listen, Beth, to anything significant."

"You mean to tell me, John Brady, that you don't consider Lizzie's love life significant?" Mary quirked her lips. "And satisfy my curiosity, if you will. Why do you still call her Beth when everyone else calls her Lizzie?"

"Because he's a mule, Mary, who refuses to change. Don't even try. It's impossible."

Brady crossed his arms on top of his Bible. "Are you two troublemakers about done? Maybe we should just forego Psalms to study a chapter on respect for authority."

"But aren't you even curious?" Mary asked.

"Nope." Brady took another sip of coffee and flipped the pages to Psalm 10.

"Well, okay, but as Lizzie's friend *and* a man, I think you'd be the perfect person to advise her as to what to do when a man gets fresh."

The coffee pooled in his mouth. He quickly swallowed and locked his gaze on Lizzie, his tone suddenly curt. "He's pressuring you, Beth?"

Her lips parted and she looked away. A soft hint of rose tinted her cheeks. "Not exactly. I mean, yes, I guess maybe a little, but we've been seeing each other for several months now and I . . . well, I just figured that . . . well, that . . ."

"What?" Dread slithered in his gut.

She bit her lip and avoided his eyes. Her voice dropped to a whisper. "It's just that I'm starting to like it, Brady. A lot."

"Tom?"

She finally looked up, and he read the embarrassment in her eyes. "Yes, Tom, of course. And . . . kissing him."

He winced, as if he'd been stung.

Mary laid a hand on Lizzie's arm, then leaned forward, the blue of her eyes intense. "What's she supposed to do, Brady? What's any good girl to do when she *should* say no but *wants* to say yes?"

He took a deep breath to ease the fury in his gut, then forced it out slowly, quietly. Two sets of eyes fixed on him, full of expectancy and more than a little hope. He tightened his jaw. "Well, the Bible says to flee fornication—"

Lizzie put both hands to her red cheeks. "Sweet mother of Job, Brady, you know I'm not talking about that—"

"I know you're not, Beth, but hear me out. It's natural to have attraction to the opposite sex. God made us that way. But listen to the wording here—*flee*. Not turn. Not walk away. Not don't do it, but 'flee.' That means run . . . without looking back, lest you change your mind. Flee like your life depends on it. Because it does."

Lizzie huffed out a sigh. "Now you're just being melodramatic. How can your life depend on a kiss?"

He lunged across the table and grabbed her hand, pinning his firmly on top. His tone was deadly calm. "Stop it, Beth. Don't diminish the Word of God. Our spiritual life—and death—hang in the balance depending on how we heed it. Kisses are not the problem. It's the desire they ignite that can weaken our will to please God. Guard your affections and stay strong. Because when it comes to kisses, men are weak . . . and quite skilled at disarming women."

She pulled her hand away to hug her arms close to her body. "Nobody's going to disarm me, Brady. You know me better than that."

"I do know you, Beth, and that's why I'm cautioning you. For as long as I can remember, you've had your nose buried in a book, enamored with romance. More than any little girl I've ever met, you've been spellbound by happily ever after. I just worry that when all those fairy-tale notions of romance meet a smooth-talking guy, it could be a deadly combination. Trust me, Beth, men can read a woman like you."

She slowly rose to her feet, visibly shaken. "*A woman like me?* And that's what you think? That I care more about romance than doing the right thing? You think a few kisses will turn my conscience off, is that it? That I'll just lie down and let them have their way?"

He shot to his feet. "Don't talk like that!"

"Why? You have. You and your holier-than-thou lecturing. Too bad it slipped your mind the night on the porch." She seized her notebook from the table with trembling hands and slammed the chair in. She got as far as the door that divided the two rooms.

Brady grabbed her arm and pushed her to the wall in the front room, well out of Mary's view. His breathing was ragged and his voice low as he gripped her shoulders. "I did exactly what I needed to do, Beth, I fled. So don't go flinging stones."

"No, instead I should let you fling them, is that it? Well, congratulations, Brady. You followed the Word of God—you fled my sinful advances. Only from my vantage point, it looked a lot more like a coward running away."

His hands flinched from her shoulders. He took a step back while his anger fused into white-hot calm. "You're changing, Beth, and I don't like what I see."

"Really? Well, Tom does, which is a good thing since he's the one I'm looking to please. Excuse me, I'm late." She pushed past him.

He clenched her arm. "What about God, Beth, you looking to please him?"

"You wouldn't believe me if I said I was, so why don't you just take care of that for the both of us?" Tears filled her eyes as she jerked free and ran out the door, slamming it hard.

Brady stared out the window while every muscle in his body twitched with anger. He took a deep breath and released it before returning to the back room.

Mary's eyes circled in shock. "Brady, I . . . I'm sorry. I shouldn't have brought it up."

He sagged into the chair and attempted a smile, which failed miserably. "No, Mary, it's not your fault, it's mine. God knows I didn't handle it in the best way. Even so, I'm glad you brought it up, because it shows me how I need to pray for her."

"You're going to pray for her? Even after all she said to you?"

"I love Beth as a sister, so yes, I'll never stop praying for her. But even if I didn't love her, I'd pray for her, even when she wounds me to the core. God commands it."

Mary shook her head. "I don't know, Brady, it seems impossible. I'm not sure I could."

"If I can, you can. It just takes practice . . . and a lot of prayer."

She squinted to study him. "You seem to love God an awful lot."

He sighed and reached for his coffee. "Yeah, well, he who's forgiven much, loves much."

"You? What do you need to be forgiven for? All I see is a man with a clean heart."

His eyes met hers. "We all have our demons, Mary, especially me. Which is why I love God so much. I need him—desperately. We all do."

A hoarse laugh erupted from her throat. "I'm not sure God can forgive everything."

"He can and he will. You can count on it. The Bible is riddled with sinners he's forgiven—cheats, murderers, prostitutes, you name it."

She smiled. "Forgiven much, love much . . . that's from the Bible?"

He nodded, taking a slow sip of coffee. "A woman who the Bible calls a sinner—probably a prostitute—repented by washing Jesus' feet with her tears and drying them with her hair. Jesus forgave her, telling those around him that her sins, which were many, were forgiven because she loved him enough to repent. And he who's forgiven much, loves the forgiver much."

She gave him a sad smile. "How I wish I could believe in forgiveness."

"Why can't you?"

She focused on her hands clenched in her lap. "I just think there are some things that even God can't forgive."

Brady rose to his feet and moved to her side of the table, suddenly feeling an unlikely kinship with this gentle woman. He sat on the chair beside her and gently lifted her hand from her lap, cradling it in his. "God can forgive anything, Mary—that's how great his love is. His forgiveness is endless and overflowing. All we have to do is ask."

She looked up, her blue eyes misty with tears. "Oh, Brady, if only I could believe that—really and truly believe that—then I would confess everything."

He smiled and carefully wiped a tear from her cheek. "Then that's where we'll begin, Mary. We'll pray . . . for a tiny seed of faith."

## 8

Lizzie finished applying just a touch of eyeliner and smudged it exactly like Charity had taught her to do. She stepped back to study the effect in her dressing-table mirror and chewed on her lip. "Not too much," Charity had said with a smile. "You don't want to look like Millie, after all, only like a woman with haunting eyes." Lizzie's lips skewed into a half smile. "Haunted eyes" was more like it, she thought with a sinking feeling—compliments of John Brady and not Helena Rubinstein.

Lizzie took a deep breath and reached for her rose lipstick, outlining her lower lip to exaggerate it a bit. With newly acquired skill, she carefully de-emphasized the width of her mouth to create the perfect "cupid's bow." All at once, queasiness rolled in her stomach, and she touched a shaky hand to the slicked-down chestnut waves that framed her face. She was glad she was seeing Tom tonight. The fight with Brady had completely unnerved her, and she was bent on proving him wrong.

*How long will ye love vanity, and seek after falsehood?*

The lipstick in her hand clattered to the glass surface of her vanity table. Conviction prickled her conscience at the memory of a recent Scripture she had studied with Brady. With a hitch of her breath, she blinked at her painted face and suppressed a shiver. But she wasn't seeking after falsehood, she wasn't! She was simply searching for love, for a man who would sweep her away.

*But know that the LORD hath set apart him that is godly for himself . . . stand in awe, and sin not.*

Her fingers quivered as she retrieved the lipstick and slipped it into her purse, visibly shaken. "I know I'm set apart for you, Lord, and I will be true to your precepts." She drew in some air as she thought of Tom's insistent kisses and released it slowly in one long, shallow breath. "Oh, Lord, please, keep me strong."

"Gosh, Lizzie, you look just like Millie. Does Tom like all that stuff?" Katie barged into their room and flopped on her bed, belly down and feet dangling over the headboard.

Lizzie took another peek in the mirror and worried her lip. "I think so. At least he seems to."

"Doesn't he get red goo all over his mouth?"

Lizzie spun around. "What?"

"When he kisses you? Doesn't he? I would hate that."

"Katie Rose, you shouldn't be talking about such things."

"*Well*, Lizzie Marie, maybe you shouldn't be doing them."

Lizzie quickly shoved the rest of her makeup into her clutch, avoiding her sister's eyes. "Honestly, Katie, you sound just like Brady. There's nothing wrong with a simple kiss, you know. And nobody likes a prude."

Katie propped her head in her hands and grinned. "Charity might agree, but I bet Faith would give you a run for your money."

Lizzie forced a smile and then blew her a kiss. "Good night, Katie Rose. I'll try not to wake you when I come in." She rushed out of the room and down the stairs to enter the parlor where her mother and father were reading. She smiled and folded her arms. "Goodness, you two are all alone? Now there's a rare sight. Where's Steven?"

Patrick looked up from his paper. "Sean railroaded him into helping with inventory at the store. Promised him enough to buy the latest Mysto Magic set." He squinted. "You look very pretty, Lizzie . . . but can you honestly see with all that black stuff on your eyes?"

She ignored the heat in her face and gave him a patient smile, followed by a kiss on the cheek. "Yes, Father, I can. It's the style, remember?"

His lips squirmed to the right. "Mmmm . . . and it's rather odd having a date on a Monday night, isn't it? What time is Tom coming?"

Lizzie glanced at the clock on the mantel. "Any minute now. And believe me, it wasn't my idea to go out tonight. Between school and work, I'm exhausted. But the new Valentino movie just opened at the Copely, and Tom can't wait to see it."

Marcy pressed her open book against her chest and sighed. "No matter how tired I was, I believe I'd still want to see that man in a movie."

Patrick lowered his paper. "A little less drooling, if you will, darlin'. And what's this Valentino character got that I haven't?"

Marcy smiled coyly and turned a page in her book. "A wife who doesn't have to keep dinner, no doubt."

Patrick's lower lip puckered slightly. "Ah, a barb to the heart from the love of my life." He glanced at Lizzie, apparently hoping to entreat her sympathy. "I'm late for one meal this week, and it's an unforgivable crime."

Marcy never glanced up from her book. "It was two, and if it were unforgivable, Patrick O'Connor, you'd be sleeping on the couch tonight."

Lizzie grinned. "I'll be sure and cover you up when I come in, Father."

The doorbell rang and Lizzie laughed, hurrying to answer it.

"I hope that smile is for me," Tom said, hands tucked in the pockets of his tan linen knickers. He grinned and folded his arms, then leaned against the frame of the door.

To Lizzie and every other girl, he was the epitome of a college man with his cream V-necked sweater, red Windsor necktie, and classic spectator shoes. A tweed newsboy cap perched low on his head, hinting at sandy hair cut short on the sides in the fashion of the day. His gaze traveled the length of her, producing an indecent grin. "You look beautiful, doll," he said, reeling her into his arms out of sight of the open door. His mouth burrowed deep into the crook of her neck, tasting her skin. "Mmmm, you taste good too."

A dangerous heat stirred within, and she pushed him away. "Tom, stop! My parents are right in the parlor."

He laughed and fanned his hand down the back of her waist with a familiarity that both shocked and excited her. "That's why I didn't go for your sweet lips, Lizzie, although God knows I want to. Can't say hello to the folks with lipstick on my face, now can I?"

He ushered her into the house with all the practiced authority of a college man, hat in hand. "Good evening, Mr. and Mrs. O'Connor. Thanks for letting Lizzie go out on a school night. I've been jazzed to see the new Valentino movie, and this is the only time I can go."

Patrick glanced up from his paper. "Hi, Tom. That's fine, just have her home early."

"Hello, Tom. You look very handsome tonight." Marcy smiled over her book.

"Thank you, ma'am. And yes, sir, I will—right after. Have a good evening."

He steered Lizzie into the foyer where he snatched her jacket from the coat rack with a flick of his wrist. He slipped it over her shoulders and latched an arm to her waist. His warm breath tickled as he leaned close to her ear. "But I didn't say after what."

Patrick yawned and dropped his trousers. He stepped out of

them and unbuttoned his shirt, launching it at the hamper with little success. It skimmed the top and landed on the floor. He picked up the pants and draped them over the wooden valet with little more ceremony than the shirt.

"Really, Patrick, the hamper's not there to take potshots at, you know. Would it be so very hard to open the lid and toss the shirt in?"

He slipped his pajama bottoms on and shot her a boyish grin. "No, darlin', but not near as much fun." He skimmed a thick hand across the dark hair on his chest and put his nightshirt on.

She sighed and continued brushing her hair while she eyed him in the mirror. He scooped up the shirt and deposited it into the hamper. With another yawn, he dropped on his side of the bed, spread-eagle, ignoring the covers beneath.

Marcy doused the light and hurried to join him. She tunneled beneath the sheets, then yanked to wrest her blanket from beneath Patrick's bulky frame. "Sweet saints, aren't you cold?"

Nothing moved but his lips. "No, darlin', I'm hot."

She cuddled close to his side. "Yes, I know. It's one of your greatest attributes on the coldest of nights. But if you've any mind to spoon tonight, I suggest it will be *under* the covers."

He chuckled and turned on his stomach, hoisting a sturdy leg over her body. "I don't know, I think this may be the safest way to spoon for a man with sleep on his mind."

Her answering yawn rose several octaves, in the cadence of song. "Not if the woman doesn't fall asleep first. I'm cold, Patrick, warm me up."

He clamped an arm to her waist. "Don't tempt me, Marcy, I'm way too tired."

She grinned in the dark. "Good night, Patrick. I love you."

"Good night, darlin'. Sleep well."

His body transferred warm contentment to her bones, and she breathed in deeply, filling her lungs with the scent of their room. The faint smell of musk soap and pipe tobacco brought a soft tilt to her lips, and she whispered silent gratitude for the man beside her.

All at once, he jolted awake. "Blast it all, Marcy, I almost forgot. Sam called. He's in town."

It was her turn to jolt. "Sam . . . O'Rourke?"

"Of course, Sam O'Rourke. What other Sam do we know? He wants to take us to dinner Friday night. Are we free?"

She tried to think, but her mind wouldn't focus. Sam O'Rourke? Here? *Now?*

"Marcy?"

"I'm thinking, Patrick, I'm thinking." She pressed a hand to her temple. Tuesday was bridge, Wednesday she'd promised to help Faith sew a dress, Thursday was Katie's play practice, and Friday was . . . She stopped. Oh, Lord, no . . . they were free!

"If you don't want to go, just say so, but I would think you'd be as anxious to see him as me. After all, it's been over twenty years."

"Almost twenty-five, to be exact. Why don't you meet him, and I'll just stay home?"

He drew her around to face him. "Marcy, it's time to forgive and forget. What Sam did, losing our money in that scam investment, well, it all happened a long time ago. And don't forget he lost money too. For pity's sake, he was my closest friend, more like a brother, really, and the best man at our wedding. Can't we spend one evening with him, for old time's sake?"

Dread soured her tongue. "If that's what you want."

"I do. Now, I'll call him tomorrow and handle the details. I want you to go out and buy something new, something pretty that won't make this such a chore, all right?"

She nodded.

He kissed her on the nose and rotated her back into a spooning position. He tucked his arms firmly around her waist and sighed against her neck. "I love you, Marcy. Sweet dreams, darlin'."

She stared in the dark, seeing nothing but Sam O'Rourke's smile on the walls of her mind.

Dreams? Undoubtedly.

Sweet? Dear Lord, she hoped not.

ᘜ ᘔ

"Come on, Lizzie," he whispered. "Don't you like me?"

Lizzie tried to scoot to her side of the swing, but Tom lured her back with another heated kiss, no doubt intended to numb her conscience. She shivered. It was working.

"You know how I feel about you. I've been after you for years. Now you're my girl, and I just want to love you." He scooped her close and kissed her deeply while his hands roamed from the nape of her neck to the small of her back. A delicious heat pulsed inside of her, dulling her will to stop. His hands swept to the curve of her hips and he moaned, whispering against her cheek with labored breaths. "I love you, Lizzie." He kissed her again while his palms skimmed up the sides of her waist, triggering an alarm inside her brain.

Her mouth wrenched from his. "Tom, no!"

He pressed his mouth to her ear, tickling her earlobe. "Come on, Lizzie, you know I'm crazy about you, and I can tell you like it."

"But it's not right."

"It is if I love you."

She pushed him away. "No, Tom, it's not."

He exhaled and sat back on the swing. "Look, Lizzie, I'm a man in college now. Do you know what that's like? It's a new world out there. There are modern women everywhere, throwing themselves at guys like me. But I don't want them—I want you."

She shivered, caught off-guard at the jealousy that stabbed within. "You have me, Tom."

"I know, Lizzie, but I want *all* of you."

Shock heated her cheeks. "You can't mean—"

He kissed her lightly on the lips. "Not right away, doll, but when you're ready. Until then, I want to hold you, touch you . . ." He pressed a kiss to the lobe of her ear. "You know, Lizzie, I've had chances to go to petting parties—"

"No!" She pulled away as tears stung her eyes.

He gripped her arms. "But I wouldn't . . . because of you. You're my girl, the only one that I want to do that with."

He smiled and stroked her cheek with his thumb. "Just think about it, okay?" He stood and lifted her to her feet, then walked her to the door. He bent to kiss her gently on the mouth. "Good night, Lizzie. I'll be dreaming of you. Think about me too, okay?" He chucked her on the chin and bounded down the steps. His whistling faded down the street.

She leaned against the door and closed her eyes, guilty over heat that still pulsed from his touch. Think about him? Shame shivered through her. As if she had a choice.

ᴄ᷿ ᷿ᴏ

Brady rolled his neck to clear the kinks while he stared at the dripolator. He glanced at the clock and winced. Five thirty a.m. Well, it wasn't the earliest time he'd come into the shop, but it had all the markings of one of the most difficult, given his workload. He glanced at the new stack of orders Collin put on his back table last night, higher than the old stack that never seemed to dwindle. He reached for the old work orders and began to sort, releasing a weary sigh. He needed to get a jump-start on the day, something he couldn't do until strong, hot coffee flowed in his veins. He peered up at the brand-new Silex coffee machine, willing it to hurry. It steamed and spit in response, sputtering dark liquid into the pot at a snail's pace.

He scanned the first order and groaned. A sixteen-page addendum to the St. Stephen's bulletin, extolling the virtues of their financial campaign. It alone would eat up a good chunk of his morning, precious time he didn't have. He and Collin needed to talk. The prospect of hiring additional help was something they could no longer ignore. That is, if he wanted a life. His lips twisted into a near smile. Not that his was worth having, right at the moment.

The heady aroma of coffee teased his senses as he fanned through the rest of the orders, contemplating a plan for getting them done. Not an impossible task, he supposed, if he spent his time wisely and worked straight through. He suddenly thought of Mary, so hungry for God she now came five days a week. She seemed determined to spend her lunch hour with God's Word—and him. He sighed. Maybe he should cut back to the original three days. It might be the best thing to do. Wiser, more productive.

*And certainly safer.*

The coffeepot gurgled with a final groan, hissing to indicate its cycle was through. Brady rose and poured himself a cup while thoughts of Mary furrowed his brow. He sat back down and reached for the pile of papers. She was finally able to relax with him and had developed a trust he suspected was rare for her. She seemed to admire him, open up to him, cling to his every word. All at once, his gaze fell to the work orders in a cold stare. *Dear God, no.* Could she be falling for him?

Lizzie had, despite his doing everything in his power to prevent it. Although Mary was close to Lizzie in age, she was not as wide-eyed and naïve, he was sure, regardless of the sweetness of her face. His jaw tightened. He knew all too well that tragic eyes often came from ruin of innocence.

He dropped his head in his hands and began to pray for wisdom.

"Brady?"

He spun around, his heart jolting in his chest. "Beth! What are you doing here?"

She moved into the back room like a ghost with sunken eyes and pale cheeks. The shingle haircut she was so proud of, usually carefully waved and hugging her face, now wisped below her ears in soft, unruly curls—clear evidence of a restless night's sleep. She avoided his eyes as she sank into the chair across the table.

"Beth? What's wrong?"

She looked up then, and his heart squeezed in his chest. Those near-violet eyes, so soulful, so sweet, now stared back like a little girl lost, heavy with tears. He fought the urge to pull her into his arms and leaned over the table instead. "Talk to me, please."

She shook her head and wetness spilled loose, glistening her cheeks. She fanned a hand to shield her eyes, as if she couldn't bear his gaze. "You w-were right, Brady. I should h-have listened."

The blood stilled in his veins. "About what?"

She sniffed and swiped her face with the corner of her sweater, prompting him to pull a clean handkerchief from the pocket of his work apron.

"Here, use this."

She took it and started to cry. "Oh, Brady, I'm so ashamed. You . . . tried to w-warn me, but I didn't believe y-you."

His jaw felt like rock. "What happened, Beth?"

"N-nothing, y-yet, but I . . . I'm scared." She laid her head down and sobbed, the sound of her weeping lacerating his heart. He leapt up and rounded the table, then pulled her up from her chair and into his arms. He held her tightly, stroking her head with his hand. "It's okay, nothing's going to happen. That's why you're here—to pray about it and make sure."

She clung with all her might while she shook in his arms, and he laid his head against hers, breathing in her scent. Lilacs and soap drifted to his nostrils, and a rush of love welled as he closed his eyes. This was his Beth, sweet and clean, innocent to the core. *Oh, God, please keep her that way.*

He lifted his head, aware her weeping had stilled as she sagged against him. Her tentative arms encircling his waist now slid higher to a more intimate embrace. He caught his breath and took a step back, fisting her wrists with a gentle hold. "Sit down, Beth, please."

He quickly released her and returned to his seat. "What happened? Why are you scared?"

She slumped in the chair and blew her nose. "Because it's hard to stop. And Tom has no intention of stopping."

"Break it off, then. He's no good for you."

"It's not that easy, Brady."

"No, but you can do it."

"No, that's just it—I can't! Tom makes me feel things I've waited a lifetime to feel. Alive and in love and desired."

"Desire isn't love, Beth, I've taught you that."

She pressed forward. "Yes, Brady, you did—with *words*. But when Tom kisses me, touches me, tells me he wants me . . . it *feels* like love."

Brady reached to gently touch her arm. "And what's it feel like in the morning, Beth?"

She shivered and looked away.

He exhaled and leaned back in his chair. "I can tell you what it feels like. Like sin. I've been there more times than I can count. A sick feeling, bitter regret, guilt so heavy your shoulders ache. And death—dark, cold, hopeless death. The 'wages of sin is death,' little buddy, and trust me, nobody gets away with it."

She nodded and wiped her eyes with his handkerchief. "I know. I can see that now." She looked up with sorrowful eyes. "He doesn't really love me, does he?"

"I believe he cares for you, but that's not love. Real love gives, not takes."

Her voice was quiet. "Tom would say, if real love gives, then I should give what he wants."

A faint smile touched his lips. "And you would say no, real love gives what God wants."

She hung her head. "It does, doesn't it?"

"You ready to pray about this?"

"To pray, yes. To quit seeing Tom? I'm not so sure, at least not yet. But I'm willing to pray. For God's strength . . . and that he'll show me what to do."

"That's a good place to start."

She sighed. "Yes, but either way, I doubt Tom will like the outcome."

He reached for her hand and smiled. "There's no doubt at all. He won't."

❦ ❧

If ever there were a night for Patrick to sleep on the couch, this would be it. With barely contained fury, Marcy waited for Sam to return from the washroom. She folded her arms and tucked them close to her body, vowing to lock her husband out of their bedroom for the first time in over twenty-six years.

She exhaled and began tapping her fingers on the table, then glanced at the front for some sign of Patrick. Her hand fidgeted with the base of the water glass before she finally reached for her purse. Her fingers were itchy to keep busy, so she applied a coat of lipstick and powdered her nose. Seconds ticked by as she fumed, reflecting back on the evening—the evening Patrick had insisted they attend. Against her wishes.

"For old time's sake," he had said. But "old times" weren't all that he supposed them to be, and now here she was, face-to-face with her past. While that stubborn Irishman was, once again, putting the *Herald* before her.

Her insides had been a jumble as she dressed, angst bubbling in her stomach like vinegar in a fry pan. She slipped into the new butter-yellow frock Patrick had helped her pick out. "It brings out the blue of your eyes, Marcy, and the glints of gold in your hair," he said, ignoring the cost. He flashed his heart-melting grin before finalizing the decision with a kiss. "I want to show you off, darlin'," he had whispered.

But he hadn't realized to whom.

When he had called to say he'd be late, some of her anxiety had edged into anger. "I'll meet you at the restaurant," he promised, and she had begged him to hurry.

"I will, Marcy, as quickly as I can. Just one crisis to avert, and I'll be on my way."

She had hung up the phone in the hall with a lump in her throat, desperate to avert a crisis of her own. She glanced at her reflection in the mirror. Sky-blue eyes stared back, etched with concern. Anxiety had paled her cheeks, so she'd blotted her lipstick and rubbed in a bit of the color. She scrutinized her hair and wrinkled her nose. She was so tired of chignons, despite the pretty mother-of-pearl comb she wore, and had been sorely tempted to get it bobbed for ease of care. But Patrick had pleaded, and she had succumbed. She sighed and leaned close to the mirror to study her face with a critical eye, grateful for the creamy skin inherited from her mother. Even with her fair share of laugh lines and faint wrinkles, it glowed as softly as Charity's in the right light. Some said she looked closer to thirty-five than forty-three. Her lips tipped into a faint smile. Mmmm . . . maybe in a dark room.

She returned to the present to see Sam heading her way and quickly took a drink of water. He strode to the table with a confident air that had been one of his many hallmarks, and she found herself wondering why he never married. Although not as handsome as Patrick, he had a definite charisma that had never left him wanting for a woman on his arm. Even now his easy smile lit his ebony eyes with an almost roguish glint, turning female heads as he crossed the room. He eased into the booth and teased her with a grin, looking so much like the pirate he was—dark hair slicked back and hard-chiseled features.

He nodded at her uneaten dessert. "You've changed. The Marceline Murphy I knew would never leave that on her plate."

She laughed, and it dispelled some of the edginess she felt. "I suspect we've all changed a good deal. Hopefully, for the better."

He leaned back in the booth and studied her through lidded eyes. "You haven't. Other than your appetite for desserts." He paused before leaning in to rest his arms on the table. He lowered his voice to a whisper. "You still take my breath away, you know."

It had been years since she blushed to the roots of her hair, and his low chuckle did nothing to help.

"Well, I can see I've embarrassed you, Mrs. O'Connor, so I do apologize. But as you know, I've never been a man to mince words."

She fumbled for her napkin and dipped it in her water glass, then closed her eyes and patted her face. She was certain the breath in her lungs had seldom been so shallow.

He touched a gentle hand to her arm, and she jolted. "Don't tell me you're not used to hearing such things, Marcy. Knowing Patrick as I do, I would think you'd hear them warmly and often. I know if you were my wife—"

"Well, I'm not and well you know it, Samuel O'Rourke." Her chest heaved with ragged breaths as she pressed the cool cloth to her cheek. Her glance skittered to the door. "Where in the world is Patrick?"

Sam picked up the check and reached into his suit coat. "Oh, didn't I tell you? That phone call I took at the front desk was from him. He's running late and said he'd meet us back at the house."

The cool napkin adhered to her skin. "The call you took more than an hour ago? That was Patrick?"

He placed several crisp bills on the table and gave her an intimate smile. "I know your fondness for dessert, my love. I didn't want to ruin it for you." He stood and offered his hand. "Patrick has had you for over twenty-six years, Marcy. I only have tonight."

She shot to her feet and slapped his hand away. "Keep your hands to yourself, Sam O'Rourke, and I am *not* your 'love.'"

He blocked her path. "You were once, or have you forgotten?"

She butted him out of the way with her purse. "I haven't forgotten what a wolf you were, and apparently you haven't changed, either." She stormed toward the door.

He cupped her elbow before she exited the front entrance. "Marcy, please . . . forgive me. I was way out of line." He offered her the thin wrap she'd left in the booth. "Truce?"

She snatched it from his hands. "I want to go home. Now!"

"Yes, ma'am." He turned to hail his driver, and within minutes, he was ushering her into the back of his private car, extending his hand to help her in. Ignoring him, she climbed inside, then scooted to the far side of the seat. He eased in beside her and gave the glass partition two hard raps, indicating for the driver to go. He sat back and she wedged her purse neatly between them. With a grin, he casually placed his arm along the back of the seat. She turned and fixed her gaze out the window, all but holding her breath as they jostled along cobblestone streets.

The tips of his fingers lighted upon her shoulder, almost searing her skin through the chiffon of her sleeve. "Marcy, for the sake of our past, let's not fight. I'm leaving in the morning and may never see you again. Won't you give me these few precious moments?"

She turned sharply and saw the loneliness in his eyes. She expelled a soft breath and gently removed his hand from her arm. "All right, Sam, for the sake of our past and your friendship with my husband—truce."

He sloped back in the seat and visibly relaxed. "I came here this weekend for one reason only—to see you and Patrick and set things straight." He reached inside his suit coat and withdrew a piece of paper. His gaze locked on hers as he tucked it in the pocket of her clutch. "Here's a check for the money I owe you, every dime."

He looked away and threaded a hand through black hair grayed at the temples. "You know, I never intended to say those things to you at the restaurant back there, truly. But when Patrick didn't join us and I found we were alone . . ." His gaze returned, stifling her air. "I suddenly remembered things I've missed. Like that lopsided tilt of your smile when you're teasing, or that little-girl glow when you laugh." A grin creased his lips. "The look of panic in your eyes when I would get too close . . ."

She laughed and he took her hand lightly in his, his eyes suddenly serious. "It all came rushing back, Marcy, and I found myself wishing . . . that you'd married me instead of Patrick."

"You weren't the marrying kind, as I recall."

"I was a fool."

She squirmed and tugged her hand free. "Sam—"

"No, hear me out, please. I know you love him, and there's nothing I can do about that. You belong to him, and rightly so. But he's not here now, and I am. And I can't help but wonder . . . what might have happened if I hadn't ruined it between us." His voice dropped to a whisper as he stroked a calloused thumb against her cheek. "Can't help but wonder . . . what it would be like to kiss you again."

His words caught her by surprise, and her lips parted in shock. In the catch of her breath, he took full advantage and drew her close, mating his mouth with hers. Panic seized in her chest, and she tried to push him away, but his grip tightened as he deepened the kiss. She managed to bite his lip and he jerked away, retaining his hold. A glint of anger shone in his eyes.

"Still the hellcat, I see. I imagine Patrick must enjoy that immensely."

He tried to kiss her again, and she wrenched to the side, struggling to get free. "Let me go, you lout, or I'll tell Patrick everything."

His laugh was bitter. "No, I don't think you will, Marcy. Because somehow, someway, it would all slip out, and you can't afford that. It wouldn't do for Patrick to know I was the reason you played so hard to get, the reason you took so long to say yes. He may have won your hand, my love, but at the time, I had your heart, remember? And I don't think you would want him to know that. Sometimes it's best to let sleeping dogs lie."

Her chest heaved with indignation. "Sleeping dogs? Or lying ones?"

He grinned. "Perhaps a bit of both, my love." He immobilized her arms so she couldn't move and nestled his lips along the curve of her ear. "Either way, there's no sense in dredging the past."

"You mean, along with the slime?" She jerked a knee hard into his gut and twisted away. He released her with a grunt. Her pulse raced frantically as she groped for the comb from her hair, finally jerking it free. Loose curls spilled in defiance as she brandished the comb in his face. "So help me, Sam O'Rourke, if you lay one more finger on me, I will gouge out that lecherous look in your eye! You haven't changed one bit, which is exactly why my name is O'Connor."

The car lurched to a stop, and she turned to fling the door wide. In a flash of his thick arm, he heaved it closed again, butting her hard against the back of the seat. "I suggest you hear me out, Mrs. O'Connor, if you value your marriage. You and I may not part on the best of terms, but your husband is my friend. If you so much as breathe a word of this to Patrick, I'd be forced to do the same. I'm sure he'd be shocked to learn he wasn't the first man his wife kissed on the morning of her wedding."

With a set to his chin, he removed a handkerchief from his pocket and wiped his mouth. He bent to retrieve the comb she had dropped and pushed it in her hand. "I suggest you make yourself presentable. We wouldn't want Patrick to wonder what's kept us."

She turned away, unwilling for him to see the tears in her

eyes. With shaky fingers, she wound her hair into a semblance of a chignon and gouged the comb in until it hurt. She flailed at the door handle, relieved when it swung open. The brisk night air helped to cool the humiliation in her cheeks as she stepped out onto the dark street. This time he didn't stop her. She slammed the door, and her hands trembled as she adjusted her dress.

He got out on the other side and rounded the car. He assessed her in the shadowed light, then lowered his voice to resume a teasing tone. "Your hair is a bit disheveled, my love, a wee bit like you just rolled out of bed, but nothing that would give suspect, I don't think."

He smiled and latched her arm firmly onto his. She tried to break free, but he tightened his hold.

"It's a pity you and I didn't end up together, Marcy. I could have tamed a bit of that stubborn streak in you. Not all, mind you, but enough."

A shadowy figure rose from the swing on the porch. "I was beginning to think you ran off with my wife, O'Rourke."

Marcy caught her breath and pressed a hand to her chest. "Patrick! You scared me."

Sam ushered her to the steps and released her arm with a chuckle. "I certainly gave it my best effort, old man, but I daresay the woman is set on you."

She was grateful for the dark that hid the fire in her cheeks and hurried to where Patrick stood on the porch. He smiled and circled an arm to her waist. Relief ebbed through her like a tidal wave.

"So, did you two have a good time, darlin'?"

Sam's eyes locked on hers. "I don't know about Marcy, but I certainly did. Your wife is a beautiful woman, Patrick. I'd think twice before not showing up again."

Patrick squeezed her waist. "Yes, no doubt there will be penance to pay for this latest infraction of mine, Sam, but thank God Marcy is a forgiving woman."

Sam grinned. "Is she, now?"

"Come on in. There's a fresh pot of coffee on the stove, and we've got years to cover." He herded Marcy inside while holding the screen door for Sam. He closed the door and turned, hand suspended on the knob. She could feel the heat of his gaze. "Marcy, are you all right? You look tired."

She attempted a smile and took a step back, then brushed a hand to her forehead. "I . . . am tired, Patrick. If you and Sam don't mind, I believe I'm going to head up and let you two catch up."

Patrick moved to her side and pulled her into his arms. He kissed the top of her head. "Of course we don't mind, do we, Sam?"

"Not at all. I'm afraid I've worn her out, Patrick. My apologies, Marcy. It was wonderful seeing you again. Good night."

Patrick lifted her chin to bestow a quick kiss. He hesitated for a split second before retrieving a handkerchief from his pocket. He gently wiped the side of her mouth. "You must have brushed up against something. Your lipstick is smeared." He shoved it back into his suit coat and smiled a smile that didn't quite reach his eyes. He gave her a gentle kiss on the lips. "Good night, darlin'."

"Good night, Patrick. Sam, thank you for dinner."

Her legs felt like lead as she mounted the steps, well aware that two sets of eyes burned a hole in her back. She braced herself against the need to shiver, then reached the landing and fought the urge to run. Once hidden in the safety of the hall, she flew to the bathroom and scoured her mouth with a soapy washrag, desperate to purge her lips of the residue of Sam's mouth. She brushed her teeth three separate times and gargled with lilac water, but the stain of his lust still burned like the fear in her throat. *Dear God, please protect Patrick from the truth.*

She turned and made her way down the dark hall, grateful that Lizzie had taken Katie to a last-minute play practice. A shudder rippled through her. She needed to escape. To strip off her clothes and crawl into bed, where sleep could take her far, far away. She flipped on the light in her bedroom and suddenly sagged against the door, not putting much hope in the prospect of sleep. She had a feeling that slumber—like Sam O'Rourke—would be anything but a friend tonight.

❦ ❧

Patrick dismissed the uneasy feeling in his gut and turned to Sam with a smile. "So, you up for a cup of coffee?"

Sam laughed. "I'd much prefer a good scotch like old times."

"As would I, my friend, but then the eighteenth amendment isn't particularly concerned with your preferences or mine." Patrick grinned. "Not to mention the fact that I'm clean out."

Sam's teeth flashed in a return grin. "But I'm not." He disappeared out the door and returned a few moments later, bottle in hand. "I trust you still have whiskey glasses?"

Patrick chuckled as he rose to his feet. "You never have been a good influence." He retrieved two glasses from the kitchen and set them on the table. Sam filled each three-quarters full and then raised his glass in a toast. "To good influences—may they be few and far between." He gulped half of his drink and settled into a chair.

Patrick swallowed some whiskey and eyed him over the glass. "What brings you to Boston? Business?"

Sam smiled and twirled his drink in his hands. "Of a sort. I'm looking for investors for a business venture I'm putting together. Interested?"

Patrick grinned and raised his glass before taking another quick swallow. "Only in your whiskey, my friend. It doesn't burn quite as much when it goes down."

Sam laughed. "I suppose that's a natural reaction after the last time I invested your money. But I've paid it all back, you

❦ 163 ❧

know. Gave Marcy a check tonight. We're all clear, my friend, and ready to begin again." He emptied his glass and stood up to pour more. He held the bottle out, but Patrick waved him off.

"No, better not. I'm already this close to sleeping on the couch after not showing up tonight. Marcy might not look too favorably upon me if I came to bed drunk."

"You're a lucky man, my friend, going to bed—drunk or otherwise—with a woman like that. She's something special, Patrick. Always has been."

Patrick took another drink and wondered why the compliment bothered him so.

The front door wheeled open, and Lizzie and Katie trudged in, apparently as exhausted as Marcy had been. Patrick glanced at his watch and frowned. "Don't tell me you had practice until now? Sweet saints, they must have it near perfect."

Lizzie smiled and propped two hands on Katie's tired shoulders. "No, play practice was over at nine, but your daughter insisted on a fountain soda."

Katie yawned and lumbered over to give Patrick a hug. "Good night, Daddy."

"Before you girls head up, I'd like to introduce you to an old friend of mine. Sam, these are my two youngest girls, Lizzie and Katie. Girls, this is Sam O'Rourke."

Sam stood to his feet, drink in hand. He smiled and raised a toast before taking a sip. "Hello, Lizzie, Katie. Patrick, I do believe Lizzie favors you, and Katie, her mother."

Patrick studied the girls and felt his heart glow warm with pride. "I'm not sure that's a compliment to Lizzie, but they're both beauties, that's for sure."

Katie yawned and gave him a tired nod while Lizzie smiled. "It's very nice to meet you, Mr. O'Rourke." She leaned to give Patrick a kiss. "Good night, Father. Is Mother in bed?"

"Yes, she went up a bit ago, but she may be asleep by now. She looked pretty beat."

Lizzie draped an arm around Katie's shoulders. "Come on, Katie Rose, before you fall asleep standing up. Good night, Mr. O'Rourke, Father."

Sam sat back in the chair and watched the girls ascend the stairs. His eyes were pensive as he took a quick swig of whiskey. "They're beautiful, Patrick. Just like their moth—"

The glass suddenly slipped from his fingers and tumbled in his lap, prompting a curse from his lips.

Patrick jumped to his feet. "I'll get something to wipe that up." He hurried to the kitchen and returned with a wet rag. He handed it to Sam and watched as he blotted his pants. All at once the blood chilled in his veins. A rose-colored smudge marred the far right side of Sam's collar, the exact shade of Marcy's lips.

Patrick turned away, stunned at the barrage of thoughts in his brain. Lipstick smeared on the side of her mouth. The disheveled hair. The guarded look in her eyes. His instincts had sharpened, but he'd merely brushed them aside, ignoring the unfamiliar coolness he had sensed in her manner. He had written it off as nothing more than wifely annoyance. But what if it were more? His pulse began to throb at the side of his head. What if it were guilt?

"Sorry. I'm afraid I become clumsy when I tip the bottle too much." He poured himself more whiskey and sat back in his chair. "As I was saying, your family is beautiful, Patrick. You're a lucky man." His lips twisted into a wry smile. "In fact, I think I may be jealous."

Patrick turned to face him, his nerves twitching under his skin. "Enough to make advances to my wife?"

"What?" Sam's lips went pale.

"You heard me. You care to explain why my wife's lipstick is staining your collar?"

Sam froze for a split second and then calmly set his glass down. "You're letting your imagination run away with you, my friend. Marcy tripped on the cobblestones, and I caught her before she fell."

Patrick stared, his teeth aching from the tension in his jaw. He hadn't seen Sam O'Rourke in over twenty-five years, but he could still sense when he was lying. Sam had been his best friend since the second grade, the two of them inseparable. Until Marcy. The taste of nausea soured his stomach. Marcy had dated Sam before him.

"You're lying, O'Rourke. What did you do to her?"

Sam stood to his feet. "Nothing. Don't let her come between us again, Patrick. We were good friends once."

Patrick took a step forward, his fists clenched at his sides. "So help me, God, if you hurt her . . . Answer me! Did you touch her?" He grabbed the lapel of Sam's sack suit and fairly spit the words in his face. "Did you?"

Sam pushed him back with a sneer. "And what if I did? Who's to say she didn't like it?"

Patrick slammed a fist against Sam's jaw, sending him careening into the chair. "Get out—now!"

Rubbing his jaw with the back of his hand, Sam stared up with cold fury in his eyes. "You think I'm lying? Why don't you ask her? Ask why it took her so long to say yes to you."

Patrick lunged and hauled him out of the chair, flinging him toward the door. "You're nothing but a vicious liar, and I can't stomach liars. Get out!"

Sam was breathing hard when he turned at the door, his eyes little more than slits. "A surprising declaration since you're married to one. You think you're the man she loved when she said 'I do'? Ask her sometime, about the morning of your wedding."

He slammed the door behind him, leaving Patrick in a stupor. Despite ragged breaths that heaved in his lungs, his body felt numb. He closed his eyes and almost staggered at the heaviness shrouding his mind. *The man she loved when she said "I do"?*

Cold comprehension pushed pain aside to allow his rage to rise. He remembered with painful clarity how she'd been the only woman immune to his charms. He had always had his pick of the lot. Until Marceline Murphy, a beguiling lass who had remained aloof. But he had persisted until she'd said yes, a sweet conquest that had taken him far too long. Everything suddenly shifted in his mind, becoming all too clear. Had she been in love with someone else? Had his marriage begun as a lie?

With lethal calm, he locked the front door and returned to the parlor to douse the lights. His gaze fell on his half-finished glass of whiskey, and he bolted it down in one burning swallow. He snatched the bottle of whiskey and strode to the kitchen, pouring it out in the sink along with the hot coffee. The steam rose like his ire. He mounted the stairs as if in a trance, feeling his temper sharpen with every step he took. He stood at the door and stared at their bed. Beneath the covers lay the woman who had shared his life and given him joy. Now the poison in his mind said she was no more than a stranger.

He entered the room and closed the door, shattering the silence with a sharp snap of the bolt—a perfect complement to the edge in his voice. "Don't pretend you're asleep, darlin', we both know that you're not."

Marcy squeezed her eyes shut. Fear shivered through her at his icy tone. She held her breath, praying he would believe she was asleep.

She was met with a cool blast of air when he snatched the covers from her body and flipped on the light. "Get up, darlin', I'd like to hear all about your evening."

Marcy sat up and put a hand to her eyes, squinting at the blinding light. "Patrick, have you been drinking?"

His laugh was not kind. "Yes, Marcy, I have. A man will often do that when he learns his wife has been unfaithful."

She pressed back against the headboard, alarmed at the brutal look in his eyes. "That's a lie! I have never been unfaithful."

His look pierced her to the core. "Not physically, I'm sure. At least, not until tonight."

Fear paralyzed her. "I fought him off, Patrick, I swear I did. He's a liar."

"Funny, he said the same about you."

He took a step forward, and she cowered back. Her husband had never laid a cruel hand on her. But this man was not her husband. "Patrick, you're tired, and you've been drinking. Come to bed, and we'll discuss it in the morning."

"Did you kiss him?"

"No, of course not!"

"Did he kiss you?"

She gasped for breath.

He gripped her arm and shook her. "Answer me!"

"Yes!"

His eyes glittered like ice. "Well, Mrs. O'Connor, and how do I compare?"

She stared in shock, tears welling. "How dare you act like I enjoyed it!"

He stepped back, a total stranger with distant eyes. He moved to the bureau and opened a drawer, spilling clothing on the floor as he rooted through it. His back was so rigid and his manner so cold, she barely recognized him. "Do you love him?"

"What? No! How can you think that?"

He slammed the drawer shut and turned, a pair of clean socks and underwear fisted in his hands. There was no love in his eyes. "Have you ever?"

Her heart stopped. She swallowed the fear that cleaved to her mouth. "Once. A long time ago."

"When you married me?"

She remained silent, a lie weighting her tongue like forbidden fruit waiting to be tasted.

"What happened the morning of our wedding, Marcy?"

The blood drained from her face. "Nothing, Patrick, I swear."

"You're lying. Tell me the truth!"

Her fingers quivered as she pushed the hair from her eyes.

"H-he came to see me . . . at the house . . . h-he begged me not to marry you."

"And why would he do that, darlin'?" His term of endearment hissed from his lips like a curse.

She leapt from the bed and ran to his side, clutching a hand to his arm. He slung it away and moved to the closet with deadly calm.

She stared in horror. "What are you doing?"

He snatched a clean shirt and turned. "Did you kiss him then too?"

"What?"

"What else happened?" His voice stung like a slap.

"Patrick, don't do this. It was a long time ago. And it doesn't matter now. I love you!"

"But not then."

The truth hung in the air like a cloying mist, burning the air from her lungs. She looked away, unable to bear the pain in his eyes.

"The truth. I want the truth. *Who* were you in love with when you became my wife?"

She put a hand to her mouth and began to cry.

"Who, Marcy?"

She forced the truth from her lips. "Sam." It was a mere whisper, but she felt him flinch from across the room.

"I see. Well, it seems as if Sam's not the only one adept at lying." He strode to the door.

"Patrick, wait! Don't leave, please—I love you."

She barely recognized the man who turned. "Somehow, Marcy, that doesn't carry a whole lot of weight right now. If you need me, I'll be at the *Herald*."

"No!" She followed him downstairs, her chest heaving with sobs. "Patrick, please, can't you forgive me . . . for the sake of our marriage?"

He unbolted the door and swung it wide. It ushered in a cool breeze far warmer than his eyes. "I don't know, Marcy.

Maybe. But I can tell you one thing, darlin'—it won't be any-time soon."

The door slammed behind him, effectively severing her hope. A frightening loneliness shivered through her, and she listed against the door, stunned at how easily love could be shattered. With a low moan, she turned and mounted the stairs as slowly as a woman twice her age, barely able to breathe. Like a sleepwalker, dully and without purpose, she finally collapsed in a heap on her bed. She shut her eyes to block out the pain, but it only droned on in her brain—a mind-numbing lament, suffocating until she thought she would die.

*Oh, God, help me! Please! Restore our peace and heal my marriage.*

She forced her lips to pray, soundless utterings that seemed to silence the torment inside. She took a deep breath and allowed his peace to quiet her mind, as it had done so many times in her past.

Her husband had left. But God would not. The only balm to her tortured soul.

But more than enough.

# 9

Brady wiped the sweat from his face and opened the door of his flat. He tossed the towel over his shoulder and spiked a hand through his hair, which was pasted to his head from his workout at the gym. He stopped midway to blink. Cluny sat ramrod straight on the couch like the garden gnome in the neighbor's yard, displaying a nervous amount of teeth in a cast-iron grin.

"What are you doing, bud?"

His throat bobbed like he'd just swallowed a canary. "Sittin'."

Brady glanced out the window, taking in the blue of the sky on this, the warmest day they'd had so far. He tossed his keys on the coffee table. "When you can be outside?"

Cluny picked at a seam in the couch. "Thought I'd wait for you . . . that maybe we could shoot some pool."

Brady slacked a hip and smiled. "Also inside. You have a sudden aversion to fresh air?"

"Basketball, then."

Brady rolled the back of his neck. He stripped off his damp shirt and headed down the hall. "Okay. Let me just clean up a bit. I can't stand myself."

Cluny followed him to the bathroom and slacked a leg against the door. "So when we going to Lizzie's house again? I got a hankering for a home-cooked meal."

Brady cupped several handfuls of water to his head and chest, then soaped his hair and under his arms. He doused his head under the sink and then his torso. "Not anytime soon, bud. Hand me that towel on the rack, will ya?"

Cluny tossed it, and Brady dried off. "Much better." He pushed past Cluny to get a clean shirt from his room. Miss Hercules lay sprawled on his bed, watching him through sleepy eyes. He slanted a brow and buttoned his shirt. "You could use some fresh air too, you bed jockey."

Miss Hercules yawned and rolled on her back.

Brady's lips quirked. "Come on, you mangy mutt, we're going outside."

She jumped off the bed and shook, sending a cloud of hair floating like slivers of feathers in a snow globe. Brady leaned into his closet and scooped up his brand-new basketball, purchased the week after Cluny had come to stay. He cinched the back of Cluny's neck and led him down the hall. "Come on, kid, I'm going to give you an education today."

Cluny laughed. "Not if I give you one first."

Brady stopped at the door and patted the pocket of his trousers. "Keys . . . where did I put my keys?"

Cluny rolled his eyes. "On the table by the couch, remember? Shoot, Brady, if you're gonna educate me, first ya gotta remember how."

"Very funny, kid." He reached for his keys, and something caught his eye. The cushion of the couch was cocked, raised just enough for him to notice. Brady paused, hand hovering over the keys as he squinted at the sofa. "What the—"

"Brady, let's go!"

He ignored the urgency in Cluny's voice and lifted the cushion. In slow motion, he reached for his M1910 canteen, standard military issue that soldiers were allowed to keep. He rose to his full height and stared at his one souvenir from the war. He glanced at Cluny, the smooth aluminum of the canteen cool against his palm. "What's this doing there?"

Cluny's face was so pale that his freckles looked like splotches of dirt. His words came out in a high-pitched rush. "M-me and Johnny Landers . . . we were playin' war . . . I'm sorry, Brady, I won't touch it again, I promise. Here, I'll put it back in your room." Cluny rushed forward and extended an unsteady hand.

Brady studied him with a smile. "Don't worry, bud, I don't mind, but ask me next time, okay?" He ambled to the kitchen, shaking the canteen. He unscrewed the cap. "What'dya put in here anyway, soda pop?"

"Brady, no!"

Cluny's shriek halted him dead in his tracks. Fear prickled the back of his neck as he lifted the open canteen to his nose. The distinct scent of oil of juniper invaded his senses, draining the blood from his face.

*Gin.*

Brady walked to the sink and poured the poison out, his hand shaking as the vile liquid gurgled down the drain. He hurled the canteen into the sink with a deafening clatter and slowly turned to face Cluny, whose back was now pasted hard against the front door.

"Brady, it was Johnny's idea, and I only took one sip, I promise! His older brother made it at college, and I swear I'll never touch it again."

A vein pumped in his neck as he moved forward in a slow, deliberate pace. He jerked the boy hard by the collar until he began to cough. Brady leaned close, his voice savage. "If you so much as come near my home or me with this trash ever again, I'll throw you out on your ear, do you hear?" He shoved him away, causing Cluny to tumble against the door. "Now, get out. I don't want to see your face for a while."

Tears of shock welled in the boy's eyes before he fled from the room with Miss Hercules close on his heels. Brady slammed the door to release his frustration. The walls shook, and several of his framed pictures crashed to the floor.

He was seething as he returned to the kitchen and stood, his gaze glued to the canteen in the sink. The stench of alcohol was strong in his nostrils, forcing him to swallow hard as his throat went dry. He closed his eyes and prayed for strength, feeling the pull of his past—like sticky venom, seeping into his soul. He licked his dry lips and felt a shudder ripple through him while painful memories barraged his mind. With a gutteral groan, he jerked the canteen from the sink and hurled it into the waste can, fingers quivering from the motion. His breathing was labored as he put his head in his hand.

He felt like death and he hadn't even taken a drink. But the scent alone triggered reactions in his body that reminded him just how weak of a man he was. He thought of Cluny and felt a stab of grief. Even now, without tasting a single drop, the poison had traveled his bloodstream in the form of fury and shame, unleashing his temper. To Cluny he was a hero, to the world a man of God, but the reality remained, buried so deep that he ached to the core. To himself, he was little more than a failure, hopelessly flawed.

"God forgive me," he whispered, more out of desperate habit than belief, knowing full well that God had forgiven him long, long ago.

Asking for forgiveness was one thing. He drew in a deep breath before releasing it again in one long, desolate shudder.

But accepting it—now that was something else altogether.

"Are you sure you don't mind?"

Lizzie glanced at Mary over the stack of books in her hands and smiled at the pucker on her brow. Over the last two months, she'd become as close to Mary as she was to Millie, the three of them almost inseparable, inside work and out. Mary Carpenter proved to be the perfect foil to Millie Doza—sweet, shy, and somehow worldly in a way that Millie only dreamed about. When Millie would get a bit wild, Mary could temper her with a maturity that seemed far beyond her years, often earning a begrudging respect from her free-spirited friend.

"Why would I mind? I've been wanting to return these books for a while now, and it's right on my way home. Besides, I kind of like the idea of popping in and giving Brady a little trouble. He's been pushing us pretty hard the last few weeks. Let's face it—he's a slave driver."

Mary grinned and hefted her own stack of books in her arms. "Yeah, but it's good for us. *He's* good for us." She sighed. "I wonder what it would be like to be married to a man like him."

Lizzie rolled her eyes. "I'd advise not thinking about it, Mary. It's a road I've traveled way too many times, and I've always run into a dead end. Brady will live and die as a bachelor, I'm afraid. And more's the pity." Her sigh matched Mary's. "He's a pretty special guy."

Mary giggled. "Listen to us, will you? Two love-struck girls. Wouldn't Brady laugh?"

"Probably not. He always gets this look of panic in his eyes whenever any woman looks his way. Trust me, I've seen it more times than I care to admit." She stopped in front of Brady's flat and nodded up. "Well, here it is. Shall we go in and surprise him?"

Lizzie drew in a silent breath, glad that Mary was by her side. She helped to calm her whenever Brady was around, taking her mind off what she couldn't have. But all the same, her pulse skipped a beat as she stood outside his flat and gave a timid knock.

The door opened a crack, and immediately Lizzie sensed something wasn't right. His face looked haggard, as if he hadn't slept in days, and his eyes were guarded, dark with something she couldn't read.

"Oh, Brady, I'm sorry. Are . . . we disturbing you?"

He looked away and cleared his throat. "No, Beth, I was just reading."

Mary took a step back. "We can come back another time if you like—"

"No, that's not necessary." He glanced at the stacks of books in their arms and attempted a smile. "Come on in. You can put the books on the table."

Lizzie stepped past, and her eyes surveyed the room. She'd been in his flat several times before, but a long time ago, when she'd gone there with Collin. She scanned an impressive wall of books lining a beautiful bookcase he'd built himself. Her gaze moved across the room to where his Bible sprawled open on the couch. She nodded at it with a smile. "You never get enough, do you?"

He glanced at it and looked away, avoiding her eyes. "No. Apparently not."

For some reason, she felt uneasy, as if they'd invaded his privacy. She found herself wanting to leave and slowly backed toward the door with a tinge of heat in her cheeks. "I have to go, Brady, but Mary wanted to return your books, so I brought mine along too."

"That's fine, Beth."

She smiled and glanced at Mary on her way out. "Cheer him up, will you? He looks like he could use a good friend."

Brady watched Beth slip out the door. His eyes followed her, lost in a cold stare long after she was gone. He took a deep breath and turned. "You didn't have to return them all at once, Mary. You could have kept them for a while, you know."

Her smile was hesitant. "Well, actually, Brady, I was hoping to browse the library Lizzie's always bragging about. That is, if you don't mind?"

He nodded and she wandered over to the shelf to peruse the titles, gently running her fingers along the spines.

He studied the graceful curve of her shoulders as she selected a volume and opened the book in her hands. All at once, his gaze traveled the length of her, and out of nowhere, thoughts of attraction flashed in his mind, flooding him with shame. He quickly turned away and strode to the kitchen with keen resolve, leaving the front door gaping wide. "Would you like some coffee?"

She smiled over her shoulder. "That would be nice, thank you."

He clattered around in the kitchen until the aroma of coffee perked in the air. When he returned, she sat perched on the far end of the couch. She thumbed through his Bible and looked up with a smile. "Why are there marks everywhere?"

"It's my way of studying, committing it to memory."

She nodded and flipped a few more pages. "You must have had this a long time. It's pretty battered."

He smiled and fanned his fingers though his hair. "Yeah, well, it's the first one I ever got, so it's been through a lot, I guess. Like me."

"When'd you get it?" She looked up, curiosity piqued in her eyes.

"Too long ago to remember. From a good friend who convinced me that God was real."

She scrunched her nose. "You needed convincing?"

He laughed and dropped down on the other side of the sofa. "Oh yeah. I didn't even believe he existed. Or if I did, I just didn't care."

"Why?"

He managed a faint smile. "Why all the questions, Mary? I thought you came to get books, not pick my brain."

She hugged his Bible to her chest. "I did, but the other is so much fun. Like reading a great mystery and unraveling the plot."

He shook his head and laughed. "It's a mystery all right. How a God like him could love a wretch like me."

She scooted closer, the Bible still clutched in her arms. "Talk to me, Brady. I want to know what you did that you think only God can forgive."

He shifted on the couch and butted his back against the armrest. His heart was racing. The smile on her face was innocent, but her proximity was not. "I don't like to talk about it, Mary. God's already forgotten it, so I do as well. 'As far as the east is from the west, so far hath he removed our transgressions from us.'"

"Psalm 103:12," she whispered.

He smiled. "You've been studying."

She closed the Bible and rested her head on the back of his sofa. Her eyes never left his. "Not just the Bible, you know."

He cleared his throat and stood. "Mary, I have some things I need to get done. I think you better go."

She sat up, flustered. "Brady, please, let me stay. I can't go home. Not right now."

"Why?"

She looked away. "Because I can't, that's all. Please believe me."

"Well, you can't stay here."

Fear flecked in her eyes. "Why not? I'll be safe here."

"No!" Heat chafed the back of his neck. "Why can't you go home?"

"Because *he* might be waiting."

"Who?"

She stared at her hands, limp on the Bible. "The man I ran away from, back in New York." Her gaze locked on his. "Please, Brady, let me stay. Just for a while? And then I'll go to Lizzie's if I have to."

The blue of her eyes blurred with tears, and compassion swelled in his chest. He sat down and put an arm around her shoulder. "Oh, Mary, I wish there was something I could do, some help I could give. But God can and will . . . if we pray."

She turned and clutched him tightly. He hesitated before slowly hugging her back. He felt her shiver and gently lifted her chin with his finger. "Let's pray, then what d'ya say we take a walk and get some fresh air?"

"What would I do without you?" she whispered. Her eyes softened, and her expression was almost worshipful.

His gaze settled on her mouth, causing his cheeks to heat. She pressed in to hug him again, and the nearness of her body caused his heart to pound. He closed his eyes. The temptation to kiss her was almost more than he could bear.

*No, my son.*

"Brady?" A timid voice sounded from across the room.

For a split second he was paralyzed. He glanced up at the open door where Cluny stood, confusion glazing his eyes.

"What are you doing?" Cluny whispered.

In a jagged beat of his heart, Brady pushed Mary back and staggered up. A sick feeling roiled in his stomach. "Nothing, we were doing nothing." He pulled Mary to her feet and then to the door. "Mary, please forgive me. You have to go."

"But, Brady, why?"

"Just go now, *please.*"

She blinked and shoved the hair from her eyes. Her gaze skittered first to Cluny, and then back to Brady. "I'll see you on Monday, then?"

He stood, eyes trained on the floor. "No . . . work is . . . well, it's really busy right now. Give me a couple of weeks, okay?"

She didn't answer, and he looked up in time to see the hurt on her face before she hurried out. Brady felt a stab in his chest and shut the door, turning to face Cluny alone. He nodded toward the couch. "We need to talk."

Cluny shoved his hands in his pockets and shuffled to the sofa without a word, parking himself as far away as he could.

Brady sat and put his face in his hands. "I owe you an apology, Cluny, for screaming at you like I did. I'm sorry, I . . . I lost my head."

Cluny folded his arms and scooted into the crease of the

couch. "From the looks of you and that gal, Brady, I'd say you lost more than your head."

"No, it's not what it looked like, bud—Mary's only a friend and nothing happened." Brady closed his eyes, remembering the desire her simple hug had provoked. "But it could have, being alone with a pretty woman in my apartment like that. That's never a good thing." He opened his eyes to confront the boy head-on. "So I owe you a second apology because I was wrong. Again." Brady exhaled and leaned back on the couch. He rubbed the bridge of his nose and stared straight ahead before letting his arms drop limp at his sides. "Remember the night we went to the O'Connors'? When I told you I was sick?"

"Yeah, I remember. I thought you were gonna die."

"Well, I am sick, Cluny. Spiritually. That's why I screamed at you about the canteen . . . and that's why I'm embarrassed you found me hugging Mary like you did. I'm sick, kind of like Pete across the hall."

Cluny cocked his head. "You drink too much? I've never seen you drink before."

"No, not alcohol . . . at least not anymore." He paused, finding it difficult to put into words. "Somebody like Pete, well, he can stop drinking and he's fine. He'll be a great husband to Eileen, a good neighbor to us, a great guy all around. But when he takes a drink of alcohol, it's like it controls him, changes his personality, he can't seem to stop. You understand?"

Cluny nodded. "But I thought you said you don't drink?"

"I don't. But I'm kind of sick like that too, when it comes to both alcohol and . . ."

He squinted at Brady. "Alcohol and what?"

Brady swallowed hard, then turned to look Cluny straight in the eyes. "I . . . have a problem with temptation and . . . women. Do you know what I mean?"

A spray of pink deepened the freckles on Cluny's face. He nodded. "Would you and Mary have . . . you know, done more than hug . . . if I hadn't come home?"

"No. Because it's not right. I know that, and I would have sent her home immediately if you hadn't walked in. But sometimes it's hard to say no when your body says yes. Which is why I stay far away from women. Because that kind of intimacy is a gift from God, little buddy, and leads to things God intended between a man and his wife. That means you stay far away from temptation—whether it's Johnny Lander's bathtub gin or—" Brady swallowed hard. "Or other things. Okay?"

Cluny nodded.

"Promise me, Cluny, especially about the alcohol. Tell me you'll stay far away from it because it can destroy your life. I can vouch for the damage it's done to my past and what it's doing to Pete right now. I love ya, bud, and I just don't want the same thing to happen to you."

Cluny hurled himself into Brady's arms. "I'm so sorry for bringing that stuff home. I won't do it again, I promise."

Brady closed his eyes and squeezed the slight boy, wondering for the thousandth time what he would do when Gram finally came home. "Just promise me you'll steer clear of all of it. And I promise I'll do the same. Deal?"

Cluny pulled away and stuck out a hand. His freckles made way for a grin that stretched ear to freckled ear. "Double deal."

❧ ❧

Brady stood in the doorway of Father Mac's study with a stomach as jittery as that of a seven-year-old pickpocket making his first confession. He glanced inside and drew a bit of calm from the quiet and steady feel of the room that reflected the same warmth and comfort of its owner. From its floor-to-ceiling bookcases overflowing with rich, leather-bound books, to the mahogany-slatted windows that washed the room in hazy ribbons of light, Father Mac's study exuded a sense of peaceful solitude and humble reverence. Like the man himself.

He'd been reading, apparently, legs crossed on his desk and a book in his lap, but his eyes were now closed. One hand relaxed on the open pages while the other hung limp over the arm of the chair. His head rested against a crocheted doily knitted by Mrs. Clary, no doubt, providing a halo effect that brought a quirk to the corner of Brady's mouth.

He cleared his throat. "Father Mac . . . can we talk?"

Matt's dark eyes blinked open, and a sleepy smile lit his face. "Father Mac, is it, now? Well, this must be serious. Conviction, evidently, over your treatment of the clergy."

Brady smiled, but his eyes were sober. He settled into a chair. "I wish it were that easy, Matt."

Father Mac swung his legs off the desk and closed the book. He sat back to study him, the seriousness of his face a mirror reflection of Brady's. "What's the problem, John?"

Brady looked away, choosing to focus on the shafts of sunlight streaming across the scarlet and gold hues of the fringed Oriental rug. "I need counsel, Father, on a problem I had." He swallowed the pride in his throat. "Have. Something I struggled with a long time ago. I thought it was gone, but . . . well, lately I've had . . . thoughts."

"Thoughts?" Father Mac's voice was barely audible. "What kind of thoughts?"

All courage suddenly fled, and Brady steeled his jaw. So help him, if he could turn around and walk away now, he would. What had possessed him to come here?

"John? What kind of thoughts?" Father Mac persisted.

He forced himself to look up and cleared his throat. "Thoughts of . . . desire." He swallowed hard and lowered his voice to a whisper. "About Beth O'Connor."

Father Mac sat back in the chair, hands steepled and poised low on his chest. His brows knitted into a frown. "What do you mean?"

"I mean lately, I find myself thinking about her as a woman and not as I did before, as a little sister." He sighed and dropped into the chair, emotionally drained. He put his head in his hands. "I find myself wanting her, Matt. Thinking about her, touching her . . ."

"In an impure way?"

"No! Yes . . . I don't know. All I know is, I crave holding her, kissing her."

"It's not a sin to kiss a woman."

"It is for me. With her." Brady's voice was barely a whisper.

"Why?"

He didn't respond.

"I know you've always seen Elizabeth as a sister, but the fact is that she's not. You're clearly smitten by her, and from rumors I've heard, she with you. Why are you fighting it?"

"Because it's wrong."

"Why?"

Brady looked up, desperation straining his voice. "I don't know! All I can say is that when I think of wanting her that way . . . it feels wrong, dirty, like I've committed a horrible sin."

Father Mac studied him in silence. His finger absently traced the rim of his lower lip. "What aren't you telling me?"

Brady's look was fierce. "So help me, God, I'm telling you everything that's bothering me, Matt. I can't have these thoughts about Beth."

"Because you feel shame?"

"Yes."

"But they're not impure thoughts, correct? Thoughts that arouse you to the point of lust?"

Blood heated Brady's cheeks. "No, of course not. I don't allow myself to go that far."

Father Mac's eyes darkened. He stared, not saying a word, then finally exhaled. "You're keeping something from me. Something from your past that's warped the way you see that girl. I can feel it."

Brady shot to his feet. The air in his lungs thickened with

rage, choking him. "Sorry I wasted your time, Father, but I need to go." He started for the door.

Father Mac's voice rose, the steel of his tone as pointed as the shards of fear prickling in Brady's gut. "You go, but you go knowing that the devil doesn't want this dealt with. He's got a grip on you, John, something from your past, a stronghold that keeps you from all that God has for you."

Brady whirled around, his eyes hot with fury. "You're spouting fairy tales, Matt. Satan has no hold on my life."

Father Mac's gaze burned into his. "No? Then why are you so angry?"

"Because you're crazy—"

"And you're afraid. He's got you by the throat. You walk out that door, and he wins and you lose. And all because you refuse to deal with your past."

Brady's teeth clenched so tight, a nerve quivered clear to the back of his jaw. His eyes itched with anger as he glared, moving to the desk with slow deliberation. He shoved the chair hard and sat down, arms folded thick across his chest. "Five minutes," he hissed, "you've got five minutes to have your say, and then I'm gone."

Father Mac sank back into the chair. The tension in his face eased into cool professionalism. He released one long, slow breath and made a quick sign of the cross. "You're not leaving until we pray about this, John. We're going to try and lift a burden off your shoulders that's been there way too long." He rose and walked to the door, closing it with an ominous click. He sat back down and propped his feet on the desk. "But first, suppose you tell me all about John Morrison Brady. And start from the beginning."

❧ ❧

The bell over the door jangled, and Collin looked up. He slacked a hip against the work counter where he was welding a broken lever on a mimeograph press. "Hey, where'd you go? I never even heard you leave." He squinted through goggles, eyeing Brady from head to toe, then blinked. *What the . . . ?*

Instead of sporting ink on his face, his partner stood there dressed like a wealthy playboy fresh off the pages of *Vanity Fair*. Collin's jaw dropped a full inch. That getup had to cost him half his week's salary—plaid linen knickers sported by the country club set and a cream V-necked vest with snazzy bow tie. A straw boater perched back on his head, revealing a more stylish, shorter haircut.

"Where in blazes have you been and what in the world are you wearing? Did you give yourself a raise or something?"

"Pardon me?"

Collin's brow furrowed. "The glad rags. Who are you trying to impress?"

Brady's lip curled into a smile. He removed his hat. "No one. I'm looking for John Brady. Is he here?"

Collin shoved his goggles up and stared, his mouth gaping about as wide as the open door. He flipped off the control switch on the welding gun and set it down.

Standing on the threshold was the exact image of John Brady, albeit shorter hair and a decidedly bolder look in his eyes.

Collin blinked. "St. Peter's gate, who are you?"

"Michael Brady, John's brother." He nodded at the gold-embossed lettering on the front window. "I take it you're McGuire?"

Collin grinned and wiped his palms on his work apron, then hurried over and extended a hand. "Collin McGuire, Brady's partner. I swear to heaven I'm going to box his ears but good. He never even mentioned he had a brother."

Michael grinned and shook his hand. "Get in line, Collin. I'm here to take him on too. Haven't heard from him in over eleven years."

Collin folded his arms and shook his head, shocked at seeing

Brady's double right before his eyes. "A twin, imagine that. Sweet saints above, he's got some explaining to do."

Michael looked around. "Is he here?"

The sound of a press clanging in the next room suddenly registered. "Yeah, he is. Come on back." He swung an arm around Michael's shoulder and led him to the rear. The tendons in Brady's back shifted as he fed paper into the machine. "Hey, buddy, you got company."

Brady glanced over his shoulder, and Collin stiffened when the smile grew cold on his partner's lips. Collin sidled over and slapped him on the back to cover his own unease. "Why didn't you tell me you had a twin? So what if he's better looking— that's information I could have used. He shocked the living daylights out of me."

Michael grinned and motioned his head toward Brady. "Him, too, apparently. It's good to see you, John. How are you?"

A lump shifted in Brady's throat. His eyes darkened to near-black, providing a stark contrast to the abrupt pallor of his cheeks. "What do you want, Michael?"

"We need to talk."

"I don't have anything to say to you." He turned back to the press, shoving too much paper into the feeder. The machine sputtered and jammed, eliciting a rare curse from Brady's lips.

"No, but I have a lot to say to you. Lucille is dead."

Brady flinched, and Collin watched his broad shoulders sag as if the lever on the press had gut-punched him. He rammed it to the off position. "Collin . . . can you leave us alone?"

Collin's eyes flicked from Brady, to his brother, then back again. "Sure. I have deliveries to make. You okay?"

"Yeah."

"I'll be back in about an hour. Need anything while I'm out?"

"No. Thanks."

"Okay, see you later. Nice to meet you, Michael."

"You too, Collin."

The dead silence between the brothers was awkward as Collin hefted several boxes onto the wooden delivery cart. He shot a worried glance in Brady's direction, but his partner only stared at the floor, fists clenched at his side. Collin exhaled and shoved the cart into the alley, then closed the door with a silent prayer.

Brady wheeled around. "I'm sorry Lucille is dead, but what's that got to do with me?"

Michael propped against the counter and folded his arms. "A lot, John. She left us a bloomin' fortune—Helena, you, and me."

"I don't want her filthy money. You two can have it all."

Michael laughed. "Believe me, we'd like nothing better, but unfortunately, it seems our wicked stepmother tied all of our hands with a minor stipulation in her will."

"And what would that be?"

"That before Helena and I can collect one red cent, you have to go back to Forest Hills and sign all the papers. She divided the bulk of the estate between the three of us, but she left the house to you. After she got sick, she changed, John, turned into a real religious fanatic. I think she wanted to make it up to you. Wanted you back in Forest Hills so we could be a family again."

Brady studied his brother, shocked to realize he had no feelings toward him one way or the other. Not love. Not hate. God had healed him of bitterness toward his family a long time ago. But even so, no love remained. But then, he and Michael had never been close, not like twins were supposed to be. At least not since his father had married Lucille. She had taken an immediate affection to John, preferring his quiet and deep personality over Michael's swaggering ways, inciting irreparable jealousy. Once inseparable, they suddenly had separate lives—Michael spending his time with friends, while John spent his with Lucille. She had fawned over him, trusted him, leaned on him for strength after their father had died, severing any closeness his brother and he might have shared.

Brady sighed and dropped into a chair. "Nothing can make up for what happened to me."

"I know, John, and I'm sorry. I suppose I'm as much to blame as Lucille, for not speaking up, for letting her do what she did. Will you forgive me?"

"I already have, Michael, years ago."

"Then you'll come?"

Brady rose to his feet. "No, I won't. You and Helena will have to contest the will or find another way to get your payoff. I'm through with Forest Hills." He glanced at the clock. "You need to leave now. I'm expecting someone."

"Sorry, John, but I can't. I'm here to stay until you agree to go back."

Brady's shoulders tensed as he glanced at the front window for some sign of Beth. "I don't want you around, Michael. I'm warning you now—stay out of my life."

"It's been eleven years, John. I think we need to talk, get to know each other again."

A sharp rasp of air crossed Brady's lips. Michael's gaze followed his. Brady gripped Michael's arm and yanked him out of view just as Beth passed by the window. "So help me, God, if you breathe a word while she's here, you'll never get a dime." He shoved him into the supply closet at the exact moment the bells rattled over the door.

Michael grinned. "So, you got yourself a girl, eh, John? What, you don't want that pretty little thing to meet your long-lost brother?"

"Shut up, Michael, she's not my girl."

"Brady?" Beth's voice jolted him from the front of the shop.

Sweat broke out on the back of his neck. "I'll be right out." He gritted his teeth. "Not one word, or so help me—"

"Say you'll sign the papers."

"No," he hissed.

"Then at least let me stay at your place—so we can talk."

"Brady? Why can't I come back?"

"No, Beth, wait! I'll be right out." He lowered his voice to a hoarse whisper. "One night."

Michael flashed another grin before ducking back in the closet. "Nope, I need time. Enough to convince you. Give me your word, John, or I'll blow your cover."

"Brady?"

"All right, but then you're gone. Do you understand?"

"John Brady!" She appeared at the door, hands on her hips and a teasing smile on her lips. She crossed her arms and tilted her head. "The way you're acting, I would think you have a woman in that closet."

Brady spun around. He managed an off-center smile to deflect the heat crawling up the back of his neck. "Yeah, Beth, you know me so well. I stash women in my closet all the time."

She giggled and shimmied into a chair, looking especially pretty with a soft glow in her cheeks and concern in her eyes. "Actually, I was pretty anxious to see you. You weren't yourself on Saturday, almost depressed, it seemed, so I was hoping Mary cheered you up."

The heat in his neck shot straight to his face. "Well, she didn't stay long. Did she . . . mention anything?"

"No, she wasn't in today. Mr. Harvey said she called in sick."

"Oh. Beth?"

"Yes?"

"Can we do this another day?"

She blinked. Confusion shifted into concern. "Is something wrong? You're not yourself, Brady. Not Saturday and not today. You've never canceled before, not when it comes to our Bible study."

He tried to fake it. "Nothing's wrong. I'm just bogged down with a lot of extra work." He took her arm and pulled her to her feet. "Come on, I'll see you on Wednesday."

Distress darkened her eyes. All at once she wrapped her arms around his waist and hugged fiercely. "Oh, Brady, something's wrong, I can feel it. And I'm worried. What is it?"

His arms encircled her and he closed his eyes, almost forgetting about Michael. "Nothing's wrong. I'm fine, I promise. Go on now and scoot. I'll see you on Wednesday, okay?"

She stared for several seconds, then nodded and backed toward the front of the shop. She finally turned and hurried the rest of the way out, giving a tentative wave. Clattering bells brought relief as the door closed behind her.

Michael strolled from the closet. His long, low whistle burned Brady's cheeks. "*Bible study?* With that pretty thing? You're boggling my mind, little brother. Who's the doll?"

"None of your business. Get out."

"Oh no, John, you promised me a week's lodging. Besides, we have to talk."

"No way. I don't want you around."

Michael's brow shot up. He glanced out the window in the direction Lizzie had taken. "Apparently. And I suspect one of the reasons is our little . . . what did you call her? Beth? Who actually didn't look so little from where I was standing. You're in love with her, aren't you?"

"Get out, Michael. Now!"

"Does she know your past?"

Brady's hands knotted into fists as he took a step forward. "I'll hurt you, I swear I will."

Michael sauntered over to the door, hands deep in his pockets. "Oh no you won't." He turned with a faint smile. "You don't want her to know, do you? It wouldn't do for the man she admires to have such a sordid past, would it? Besides, a man who teaches Bible shouldn't renege on his word. Let's face it. You have no choice. Give me your key, John."

Brady fought the urge to knock him down. He reached in his pocket and threw his keys across the room.

Michael caught them, midair. "Thanks. Rumpole Street,

right? Guess I'll see you at home." He smiled and opened the door.

"Michael!"

Michael turned slowly, his smile thin on his lips. "Yeah?"

"I'm keeping a kid and his dog at my place while his gram is out of town. Name's Cluny. Stay away from him."

"Sure, John. That's real nice of ya. First, teaching the Bible to a pretty little girl, then playing big brother to a lonely little kid. You've turned into a regular father figure, haven't ya? Just like Pop." He grinned and strolled out the door, leaving Brady with a sick twist in his gut.

Yeah. Just like Pop.

He slumped in the chair and put his head in his hands. Only Pop was dead, no longer haunted by his past. While he was still here . . . with a past that was alive and well.

## 10

Mitch stretched out on the couch and did his best to focus on the newspaper, refusing to be distracted by Charity's good mood. She had been humming softly all evening, perky and attentive to a fault. The more she hummed, the deeper he buried himself in the news. It was their new Wednesday night tradition—she was up, he was down.

"So, what do you think?"

Mitch lowered his paper to glance at his wife, who sat on the loveseat with a mountain of knitting yarn in her lap. Runt slept at her feet, partially hidden by a pale yellow and green baby blanket piled high on his back. Charity held the blanket up and peeked around it. She chewed on her lip. "You think it needs to be bigger?"

He grunted. "It's a baby, Charity, not an elephant. It'll be fine."

"I suppose so. But I just want everything to be perfect." She laid the blanket aside and lumbered to her feet, breathless from the attempt. "Goodness, I'm tired!" She put her knitting away and waddled over to plant a kiss on his forehead. She stroked his cheek, bristly with a day's growth of beard. "But not too. I'm going up. You coming?"

He grunted again and raised the paper so she couldn't see the frown on his face. "I think I may just stay up and read awhile."

The paper buckled in his lap with a loud thwack of her hand. She folded her arms over her stomach and hefted her chin. "A deal is a deal. This is Wednesday night, and you are not going to stay down here and fall asleep on the couch."

He groaned and dragged a hand through his hair. "Come on, Charity, you're close to seven months, and that's too far along. I don't care what the doctor says, I'm not comfortable with it."

"But you promised! I acknowledged your concern for the baby and stopped harping six days a week, and all you have to do is satisfy my need for marital joy one night in seven."

He ground his jaw and jerked the paper back up. "Forget it. I'm the head of this house, and I say no. Go to bed, little girl."

The silence unnerved him as he stared at the paper, seeing nothing but the look of hurt on her face.

He heard something swish to the floor and jerked the paper aside. His jaw dropped. "What the devil are you doing?"

She calmly stepped out of her shift now pooled on the floor. She smiled and kicked it away. "I've lived up to my part of the bargain, Mr. Dennehy, and you're going to live up to yours." She began unbuttoning her lacy camisole.

He jumped up from the couch and grabbed her hands in his. His tone was pleading. "Charity, please, stop. You know I can't handle this."

She reached up and unpinned her hair, giving him a seductive smile. "I know." She stepped up on the couch with amazing dexterity and wound her arms around his neck. "I love you, Mitch Dennehy. You're going to make a wonderful dad." She leaned down and kissed him full on the lips.

He groaned. "Charity, please—"

"Kiss you again? My pleasure."

She did, more deeply this time, and the heat started to build until he knew he was dead in the water. He picked her up in his arms and laid her gently on the carpet, pitching the newspaper out of the way. He lay down beside her and held her, more in love with this woman than he ever dreamed possible. "Charity, I love you—so much." He pulled her as close as he could and gave up, losing himself in her kiss.

"Oh!" Her body stiffened against his before she pushed him away. "Oh, God help me—"

He jumped to his knees. "What's wrong? Are you all right?"

She pushed hard against the sofa. "Mitch, help me. I'm scared!"

He bounded to his feet and picked her up, placing her on the sofa as if she would break. He swiped his shoes from the floor and shoved them on, then scooped his keys from his suit coat in the hall. She was writhing in pain, and fear heaved in his chest. He tore the quilt off the loveseat and wrapped it around her body, then snatched her dress and shoes off the floor before hoisting her up in his arms. "We're going to the hospital—*now!* I'm not taking any chances."

She nodded and seized up in pain, her breathing jagged.

*Dear God, please protect her.*

He rushed to the door and opened it wide. "Runt, stay!" he commanded. And with a prayer on his lips and his wife in his arms, he fled from their home, slamming the door behind.

❧ ❧

"Top of the morning to ya, Mr. Dennehy."

Mitch mustered a tired smile, which collided with a yawn as he shuffled through the front door of the *Boston Herald*. "Good morning, Angus . . . although I've had better."

The night watchman bobbed his bald head and sat up straight in his chair at the front desk. He grinned, revealing a near toothless smile. "Yes, sir, you look a might worn right now, but no more so than Mr. Patrick. He's been working every night, all night, for almost a month now. I swear, I never seen two people work to the bone for this newspaper like you and the boss."

Mitch glanced at his watch and frowned. "Patrick's here? At five in the morning? And what do you mean he's been here every night for almost a month?"

"Yes, sir, he has. Moseys out 'bout six most nights, then comes traipsin' back 'bout midnight or so and works all night." Angus's eyes narrowed a bit as he leaned forward, lowering his voice as if someone might hear. "If truth be told, I suspect it ain't all work, though, 'cause once he was snoozin' up a storm on that there couch of his."

Mitch frowned. "Thanks, Angus. If you feel like fresh coffee, I'll have some brewed in about twenty minutes. Just come on up."

"Thank ya kindly, sir, but I'll be going straight home to bed, come six o'clock. Best not be tippin' any if I plan to sleep, know what I mean?"

"Afraid I do. Hope you get more sleep than I did last night." He strode to the stairs and took them two at a time, despite the weariness of his sleepless night. First, Charity with her false alarm, keeping them at the hospital half the night, and now Patrick with this strange behavior. It was unnerving and hardly conducive to sleep. He hurried toward Patrick's office with an uneasy feeling, nodding at the few night-shift workers in the newsroom. Patrick's door was closed, so Mitch knocked. No answer. He opened it and walked in, easing it shut.

Patrick looked like a man who had had an equally restless night. His long body bridged the length of a short leather couch that God had never intended for sleeping. One leg tented beneath a thin blanket while the other draped over the side of the tufted seat, revealing a long, tapered span of black sock. His parted lips emitted a series of nasal grunts as he snored, while one arm was tucked deep beneath his unruly head as a makeshift pillow.

Mitch blinked. The uneasy feeling in his gut started to rise to his chest. *Why would Patrick be sleeping at the* Herald? *And more importantly, why would Marcy let him?*

He backed toward the door, not sure he wanted to know why his father-in-law was not sleeping at home.

Patrick grunted and rolled on his side. One shirted arm dangled over the edge. Mitch held his breath and turned toward the door.

"What the devil are you doing here?"

An inward groan rolled in his chest as his hand adhered to the knob.

"Mitch?"

He sighed and turned. Patrick sat up, and the blanket slid to the floor, unveiling a rumpled shirt and trousers that looked even worse. Kind of like he had slept in them.

Mitch's lips quirked. "Couldn't sleep, that's all. Charity had false labor, so we spent half the night at the hospital."

"What? Is she okay?"

"Yeah, she's fine. Doctor says it's nothing to worry about. Happens all the time."

Patrick scratched the back of his head and squinted. "Come to think of it, I do remember Marcy going through that with Sean, but we didn't know what it was at the time. Just scared the daylights out of us."

Mitch slacked a hip and smiled. "Yeah, it pretty much does."

Patrick gave him a lidded stare. "I suppose you're wanting to know why I am in so early?"

"I am, but it's your business, Patrick, not mine."

"You're right. It is my business, and that's what I admire about you. Tight-lipped, like a man should be."

"Yes, sir."

"But, regrettably, your wife isn't. I'd like your word that there will be no mention of this—not to Charity or Collin, or anyone. Is that clear?"

Mitch studied the man he'd come to respect more than anyone he knew. The man he loved as a father and a friend. He saw something in his eyes he'd never seen before—loneliness, bitterness, hurt—and his gut constricted. "I don't know what's happened, Patrick, but are you sure . . . sure you're doing the right thing staying here?"

Patrick stood and attempted to slap the wrinkles from his trousers. He straightened his shoulders and shook at the cuff of his sleeve. "Doesn't matter. At the moment, I have no interest in doing the right thing."

"I see. And Marcy? She's okay with this?"

Patrick bent to retrieve the cover from the floor. He rose to his full height and turned away, his back rigid like a man bent on a course no matter the cost. "At the moment, that doesn't matter either, I'm afraid." He finally looked up, and Mitch winced at the pain he saw. "Not a word, Mitch, do you hear? I need time to heal."

Mitch nodded and opened the door. He paused. "Don't take too long, Patrick. Your time for healing may be Marcy's demise. And yours."

He closed the door behind and put a hand to his eyes. Total exhaustion sapped all strength. He exhaled heavily and moved toward his office like the zombie he was. He shut the door and sank into his chair with a low groan and a soft swoosh of the leather seat. His head sagged back and he closed his eyes.

Not to think, not to plan, and not to sleep.

To pray. The only thing he could do.

"Tom Weston, are you going to tell me where we're going?"

"Nope. It's a surprise." He adjusted the blindfold over her eyes, his warm words breezing against her ear. He tightened his hold around her waist and led her down Donovan Street, his deep chuckle in perfect harmony with the symphony of summer. The sounds of locusts and bullfrogs buzzed in her brain, laced with children's shrieking and dogs yipping. Wonderful smells teased her senses—honeysuckle, fresh-mown grass, and the faint scent of Bay Rum from Tom's fresh-shaven cheek. Lizzie sighed and leaned into his embrace, tingling with the thrill of romance.

"We're almost there," he whispered, his voice husky with promise. A soft mat of grass met the soles of her new Mary Jane shoes, and the street sounds of autos and children grew fainter. The earthy smell of woods and moss intrigued her, quickening her pulse.

He stopped to warm her lips with a kiss. "We're here," he whispered, then removed the scarf from her eyes. "What do you think?"

She blinked at the mirror reflection of O'Reilly Lake, aglow with the colors of dusk. "The park? But I thought we were going to dinner?"

He grinned and foraged beneath a willowy forsythia bush, unearthing a blanket and basket. "We are. A moonlight picnic for two—to celebrate the three best months of my life." He shook out the blanket and dropped the basket on top, unlatching its carved mahogany lid. The inside was cushioned with a red-and-white check gingham napkin topped by a dainty bouquet of daisies, which he presented to her with a proud gleam in his eye. "To the girl I dream about every night."

Lizzie laughed and sank to her knees, clutching the flowers to her chest. Her heart swooned. "Oh, Tom, this is the most romantic thing anyone has ever done."

"Well, it's only the beginning, Lizzie, of a night to remember." He positioned a thick candle on a china plate and struck a match. "My mother helped with the basket, of course, but the idea was all mine." He lit the wick, and his smile was dangerous in the glow of the flame. "Of course, she was under the impression our picnic would be at noon."

She slid to the side and sat, sniffing the daisies to obscure the uncomfortable heat in her cheeks. The light of day had faded to a purple hue, streaking the sky with various shades of warning that darkness was well on its way. Lizzie adjusted the hem of her skirt to cover as much of her stockinged legs as possible. Here near the lake, the chant of the locusts and bullfrogs drowned out the rest of the world as their incessant song vibrated in her ear. Or maybe it was her pulse. She peeked at Tom over the soft petals of her flowers, thinking they shouldn't even be here, alone on a picnic in the dark. And yet he had never looked more handsome, shadowed by flame. He unscrewed a jar and poured orange juice into two crystal goblets. He handed one to her and raised a toast. "To the girl I intend to marry."

Lizzie blinked wide and almost dropped her glass. "Oh, Tom!"

He smiled and clinked his drink to hers. "To us, Lizzie."

"To us," she whispered, feeling both excited and unsure all at once. She sipped and almost choked, spraying a mist of juice all over her skirt. "Sweet mother of Job, what in the name of heaven is in this?"

He grinned and unpacked the rest of the basket. "Bathtub gin, our very own fraternity brew. Trust me, it gets better the more you drink."

Lizzie tossed the swill into the grass. "Tom Weston, how dare you try to get me drunk, not to mention break the law."

"Come on, Lizzie, I'm not trying to get you drunk, I just wanted to celebrate, that's all. Give me some credit, will you? I would never take you home drunk. It's too risky."

Her eyes narrowed. "This whole evening is starting to appear too risky."

He moved to her side and pulled her into a hug. "No, doll, I promise. I'm crazy about you and just wanted to tell you in my own way. Are you hungry? My mother made roast beef sandwiches, her special fruit salad, and the best turnovers you've ever tasted." He nuzzled her neck. "Come on, you know I love you, don't you?"

She closed her eyes to enjoy the warmth of his lips grazing

her skin. She sighed and pushed him away. "Sometimes I wonder. You seem to have a one-track mind, Tom Weston, and you already know how I feel about that."

He bussed her cheek with a quick kiss and commenced divvying out the food. "I know, which is exactly why we are going to eat instead." He winked. "I have to feed one of my appetites, you know."

The night took a turn toward the perfect evening. The moon hung heavy over the lake like an overripe orange, trickling its golden stream of light across inky depths. The air was sweet and warm, coating her skin with the moist scent of night. She sat back against the smooth trunk of a towering oak with a contented sigh, her legs stretched out and crossed on the blanket. She was dazed by the beauty of the stars, if not the few sips of juice Tom had finally convinced her to take. The sandwiches had been wonderful, and the company even better. They'd talked forever, laughing at his stories of college life and her adventures with Millie and Mary. He wanted to be a lawyer like his uncle, and Lizzie thrilled at the dreams in his eyes.

Since the morning she'd prayed with Brady, she'd found a new courage to share her faith with Tom, and as if her prayers had been answered, his bold advances had seemed to wane. She was slowly beginning to trust him. Not like Brady, of course—nothing with Tom was ever like Brady—but maybe, down the road a bit, she might even fall in love with him. Thoughts of Brady suddenly dampened her mood, and she shook them off with a deep sigh, choosing to think of Tom's affection instead.

She closed her eyes and felt warm and safe in his presence. They'd drifted into comfortable silence. He lounged at the far edge of the blanket, his hands clasped behind his head and legs sprawled with one knee tented. She opened her eyes at his gentle rustle of movement, and caught her breath when he moved to sit beside her.

"Lizzie, I have something to ask. But first, you gotta know

I'm stuck on you in a big way. College was crawling with dolls, but I don't want some pushover dame who will give me whatever I want. I want you. You're younger, but you're so different. In some ways, you're way older than the Janes I ran into at school. I don't know, more innocent, more mature, and yet . . . there's a fire inside of you that drives me crazy." He pulled something from the pocket of his trousers and held it up. "I love ya, Lizzie, and I'm asking you—will you wear my pin?"

She sat up with a catch in her throat and put a hand to her chest. *A boy's pin—one step from engaged!* "Oh, Tom, do you mean it?"

He grinned and fastened it to the collar of her blouse. His fingers lingered to gently knead her shoulder. "Of course I mean it, you goose. You've got me goofy over you."

He pulled her close to give her a kiss, and euphoria took her away. *Pinned!* She returned his kiss with an intensity that made him moan.

"Oh, doll, I love you." He stroked her hair while burrowing his lips into the sensitive curve of her neck, forcing tingles of heat to prickle her skin. His hands skimmed down her arms, past her waist, gliding the curve of her hip. He kissed her again, his mouth probing hers.

She jerked away, alarmed at the desire he provoked. "Tom, no! We need to stop—"

He answered her with another deep kiss that took her breath away. His mouth moved to her ear where he playfully flicked the soft flesh of her lobe with his tongue. "It's okay, Lizzie, you're my girl now. We love each other, so it's all right." His hand fanned the length of her.

She heaved it away. "No! It's wrong and you know it."

He took her face in his hands. "Not anymore. Things are different now. We belong to each other." He pressed a gentle kiss to her cheek, and his eyes were dark and pleading. "Lizzie, I need you. Besides, it's dangerous for a guy to stop."

A cold slither of guilt collided with the heat of his kiss. *Real love gives, not takes.*

She shoved him back. "If you loved me, you wouldn't push."

"And if you loved me, I would think you'd want to show it. Not tempt me beyond my control and then say no."

"What?"

"Admit it, Lizzie, you kiss like a girl who's looking for more."

She sat up. "How dare you! I wear myself out telling you no."

"Yeah, you tell me 'no,' all right, but your body tells me 'yes.'" He shifted to prop his elbows, then arched a brow. "Don't deny it, Lizzie. You talk God and religion, but the way your body responds, the way you kiss, tells me it's not God you're looking for. On the outside, you're this chaste and proper girl, but inside . . . well, let's just say if I didn't know better, I'd think you were a regular at some of those petting parties."

For a split second, she was too shocked to speak or move. And then the crack of her slap rang in the air. Wetness stung her eyes, and her fingers shook as she fumbled to unlatch the pin from her blouse. She stood and threw it in his face. "Here, pin this on one of the girls at those petting parties you never go to. And so help me, Tom Weston, if you ever darken my door again, I'll tell my father."

"Lizzie, wait!"

She snatched her clutch from the blanket and lashed through the bushes. She ran blindly through the dark while tears streamed her cheeks, stopping to catch her breath at the far edge of the park. Her chest heaved with hurt as she leaned against a tree and slid to the ground. Sobs choked in her throat. *Oh, Brady, you were right! I am such a fool.*

Desperation, like bile, rose in her throat, and she had an overwhelming urge to see Brady. To talk, to pray. She looked at her watch in the glow of the lamplight and pushed the tears from her eyes. She couldn't go home and face her parents, not yet, especially with a tearstained face.

She stood to her feet and straightened her skirt, her chest heaving with hurt and shame. She began walking toward Brady's apartment at a brisk pace and then broke into a run. She hurried up the steps and opened the door to the sounds of children's laughter and the strains of a radio. The smell of fried chicken was heavy in the air, mingling with the faint scent of dog and pipe tobacco. Lizzie drew in a deep breath and knocked on the door.

"Who is it?"

She clutched her arms, gasping for breath. "It's me—Beth."

"Beth? Come on in, the door's open."

She peeked inside, blinking into the dark. Her eyes adjusted to the light, and she saw his shadow sit up on the couch. "Beth? Are you all right—you sound out of breath. What are you doing here?"

More tears bubbled, and she choked back a sob. "Oh, Brady, you were right—Tom doesn't love me. He . . . he j-just wants what he wants."

He rose to his feet and she ran across the room, flinging herself into his arms. Without a word, he sat her down on the sofa and tucked her close. She could smell the clean scent of his soap, and she closed her eyes, letting the strength of him seep into her soul.

"What happened?"

She shivered and pulled away. "Y-you s-said that men can read a w-woman like me, and you were right. All this time I thought Tom was listening when I talked about God, that he respected me. B-but h-he treated me tonight like some kind of loose woman."

She wiped her eyes with her hand. He produced a handkerchief, and she took it and blew her nose. "He . . . h-he said the way I kiss . . . and the way I respond . . . tells him it isn't God I want." She pressed the handkerchief to her eyes to stem the onslaught of another bout of tears. "Oh, Brady, when he said that, my heart ripped in two . . . because I realized, for the very first time, that it's all true. I've lived in this dream world of romance for so long now, that it's become my god, the craving of my soul. I wanted Tom's kisses, his attention. It made me feel good inside, warm and alive with passion. But when he said those things tonight, I realized . . . that without God in the middle, it's nothing but lust—heat that burns but doesn't keep you warm. A flash of fire that leaves you feeling empty and dirty and cold, like charred remains."

She shifted to face him head-on. "Brady, I need you to pray with me. I want God to be the fire in my soul, not lust or romance. I want to live for him, not for myself or shallow dreams. Because for the first time tonight, everything you ever taught me finally makes sense. Love and romance is a very good thing, but I know now that it pales in the face of love and romance with God in the center. I want that, Brady, with all my heart. So I broke it off with Tom tonight. Because I want to do things the right way." She swiped at her eyes. "Will you pray for me?"

She couldn't read his expression in the darkened room, but he nodded and pulled her close. His whisper was soft against her neck. "This prayer belongs to you, Beth, and I'll pray silently."

She blinked over his shoulder. A sliver of disappointment prickled. He wouldn't lead her in prayer? She took a deep breath and released it again. But then, he was a very wise man. He apparently knew this was a prayer she needed to voice for herself. She closed her eyes. "Oh, Lord, forgive me for losing sight of you in my life, for being led astray by my hunger for love and romance. Your Word says that as the serpent beguiled Eve in his craftiness, so can we be corrupted from the simplicity and purity of Christ. This happened to me with Tom, and I'm asking for your forgiveness. Help me to live for you and to find a man who will love me as much as he loves you. And,

Lord, please bless my dear friend, Brady, for being a man who seeks you with all of his heart and for being the best friend I've ever had. Whatever his past or his fears, please get him through it so he can experience the joy I know you have for him. Amen."

She exhaled, marveling at the sudden lightness of her heart. She pulled away and smiled. "What would I do without you?"

He stroked the curve of her jaw with the pad of his thumb, studying her in the shadowed light. "You'd get along, but I hope you never have to. You're an amazing woman, Beth."

Her blood warmed at the heat of his touch. His gaze settled on her mouth, and her breathing slowed. He bent close in an unhurried manner, and her lips parted in shock as he caressed her mouth with his own. His lips moved over hers, carefully, tenderly, as if she were fragile enough to break.

She startled back, her eyes awash with hope. "Oh, Brady, I'm so in love with you. I've never stopped—you have to know that."

"I know, Beth," he whispered, his mouth lingering over hers. He leaned to taste her lips again with a gentle touch that slowly intensified, sending warm contentment purling through her veins. "I love you too."

She broke free to search his face, not daring to believe. Her heart pounded in her chest. "Oh, Brady, do you mean . . . as a sister, a friend? Or as a woman?"

His warm chuckle feathered her ear. "You tell me," he said, and then his mouth met hers with a hungry kiss, deep and long, leaving little doubt as to his answer. She was breathless when he finally released her. "Let's get you home before I lose my perspective on Scripture." He tugged her up from the sofa and pulled her toward the door, then kissed her on the forehead. "Wait right here while I get my shoes, and then I'll walk you home."

She watched him disappear down the hall, half giddy with

a rush of joy pumping in her chest. Walk? She grinned. Float might be a better word.

⌖ ⌖

Brady yawned and reached for a rag to clean the press. The first glimmers of dawn filtered through the back window with a pinkish hue, the only daylight he'd probably see until he headed home again at dusk, given his workload. He blinked to clear the sleep from his eyes and bent over to wipe the plate cylinder of the offset. The aroma of fresh-brewed coffee merged with the pungent smell of ink.

His mind drifted to Beth as it often did in the early hours of the morning when hope dawned as fresh and innocent as the new day. And then, in the rise and fall of the breath in his lungs, he reflected on his life and was once again reminded how reality had a way of dashing all hopes. His thoughts turned to his brother and he scowled, confirming his cynicism about life—that is, his life, anyway. Michael had not contributed much happiness to his youth; there was no reason to believe he would fare much better with Brady's life now. No, the sooner he was gone, the better. Although "better" was something Brady hadn't seen in quite a while now—at least not since Beth had become a modern woman, bent on loving him. He missed the simplicity of his life before that, her childlike wonder and little-girl innocence. A time when her smile hadn't quickened his pulse or her glance tightened his gut. Or when thoughts of her kisses didn't dredge up guilt from his past.

Brady released a heavy sigh that stopped short when two slight arms squeezed his waist from behind. He spun around. The motion flung a dirty rag into Beth's face.

She laughed and ducked out of the way. "Goodness, remind me not to sneak up on you again." She tiptoed to give him a warm kiss on the lips and snuggle close.

He stood rooted to the floor like their two-ton web-fed press, heart drumming like its steel rotors. The rag dangled in his hand—pale and limp—as if the wind had been knocked out of it. Just like him.

"What are you doing?" he asked, his voice little more than a croak.

"Kissing you good morning, silly. No objections, I hope?" She pressed her cheek to his chest and closed her eyes. "Oh, I am so crazy about you, John Brady, that I haven't slept a decent wink since Saturday night. Which is why you're in the shop early too, I hope, judging from the racing of your heart."

He blinked and peeled her hands from his waist. "Beth, what are you talking about?"

She stepped back to purse her lips and fold her arms, all with a knowing smile. "Don't go shy on me now, acting like you don't know what I'm talking about. I've waited way too long for you to profess your love to me. And now that you have . . . *and* sealed it with a kiss . . ." A bit of color stole into her cheeks. "Or several, I should say, well, I'm not about to let you get away."

She stood on tiptoe to kiss him again. He fended her off, his grip gentle on her wrists as he set her in the chair. He sat across the table and leaned in, the thick tendons of his arms tense below his rolled-up shirtsleeves. Anger twitched in his jaw. "I *don't* know what you're talking about, Beth. I wasn't home Saturday night. Cluny and I worked out at the gym, then I took him to Robinson's for a soda."

She blinked. "B-but . . . you kissed me . . . at your apartment. You told me you loved me."

His neck stiffened. *Dear God, I'll kill him.* "I'm sorry, Beth, but it wasn't me."

"But you *kissed* me!"

Jealousy twisted in his gut. "My brother, apparently."

"Your . . . b-brother?"

"Yes." He forced his voice to remain calm. "Are you all right? Why did you go there anyway? Was something wrong?"

Tears pooled in her eyes and she nodded. "I needed to pray because I . . . I broke it off with Tom."

His eyes softened. "Beth, I'm sorry you were hurt, but I'm not sorry you broke it off. He wasn't good for you." He reached for her hand. "My brother . . . what did he do? He didn't hurt you, did he?"

She twitched away, as if stung by his touch. "No. But he looks just like you and I . . . well, I thought—"

"He's my twin. I haven't seen him in over eleven years. Not until this week. Tell me the truth, Beth, did he do anything . . ."

She staggered to her feet, her face void of all color. "Yes, Brady, he did. He gave me hope. Hope that finally, the man I've been in love with all these years was ready to love me back. Do you, Brady, do you love me? Or are you going to crush my heart again?"

The hurt in her face was like a kick in the gut. He rose to his feet slowly, his breath shallow as his gaze locked on hers. "I do love you, Beth, you know that. But not that way."

Her eyelids flickered closed. In slow motion, she pressed a palm to her face and began to cry.

He jumped up to circle the table.

"No!" Her hand quivered as she warded him off, and her eyes glinted with wet anger. "Don't you dare touch me again, ever! You have hurt me for the last time."

"Beth, please—"

She fled from the room, and he cut her off at the door. He gripped her arms. "Can't we talk, please—"

She twisted to break free. "Let me go, I can't bear for you to touch me!"

"No! I am not letting you go." He scooped her up and carried her to the back, his jaw set like rock as she thrashed in his arms. He dumped her in the chair and squatted before her, maintaining a tight hold. "Stop it, Beth! You're acting like a spoiled little girl. Why don't you act like the woman you profess to be and calm down and listen to reason?"

"I'll start acting like a woman when you start acting like a man who's not afraid of his feelings. You're a coward, John Brady, through and through." She thrust her chin in his face. "But I'll bet your brother's not."

He sucked in a sharp breath and stood to his feet. Rage pumped in his veins, but he fought to keep his tone deadly calm. "Beth, you know that I love you and want what's best for you. But I'm telling you flat out—what's best for you doesn't include me or my brother, so get both ideas out of your head right now."

"Or what?"

His lips clamped tight.

"What, Brady? What are you going to do? I'll tell you— nothing, absolutely nothing. Just like always. Because you can't—you don't own me, not my heart and not my soul. At least, not anymore." She rose to her feet, her manner as deliberate and cold as his. "In fact, I think it's best if we just end our friendship right here and now."

She may as well have slapped him full across the face. The impact of her words had the same effect: his heart was reeling. Without a word he pulled her to him with an intensity that silenced her. He tucked his head against the crook of her neck and closed his eyes. Pears soap and lilac water flooded his senses, renting his heart at the thought of losing this woman forever.

*Woman.* His heart turned over. *God help me.*

No longer his "little buddy." But still, God willing, his friend.

He could hear his breath, shallow against her throat, keeping time with his pulse, and he willed both to slow to a place of calm, where wisdom and self-control took reign. He suddenly became aware of the strain of his palms against her back and slowly relaxed, sliding his hands up to rest on her shoulders. He lifted his head to meet her gaze, not as a mentor, but as a man pleading for mercy. "Beth, I need your friendship, your prayers. Now more than ever before. Please . . . please don't shut me out."

Tears welled and her mouth trembled open. One short heave shivered her chest before she flung her arms around his waist and began to cry. He stroked her hair and soothed her with low whispers until her weeping stilled and she lay spent in his arms. With a gentle kiss to her brow, he steered her to the chair, then knelt beside her. He pulled his handkerchief out and began to wipe the tears from her face. "Beth, if you love me—"

"Oh, Brady, I do—"

He silenced her lips with a touch. "Then be my friend and only my friend."

A lingering heave shuddered her frame, and she looked away. Her shoulders fell. "All right, Brady, whatever you want."

He brushed a finger to her chin, lifting her gaze. "I love you, Beth, make no mistake about that. So much so that everything I say and do is filtered through that love. I'm asking you to trust me and know that I am only looking out for your welfare." He paused and shifted from his knees to a squatting position. "That said, I'm asking you to stay away from my brother—"

"I'm not interested in your—"

"No, I know. But you're a beautiful girl, Beth, and I don't trust him. He's got a jaded past—" He scrubbed a hand over his face. "Like me, I guess, only Michael has no faith in God to save him. And you and I both know that faith in God is everything. It's the air we breathe, the pulse of our soul. Promise me, Beth—with all of your heart—that when you fall in love, it will be with a man who seeks God."

She cupped his face in the small of her hands and gave him a trembling smile. Wetness shimmered in her eyes and spilled down her cheeks, making her look so much like the little girl he longed to protect.

"Oh, Brady, I already have. And he does. With all of his heart."

# 11

"You look exhausted, darlin'. Why don't you go to bed?"

Lizzie looked up to glance at the clock. Ten fifteen. She sighed and closed her book with a thud, then gave her father a weary smile. "I am tired, but I'm not sure I'll sleep."

He squinted over his newspaper. "Because of Tom?"

"No, I'm fine about that. I'm glad I broke it off."

"What, then?"

She rose and hugged the book to her chest. "I don't know. I suppose I'm just a bit blue tonight, nothing a good night's sleep can't cure." She leaned to kiss his cheek. "Good night, Father. You coming up soon?"

He squeezed her hand, then disappeared behind the paper once again. "In a bit, darlin'. Sleep well."

"I'll certainly try."

She needed to. It had been a grueling day. Not because of her breakup with Tom. No, that had lifted a huge burden from her shoulders, dispelling a heaviness that had mounted over the last three months. She was grateful it was over, although Tom apparently felt otherwise. He had called a number of times, but she had refused all calls, asking her mother to turn him away.

With a tired sigh, she headed for the bathroom to brush her teeth and wash her face, then tiptoed into her bedroom. She listened for the sound of Katie's even breathing. As quietly as possible, she undressed and put on her nightgown, then slipped under the sheets. She curled into a ball and let her thoughts drift to the true source of all her sadness.

John Brady. A man she loved but couldn't have. Elusive as the wind.

Wind. The Scripture they'd studied last week came to mind.

*O LORD my God, how great you are! . . . You ride upon the wings of the wind. The winds are your messengers; flames of fire are your servants.*

She stared at the ceiling. John Brady to a T.

A man aflame for God and a mighty wind, one who carried the Word of God to all who would listen. She, too, had ridden on the wings of that wind, allowing him to breathe hope and change into her life. And in the process, he had become for her a flaming fire, a man who'd set her heart ablaze, along with her passion.

Wetness pricked at her eyes and she let it have its way, sluicing down her cheeks until it soaked her pillow. She shivered. If only she could dispel her longing as easily. A broken sob escaped her lips.

"Lizzie? Are you crying?"

She froze. "Oh, Katie, I didn't mean to waken you. I'm sorry."

Her sister sat up in bed and rubbed her eyes, moonlight spilling across her face. "What's the matter? Do you miss Tom?"

"No, darling, I don't. Not even a little."

Katie maneuvered her legs over the side of the bed and lumbered to her feet. She padded over to Lizzie. "Good. I don't miss him, either. He always called me 'kid.' "

A smile tugged at Lizzie's lips. "You know, Katie Rose, when it comes to maturity, I do believe you may have it all over Tom Weston."

Katie's teeth flashed white in the dark. "Lizzie? Are you lonely? 'Cause if you want, we can cuddle."

More wetness rimmed Lizzie's eyes, but this time it felt

good. She lifted the covers. "Sure, Katie, I would really like that."

Her sister burrowed in, and Lizzie gave her a tight hug. She rested her head against her sister's soft hair. "I love you, Katie Rose," she whispered.

"I love you too, Lizzie. You're way too good for Tom." She yawned and nestled close, releasing a contented sigh.

Lizzie smiled in the dark with Katie snug in her arms, and wondered what she would ever do without her family.

Or God.

Or Brady.

Katie's even breathing finally resumed.

Lizzie sighed.

So had her heartbreak.

❦ ❧

Patrick waited a full thirty minutes after Lizzie went upstairs before he set the paper aside and stood to his feet. At long last, everyone was in bed. He checked the kitchen door and turned out the lights, feeling well beyond his years as he slowly mounted the steps. Sleeping at the *Herald* was taking its toll, but no more so than the wound in his heart. The couch at the *Herald* robbed him of a decent night's sleep, to be sure, but his bitterness robbed him of far more. And yet, for the first time in his life or his marriage, he had no will to fight it.

Marcy's love had been sustenance to his soul and strength to his bones. Without it, he was empty, weak, a shell of despair that grew more brittle each day. The love he once thrived on was now tainted, and it was difficult to be in the same room with her, let alone the same bed. In the beginning, she had pleaded and begged, shedding more tears than she had in their lifetime together. The sight of his wife's tears had once pierced him beyond measure, but now they only fell on a hardened heart, one too wounded to care.

And so they'd come to terms. She would give him time—to stew, to pray, to heal. And he would give her a semblance of normalcy. Home for dinner, time with the family, and then leave when his children were in bed and all was right with their world.

While Marcy and his ripped apart at the seams.

Patrick was certain his children sensed the tension. It couldn't be helped with a family as close as theirs, but a mundane routine settled in, assuaging his worry. They now expected the hours he kept—up late at night and gone before they rose in the morning. Once, Katie had informed him, she'd fled to their room after a nightmare, but Marcy had quickly ushered her back to her bed, where they apparently snuggled until dawn. Patrick sighed as he trod down the hall. Marcy was a wonderful mother, no question about that.

*And a wonderful wife?* He stiffened as he opened their door. He no longer cared.

He moved to his closet to retrieve the clean clothes he'd set out, noting the silence of the room. He knew she was awake; he could feel it in his bones. Living with a woman for a quarter of a century did that to you. Sharpened your senses, made you aware. Like an unspoken language between once-kindred hearts.

He stilled as she stirred in the bed.

"Dinner will be early tomorrow because of Katie's play—five o'clock." Her voice sounded lifeless and far away.

Like their marriage.

"I'll be home early, then," he said.

"Then the children are having dinner at Charity's on Friday, so you can work as late as you like. Charity says it's to give us a night off."

He hesitated, fingering the clean clothes draped over his arm. "I have plenty I can do." He turned toward the door.

Her voice reached out, little more than a frail whisper. "Patrick, I love you."

He paused, hand on the knob. A flicker of response flared and quickly died out. "Good night, Marcy."

He opened the door and jolted at the sight of Lizzie in the hall.

"Father, I'm so glad you're still up. Is Mother awake?"

Marcy sat up in the dark. "Lizzie, is that you? Are you all right?"

Patrick's pulse skipped a beat. He quickly stashed the clean clothes on the bureau. "What's wrong? Can't you sleep?" He steered her to his side of the bed. She crawled in next to Marcy while he sat beside her, his arm encircling her waist.

She shook her head while Marcy scooted close.

"What's the problem, darlin'?" Patrick asked.

"The same old thing, I'm afraid," she said, leaning her head on his shoulder. "Feeling sorry for myself because I'm in love with a man who won't love me back."

"Brady? We're back to that again?" Marcy brushed the hair from Lizzie's eyes and stroked her face.

"It would seem so."

"Did something happen to stir the pot?" Patrick kicked off his shoes and stretched his legs out on the bed, cupping her closer.

Her laugh was bitter. "Yes, Father, Tom happened. Proving quite neatly that no other man can even come close."

"Darlin', one relationship is hardly a measure. There'll be plenty more."

She sighed. "I don't know, Father, how do you get over someone who's held your heart in their hands for so long? And what do you do when they constantly turn your love away, leaving you battered and bruised?" A sob broke free from her throat to pierce the darkness.

His arm stiffened, paralyzed over her shoulder.

Marcy's voice rose, quiet and strong, to counter her daughter's pain. "You run to the arms of the Almighty, Lizzie. 'Because thou hast been my help, therefore in the shadow of thy wings will I rejoice.' That's the only place our hearts are safe, the only place they can heal."

Patrick watched as Lizzie fell into her mother's arms with another hoarse sob. Marcy held her tightly, her eyes squeezed shut and her own face sodden with tears over her daughter's shoulder.

Pain seared his heart and he turned away, unwilling to witness his wife's grief.

He startled at the touch of her hand on his arm. "Patrick, will you pray? That Lizzie can be set free from this torment? And that God will restore her joy?"

He stared at his wife's hand for several seconds, and then up into her eyes. His heart clutched in his chest. He pulled Lizzie from Marcy's arms to his, resting his head against his daughter's. His heart, riddled with bitterness, was in no condition to pray. But pray he would, if not for himself, at least for her.

"Lord God, we bring Lizzie before you, and ask that you heal the grief in her heart. Your Word says you are the lifter of our heads and that your joy is our strength. Lift our daughter's head, oh Lord, and be her strength during this time of heartbreak. We pray that you free her from these ties to Brady and help her to move on to where you want her to go. In your time, Lord, we ask that you bring a godly man who will love her with all of his heart. But until then, fill her with your joy and your peace. Amen."

Lizzie sniffed against his shoulder and gave him a squeeze. "Thanks, Daddy. I love you."

He pressed his lips to her hair. "I love you too, darlin', with all my heart."

Marcy hugged her. "Lizzie, would you like me to come in for a while, just until you fall asleep?"

"No, Mother, I've already kept you and Father up late enough. You two go to bed, and so will I. I promise."

She rose and kissed each of their cheeks. "I love you both

so much, I don't know what I'd do without you. Thank you for praying with me. Now please get some sleep."

Patrick rose and followed her to the door. "I have a bit more to do downstairs, I'm afraid. You two will be long gone before my head even hits the pillow."

He felt Marcy's pull from the bed. "Patrick, whatever's keeping you . . . can't you . . . just this once, set it aside for tonight?"

Lizzie stood on tiptoe to give him a quick kiss. "You do look tired, Father. Why don't you call it a night?"

He stroked the curve of her jaw with the pad of his thumb. "All in good time, Lizzie, all in good time. Good night, darlin'."

He watched her disappear down the hall, feeling Marcy's gaze in the dark. His sigh filled the room. Slowly, he returned to the bed to put on his shoes.

The press of Marcy's hand, gentle on his back, jarred him. "You don't have to go, you know."

He dared not look at her. Prayer had softened his heart and threatened his pride. He stood and walked to the bureau to gather the clean clothes in his arms. "Yes, darlin', I do. Good night."

And with a resolve he didn't fully understand, he twisted the knob and shut out his wife, closing the bedroom door along with his hardened heart.

❧ ❧

Brady made his way home in the fading light of dusk, the air still so thick, it drenched the back of his shirt. Despite the stifling ninety-degree temperatures, people milled on the sidewalks and lawns, thick as flies at a summer barbecue. The smell of fresh-mown grass hung heavy in the air, tinged with the sweet scent of honeysuckle. As he strode down Rumpole Street, he waved to his neighbors, several of which were dousing their gardens or their kids. In one front yard, children swung on rope swings, cooling off in the breeze, while moms and dads chatted beneath leafy oaks as limp as the flag on the post office pole.

But tonight, his thoughts were far from the city heat wave and its happy victims. Instead they festered on his brother, unleashing a heat wave of his own that burned in his eyes. Here less than a week and already Michael had almost destroyed his relationship with Beth. He had forgiven his brother long ago for their past, but he had no intention of beginning again with the future. One way or the other, Michael would have to go.

"Hey, Brady, wanna play?"

At the sound of Cluny's voice, Brady looked up, shaking off his thoughts. He stopped dead in his tracks a quarter block from his building, his smile waxing into shock. There was Michael next to Cluny, leaning against a light pole with hip cocked and arms folded.

Miss Hercules let loose with an unladylike woof and bounded toward him. She planted two dirty paws on Brady's chest while Esther gave him a gap-toothed grin, balancing one leg like a stork in a game of kick the stone out. She hopped in the air and kicked at a rock, sending it pinging into Cluny's leg.

"Hey, watch it, will ya, Mullen? Come on, Brady. Wanna play? Michael's won twice. Think you can beat him?"

Michael grinned. "I doubt it, Cluny. He wasn't much good as a kid, sure couldn't beat me now."

Brady glared. "I need to talk to you inside. *Now.*"

Esther rolled her stone into the next chalked square, then implored Brady with pleading eyes. "Come on, Brady, we just started this game. Can't you talk to Michael later?"

Brady tugged on her pigtail. "Sorry, Ess, but this can't wait. Why don't you and Cluny finish the game, and I'll take you both to Robinson's for a soda after?"

She thought about it and then grinned. "Okay. Come on, Cluny, I'll show you how it's done."

Cluny grunted and hiked up his pants. "In your dreams, Mullen."

Brady nodded to his building, giving Michael a look of warning.

Michael leaned down to whisper something in Cluny's ear, then sauntered toward the flat with Brady close on his heels. The sound of Cluny's laughter rang in their ears. Brady followed him into his apartment and shut the door hard, bent on unleashing his anger.

"Why'd you do it, Michael? Why'd you lie to Beth?"

Michael eased back onto the sofa and hiked a leg up on the table. "Come on, John, you're so big on the truth, and that's all I told her. You going to deny you love her?"

"It's none of your business what my feelings for Beth are. You deceived her and got her hopes up. You hurt her, Michael."

Michael rolled his neck while studying Brady from across the room. "No, John, you hurt her, and apparently not for the first time. What's your problem, anyway? She's a beautiful woman, and from what I can tell, the beauty runs way deep. I've never met any girl like her. If she wasn't so all-fired bent on God, I'd be tempted to give her a shot."

The muscles in Brady's neck were knotted as tight as his fists, but he kept his tone calm. "I love her as a friend. Nothing more. I just don't want to see her hurt, that's all."

"You sure have an odd way of showing it. The woman is goofy over you. I only saw you together for a few moments, but it was enough to convince me of one thing. You can espouse the virtues of God till you're blue in the face, little brother, but if you stand there and tell me you love Beth only as a friend, I'd have to say you're lying through your teeth."

The hackles rose on Brady's neck. He moved to the window to thrust the sash up, then turned to glare. "You wouldn't understand."

Michael shot him a narrow gaze. "Try me."

"I've known Beth since she was thirteen. She's like a sister to me."

A glimmer of surprise reflected in Michael's eyes. "Oh, I get it. You're attracted to her, but you see her as family. Gee, that sounds a bit familiar, John."

Brady jerked forward. "Get out, Michael, now. I want you gone."

He laughed. "Well, that makes two of us, little brother, but you and I both know we have unresolved business. I'm not going anywhere until you agree to sign the papers."

"I don't care where you go, but you're not staying here."

Michael sat forward to straddle the edge of the couch. For the first time, his face was void of its usual confidence and humor. "Look, John, I came here to get you to sign the papers, it's true. But that's not all. For some cockeyed reason I actually had this far-fetched idea that maybe, just maybe, we could heal our relationship, get back on track as brothers, as a family." He turned away and threaded a hand through his hair. "I've missed you. Both Helena and I have. With Lucille gone, you're the only family we've got. Can't we start over?"

Brady stared, shock warring with anger. He looked away. "I don't know. There's a lot of pain in our past. I don't know if I can handle it."

"Maybe you need to. Ever think about that?"

Brady exhaled and nodded. "Yeah, I have. But I need more time."

"You've had eleven years."

He looked up. "To forgive. But only a week to get to know you again."

His brother paused, as if weighing his words. He exhaled softly. "I need you, John. Not just to sign the papers. But as a brother and a friend."

Brady stared out the window, his eyes lost in a cold stare. "Someday, maybe."

He heard the swoosh of the sofa as Michael rose to his feet. "Someday? Well, tell me, John, what exactly would your Bible tell you to do?"

*But whoso beholdeth his brother in need, and shutteth up his compassion from him, how doth the love of God abide in him?*

Michael's words hit their mark and Brady closed his eyes, releasing all the fight inside with one long, weary breath. "All right, Michael, you win."

He heard his brother take a step forward. "You'll come back, then?"

"No, I already made that clear. But you're welcome to stay awhile longer."

"I appreciate it, John. But I'd appreciate it a lot more if you'd come back with me. What can I do to convince you?"

"Nothing."

"Not even the threat of seducing Beth?"

Brady wheeled around, his fury rekindled. "You wouldn't dare, not after that heartfelt speech about family."

Michael shrugged. "I don't want to, trust me, but what choice do I have? You're being a mule, and you know it. What's it going to cost you? Maybe some time, and then you're a rich man. What more could you want?"

"To be free of my past, not to reclaim it."

Michael eyed him through weary eyes. "I'm tired of pussy-footing with you, John. If Beth is the only thing you care about, then maybe you'll care enough to keep me away from her. Sign the papers or I'll make a play for her. She's already half in love with me because of the way I look. Couldn't be too hard to take her the rest of the way."

Muscles twitched in Brady's face. He thought of Beth and her commitment to seek a man who loves God. He waged a bet and put all his fears on the table. "It won't work. She's not interested."

"No? Well, I don't know about you, little brother, but I've had a lot of success with women. Come on, John, we're good-looking men, don't you know that? It shouldn't be long before she's looking at me the way she looks at you."

Brady took a step forward and shoved Michael hard. His

jaws ached with fury. "Get out—*now!* I'm taking Cluny and Ess to the drugstore, and you better be gone when I get back or so help me, God—"

Michael stood his ground. "You think God'll 'help' you beat me up, is that it? You know, it's a funny thing about your God, John. You preach him a lot, but when it comes to the deep, dark secrets inside, you pretty much do whatever you please."

Brady's fist froze midair, inches from his brother's face. He took a step back and released a choking breath. His arm quivered to his side.

"Thanks for proving my point. I'll be gone when you get back, but I'd give it some thought. I don't want to move in on your girl, but you leave me no choice. I'm not going to let your pride and fear of the past rob Helena and me. Think about it, John. You have everything to gain and nothing to lose."

He walked out of the room, leaving Brady shaking with rage.

Everything to gain. A house and a past he swore he'd never return to.

And nothing to lose.

Except for his peace.

❧ ☙

Marcy stood at Mrs. Gerson's kitchen window, in bleak harmony with the rivulets of water that slithered down the pane. It was a slow and steady rain, endless weeping from a gray and dismal sky, and Marcy felt a kinship with it. It showed no signs of letting up, much like the grief in her heart over the loss of her husband. A silent mourning over a spouse who was still very much alive, but whose love was as cold and dead as any corpse.

She felt the chill of a shiver and clutched her arms to her waist. A shrill whistle pierced the air, and she turned to see Mrs. Gerson rise to serve the tea. Marcy watched her blind neighbor move with the ease of a sighted woman, and knew she had come to the right place. Small and frail, Christa Gerson could barely see more than shadows, but she possessed a vision far beyond mundane tasks. She hobbled to the table with the teapot and smoothed a wrinkled hand across the surface until she located the cup. A soft smile lifted the corners of her mouth as she poured first one cup and then the other.

"Sit, Marcy," she said quietly, as she returned the teapot to the stove. "The tea will warm you."

Marcy buffed her arms and sat down. "Warm" was something she hadn't felt in quite a while now, despite the sweltering summer days. Not since Patrick had left her bed almost five weeks ago, depriving her of a love that had been as constant and second nature as the beat of her pulse. His departure— emotionally, if not physically—had left her plunging into a dark hole, beginning with heartbreak and grief, and bottoming out with anger and bitterness. She could feel a thick callous taking form on her heart, and it scared her. Love was a fragile gift, too easily hardened. *And too easy to slip away* . . .

She took a sip of her tea and focused on Christa, who waited patiently, a painted china cup held to her lips. Her snow-white head bent as she blew on the hot liquid. Steam misted vacant eyes that were half closed. Marcy suspected she was praying, and the thought warmed her more than the cup in her own hands. Mrs. Gerson had been a godsend for Faith during those troubled years that Faith had struggled with Charity, and Marcy marveled now at the wonder of God's provision in their lives. Reading the Bible to the blind woman down the street had changed her daughter's life forever, infusing her with a passion for God's Word like Marcy had never seen. That passion had carried her daughter through some of the worst times of her life. And Marcy as well. She swallowed another taste of tea and set the cup down.

She hadn't realized she'd expelled a heavy sigh until a wrinkled hand lighted upon hers. At Christa's touch, wetness sprang to her eyes, and she fought it back with a lift of her chin.

"No, I will not cry," she said in a harsh tone. "Patrick O'Connor has already wrung enough tears from my eyes."

"Like this dreary rain outside, Marcy, your tears will cease. Now suppose you tell me what happened," the old woman whispered.

Marcy nodded and started at the beginning, spanning from her relationship with Sam O'Rourke before she'd met Patrick, to the night her husband had left. It felt so good to unleash all the hurt and loneliness that night had wrought, but as she disclosed the coldness of her husband's behavior over the last weeks, her voice took on a steely quality. "I've tried, Christa, to reach him in every way I know how. I've begged his forgiveness over and over again, but it's as if his heart has turned to stone."

Christa nodded. "In a way it has. Bitterness will calcify a heart faster than anything."

Marcy hesitated "Yes, I know. I'm experiencing it firsthand. And I can't help but worry . . . that our love will never be the same."

The old woman leaned forward. "Bitterness is a natural reaction, Marcy, given Patrick's rejection. But for your sake and his, you must fight it. Your marriage depends upon it."

Marcy shot to her feet. Her voice was shrill. "Why me? Why not Patrick? He's the one who's bitter, Christa, the one who started this. I have begged for his forgiveness more times than I can count, and yet I've done nothing wrong! It's him. He's the one who needs to deal with his bitterness—he's the one who's wrong!"

"Yes, Marcy, he is. Patrick has allowed his own hurt to blind him to the truth, which is shocking, because we both know he's not that kind of man. Which merely underscores the true depth of his hurt. A hurt now steeped in sin."

Marcy sank back into her chair, her anger abated by sorrow. For the moment. She drew in a cleansing breath and exhaled. "So, what do I do?"

"Well, you have no power to change him or the bitterness that's taken root in his heart. But you do have power to change yourself."

"What do you mean?"

Mrs. Gerson took another sip of tea and smiled. "The same bitterness closing off Patrick's heart wants to close yours, but you will not let it. You will fight it for the sake of your marriage because Patrick is too hurt to do so. Because you see, Marcy, the kind of love you and Patrick have is deep and abiding. A set of scales, if you will, with Patrick on one side and you on the other." She held out her hands evenly, palms up. "A choice, really. Do I love him enough to forgive? Or do I love myself more, wanting to hurt him like he's hurt me?" She tipped her hands off-kilter, one up, one down, and then smiled. "The kind of love you and Patrick share always tips the scales in the other's favor. Patrick can't do that right now, Marcy, but you can."

Marcy swallowed hard. "How?" It was a whisper, a faint surrender.

"Fourfold, my dear. First, you repent for any bitterness you've held up until now. Second, you learn from the Master. Once, when Jesus was asleep in a boat with his apostles, a storm threatened. The Bible says that Jesus rebuked the winds and the sea, and there was a great calm. You will do the same. When bitterness comes, you will rebuke it in Jesus' name, and he will send the calm. Third, you will put feet to your faith, because action speaks louder than words. And love, my dear, speaks louder than anything. That means you will demonstrate your love for Patrick—a love note, a favorite dessert, a kind tone—regardless of how he treats you. And finally, my dear, you will pray. Pray for God to soften his heart, to wrest him free from the grip of sin, and to bless him. And this, Mrs. O'Connor, is the most powerful step of all. Because if you are faithful to the first three, your prayers will unleash the power of heaven."

Marcy's spirit quickened.

Mrs. Gerson rose to retrieve the tea, then turned at the stove with a sparkle in her eye. She stared straight at Marcy as if she could really see. "And do you know why?"

Marcy held her breath and shook her head.

A soft chuckle rumbled from the old woman's lips as she hefted the teapot with an elfin grin. She toddled to the table, and Marcy could have sworn she saw her wink. "Because, my dear, like natural laws of gravity, there are also spiritual laws. Such as 'the fervent prayer of a righteous man availeth much' or 'if I regard iniquity in my heart, the Lord will not hear me.'" She settled into her chair with a peaceful smile and leaned forward. "Which simply means, my dear Marcy, if you do your part—" she nodded heavenward "—as sure as the sun rises . . . he will do his."

❦ ❧

Mitch shoveled the last piece of cherry pie into his mouth and pushed the plate away.

Charity studied him from across the dinner table, chin propped in her hand and mouth slack. "Sweet saints, are you finally done? That was your *third* piece of pie! If I ate like you, I'd be big as a house."

He unbuttoned his vest, eyeing her with a faint smile. "Two. And if you ate like me, little girl, we wouldn't be married."

Collin chuckled and took a sip of his coffee. "Good job side-stepping the 'big as a house' remark."

Faith slapped him with a napkin. "Collin, you know she's sensitive about that."

He hauled her onto his lap and snatched the offensive napkin from her hand. "She's the one who said it first, and if you plan to go after me, Little Bit, I suggest you use something more deadly than a napkin." His lips dove for her neck.

Charity clinked a spoon against the side of her water glass and gave Collin a less-than-patient smile. "Save it, McGuire.

Now, if you can keep your hands off my sister long enough to discuss pressing family matters, I'll be a happy woman."

Mitch chuckled. "Instead of a jealous one," he mumbled under his breath.

She singed him with a lidded gaze. "I heard that. Keep in mind that hell hath no fury like a woman almost eight months pregnant." She glanced around the table. "Anybody need anything before we get started? Sean? Katie? Steven?"

"Do I have to stay? I'm only fourteen—what can I possibly add to this discussion?" Steven's lanky legs hovered over the edge of the chair, poised for escape.

"No, I suppose you and Katie can go into the parlor if you like—"

Steven fired out of the room before the last word could roll off Charity's tongue. Her lips twisted. "*Et tu*, Katie?"

"Not on your life. I'm staying. Sean and Steven are never home. It's Lizzie and I who really know what's going on in that house."

"Katie's right. She should stay," Lizzie said. She scooted Katie's chair close so she could braid her hair.

Charity folded her hands. "Okay, we need to discuss what's been going on in that house over the last several weeks."

Sean leveled beefy arms on the table. "Yeah, I'd like to know myself. I'm not around a lot these days, I know, but I don't have to be to see that Mother's not been herself."

"That's the understatement of the year," Faith muttered. She leaned back against Collin's chest. "I haven't seen her this depressed since you and Father went to war."

"Me, either," Lizzie said.

Charity grunted and settled back in the chair with great effort. She sighed and locked her hands over her sizable stomach. "Well, something is wrong, and we are not leaving this room until we get to the bottom of it." Her piercing gaze landed on

Lizzie. "You said that Mother goes to bed early every night while Father stays up?"

"Every single night. There have been occasions, of course, when Mother would do that every now and then, but not every night. They usually like to go to bed at the same time, it seems. But not anymore. Father stays up reading as far as I can tell. In fact, the other night when I kissed him good night in the parlor, he said he was going to read for a while. But then when I went to their room about thirty minutes later, he was leaving again, fully dressed, with clothes draped over his arm."

Collin frowned. "Well, he could have been putting them in the bathroom so as not to waken Marcy in the morning. He goes in early, I know. Faith hasn't ridden to work with him in weeks because of it."

"He's not sleeping in the parlor, is he?" Charity leaned forward in shock.

Lizzie shook her head. "No, I don't think so. I would have noticed because I left the house before dawn at least two mornings."

Charity wrinkled her nose. "Sweet saints, Lizzie, whatever for?"

Lizzie blushed. "Don't ask, but suffice it to say that Brady was involved."

"Gosh, Lizzie, we need to put you on the payroll. You get there earlier than I do." Collin shot her a grin.

Charity dismissed Collin with a lift of her chin. "Well, they must sleep together, at least, even if they aren't talking all that much."

"They weren't on the night of my nightmare."

All eyes focused on Katie.

Lizzie's fingers stilled in Katie's hair. She bent forward to meet her sister's gaze. "What do you mean?"

"I mean that I had a nightmare the night you stayed at Millie's. I ran into their room, and Mother jumped from the bed like she was having one too. She rushed me out like the house was on fire, but not before I saw that the bed was empty."

Faith shivered on Collin's lap. "What time was that?"

Katie scrunched her freckled nose. "Had to be close to three in the morning at least. Mother ended up sleeping with me until dawn."

"Did you ask her where Father was?" Charity scooted to the edge of the seat in suspense.

"Yeah, but she acted like he was in the bathroom."

"Maybe he was," Collin said.

"Naw, the door was wide open and he wasn't in there."

Sean frowned. "Didn't you wonder where he was?"

Katie tilted her head in thought. "Kind of, but Mother was fussing over me so, that I guess I didn't think too much about it. Not until now."

Charity pursed her lips and shook her head. "Something's terribly wrong. I can feel it. If Father's not sleeping in their room, and he's not sleeping in the parlor, where in the world is he sleeping?"

"You don't know for a fact that he's not sleeping at home."

The room fell silent as six sets of eyes converged on Mitch.

"What?" he asked. "It's just an observation."

Charity crossed her arms on the table and squinted at her husband. "No one even considered the possibility of him sleeping anywhere but home, Mitch. Why would you?"

An uncommon ruddiness crept up the back of his neck. "I just meant that, well, if he's not in his room and he's not on the couch, where else might he be?"

Charity rose to her feet, searing him with a cold gaze. "I don't know—our old room, maybe? Or the hammock on the back porch, or even the basement? Where *else* might he be, Mitch? Since you work for the man, maybe you would know."

The color fused to his cheeks, a rare sight, indeed. His jaw began to grind, a dead giveaway he was hiding something.

Charity pushed her chair away in an abrupt motion and

rounded the table, her eyes never leaving her husband's flushed face. "You know something, don't you? You better spill it now or so help me . . ."

He shot to his feet. "Don't you dare threaten me. Pregnant or not, I won't stand for it."

She stood so close that her stomach obscured his hips, deepening his color. She stared up with heat in her eyes and pummeled a swollen finger hard into his chest. "These are my parents we're talking about, you mule-headed Irishman, and I don't give a fig about your male ego at the moment. You know something, don't you? I can see it in your eyes, and you sure in the blazes better come out with it now if you value our happy home."

He fisted her hand and lowered her finger with calm deliberation, despite a dangerous tic in his cheek. "I know about as much as you do, give or take a few minor details."

She folded her arms. "Well, then, I suggest you divulge the 'details' and quickly. I knew you were way too quiet tonight. Tell us what you know, Mitch." She swallowed her pride and humbled her tone. "*Please*."

He sank back in the chair and blew out a heavy breath that sounded like a groan. He put his head in his hands. "I swear, Charity, if I lose your father's trust over this—"

"You won't. I'll tell him I badgered till you bled."

He focused on the table in a dead stare, his fingers buried in his hair. He made them wait, apparently contemplating his fate. A moan merged with a sigh. "He's sleeping at the *Herald*."

The room was a morgue. He looked up, as if to gauge their silence. Whatever everyone had expected, this wasn't it.

"Every night?" Faith slid off of Collin's lap and thumped into her chair, appearing to be in a near stupor. "For how long?"

"Almost two months, at least according to Angus."

Faith blinked. "The night watchman? How in the world did you find out?"

Mitch rubbed the bridge of his nose. "By accident, a month ago. I took Charity to the hospital for false labor—"

Collin leaned forward. "What?"

"Go on," Charity and Faith's clipped voices cut him short, their gazes glued to Mitch's face.

"Well, we didn't get home until about three in the morning and obviously I was too keyed up to sleep, so I went in to work. Angus made a comment about Patrick and me working long hours, and then he just spilled it. Said Patrick's been sleeping on the couch in his office every night. Leaves at six or so after work, then comes back at about midnight or so."

Charity felt like a sleepwalker as she lumbered back to her chair. She sank into the seat, her body numb. "Dear Lord, that can't be. Not our parents. Everyone knows—their marriage is the bedrock of all marriages."

"Yeah, well, 'rock' is the appropriate word, because at the moment, Marcy and Patrick's relationship is on the rocks."

"It's not funny, Mitch," Charity lashed out, knuckles clenched white.

His eyes softened as he stared at his wife. "I'm not trying to be, Charity. I'm just as grieved about this as all of you. It's about eaten my insides out knowing what's going on. I love them too, you know." He took a deep breath. "That's why I confronted him."

Faith jolted to her feet. "You talked to Father? What did he say?"

"Not a lot, I'm afraid. But what he did was very telling. He seemed wounded and bitter, not concerned about what this might be doing to Marcy or if it was the right thing to do. He said he needed time to heal. And that was all. Other than asking me to keep quiet."

Charity dragged her fingers through her hair. "And you agreed?"

His eyes narrowed. "I didn't see that I had a choice, Charity. He's my father-in-law and my boss. He said it was his business, and it is."

Charity lunged to her feet and slammed her fist on the table.

"No! It's not just his business, it's all of ours! How dare Patrick O'Connor think that the people who love and depend on him have no right to know? And how dare you, when you know those two people are the foundation of this family?"

Lizzie rose to put an arm around Charity's shoulders. "Charity, please calm down, for your sake and the baby's. We'll work this out. Whatever pain is in Father's heart, it can't win out. Not when he and Mother have raised children who pray."

Charity sagged into the chair with tears in her eyes. "I'm sorry, everyone. I just . . . can't bear the thought of Mother . . . and Father . . ."

Faith squeezed Charity's hand. "None of us can. Which is why we're going to do something." Her eyes scanned the table. "We need a spokesman to talk to Father. A man, and preferably not one of his children."

Mitch groaned. "Oh, that pares it down neatly. Why don't you girls talk to Marcy?"

Faith arched a brow. "You don't think we've tried? Mother's lips are sealed tighter than the U.S. Treasury. She's protecting Father, there's no question about it. So we need someone to reason with him, talk to him. And from where I'm standing, that's either you or Collin."

Collin shifted in his chair. "And I'd do it in a heartbeat, but I don't see him every day like Mitch does. Besides, he's like a father to me, while Mitch is more of a . . . peer."

Mitch broiled him with a glare. "Thanks. An endorsement and a slam."

"He's right, Mitch. Father respects you," Faith insisted, her eyes pleading.

Collin folded his arms. "Thanks, Faith, I appreciate the support."

She dismissed him with a sweep of her hand, focusing only on Mitch. "Will you do it? For us? For your wife?"

Mitch studied her for a long moment, then exhaled his dissent. "He's not going to like it."

Faith's jaw tightened. "We don't care—he's wrong. And if that bothers him, tell him he shouldn't have raised a God-fearing family. Will you do it?"

"Do I have a choice?"

Charity rose and raised her chin. "No."

Mitch's lips flattened as he stared at his wife. "I didn't think so."

"When?" Charity asked.

"When I feel the time is right."

"Monday." Her gaze connected with his as she rubbed her swollen belly.

His brows dipped. "When-I-feel-the-time-is-right."

She leaned in, took advantage of the easy tears in her eyes, and enunciated as clearly as he. "Monday-Mitch-no-later. When this baby arrives, I need there to be two loving, happy grandparents waiting in the wings."

"Don't push me, Charity . . ."

She clutched at her stomach. A small cry of pain wrenched from her lips.

Mitch shot to his feet. "What's wrong?"

She pressed a frail hand to her chest and took a deep breath. Her voice was a hoarse rasp as she leaned over the table. "Monday, Mitch. I can't wait any longer. Please."

He blinked, his mouth settling into a mulish press. "You're milking this pregnancy."

She lowered herself into the chair with difficulty, finally settling in with a low groan. She sighed and folded her hands on her belly, then gave him a timid smile. "I know, Mitch, but I'm carrying your child. Humor me."

He gave her a hooded stare. "What happened to the compromise we were supposed to have in this marriage?"

She fought the twitch of a smile. "It'll come back when I'm not pregnant, I promise."

Collin and Sean snickered.

Faith rose and stood behind Mitch. She grinned and kneaded

his shoulders. "Don't worry, Dennehy. After the baby's born, she'll be right back where you keep her—under your thumb."

He swabbed his face with his hands and grunted. "Yeah, right."

Charity scooted to the edge of her seat and steepled her hands on the table. She flashed a pretty smile. "Well, I don't know about anyone else, but I certainly feel better. Shall we pray?"

❦  ❦

Lizzie stared out the kitchen window, her eyes trained on a threesome of little girls playing in the neighbor's backyard. Plumed hats and their mothers' hand-me-down jewelry painted a pretty picture for an afternoon tea party. Their giggles floated in the thick, warm air. On the other side, twelve-year-old Libby O'Shea coasted on a homemade swing, toes touching a blinding-blue heaven dolloped with clouds.

Lizzie breathed in, filling her lungs with the scent of July— Mother's rambling cottage roses and freshly laundered linens swaying stiff in the occasional breeze. Life had once seemed so simple—as free and uncomplicated as pumping high on the wooden swing Father had hung on the oak. Lizzie closed her eyes, remembering the tingle of air against her skin as she'd sailed, like Libby, into an endless sky. She sighed and opened them again to the sink of soapy water that now withered her hands. Life was no longer that simple.

Somewhere along the way, her high-flying fairy-tale dreams had taken a sharp dive into reality, shriveling her wide-eyed hopes faster than her skin in a tub of hot dishwater. First with Brady, and now with her parents. Growing up, it had been so easy to escape between the covers of a book, where heartbreak seldom thrived and happily ever after was a given. Reality was not so kind, she was discovering.

Nor as forgiving.

She was grateful that God was. She reflected on Tom's assessment of her faith, and her cheeks burned as warm as the water chafing her hands. At least God's forgiveness allowed her to begin anew. But what about the next time a man turned her head? When his kisses warmed her skin. Could she be strong?

The screen door squeaked open, and Lizzie glanced over her shoulder. "What are you doing here? I thought Collin's mother's birthday party was today."

Faith hefted a box of homegrown tomatoes and cucumbers onto the table, then brushed her hands down the smooth lines of her navy cotton skirt. "It is, but I wanted to drop these vegetables off first." Her gaze flicked to the backyard where Marcy's once thriving garden now toasted brown in the sun. "I know Mother hasn't felt much like gardening, and since we're having a banner year, I thought I'd surprise her. Where is she?"

Lizzie fished the last of the pots from the rinse water and began to dry. "Upstairs, taking a nap."

"Again? She's taking naps every afternoon, it seems. She's never done that before."

"She's doing a lot of things she's never done before. Naps, sleeping late in the morning, staring out windows, spending time with Mrs. Gerson."

Faith pulled out a chair and sat down. "Well, that's the first good thing you've said. Mrs. Gerson is the best person for Mother right now. She was my spiritual mentor for so many years, that no one could see me through a crisis like her. She's exactly what Mother needs." Faith huffed. "Now, Father? What he needs is—"

"A swift kick in the behind?"

Faith's lips zagged into a droll smile. "You're too kind, Lizzie, but you certainly get my drift. I love our father more than any man on the face of this earth except Collin, you know that, but I'm not very proud of him right now. He taught us to face our fears and hurts, not to run away. I don't know what kind of pain he's dealing with, but I do know he's not dealing with it in the right way, not when he's wounding Mother like he is. I only wish Mitch were talking to him tomorrow instead of Monday."

Lizzie joined her at the table. "Well, you and I both know he can't say anything at Sunday dinner. Mother would be humiliated if she had any idea. And only God knows how Father would react. It's way too risky."

"I suppose." Faith squinted at her sister. "You don't seem yourself this morning. Is all this troubling you . . . or . . . is it Brady?"

Lizzie tried to smile. "Both, of course, but there is something else."

Faith folded her arms and leaned in. "Give."

"Want some iced tea?" Lizzie jumped up and scurried to the icebox.

"Yes. What's on your mind, Lizzie?"

She paused, taking her time to pour the tea. "Faith, you like it when Collin kisses you, don't you? I mean, it's wonderful, right?"

"Yes, of course . . ."

She sliced a lemon into wedges and plopped one into each glass. She set them on the table, careful to avoid her sister's eyes. "Well, you were engaged for almost a year. When Collin would kiss you, how . . . I mean . . . well, how did you manage to . . . to—"

"Stop?"

Lizzie blushed. "Yes."

"Did you have trouble stopping with Tom?"

"A little . . . I always did stop, of course, so nothing ever really happened . . . but it could have. More easily than I liked."

"Is that why you broke it off?"

She nodded and searched her sister's face. "Is something wrong with me, Faith? Tom said that my kisses, the way I responded to his, well, he made it pretty clear that even though I told him no, my kisses said yes. I think deep down he thought I was . . . loose."

Faith laid a hand on Lizzie's arm. "There's nothing wrong with you, Lizzie. We're a passionate family—about God and about love. And romantic love feels really good. God made us to desire it, to gravitate toward it like a moth to flame. But the irony is that unless God's in the center of it, you can get singed pretty badly." She took a quick sip of tea and closed her eyes. "But, oh my, when he *is* in the center of the love between a man and a woman, you can't imagine the rightness of it, the freedom, the joy. No guilt, no shame. Just becoming one with your husband. And in the process, one with God."

Lizzie forced herself to breathe. "Oh, Faith, that's what I've been looking for my whole life. But I'm so scared that I'll ruin it, taint it with my weakness. Wasn't it hard for you and Collin to stay pure until your wedding night?"

Faith grinned. "Little sister, you have no idea! That man can heat my blood with a look, much less a kiss, and although his commitment to God was as strong as mine during that year, the closer we got to the wedding, the harder he'd push, testing the limits of my self-control."

"How did you get through it?"

A faint smile softened her lips. "Passion for God. I begged God for it, cried out for it. I wanted a passion for him that would rival my passion for Collin. And so I prayed, day and night and always before I'd see Collin. Prayed that God would strengthen us to honor him. After all, it was God's love that brought us together. I never wanted to betray that love for a moment's pleasure. Not when I knew I could have a lifetime of pleasure sanctioned by him."

She idly traced a finger through the moisture beading the side of her cool glass, her eyes lost in a faraway stare. "It's hard, Lizzie, there's no question about it. But if you really love someone, then you want the best for them. And the 'best' is clearly laid out in Deuteronomy 30, a mainstay in my life: life and death, blessing and curse. God begs us to choose life—his precepts—so that he can bestow blessings on us. If you really love someone, why would you choose death—your own lust and pleasure—and cut off God's blessing from your relationship and the one you love? It just doesn't make sense. So between my passion for God, my passion for Collin in wanting the best for him, and prayer—well, somehow we got through."

"But maybe you're stronger than me."

Faith wrinkled her nose. "I don't think so. But God is. Pray for fervor, Lizzie. Pray that God is the most important thing in your life, so much so that hurting him would hurt you. When that happens, and your choices line up with his, it produces an amazing ripple effect of blessings—in your life, that of your family, and for the man you eventually marry."

"Oh, Faith, I—"

A knock sounded at the door. Both sisters looked up.

"Beth, hello! I hope I'm not interrupting . . ."

Lizzie blinked and touched a hand to her cheek. "Brady?"

A crooked grin lit his face. "No, it's Michael, John's brother. I came to apologize."

Faith bounded to her feet and opened the door. "Sweet saints, Collin was right—you are the spitting image of your brother. Come in, please."

She held the screen as he sauntered past, hat in hand. He was dressed impeccably in a tan linen waistcoat and matching trousers, sporting a trace of a swagger that clearly set him apart from Brady. His smile bordered on mischievous. He said he'd come to apologize, but there was a sparkle in his brown eyes akin to that of a little boy who'd misbehaved and wasn't the least bit sorry.

Faith extended a hand. "I'm Faith, Collin's wife and Lizzie's sister. You were certainly a shock to all of us. Brady's pretty tight-lipped about his past, you know."

He grinned and shook her hand, revealing a flash of perfectly white teeth. "Yeah, well, I guess nobody was more shocked than him. I haven't seen him since we were seventeen." He gave her a narrow look. "Who's Lizzie?"

Lizzie retrieved a glass from the cupboard, grateful for something to do with her hands. Michael's similarity to Brady was unnerving. "That would be me. I used to go by Beth, but Lizzie is what everybody calls me now. Everybody except Brady, of course. He's a bit slow when it comes to change. Would you like some iced tea?"

"That would be great, that is, if I'm not intruding." He took off his jacket and draped it over a chair. He rolled his sleeves and settled in, as if intrusion were not even a remote possibility. He plopped his straw boater down and folded thick arms on the table, displaying tan muscles beneath his white linen shirt. "Slow? My brother? That's a bit like calling the Pope Catholic, isn't it?" He laughed, and the low, rich sound seemed to vibrate in the air. His eyelids closed to a squint as he studied her. "Lizzie. I like it. It suits you better than Beth."

"Are you in town long?" Faith asked, sliding back into her chair.

"I'm not sure." His eyes flicked to Lizzie as she set his glass of tea on the table. "Depends. Thank you, Lizzie." He took a large swollow, draining half the glass.

"Collin says you're staying with Brady?" Faith asked.

"Well, I was until earlier this week. But I'm afraid we had a bit of a falling out. Which is why I'm here. To apologize to your sister."

Faith set her glass down and started to rise. "Oh, well, I should be going—"

"*No!* You just g-got here and all," Lizzie said. "I mean, you know Mother will want to see you . . ."

Faith stared, obviously reading the worry in her sister's eyes. She glanced at the clock over the sink. "Well, I don't have to be home for a while yet, so maybe I'll finish my tea."

Lizzie's muscles relaxed, and she released the breath she'd been holding. Her relief, however, was short-lived.

"So, Michael, what is it exactly that you need to apologize for?" Faith asked.

His manner became serious, betrayed by a hint of a twinkle in his eyes. "Well, Lizzie came to see Brady last week, and I failed to tell her he wasn't home." His gaze wandered back to Lizzie, causing her cheeks to grow warm. "She thought I was him."

Lizzie bounced up to fetch the pitcher of tea. "Well, I needed a shoulder to cry on after my breakup with Tom, Michael, and you supplied that. Thank you for praying with me and providing comfort. I believe you did as good a job as Brady would have."

He watched as she poured him more tea, thumbs latched on the clasps of his suspenders. "I believe I could do better . . . if given the chance."

Lizzie jerked, spilling tea all over the table. Faith leapt to her feet to fetch a towel.

"I'm so sorry, Michael! Did I get any on you?" Lizzie stared in horror at the dark splotches staining his slacks.

He stood and brushed his linen trousers. "No problem, but I'll tell you what. You can make it up by having dinner with me tomorrow night."

"Oh no, I can't! We have a family dinner every Sunday."

"Monday, then?"

Lizzie's gaze darted to Faith, who arched a brow.

"I don't think so, Michael, but thank you for asking."

He reached for the sodden towel and wiped the seat of his chair before pushing it in. He tossed it back on the table. "Because of John?"

She bit her lip. "Yes, I think so."

He picked up his hat and held it loosely in his hands. His thumb grazed the rim. "He told me you two weren't dating. That you were just friends."

"No, no, we're not dating. Just friends. My best friend, actually."

"Then why would he mind?"

She was mortified by the heat burning in her cheeks, but she wasn't going to lie. "He asked me to stay away from you."

"I see. And did he say why?"

"He claims you wouldn't be good for me."

"Because . . ."

She released a sober breath. "He says you have no faith in God."

He nodded, the barest of smiles curving his lips. "I see."

He moved to the door and positioned the straw boater on his head. He gave it several firm taps. "Faith, it was a pleasure meeting you. The moment I met Collin, I knew his wife would be something special." He gave a slight bow and pressed a hand to the screen door. He turned and squinted. "By the way, what time do you leave for church on Sunday mornings?"

She pushed a strand of hair from her eyes. "Nine forty-five for ten o'clock Mass. Why?"

"See you tomorrow, then."

Lizzie blinked, her body in shock. "Church? Tomorrow? B-but I didn't think you went."

He gave her a faint smile, and his firm gaze was so much like Brady's that it caused her stomach to flip. He winked. "I do now."

❧ ❧

"Good night, Mr. Dennehy. You heading home soon?"

Mitch glanced at his watch before looking up. "Right behind you, Dorothy. Have a nice evening."

"You too, sir."

He expelled a heavy breath and rose to his feet, his lips twisting into a slight scowl. Yeah, a real nice evening—if he didn't get fired first. He plucked his suit coat from the back of his chair and slung it over his shoulder, then strode to the door with one purpose in mind. To get it over with—as quickly

❧ 241 ❧

as possible. To get the monkey off his back. He thought of his wife and sighed, fisting the knob with too much pressure as he closed his door. A beautiful monkey, to be sure, but annoying all the same.

He pinched the bridge of his nose. No, that wasn't fair. He would have done this anyway, on his own. But it would have been on his time frame, not Charity's. He wanted to see healing in the family as much as anyone. More, probably, given the fact that he had to work with Patrick, day in and day out. He was tired of the lonely bent of his father-in-law's shoulders, the hollow look in his eyes. But today certainly wouldn't have been the day he'd picked. Not when several deadlines had been missed and the paper had gone to bed late. Patrick would be in a foul mood for sure. But no more so than his beautiful monkey if he failed to get the deed done. Mitch steeled his jaw and knocked on Patrick's closed door.

"Come in."

He poked his head in. "Got a minute?"

Patrick finished scribbling on a paper before looking up. "Since when do you knock? You usually barge in with smoke coming out of your ears."

"Yeah, well, I thought there'd be enough smoke in the air." He closed the door and tossed his coat over the back of a chair and sat, elbows flat on the side arms. He jiggled his fingers nervously over the edge.

Patrick continued writing, his head still bowed over the paper. His eyes flicked up, gray and grim beneath stormy brows. "What do you want, Mitch?"

He exhaled. There was no sense in tiptoeing around. His fingers stilled on the chair. "The family knows. Everything. That you and Marcy aren't talking, that you sleep at the *Herald*, that things aren't right between you two."

Patrick leaned back in his chair. His eyes were as cold as the pewter pen clenched in his hand. "And how, pray tell, did they find out?"

Mitch sucked in a deep breath. "They held a meeting . . . to discuss the tension they've been feeling. They suspect you aren't sleeping in your room."

Patrick's brow angled dangerously high.

A nerve twitched in Mitch's cheek. "And I confirmed it."

"I see." His tone was flat, like the hard line of his mouth.

Mitch sprang to his feet, palms pressed white on the desk. "Look, Patrick, you put me in an awkward position, and I kept my mouth shut because you asked me to. But your family is bleeding over this, and something's got to be done. For pity's sake, your wife is in a depression and your family is frantic with worry. The man I thought I knew would have never allowed that. What's happened to you?"

Without a word, Patrick rose to his feet and moved to the window, shoulders stooped like a man who'd waged a battle and lost. His voice was so low, Mitch could barely decipher the words. "That man no longer exists."

"Patrick, you have to talk to me. Let me help you, please."

The light from the window blazed around him, creating a surreal silhouette as he put his head in his hand. His shoulders began to shake, and with a tightening in his gut, Mitch realized he was weeping.

"Patrick, I respect you more than any man alive. What you and Marcy have, I've never seen anything like it. Never seen two people more in love, more in tune with each other. Charity and I and Collin and Faith get on our knees and pray for what you have. As God is my witness, I have never seen a better marriage."

"It's a lie."

"What?"

Patrick turned around, his eyes raw with pain. "The marriage. It began as a lie. She didn't love me."

"I don't believe that. That woman loves you so much that she can't eat, can't sleep. She's a shell of her former self. Is that what you want?"

"No! And, yes, I know she loves me. But tell me something, Mitch. And I defy you to say otherwise. If you discovered Charity was in love with someone else when she became your wife, would it change the man that you are?"

Every nerve in his body stilled. The mere thought clotted the air in his lungs. A once-familiar taste of rage and jealousy tainted his tongue like a canker, reminding him how he'd felt prior to their marriage when Charity had been seeing Rigan or when she'd implied love for Brady. He closed his eyes and thought of Patrick, in love for a lifetime, only to discover a lie that could destroy it all. Mitch's heart pounded in his chest. Would it change him? He sucked in a harsh breath and sat down. God help him, it would.

Patrick returned to his chair and shielded his eyes with his hands. "You see my dilemma, then. It's not that I don't love Marcy. The woman is my life. Or was. Sometimes I miss her so much that it's a physical ache. But when I found out . . . something inside of me shut down, closed off. I've tried everything I know to open up again, but I can't . . . seem . . . to do it."

"How did you find out?"

A hoarse, bitter laugh erupted from his throat. "I suppose I can blame my own preoccupation with the *Herald*, along with an old friend who came to call. The best man from my wedding, actually, and the best friend I ever had. I'd known he courted Marcy before me, but he'd convinced me it was nothing more than friends. He came into town weeks ago, and I missed a dinner the three of us were supposed to have. Marcy hadn't wanted to go, and now I know why. When I didn't show, he apparently tried to pick up where they left off."

"Did she—"

"No, Marcy's too noble of a woman for that. She would never be unfaithful, at least not physically." He leaned his head on the back of the chair and closed his eyes, his struggle evident in the press of his jaw. "But the emotional betrayal . . . well, let's just say I've been wrestling with the devil."

Mitch sat back too. "Yes, the emotional betrayal. I remember it well. Your daughter turned me inside out seven different ways with her lies and deceit before we were married. But I almost lost her, Patrick, and my life would have never been the same. All because of a near-terminal illness of the soul." He paused to let that sink in.

Patrick's eyelids slitted open. The edge of his mouth flickered, giving Mitch hope. "Are ya planning on telling me now . . . or will I be reading it in tomorrow's paper?"

Mitch smiled. "I think it's something we're both pretty familiar with. It's called pride. And it's steeped in fear. Your daughter lied to me—over and over—and the thought of taking her back seared my pride something fierce. I loved her more than life itself, but she made me feel like a fool, so I cut her off, hurt her, just like you're doing to Marcy. Then the fear told me I could never trust her love again. Only it was a lie from the pit. Charity's love is the most precious gift God has ever given me, aside from his Son, and I trust her with my life."

Patrick blinked several times and looked away. The corners of his mouth twitched. "You trust her?"

"With my life, yes." His tone lightened. "When she's finagling for something she really wants? Not a chance."

Patrick finally smiled, and Mitch felt the knot ease in his stomach. He leaned forward to rest his elbows on the desk. "This is no way to live. We both know that. Your pride has cut you off from everything you hold dear—your family, the woman you love, and God. It's got to stop."

Patrick nodded, his eyes filling with moisture. He put a hand to his brow. "I know. I just don't know how."

"I know, but God does. You have to give it to him, ask his forgiveness, then pray to forgive Marcy. And when you do, Patrick, the Bible will prove itself true. 'The law of Jehovah is perfect, restoring the soul.'"

Patrick stared out the window for a long time before he wiped a sleeve to his eyes. In slow motion, he sat forward to join Mitch with his elbows firmly on the desk. He fisted his hands and lowered his head on top. His voice was rough with emotion. "I will pray, Mitch, because it's the right thing to do. And I will repent. But my heart—" An almost imperceptible trace of a shiver traveled through him. "It's raw, you understand, and I . . . I don't know when . . . how soon I . . . I can love my wife again."

"I understand. But as you and your family have taught me on more than one occasion, prayer is the first step. Taking the hand of God and gripping it like your very life depends on it. Because it does. And he will lead you home . . . to forgiveness, to healing . . . and then to Marcy."

For moments, it seemed, Patrick remained silent, head bent over the strained clasp of his hands. The bulk of his body sat in the shadows, cut off from the sunlight that sliced across his desk, highlighting only a faint touch of silver at his temples. Divided—like him—a soul half in the light, half in the shadows, wrestling with the pull of both. He finally released a struggling breath, and his hands, knuckled white, relaxed. Mitch heard a muffled rasp that might have been a chuckle. "My daughter may be stubborn like her father, but at least she had the wisdom to marry well."

Mitch smiled. "It was God's wisdom and mercy that brought us back together, Patrick, nothing more. But cheer up, my friend, because you're a blessed man. He's about to do the same for you."

# 12

Lizzie popped her head around the corner of Mary's office and smiled. "Hello, stranger. I've missed you."

Mary looked up from her paperwork with blue eyes shadowed with fatigue. A tired smile softened her lips. "I've missed you too."

"Still not feeling well after that bout with the flu?"

"No, I'm better, really. Just not sleeping all that great." She pushed at the stack of invoices on her desk and wrinkled her nose. "Blame it on the new inventory Mr. Harvey insisted I order. There seems to be more to do than hours in the day."

Lizzie strolled in and plunked into a chair. She didn't like the haggard look in her friend's face. She studied her while grating her lip in nervous habit. "I know. You haven't made one of our Bible studies in weeks. We miss you."

"Well, you, anyway."

"What's that supposed to mean? Brady misses you too."

"I doubt that, but that's okay, Lizzie. He's your friend."

Lizzie gave her a thin stare. "He's your friend too, Mary. Did something happen? Between you and Brady? Is that why you're avoiding him?"

Mary laughed and stood to face the window, but not before Lizzie saw her cheeks blot with color. She gazed out at the brick-wall alley, fixed in a stare, as if it were a vibrant summer garden. "Of course not, I just haven't had the time."

"So, ya talking about me?" Millie breezed in as if she owned the place, parking her embroidered silk skirt on the edge of Mary's desk. She crossed her legs and flung her head back in her best Theda Bara imitation, then puckered scarlet lips, the exact shade of her blouse. "Because if you're not, we can start now."

Mary spun around with a crooked smile that seemed edged with relief. "The world doesn't revolve around you, Millie Doza, no matter how much you want it to."

"Sure it does." She flicked a piece of lint off the cuff of her satin sleeve. "You two just don't know it yet."

Lizzie glanced at her watch and jumped to her feet. "Oh, sweet mother of Job, I forgot—I've got to get home."

"Not so fast, Lizzie Lou, what's your hurry? Got a date?" Millie vaulted off the desk to fasten several blood-red nails to her arm.

"No, not a date. Just . . . company."

Theda Bara's brow slithered up. "With Mr. Brady *again?*"

"It's not a date, all right?" Lizzie removed Millie's fingers from her arm with the utmost calm, but she was pretty sure the heat in her cheeks gave her away.

"You're . . . dating Brady?" Mary's tone was as astonished as her face, which bordered on stunned.

Lizzie glared. "It's not a date, Millie, how many times do I have to tell you? My family will be there." She gave Mary a wavering smile. "I've been wanting to tell you, but I haven't had the chance."

Mary sat down, her cheeks as white as the invoices pressed beneath her palms. "You and Brady . . . you're . . . seeing each other?"

Lizzie sighed. "No, Mary, not John. We both know how impossible that is. This is his twin brother, from out of town. His name is Michael, and I actually met him by accident—at Brady's apartment last week."

Mary stared and Millie snickered.

"I'm sorry I didn't tell you, but there's really nothing to it." She ignored Millie and gave Mary a timid smile. "Pretty shocking, though, isn't it? Brady having a twin?"

Mary nodded and took a deep breath.

"We're nothing but friends, honestly. I actually almost feel sorry for Michael. I mean, Brady won't have anything to do with him, which is odd in itself. He says Michael has no faith in God, but he won't reach out to him or show him God's love." Lizzie stood to her feet. "So when Michael said he wanted to go to church with me and my family, what else could I do? Besides, I'm just doing for him what Brady did for me."

"And Brady's okay with that?" Mary rose and gathered papers, her eyes trained on the stack in her hands.

"Well, Brady doesn't know about it exactly, at least not yet. But I plan to tell him on Wednesday." Her chin notched the slightest degree. "But he has no reason to be upset because nothing's going on, nor will it. I promised him when I fall in love, it will be with a man who seeks God."

"You mean . . . like his brother appears to be doing?" Mary's gaze lifted, piercing hers.

Lizzie straightened her shoulders. "No, Mary, Brady has spoiled me. It will have to be a man who not only seeks God but lives for him too. With all of his heart." She turned to go. "I'll see you both tomorrow."

"Lizzie . . ."

She turned, startled by the gravity in Mary's tone.

"I don't have a good feeling. If Brady wants you to stay away, maybe you should."

"I'm guarding my heart, Mary, and girding it with prayer. No man will get through unless it's John Brady himself . . . or the hand of God."

"Please . . . talk to Brady first. Before it goes any further."

Lizzie paused. "Mary, trust me. It's not going anywhere. Just because he looks like Brady doesn't mean he is Brady. There's no one like Brady. I know that."

Mary's eyes burned with intensity. "Do you, Lizzie?"

She blinked. "Yes, Mary, I do. I've been in love with the man since I was thirteen, remember?"

"Yes, I remember. I'm just hoping you do."

❦ ❦

"When am I gonna get muscles like you? We've been working out three times a week, and I still look like a girl." Cluny scowled as he flexed his arm. He slouched in dejection on the wooden bench and scratched his bony chest. It was a sad commentary when compared to the likes of John L. Sullivan, Gentleman Jim Corbett, and Jack Dempsey, all hanging in crooked frames on the dirty plaster wall overhead.

Brady bit back a smile as he studied the boy—scrawny, sweating, and naked from the waist up. His heart went out to the little beggar. Just turned fifteen years old and no height or muscles in sight. Why, at Cluny's age, he and Michael had been close to six foot tall with hair on their chests and faces. It had to be rough on the little guy.

"It'll come, bud, give it time. You're eating plenty, if my grocery bill is any proof, and it's only a matter of time before you shoot up and fill out." Brady leaned close and sniffed. "And if it's any consolation, you smell like a man."

A grin split Cluny's freckled face as he lifted his arm to take a whiff. "Thanks, Brady. I do, don't I? Starting to smell just like you. At least that's better than stinking like Miss Hercules."

Brady wiped his face with the towel draped around his shoulder, then flicked it at Cluny's spindly legs. "Hate to tell ya, bud, but you still reek like her too. If you want to turn the heads of the ladies instead of their stomachs, you're going to have to develop a fondness for baths."

"Yeah, yeah, yeah. I think I'll wait to get my muscles first. No sense in wasting good water until I can tempt them with more."

"You teaching this boy to tempt the ladies, Brady, is that what I'm hearing?" Collin slung an arm around Cluny's shoulders and cocked a brow at Brady.

"Yeah, Collin, spread the word. I'm a devil in disguise."

Collin leaned close to the boy's ear to whisper in a loudly conspiratorial tone. "Don't have to spread such talk, do we, Cluny, my boy? Bet every gal in town already knows, eh?" He tapped the kid on the head with a rolled-up magazine. "Here, brought you something."

Cluny laughed and hunkered down on the bench to leaf through a copy of *The Ring* magazine with Billy, George, and Dave Shade on the cover. "Wow, thanks, Collin, this is swell!"

Brady rolled his neck and flexed his fingers. "Put your money where your mouth is, Collin, and get undressed. I aim to do some punching, and it doesn't matter to me whether it's you or the bag."

"Don't tempt me, John. I'm in a punching mood myself. Butted heads with Faith again last night over quitting her job, so I'm more than ready to take both you and the bag on. But you're in luck. I need you in one piece. Three more jobs came in tonight after you left. Friday deadlines."

Brady groaned. "That's it. We have to hire somebody. We're growing way too fast."

Collin stripped off his shirt and tossed it over the bench. He kicked off his work shoes and dropped his trousers to reveal a faded pair of gym shorts. "Yeah, I know, but I want to hold off as long as possible. Not real anxious to dole out more money to somebody who won't work as hard as we do. I'm having a devil of a time as it is convincing Faith we don't need her paycheck. The more we do ourselves, the more money we can make."

"Can't spend it if you die from exhaustion, you know."

Collin stepped out of his ink-stained pants and flipped them over the bench. He sat down to lace up his boxing shoes and shot a quick glance at Cluny, who was absorbed in the magazine. He lowered his voice and gave Brady a wicked grin. "What are you exhausted for? I'm the one who works all day and then has to go home and try to get his wife pregnant."

Brady wrapped his fingers in a soft cloth before tugging a padded leather glove on with his teeth. "That settles it. I'm going first. I've got some pent-up aggression I gotta release. And since I need *you* at work, I'll have to beat the stuffing out of the bag instead."

"That might be a good idea." Collin stood to his feet, his gaze flicking to Cluny and then back. "Especially after I tell you what I know."

Brady loosened his muscles with two quick swipes of his arms. He nodded for Collin to get into position behind the bag. "So tell me."

"Lizzie's seeing Michael."

Brady was supposed to be the one doing the punching, but he felt like Collin had just landed one square in his gut. "What are you talking about?"

"He was sitting with her at Mass yesterday morning, bold as you please, like one of the family. You can imagine my surprise when he was still around for Marcy's Sunday dinner last night." Collin braced the back of the bag with taut arms, as if preparing for Brady's assault.

Brady bludgeoned the bag with several blows that slammed hard against Collin's chest, knocking the wind out of him. "I'm going to beat him to a bloody pulp."

"Yeah, I'm sure you feel like it," Collin whispered, still gasping for air, "but you and I both know that's not an option. You need to make amends and let it go. You're like a brother to me, John, but I gotta tell you—she has a right to see whoever she wants."

"Not him."

"Especially him. You better face up to it, ol' buddy. Lizzie's in love with someone she can't have, and he's as close to John Brady as she's likely to get."

The bag hammered Collin's jaw without mercy for fifteen seconds of bullet-fire pummeling. Brady's breath was ragged when he stopped. "He's the farthest thing there is from me. He's a liar and a manipulator who has as much use for God as he does for Lizzie. He's using her to get to me. I'm telling you, Collin, he's no good for her."

Collin stepped away from the bag to momentarily massage his jaw. "Well, no offense, John, but lately you haven't exactly been good for her, either. And what do you mean, he's using her? Do you really think so low of your own flesh and blood?"

"Lower," he hissed, then followed it with a curse that sounded so foreign to his own ears, heat shot up the back of his neck. "I pray to God he goes back to the devil where he belongs."

Collin arched a brow. "I'm not sure, but I'm guessing prayers don't rise quite as well when anchored by a curse." He butted his torso hard against the bag from his waist to his shoulders, obviously steeling himself against his partner's wrath. "I could be wrong, of course, but it's just an offhanded guess."

"Shut up, Collin, this isn't funny."

Collin stepped away from the bag. "No, John, I don't think it is. Actually, I think it's pretty sad. That the man who emulates Christ to me more than anyone alive is eaten up with hate for his own brother."

Few people in his life had ever been able to call John Brady on sin. At least the sins they could see. The effect of Collin's words stunned him like a blow to the head. He sagged against the bag and closed his eyes to ward off the wetness stinging his eyelids. Shame washed over him at the touch of Collin's grip on his shoulder, and his voice, low and intense, pierced him through.

"John, you were the one who taught me how to forgive,

remember? Years ago, when my own bitterness toward my mother rivaled yours for Michael? Nobody knows how to let go and give it to God better than you. Do it—for my sake as well as yours. I love you too much to see you like this."

"I thought I had, Collin. I thought I had."

"That was before Lizzie, my friend. If you truly believe he's a threat to her, talk to her, tell her why. Then pray for her and leave it in God's hands. But first you have to deal with your hate for Michael, or it will hinder your prayers like it's hindered your life." He looped an arm around Brady's shoulder and gave him a quick squeeze. "If I'm not mistaken, I believe that may have been the first lesson I was privileged to learn in John Brady's School of Hard Knocks."

Brady wiped the sweat from his forehead with the side of his arm. "Yeah, well, I was pretty sure it was going to come back and haunt me one day, and I was right. Even so, you're a good friend, Collin. I'm not sure I deserve you."

Collin grinned. "Oh, you deserve me all right, ol' buddy. Give me those gloves and I'll show ya just how much. And when I'm done pulverizing you like you did me, we'll head back to your place and deal with this foul stench in your life." He leaned toward Brady and wrinkled his nose, sniffing the air. "Both of 'em."

❧ ❧

God help her, if Mitch grunted one more time, Marcy was going to jump out of her skin. She sat on the edge of a school-style wooden bench in the large, sterile waiting room, knuckles knotted in her lap while he paced back and forth like the wipers on Patrick's new Model T. It was bad enough Charity had gone into labor early—she was not quite eight and a half months—but a muscle twitched at the back of Marcy's eye every time Mitch lurched to and fro in short, spasmodic motion. Her eyes tracked him as he made another pass, his back stiff and his throat emitting a grinding noise with each annoying stride.

She shot to her feet. "For heaven's sake, Mitch, can't you sit down?"

Lizzie looked up from her book while Faith touched Marcy's arm. "Mother, why don't we get some fresh air?"

Mitch grunted, his hand knuckle-deep in a pass through his short, cropped hair. "What's taking so blasted long?"

The look of fear in his eyes soured Marcy's stomach with guilt. She moved to embrace him in a hug, the top of her head barely reaching the midway point of his chest. "Mitch, forgive me, please. I'm on edge just like you. This is your wife and your baby, I know, but this is my daughter and my first grandchild. And so help me, God, I do believe if those nurses don't part with some information soon, I may just gouge out an eye or two." She patted his arm and forced a smile. "And trust me, they won't be mine."

He exhaled and kissed the top of her head. "I'll tell you what—I'll hold 'em down."

Her laughter melted into a sigh. She dropped onto the bench and patted Faith's hand. "Thanks for the offer, but wild horses the size of Mitch Dennehy couldn't drag me out of here right now. What time is it?"

Lizzie turned a page of her book, never missing a beat. "Eight fifteen."

"Mother, I'm hungry," Katie moaned. Tangled blond hair sprawled down the sides of her white middy blouse as she slumped low on the railway benches that bordered the room. Her navy pleated skirt draped over knees stretched so wide, you could see her white sateen bloomers.

"Katie Rose, for mercy's sake, ladies don't sit like that, for the hundredth time. And you can't be hungry. Lizzie said you ate like a fiend when she took you to Woolworth's." She eyed Steven with suspicion. "Please tell me you're reading the book due for your report on Friday and not that silly magic handbook."

Color merged with the freckles in his cheeks. "I left it at school. On accident."

Marcy shook her head and blew out a noisy puff. She put a palm to her forehead. "For the love of all that is good, where in the world is your father?"

Mitch ground to a halt. "You let him know, didn't you?"

She peeked out beneath the edge of her hand. "I assumed you did."

"No, I didn't," he groaned. "I just made a dash for the door because I thought you two would talk."

She released a slow, heavy breath. "No, we didn't. I left a note for him at home, of course, but he's probably still at work. Lizzie, would you mind giving him a call, please? I saw a phone in the hall. I'm sure he'd want to be here." She glanced at Faith. "Did you talk to Collin?"

"No, I came right here when you called, but I left a message at Clancy's Gym. He's working out with Brady tonight. I should call again, though. I'll bet he didn't get it."

Mitch resumed his roaming. "How long can it possibly take to have a baby?"

"A lot longer than eight hours, most likely," Marcy said with a crooked smile, "especially for the first one. Keep in mind that she's been in labor since noon when Mr. McKenzie and I brought her in. I swear, I was so grateful to see his car in the driveway, I almost kissed his neck." She wrinkled her nose. "I just hope he didn't miss his meeting."

Mitch came to a standstill. His blue eyes darkened to gray. "I should have been the one taking her to the hospital, not some lecherous neighbor who's always gawking at your daughters."

"Bruce McKenzie is not lecherous, Mitch Dennehy, and well you know it. For pity's sake, the poor man's a widow, so naturally he perks up when he sees a pretty girl. Besides, I already told you that Charity refused to let me call because she didn't want to put *you* through another episode of false labor. And quite frankly, I saw no reason to worry anyone. Her contractions have been steady and slow, and I know how long it can take. And you know how stubborn she is."

He jerked the tie loose from his neck with renewed anxiety. A button from his now disheveled shirt came along with it, pinging against the wall. It skittered across the black-and-white linoleum floor, spinning like a top.

Marcy arched a brow. "And she certainly knows how crazed you can be when it comes to this baby."

Lizzie breezed back in and bussed her mother's cheek. "Father's on his way. He's coming from the *Herald*."

Marcy sighed. "Naturally."

Lizzie squinted at Mitch. "Did you know you're missing a button?"

With a soft whoosh, the steel double doors flew open. They ricocheted off antiseptic-white walls with a loud bang. A rush of questionable air infused the stuffy waiting room.

"Do we have a baby yet?"

Collin and Brady were a matched set—hair rumpled and matted from sweat. They wore matching work shirts that looked like they'd been doused with a hose.

"Where have you been? I left the message with Clancy hours ago." Faith hurried over, stopping short of a hug.

Collin pushed the hair from his eyes with the back of his hand. It spiked in a stiff, wet peak. "Sorry, but Clancy forgot until we arrived at Brady's. But at least he called there, and here we are. A bit ripe, but accounted for. How's Charity?"

"No news yet," Lizzie said, glancing up at Brady. She stared at his hard-muscled chest, now sporting a sheen of sweat above several neglected buttons, and heat warmed her cheeks. She quickly looked away, embarrassed that even the overly musky scent of this man did not offend her. "We think she's fine, but we don't really know. Haven't seen a nurse in over two hours."

"Sorry we stink, Lizzie, but men don't smell real good when they work out, you know." Cluny butted through with a grin.

Lizzie smiled. "Yes, I know."

He suddenly spied Katie asleep in the chair and wriggled his brows. "Mmmm . . . Sleeping Beauty. Maybe I'll wake her up." He disappeared with a gleam of trouble in his eyes.

"Beth, can we talk?"

She turned, suddenly shy. "Sure, Brady. Outside in the hall?"

He nodded and held the door while she sidled through. She made a beeline for a bench at the other end, and he followed, settling on the far side. He seemed on edge, his back stiff against the wall and muscles knotted with tension. "There something you want to tell me, Beth?"

She studied his profile, enamored as always with the clean, strong cut of his jaw. He had sculpted cheekbones that could have been chiseled in marble. Like the busts of Greek gods she had seen in the Museum of Fine Art. His long, dark lashes, which never failed to amaze her, tapered from lids that remained half-closed, underscoring his obviously sullen mood.

She sighed. "What do you mean?"

He turned in slow motion, a Greek god with heat in his eyes. "I mean the promise you broke. To stay away from my brother."

"I'm not seeing your brother."

"Collin says otherwise."

She rose up high on the bench. "We took him to church a couple of times, yes, and sometimes he stays for dinner. That doesn't exactly qualify as 'seeing him,' you know. And Collin has a big mouth."

"Collin's my friend. Which at the moment, I'm not sure I can say about you."

Lizzie folded her arms and wrinkled her nose. Suddenly he didn't smell so good. "For the third time, I am not seeing your brother. And I'm supposed to say no when someone asks to go to church?"

"If it's him, yes. He's using you, Beth, plain and simple."

Heat washed into her cheeks that had nothing to do with the fact he'd moved close, barely inches from where she sat. She shot to her feet. "How dare you! The only one who's using me is you. Using my friendship as an excuse so you don't have to deal with bitterness toward your brother. For pity's sake, he's reaching out—to God and to me. And if you think I'm going to let you badger me into giving him the cold shoulder—"

He rose to loom over her, his lips stiff in a hard line. "He wants more than a shoulder, Beth, guaranteed. I'm warning you for the last time—stay away from him."

"*Warning* me?"

He blew out a strained breath and took her hand in his. "I'm asking you."

She flung his hand away, unwilling to be placated this time. "More than a shoulder? Not every man wrestles with the same demons as you, John Brady. And so what if your brother wants more? Maybe I should too. God knows it's probably the closest I'll come to being courted by a Brady."

She shoved him out of the way and started for the door.

"Beth, wait!" He latched onto her arm and forced her to turn. "I'm sorry. I handled that badly. But I was angry. Hurt. You promised you would stay away from him."

"No, Brady, I promised I would fall in love with a man who seeks God. But I'll qualify that right now, for your own peace of mind. I'm looking for a man who loves God with all of his heart and lives for him too. That's a pretty tall order. And unless you're looking to propose, I suggest you stop acting like a jealous suitor and more like my friend. And a brother to Michael." She removed his hand from her arm. "Have a little trust, will you? In God, if not in me?"

He pushed his hands in his pocket and nodded. "You're

right." He paused, sucking in a deep breath. "You're growing up, Elizabeth."

"Thanks for noticing."

The double door swung open, and Cluny darted through. Brady pulled Beth from the path of the door. "Take it easy, bud, you almost clobbered Beth."

"Sorry, Lizzie. Hey, Brady, do you have some change? I saw Life Savers in the vending machine in the lobby." He winked. "Katie's favorite."

Brady dug in his pocket and tossed him a quarter. "Bribery won't work, you know."

Cluny snatched it midair with a grin. "Collin says it will. Thanks!" He disappeared.

Lizzie lifted a brow. "For your information, John Brady, bribery can work. *If* the person you're bribing wants something badly enough." She turned on her heel and pushed through the door, skewing him with a look. "Maybe you should try it sometime."

"Come on, Katie, I'll buy you a roll of Life Savers. Look, I have enough for five rolls."

She folded her arms. "What do I have to do?"

"Nothing, just go with me to the lobby."

Her gaze thinned. "We'll come right back?"

He slanted a narrow hip and blew the hair out of his eyes. "No, I'm gonna kidnap you. What d'ya think? Of course we'll come right back."

She thought about it and then slowly rose to her feet. "You're lucky I like Life Savers," she muttered under her breath.

He grinned. "I am, aren't I?" He turned on his heel and pushed through the doors, waiting until she followed. He led her down the hall to the front of the hospital where a beady-eyed watchman stood guard at a curved marble desk. The lobby was dim and deserted at this time of night, lit only by a glass-domed chandelier hung low over the door. Cluny nodded to the guard before depositing his money into the machine. He gave Katie a sideways glance. "Life Savers or gum?"

"Did you hear me say anything about gum?"

He grinned and yanked on the lever. "You're a pistol, Katie Rose. Life Savers it is." A roll thudded into the open slot while change clinked into the coin return. He retrieved the candy and dropped it in her waiting hand.

She arched a brow, hand still extended. "I believe you said five."

He pulled his change from the return and tossed it in the air. "Nope, said I'd buy you *one*, but had enough for five."

She jiggled the roll in her hand. "I want five."

He grinned. "Kind of hoping you'd say that."

"You were?"

"Yes, ma'am, I was. And I would dearly love to give you five."

"You would?"

"For a price."

"A price?"

"What, are you a parrot?" He redeposited his money and repeated the procedure until four rolls of gold and blue candy gleamed in his palm. She reached and he jerked them away, slipping them into his pocket with an annoying grin. "Yes, ma'am, a price. Kind of an experiment."

She folded her arms and watched through slitted eyes as he opened a roll and popped one in his mouth. He held another in the air, taunting her. "Mmmm . . . minty."

She stared, jaws clamped tight as he rotated the little white circle an inch from her nose. She could smell the sweet scent of peppermint when he gently prodded it against the tight crack of her lips. Seconds seemed like an eternity before she finally snatched it with her teeth, almost taking his finger in the process. He jerked away.

She smiled. "A bit twitchy, are we?"

"No more than usual when you're around." He sucked on his finger as if she'd bitten clean through. "Do we have a deal?"

"What kind of experiment?"

He turned and strolled nonchalantly toward the waiting room, hands jiggling in his pockets as he ignored her question.

She bounded after him. "I-said, what-kind-of-experiment?" she demanded, each word ground through clenched teeth.

The annoyance in her tone obviously amused him. He stopped and chuckled, giving her a sideways glance. "A science experiment. To see if being nice would crack your face. You say something nice to me, I say something nice to you. What do ya think?"

She shot him a glare that only made him grin. He reached into his pocket to produce the four additional rolls of Life Savers and bounced them in his hand.

"So, you game? Think you can say something nice to me?"

She tried to leave, but he blocked her with a hand to her arm and a lift of his brow. "One measly compliment, Katie Rose, and if Life Savers were money, you'd be a wealthy woman."

She studied him with a critical eye, deciding for the hundredth time that Cluny McGee was a cocky little brat who grated on her nerves. He had way too much confidence for a boy with a sunken chest and arms no bigger than a willow twig, and enough freckles to make you lose your train of thought. Sweet saints, she hated freckles! Her eyes shifted to the glittering treasure in his hands, shimmering like gold as he rolled them in his palm. Her gaze flicked up to the piercing blue eyes that glinted as if they could read her mind. She firmed her stance and lifted her chin. "One-measly-compliment," she whispered, the very thought causing her stomach to turn. "Providing I can come up with anything. You're no prize, you know."

A slow grin traveled his lips. He pocketed the candy with the same unwavering confidence that always got on her nerves.

He crossed his arms and gave her a hard, penetrating stare. "Go ahead, then. Give it your best shot. And it's gotta be sincere."

Her forehead puckered as she flicked a strand of hair over her shoulder. "Ask for the moon, why don't you?"

The corners of his mouth flickered before his eyes narrowed. "So, fake it."

She huffed out a sigh that sounded more like a groan and crossed her arms. Biting her lip, she assessed him through a critical eye, disregarding the messy, straw-colored hair that was almost white and the annoying freckles splattered across his face like mud shot. Her gaze shifted to his eyes and suddenly locked, drawn into their pale blue depths. She shivered and looked away, irritation nettling her nerves.

"You're cocky and obnoxious and I flat out don't like you. But . . ." She swallowed hard to dispel the pride in her throat. "I suppose you have nice eyes." She took a step back and thrust out her hand.

He grinned, causing those very eyes to mock her. With a casual sweep in his pocket, he unearthed the prize for her humiliation and plopped them in her open palm. Without another word, he turned and ambled down the hall.

A swell of irritation overtook her, and she grabbed his arm. "Wait, aren't you going to say something nice about me?"

He turned and grinned, the victory in those blue eyes as sure as the cocky tilt of his chin. "Sorry, Katie Rose. Ain't enough candy in the world."

Katie blinked. Then cut loose with a kick in his shin that nearly doubled him at the knees.

"Katie Rose? What the devil are you doing?" Patrick could hardly believe his own eyes. Was the dim lighting of the hall playing tricks, or had he just seen his eleven-year-old daughter haul off and kick Cluny? Sweet heaven, but she was a bully!

Even in the dark, she turned more shades of red than he'd

ever seen on her face before, and several more when the candy in her hand spilled to the floor. Cluny scooped them up faster than Patrick could blink and handed them back to Katie, who stood still as a rock.

"Hello, Mr. O'Connor, it's nice to see you again." He pumped Patrick's hand with all the ease of a politician, not a trace of embarrassment to be found on his face. "Not much has happened, far as we know. Charity's been here since noon, but it's really Mitch who looks like he should be admitted."

Patrick nodded, as astounded as Katie. "Thank you, Cluny, for the update. How's your leg?"

"Fine, sir. At least better than your daughter's pride." He grinned and swung out his arm, allowing them to go before him.

Patrick latched a hand to Katie's neck and led her down the hall, shooting a quick glance over his shoulder at the innocent look on Cluny's face. A suspicion churned in his gut that for once his daughter might not bear the brunt of the blame. "Keep an eye on that one, Katie Rose," he muttered under his breath, "I think he could be trouble."

"Father!" Faith rushed to give him a hug, and Marcy's stomach jumped as always these days, whenever Patrick entered the room. He looked tired, his lids noticeably heavy over clear, gray eyes that still shone with a twinkle despite the fatigue in his face. There was a smattering of gray at the temple of his dark hair that only served to heighten his rugged good looks. Whether he knew it or not, the man still turned many a head. But none more than hers, especially lately, when he was so far out of reach. She smoothed out her skirt with hands far too sweaty for a forty-three-year-old grandmother, and watched as he cradled his girls, one under each arm. Something tugged at her heart. He was a wonderful father and would make an even better grandpa.

"So, what's the progress, eh?" He released the girls and bent to give her a stiff kiss, then turned quickly to shake Mitch's hand. "It's about time you see what it's like with kids underfoot. How's Charity?"

"A nurse stuck her head out a few hours ago. Apparently our girl was getting a tad testy then, which was supposed to be a good sign, she said. I'd hoped we were getting close."

Patrick grinned. "Testy, eh? I believe that's *your* trademark, isn't it, Mitch? How you holding up?"

"Well, I think Marcy may be close to having Collin hogtie and gag me with all the pacing and groaning I've been doing."

Patrick gave Marcy the perfunctory smile and took a seat on the bench across the way. His eyes flicked to hers. "A wee bit nervous, are we, Mrs. O'Connor? How's it feel to be on this side of the wall?"

Her smile was cautious but her gaze was not. "Worse, actually. At least in there, I knew what was happening. Out here, I'm shut out from someone I love, not knowing what's going on when they need me the most." She fought back a tremor with a lift of her chin. "That's an awful thing, you know."

She saw a glimmer of grief in his eyes, and the muscles seized in her chest. For months he'd been nothing but a cold, steel wall, immune to her love. No caring, no grief. Only anger and ice. Her pulse began to race. *Oh, God, are you bringing my husband back?*

He looked away and tapped his palms on his legs, then rose to his feet. "So, Collin, you and Faith plan on putting us through this exercise anytime soon?"

Collin shot him a guarded look from where he lounged, back against the wall. "Don't look at me, Patrick, it's your daughter gumming up the works."

Faith's mouth dropped open. "How can you say that? I want a baby as much as you."

"No, you *say* you want a baby as much as me, but you're not focused on it."

"What?"

Brady nudged, keeping his voice low. "Easy . . ."

"You're too focused on that silly job of yours."

Faith shot to her feet. "*Silly job?*"

"Okay, maybe not silly, but it's certainly not helping. You come home tired and spent, having given your all five days a week. That can't be good for the process, you know."

"So now it's a 'process'? I'm nothing more than a means to an end?"

Patrick clamped a hand to Faith's arm and sat her back down on the bench. He tucked her firmly to his side with a chuckle meant to diffuse the tension. "Looks like I'm going to have to fire you, darlin', if I want more grandchildren."

"Not a bad idea," Collin muttered, ignoring Brady's jab.

Patrick patted Faith's shoulder and kissed her head. "I think everyone's a bit tired, given the emotional strain of the day." He looked around. "Where's Sean?"

Marcy rose and buffed her arms. "Home in bed, sick. He was here most of the afternoon, but he was up all night with stomach problems, so I told him to go home."

"Anybody think to call Emma?" Patrick asked.

Faith and Marcy exchanged blank looks. "Oh dear. And it's too late now. With her schedule at the store, she's in bed by nine." Marcy eyed Steven, prone and snoring on a bench next to Katie, who was now yawning in Cluny's face. "Patrick, maybe you need to take the children home. It could be late."

Collin jumped up. "No, you stay. Brady and I will take them home, then I'll come right ba—"

"Mr. Dennehy?"

Mitch jerked around like he'd been shot. "Do we have a baby?"

"Yes, sir, a healthy baby girl."

"And my wife?"

The silence was deafening as the nurse scanned the anxious

faces before her. "She seems to be fine, Mr. Dennehy. She's still asleep, of course."

Air drained out of lungs collectively, and then Mitch hoisted Marcy high in the air. His laughter echoed in the sterile room. "Sweet God in heaven, thank you!"

Marcy giggled and squeezed him tightly. "Congratulations, Mitch. I'm so happy for you both."

He spun around. "When can I see her? Both of them?"

The nurse smiled. "It will be awhile yet, Mr. Dennehy, but we'll call you."

"Hey, I'm an aunt!" Katie exclaimed. "What are you going to call her?"

"Hope Marceline," Mitch said, his voice gruff with emotion. "The first name in honor of Faith's twin who was lost to polio and . . ." His gaze softened as it lighted on Marcy, "the second for a woman we happen to think is the perfect mother."

Marcy's hand flew to her mouth. Tears swam in her eyes. "Oh, Mitch!"

She jolted as Patrick touched her arm. "A beautiful name, Mitch. And no truer words."

Marcy shivered with joy, searching his face. "We're grandparents, my love. A whole new world awaits."

He nodded, his eyes as misty as hers. "It does at that."

Lizzie squealed and gave Mitch a hug. "Oh, Mitch, a little girl! I'm so jealous. I can't wait to have my own."

Patrick cleared his throat. "You can wait, darlin', trust me. All in good time."

Collin slapped Mitch on the back. "Nice going, Dennehy. But it looks like I still have a shot at the first boy."

"Mr. Dennehy?"

A sea of eyes singed the face of the nurse at the door. She hoisted her chin with a touch of rose in her cheeks. "I'm afraid we were a bit premature. You have a son."

Mitch blinked. "You mean instead of a daughter?"

"No, I mean in addition to. You have twins."

❦ ❦

Marcy stole a sideways peek as Patrick lifted Katie from the front seat. He hefted her high in his arms with a grunt, bestowing a gentle kiss to her forehead while she slumped against his chest. The poor thing had been so keyed up, she'd chattered most of the way home. Between her and Lizzie, Marcy hadn't been able to get a word in edgewise. And thank God, she thought to herself. The clip of her heart had rivaled the adrenaline pace of Katie's banter, and Marcy was more than grateful for the buffer provided.

She watched him circle around, undaunted by the dead weight in his arms, despite the fatigue she knew he must be feeling. She swallowed a deep breath and slipped out of the car, unlatching the back door to jostle Steven's arm. "Come on, son, we're home." He didn't move and she tugged, finally shifting him to his feet. He towered over her by a foot, but she braced his back with her small frame and followed Patrick and Lizzie into the house and up the stairs, each disappearing into the appropriate rooms.

She made quick work of Steven, stripping off his shoes and clothes in no time, then wrestled a clean T-shirt over his head.

"Did Charity have the baby?" Sean's voice sounded groggy from across the room.

"Oh yes! Two as a matter of fact, a boy and a girl."

"No kidding! Twins? Is she okay?"

Marcy tucked the sheet in around Steven's bed. "Yes, everyone's doing fine, even Mitch. How are you feeling?"

"The stomach's still bubbling some, but better. At least I got some sleep."

She bent to kiss his forehead. "No fever, that's good. Probably just a quick bug. I'd think about sleeping in tomorrow."

"Can't. Too much to do."

She sighed and tucked in his sheet. "We'll see. Good night."

She closed the door and glanced down the hall. Her bedroom was dark. Was Patrick inside? She pressed a calming hand to her stomach. Good heavens, she was acting like a love-struck school girl! She chewed on her lip and tiptoed into Katie and Lizzie's room to give them a kiss. Both girls were already sound asleep. Clothes and shoes littered the floor. A faint smile tilted her lips. Oh, to sleep like that again!

Her smile faded. She had once. Before Sam O'Rourke came to call.

She shut their door and paused, her fingers hovering on the knob. Was that a light on downstairs? Her stomach tightened. No . . . please, he wasn't . . .

Her throat constricted as she moved to the landing, and her eyes spanned wide at the light streaming from the parlor. In a catch of her heart, she skittered down the steps like a little girl at Christmas, hands shaking when she finally reached the door. She bit her lip, suddenly shy. "It's almost midnight, Patrick. You must be exhausted. Are you . . . will you . . . come to bed?"

He looked up from his paper, eyes limp pools of exhaustion. In fact, everything about him bespoke fatigue—heavy lids, sagging cheeks, drooping shoulders. As if he hadn't slept in days. Or weeks. A mere husk of a man, except for one thing: the hard line of his jaw, now shadowed with a day's growth of beard. He continued reading. "Not for a while. You'll probably be asleep when I come up for my things."

She listed against the door. "Y-you're leaving?"

He glanced up. "You know that."

"But I thought . . . the babies . . . you and I . . ."

He turned the page, his tone as steeled as his jaw. "Go to bed, Marcy. You need sleep."

She blinked, unable to fathom the depth of his coldness. She had done as he asked, left him alone for weeks on end. To sort out his thoughts and give him time. She had cried out to God and dealt with his rejection, praying with Mrs. Gerson to let it all go. "Keep your heart free of bitterness," Christa had warned. And she had. Obedient to a fault, weeping and forgiving until she thought she would die. And now . . . he wanted her to *go*?

Something deep inside snapped, defying all reason. With a low groan, she raised her fist and flew across the room, bludgeoning him with her rage. He leapt to his feet to ward her off, but she only struck harder, too blinded by tears to see the look on his face. "You want to leave? Well, then, go! And don't come back!"

He gripped her wrists and glanced at the door. "Stop it!" he hissed, "You'll wake the children."

"Pretense," she screamed, thrashing against his hold, "that's all you care about. Well, I won't live with it anymore, do you hear?"

He forced her to the sofa and she bit his hand. He recoiled in shock, his anger congealing into cold fury. "Really? Well, I've lived with it for over twenty-six years."

For endless seconds, she couldn't breathe. She started to shake, but forced her chin up in cold defiance. "No," she whispered, her voice as steely as his. "That would be the next twenty-six." She rose and turned her back then—on him and their marriage—moving to the door like someone he couldn't possibly know. A stranger with head high and back stiff, hardened by the very bitterness she'd fought so hard to avoid. With cold deliberation, she mounted the steps, making her way to the room they no longer shared. In an effort to purge herself of him altogether, she collapsed on her bed, seeking solace in tears. She slammed her fist to his pillow.

"I hate you!" she sobbed.

*If I regard iniquity in my heart, the Lord will not hear me.*

"I don't care!" She rose up on the bed, her face streaked with tears and her body shuddering with pain. "Over and over I've tried, and I can't bear it anymore."

*Love . . . beareth all things, believeth all things, hopeth all things, endureth all things . . .*

"No! I have endured, for almost two and half months now, and forgiven until I'm blue in the face. How many times can one person forgive?"

Silence pounded in her ears.

*Seventy times seven.*

Comprehension seared the air from her throat. Seventy times seven. *God, no, please . . .*

She tried to breathe, but the air was too thick, panting from her lips in a faint, feeble rasp. She pressed a hand to her chest, tight with the burden of decision. A choice. To lay down her pride and forgive. Or to embrace the hurt and strike back. Obedience or sin. She squeezed her eyes shut, torn by the prompting of his Spirit and the pull of her flesh. *Oh, God, I can't! Help me, please . . .*

Thoughts pelted her brain. His cruelty. His indifference. His rejection.

She put her palms to her ears, desperate to shut out the thoughts.

"No! I choose to forgive."

Gasping for air, she staggered from the bed, her mind set on a course that would cost her her pride. She groped for the light, then shielded her eyes from the glare, lips moving in silent prayer. Her pulse raced while she gathered his things, a clean shirt, pressed trousers, and a favorite tie. She bundled them in her arms. The scent of him rose, sweet to her senses, and her heart flooded with hope, purging the grief he had caused.

"Oh, God, help me . . . ," she whispered. Her breathing became deeper, unrestricted as she moved to the bureau. By God, he would have clean socks and underwear.

And she would have a clean heart.

Her pulse beat steady and strong as she padded down the stairs, no longer afraid of the light in the hall or the stranger in the parlor. She drew in a deep breath.

*Perfect love casts out fear.*

He seemed so haggard as she entered the room, and her heart longed to hold him. Instead, she placed his things on the couch, grieved at the anger she still saw in his eyes. She looked away, unable to bear it.

"Forgive me, Patrick, for losing my temper. I love you . . . and I will forever." She moved to the door, suddenly spent, pausing only to speak over her shoulder. "Good night, my love. Please get some sleep."

And without another word, she returned to their room and silently dressed for bed. When she laid her head on the pillow, it wasn't to sleep. No, it was first to pray, and then to weep. Because she knew, all too well. *The prayer of a righteous man availeth much.*

He stared at the empty door, unable to comprehend the love he'd just seen. His pulse droned in his ears as he slumped in the chair, body buzzing and mind numb.

She'd forgiven in the face of her anger. He dropped his head in his hands.

In total obedience to God. Unlike him. And total love for the man who spurned her.

Wetness welled in his eyes and he choked on a sob. An aching realization stabbed within, but its pain was kind, unlike the agony of guilt. Conviction lifted the blindness from his eyes, and he knew he had failed. He'd turned his back on God as well as his wife. And for what? Wounded pride that had yielded nothing but his demise. And hers.

Two souls for the price of one sin.

He heaved with pain, barely able to breathe. His mind grappled for the verse Mitch had given him. He closed his eyes and it suddenly pierced his thoughts, allowing a sliver of light to shatter the darkness.

*The law of Jehovah is perfect, restoring the soul.*

Oh, God, the law. To forgive. Could he really do it?

He opened his eyes in shock, revelation prickling his spine.

*The law is perfect.* Like God's love, Patrick thought, and hope surged in his chest.

He thought of Marcy, and for the first time in weeks, he could see her clearly, unscathed by his anger. A woman, pure of heart and strong of character, loving God while loving him. He thought of the damage he'd done, and his heart fisted in grief. *Oh, God, forgive me—I don't deserve her.*

He leapt to his feet, sin no longer weighting him down, and bounded the steps, two at a time. The hall was dark, but his step was light, and he prayed for mercy as never before. He neared their room and could hear her weeping, muffled and wrenching his heart like it should. He stopped in the doorway, staggered by what he'd done, and watched as their bed shivered with her grief. She didn't hear him until he knelt by her side, and when he spoke, she jerked in surprise.

"Marcy . . ."

The hitch of her breath was harsh in the dark.

He pressed a hand to her wet cheek, sick inside at the pain he'd caused. "God knows I don't deserve it, but can you . . . will you . . . forgive me for being a fool?"

His heart stopped when she didn't move or blink, seconds of agony as she stared, motionless in the dark. And then with a pitiful cry, she lunged into his arms, landing them both on the floor.

"Oh, Patrick," she sobbed.

He crushed her to him, and his voice broke. "I love you, Marcy, and I swear, I will never hurt you like this again."

He picked her up and laid her on their bed, desperate to cradle her in his arms. Neither spoke for a long while, but their silence whispered volumes. He breathed in the clean scent of her, and a rush of love overtook him. He held her face in his hands. "I don't deserve you, Marceline, but as God is my witness, I will spend the rest of my life trying to come close."

Wetness shimmered in her eyes. She kissed his mouth, softly, gently, stroking his face with the tips of her fingers. "I love you, Patrick, with all of my heart. And as God is my witness, you are the first man I have ever really loved, and you will be the last. I thought I loved Sam when I married you, it's true, but I was wrong. You taught me what real love is—with your kindness, your caring . . . your commitment. From the day I became your wife, I have felt nothing but safe and whole and cherished."

He groaned and pulled her close, his voice raspy with regret. "Until recently."

He felt her smile in the crook of his neck. "Yes, until recently. But even this, my love, has served us well. Losing you, Patrick—if only for two and half months—forced me into the arms of God in a way I'd forgotten. Sometimes, in the midst of my love for you, I tend to forget that he is my source, not you." She pulled away to search his eyes. "I've missed you, Patrick. Life is not the same without you." Her lips curved softly. "And I need my sleep."

He kissed her again, his husky groan muffled against her mouth. "Explain to me what that is, will ya, darlin'? I seem to have a lapse of memory."

She feathered his throat with soft, lingering kisses. "Really? I would have thought cold, cramped leather would have been the perfect bedding for a thick-skinned Irishman like you."

He skimmed his hand down the curve of her hip until flannel gave way to skin. Her soft moan matched his as his kisses became urgent. "No, darlin', not for sleeping . . . or otherwise." The silky warmth of her skin against his lips caused him to shudder. "And God knows how I've missed you, Marceline. And 'otherwise.'"

## 13

Brady squinted and held his breath. Father Mac's shot glided high in the air, as if in slow motion, finally arcing into the basket with a soft, clean swish. As gentle as if carried on the wings of an angel. A groan erupted from Brady's throat. "That was nothing short of divine intervention."

Father Mac scooped up the ball and lifted a brow. "Are you suggesting that there was more than pure skill involved? Nobody likes a sore loser, John."

Brady wiped the sweat from his forehead with the sleeve of his T-shirt and grinned. "What I'm suggesting is that you've been praying and practicing . . . in that order . . . since the last time I took you out. I thought priests weren't supposed to dally with pride."

Father Mac laughed and swabbed his face with a handkerchief as he headed for the rectory, basketball hooked tightly under his arm. "Consider it an object lesson. Pride goeth before the fall. My pride, your fall." He butted the back door open and turned. A glint of teasing shone in his brown eyes. "Can I nurse your wounds with some lemonade? Mrs. Clary just made a fresh pitcher."

"Sure." Brady followed Matt into the rectory kitchen where Mrs. Clary was enjoying a glass of lemonade with company. At the sight of the priest, she bounded to her feet with a warm smile on her round, dimpled face. She bustled to the china cabinet to retrieve two glasses, then glanced over her shoulder. "So, who won?"

"I believe I taught this young man a valuable lesson in sportsmanship," Father Mac said. He nodded at Mrs. Clary's guest. "And how are you today, Miss Ramona?"

A tiny, wizened woman smiled back, her dyed black hair twisted back in a severe bun. Piercing black eyes glittered with interest as she nodded. "Excellent, Father. The girls are preparing for our best recital ever." Her gaze flicked to Brady. "You are planning on coming, aren't you, Brady? My granddaughter would be so disappointed if you didn't."

Sweat that had nothing to do with basketball began to bead at the back of his neck. He grinned and reached for one of two glasses Mrs. Clary had just poured, ignoring the smug smile on Father Mac's face. "Wouldn't miss it. Truth be told, it's the only culture I get."

Father Mac took a quick gulp of lemonade and slapped Brady on the back. "Well, ladies, if you'll excuse us, John and I will be in my study discussing his rather sad performance on the basketball court today. Thank you for the lemonade, Mrs. Clary."

"My pleasure, Father."

"It's so good of you sharing time with your flock, Father Mac," Miss Ramona observed.

"'Shearing time' is more like it," Brady mumbled, following Matt to the door.

Father Mac flashed a quick smile in the ladies' direction before giving Brady a narrow gaze. "I heard that. I won fair and square, and we both know it."

Father Mac pushed the study door open and ambled to his desk, motioning for Brady to sit down. He took a sip of lemonade and propped his feet up. He eyed Brady over the rim of his glass. "So, how are you doing today? Judging from your game, I'd say not too good. I'm a big believer in prayer, but even prayer can't take all the credit for my win today. You're off your game and you look tired. Why?"

Brady's lips twisted. "Maybe I was just showing you a little mercy, letting you win. Ever think of that?"

Father Mac studied him with a penetrating gaze. "Maybe. But I don't think so."

Brady exhaled and sank back into a leather chair positioned at the front of Matt's desk. He closed his eyes and rubbed his forehead with the palm of his hand. "No, I don't think so, either. I don't know. Guess I didn't sleep well last night. Had another dream."

"About Elizabeth?"

Brady nodded and sighed, gouging his fingers deep into his scalp.

"What was it this time?"

"We were somewhere—in a park, I think—just talking and laughing. Then I kissed her."

"And how did you feel? Guilty?"

Brady opened his eyes to meet Matt's questioning gaze. "No, not until I woke up. And then maybe a little, but nothing like it's been in the past. The dream, it was . . ." He averted his gaze to stare out the window, lost in the haze of sunlight that shimmered into the room. "Wonderful, exhilarating . . ." A shallow attempt at a laugh lodged in his throat. "It actually left me breathless. Until I woke up."

"That's progress, John. There was a time you couldn't even discuss these dreams with me for all the shame and guilt you bore. God's moving in your life, my friend, through our prayers and your willingness to confront your past. He's healing you."

Brady glanced up, and a flicker of hope fluttered in his chest. "Yeah, I think he is. I can feel it, Matt, and I know you're right. But the more he heals me of the guilt and the shame, the more I seem to dream of her." He stood to his feet and moved to the window, anxious to avoid Matt's scrutiny. He leaned his palms on the windowsill and released a weighty breath, lost in a vacant stare. "That can't be good."

"Why not? You're in love with the girl. You just couldn't see that before for all the guilt and shame. But your subconscious is facing it now, and it's about time you do too."

Brady turned, realization drifting in his mind as gently as the motes of dust swirling in the sunlight. His lips parted in shock. "I . . . am, aren't I? I love her . . . as a woman and not as a sister." His eyes fluttered closed. "Dear God, I've been a fool."

A low chuckle rumbled from Father Mac's throat. "Not a fool, John, a slave. To your past. But 'if the Son therefore shall make you free, ye shall be free indeed.'"

Brady blinked to ward off the emotion that threatened. "Thank you, Father, for all you've done."

Father Mac smiled. Affection shone in his eyes. "You did it, John, you and God. All I did was lead the way." He reached for his glass and drained it. "But don't thank me yet. You've got a lot to do. A relationship to build, which is a tall order for a man who's avoided women all his life."

Brady thought of Beth. The lemonade instantly soured in his stomach. How was he going to do this? To tell her he loved her? And not lose the contents of his stomach? Even now, a tinge of guilt assaulted his mind. What if it wasn't gone? What if it came back? What if he told her he loved her and couldn't? She'd be devastated . . . and so would he. The air thickened in his throat, and his hands began to sweat.

As if reading his mind, Matt's steady tone countered the fear in Brady's gut. "You take it slowly, one day at a time. You spend time with her, get to know her as a woman, her likes and dislikes. You revel in the attraction you have for her, because it's a gift from God, meant to be tempered by his precepts. Honor him and you will honor her. The demons from your past will try to convince you it won't work, but it's a lie. You're free, John, and God has a plan for your life better than anything you dreamed possible."

Brady swallowed a cleansing gulp of air and exhaled slowly.

"Thanks, Matt. I needed that, and I believe it. But do you mind if we pray?"

Father Mac settled back in his chair and crossed his brand-new Keds—the latest fad—on his desk with an air of authority. He tucked his hands behind his head and shot Brady a lopsided grin. "Mmm . . . novel idea. Wish I'd thought of it."

❦ ❦

Lizzie's hand lingered on the knob long after the shop door closed behind her. She wrinkled her nose. "Is it my imagination, or did Brady seem a bit strange today?"

Mary ducked her head and glanced through the window, eyeing Brady bent over a press. "Maybe a little. He did seem to be in a particularly good mood. Why?"

Lizzie peered through the glass. "I don't know, he just seemed different . . . nervous, almost shy."

She turned away from the window with a sigh and started down the busy street. Lunchtime was in full sway, and the shops were crowded with patrons. She grabbed Mary's arm to dodge a delivery man with a crate of peaches. The sweet smell rumbled her stomach. "Of course, Brady's always been 'different,' I suppose, but never like this. Did you see his face when I hugged him? Dear Lord, I didn't know a man could turn that many shades of red. And I've hugged Brady more than any human being alive, except for my mother and father."

Mary giggled. "Now that you mention it, he was a bit out of character today. I literally had to bite my tongue to keep from laughing when he sat down and missed the chair."

Lizzie's hand flew to her mouth to stifle a laugh. "Oh, I know. I've never seen him do that before. Brady's always so calm and self-assured." She gripped Mary's arm. "And did you see how he was—"

"Sweating? Oh, my goodness, yes! It was literally pouring off of him, so much so that parts of his shirt were soaked."

The two girls clutched each other, laughing so hard that tears sprang to their eyes.

Lizzie wiped the wetness from her face. "That's what I mean, Mary. Something was different today."

Mary hooked an arm through Lizzie's. "Well, it can't be anything bad, because he was in a really good mood."

Lizzie chewed on her lip. "Yes, he was. So good he actually asked me to go fishing with him and Cluny sometime."

Mary came to a halt. "Brady asked you out?"

Lizzie scrunched her nose. "Don't jump to conclusions, Mary. Brady's made it perfectly clear how he feels about me, and I'm not about to toy with heartbreak again. He and I are friends, period. And nothing short of an edict from God will get me to go down that road again."

"Then why did he ask you out?"

Lizzie kept walking. "Who knows? It's fishing, nothing more. And nothing definite. He didn't even say when."

"Mmm . . . that's odd."

"Besides, I think his real motive is for me to bring Katie fishing with us. He mentioned that Cluny's a bit down because his gram is coming home. He won't be able to live with Brady anymore, so Brady wants to cheer him up. Apparently Katie is the cure."

"Awww . . . that's so cute."

"Yeah, real sweet. Katie, Cluny, me . . . and the cold fish." Lizzie rolled her eyes. "And I'm not talking about the ones in the lake."

Mary chuckled. "Any girl in her right mind can take one look at Brady and see that he's not a cold fish."

Lizzie sighed. "He is with me, and nothing can convince me otherwise. He will be my big brother until the day I die, and I have finally learned to accept it."

They reached the threshold of Bookends. Lizzie pushed the door open with a grunt. The bell rang overhead, and Millie looked up from the register. "About time. I'm starving."

Lizzie smirked. "Don't pull that on me, Millie Doza. Your lunch is long gone, and I bet there are crumbs on the counter to prove it."

Millie winked and waved her new *Photoplay* magazine in the air. She hurried toward the back of the store. "I didn't say for food, did I? This is the brand-new issue, and I'm dying to devour it."

Mary shook her head and circled the register. She squeezed Lizzie's shoulder. "As far as Brady is concerned, Lizzie, I think that's a good thing."

Lizzie bundled a stack of loose books in her arms. "What's a good thing?"

"You know, like you were saying. That you've resolved yourself to think of Brady as a brother." She snatched a pile of receipts from a sharp spike on the counter and began to tally them in a ledger. "Although the man's so ridiculously appealing, I can see how difficult that is. He could be a real sheik if he had a mind to. But, that's part of his charm, I suppose. He has absolutely no idea the effect he has on women."

Lizzie sighed and returned the books to their proper places. "Please, I've spent too many lost years dwelling on Brady's appeal. I just want to get on with my life."

"Speaking of which . . ." Mary said with a raised brow. "What's been going on with Michael?"

"Nothing more than I told you last time. Michael and I are friends. He shows up every Sunday for Mass, eats lunch with us and sometimes dinner. For pity's sake, his brother has turned him away, so somebody has to befriend him."

"Why should it be you?"

Lizzie propped her hands on her hips and stared Mary down. "Because I feel sorry for him. I don't think the man has ever been around a family before. You should see him at our house—he's like a little boy at Christmas. He plays games with Steven and Katie, talks to Mother about anything and everything, and plays chess with Father. And quite frankly, he makes me laugh, which is something I can certainly use lately, given what Brady's put me through."

Mary took a deep breath and continued logging receipts. She avoided Lizzie's gaze. "As long as he doesn't 'make' you do anything else," she muttered.

"Mary Carpenter!" Lizzie's cheeks flamed hot. "For pity's sake, he's Brady's brother. And the man is only in town for a short time. What do you have against him, anyway? You haven't even met him."

Mary glanced up, her look as searing as Lizzie's. "Brady doesn't think he's good for you. That's enough for me. And it should be for you too."

Lizzie folded her arms. "First Brady, and now you. I'll have you know that Michael Brady is a decent, God-fearing friend who has done nothing but shown me the utmost courtesy and respect."

Mary scrutinized Lizzie through narrow eyes. "And he's never tried to kiss you, not even once?"

Lizzie notched her chin. "Maybe once, in the beginning at Brady's flat, but never again. He knows there's no way I'd consider him romantically, and I told him so."

"So he comes over for nothing but pure friendship?"

Lizzie pursed her lips. "Yes, Mary, he does. He's lonely, for pity's sake. The man knows absolutely no one in Boston but his brother, who won't even give him the time of day. Besides, he only plans to be in town for a few more weeks, so why are we even having this discussion?"

Mary pushed the receipts back in the register. She stared at Lizzie for several seconds before releasing a weary breath. She shoved the register closed. "I'm sorry, Lizzie, I just care about you. My past hasn't given me much reason to trust many people, but I do trust you and Brady. I love you both."

All the frustration seeped out of Lizzie as she walked to where Mary stood with a pitiful expression on her face. She gave her a hug. "Mary, I love you too. And I appreciate your concern, but believe me, when it comes to falling in love, I'm more than a little gun-shy when it comes to both Bradys. Friendship is undoubtedly the safest course."

Mary gave her a sideways glance. "Undoubtedly. So when's he leaving?"

"I don't know, but soon."

"Humph . . . not soon enough. At least to suit Brady." Mary snatched an armload of invoices from under the counter and headed for the back.

Lizzie's tone was teasing as she called after her. "I already have a guardian angel, Mary Carpenter, so you can rest easy."

Mary turned at the door. "Rest easy? Sure, Lizzie, don't worry about me." Her lips tilted in an obvious tease. "It's the angel I'm worried about."

ᕗ ᕦ

Patrick squeezed Marcy's hand and rose to his feet. He scanned the crowded dinner table with a swell of pride. Their spacious dining room, more than enough to seat eight comfortably, was now jammed elbow to elbow with all twelve of his precious family. Charity, her first venture out in over a month and a half, looked tired but happy as she sat at the far end, a sleepy Hope in her lap. Mitch, radiating a fatherly pride that rivaled the glow of the candles, was seated at the head, where a chunky Henry dozed in the crook of his father's arm. Patrick clinked a spoon against his cider goblet and raised it in the air. He cleared his throat.

"I'd like to propose a toast to the two newest members of our family and the two people who gave them to us."

"I thought you were supposed to toast with wine," Katie said.

Patrick leveled his youngest daughter with a look that suggested silence. "In deference to the eighteenth amendment, Katie Rose, and as the head of this household, we can toast with whatever I deem fit. Just like I can administer discipline whenever I deem fit."

Katie's lips flattened. She hoisted her milk. "You were saying?"

"To Hope and Henry—may this family give them as much joy as it's given me." He arched a brow in Katie's direction. "Most of the time."

"Here, here," Mitch boomed, jarring Henry's slumber. "And to a dozen more."

Charity choked on her cider. "Oh no, I'm not drinking to that."

"I will," Collin said with a chuckle, "at least on this side of the table."

"Speak for yourself," Faith said, holding her goblet away so Collin couldn't clink.

He grinned. "I am—four more for the Dennehys, and six more for us."

"Goodness, we'll have to buy a bigger house," Marcy said with a laugh.

Patrick downed his cider. "You could be right, Marcy. It won't be long before Lizzie and Sean get married and then—"

"Oh no, not Sean—"Charity laughed. She handed Hope off to Lizzie, then stretched back in her chair with a grin. "Everybody knows he's married to the store. All you'll get out of him is inventory."

Sean flicked a pea in her direction. "Look, if you could find some poor dope to marry you—"

"Hey, wait a minute—I am not 'poor.'" Mitch said.

"Well, don't count on me for babies," Katie piped in. "I have no intention of ever getting married."

"A wise plan," Steven muttered. "It'll save on heartbreak when nobody asks." He glanced up at Patrick. "Father, may I be excused? I told Robert I'd come over after dinner."

"What? And miss the lesson I've prepared on changing diapers?" Charity gave him a look of horror.

Steven stood with a sheepish grin. "Better teach her, sis," he said with a nod toward Katie. "Spinsters have more time for that type of thing."

Katie lunged for his throat.

"Katie Rose—freeze! Steven—sit down! Everyone else—quiet! I've got something more to say." Patrick grabbed his glass of water and chugged, hoping to cool the heat crawling up the back of his neck. He put the glass down and shifted on his feet, passing a hand over his eyes while he stalled.

Marcy's touch was light on his arm. "Patrick, is everything all right?"

He nodded and cleared his throat, then grabbed her hand for support. "This . . . well, this is difficult for me because as you all know, I am a man of considerable pride." His lips skewed. "Not all of it good, I'm afraid." He took another quick sip of water and continued, his voice gruff. "I owe an apology to each of you . . . for how I treated your mother."

Marcy squeezed his hand. "Patrick, this isn't necess—"

He nodded furiously to dispel the moisture in his eyes. "Yes, Marcy, it is. I put you and this family through a lot of grief and worry before the babies were born, and I have to make it right." He stroked her cheek, stunned anew at how God could have blessed him with such a woman. "I love you, Marcy, with every fiber of my being. But because of stubborn pride, I disrespected you before your children, when God has called me to cherish you with all of my heart. Forgive me, Marcy. It will never happen again."

"Oh, Patrick, you know I've forgiven you—"

"I know, darlin', but I felt a need to ask in the presence of your children." He lifted his gaze to his family. "My children—for whom I am supposed to set a godly example, but failed miserably." He stood to his full height and scanned the table, beseeching each with humility in his eyes. "I ask each one of you to forgive me . . . and I thank you for your prayers, because I know you said them—over and over again. Don't think they don't have an effect, because they do. They saved me from myself—and your mother from further pain."

He pushed in his chair and pulled Marcy to her feet, gathering her close to his side. "Over the years, your mother and I have tried our best to teach you about prayer and forgiveness. But I can tell you right now that I bucked like the devil when God wanted me to teach you about humility. But I don't have a choice—not when I want peace in my heart and God by my side. Now, if you will all excuse us, I am taking my wife off to the parlor where I will nurse my pride over a game of chess while your mother puts up her feet to relax."

He arched a brow in Katie's direction. "Your night for dishes, I believe?"

Katie groaned. "But Mama usually helps—"

"Not tonight," Patrick said with a tone not to be questioned. "Steven will clear the table, and the rest of us will retire to the parlor where these beautiful babies will be passed around and devoured like a plate of your mother's fresh-baked sugar cookies. Collin, you up for a thrashing? I feel a surge of pride coming on."

"Hey, what happened to humility?" Collin asked.

Patrick kissed Marcy full on the lips before ushering her to the door. "Haven't you heard?" He shot a grin over his shoulder. "Doesn't apply to chess."

❧ ❧

Michael Brady stooped to snatch an acorn from the ground. He absently bobbled it in his hand as he studied the graceful girl walking beside him. The onset of dusk cast a faint pink glow across Lizzie's face, reminding him of his stepmother's prized pillar roses—creamy white and tinged with a kiss of a blush. Silky to the touch. Much like he imagined Lizzie would be.

His lips leveled flat. Not that he knew firsthand. No, he'd been on his best behavior for over two and a half months now, getting to know her and her family, biding his time. He hadn't expected it to take this long. Hadn't intended to be away for this length of time, from Queens and the lucrative printing business his father had built from the ground up. The business that would finally belong to him. That is, if John would sign it away. Michael released a quiet breath. Lizzie was to have been nothing more than leverage with his brother, a means to a signature that would send Michael back where he belonged—to his plush life in Forest Hills. And so he had set out to win, first Lizzie's trust, then her affection. He exhaled and sailed the nut hard into a passing tree. But instead of winning, he'd lost in a big way—his heart to a girl who was in love with his brother.

She didn't seem to notice—neither his pensive mood at the moment nor the fact that he was falling for her. She was too engrossed in telling her story, some humorous account of a kid at the bookshop where she worked, and he found himself smiling in spite of his mood. She had a way with words, her voice carrying softly on the crisp, autumn breeze, a hypnotic lilt to it that always held him captive. She glanced up to deliver the punch line, and he grinned, more from the look of delight on her face than the story itself. Her violet eyes sparkled in the waning light, teasing him with a heady mix of mischief and innocence.

There was no question about it. Lizzie O'Connor had completely taken him by surprise. She had this ethereal shyness that made her look as if she belonged in an eighteenth-century English garden, despite her stylish bob that now shimmered auburn against the crimson sky. But in weeks of attending church and getting to know her, the shyness had slowly given way to a playful energy, exhaustive in her thirst to explore topics and books and people she loved. He frowned. And one in particular, unfortunately.

They reached the front gate of her house far too soon, and he checked his watch in disbelief. It seemed only minutes since they'd left, but they'd been gone over an hour. It was a pleasant night, fragrant with the oaky scent of wood burning and damp leaves, and he was reluctant to go in and lose her to the family celebration he had declined to attend. He glanced at the house, awash with the red shadows of dusk and lights twinkling in the windows. His hand lingered on the latch of the gate.

"Lizzie," he whispered.

She looked up with those almond-shaped eyes, and his heart did a flip.

"Would you mind if we sat on the porch for a while?" He glanced up at the sky where the moon was on the rise, and breathed in the earthy scent of autumn. "There won't be many nights like this, with a harvest moon and warm temperatures. I'd like to enjoy it."

She smiled. "Sure, Michael. I love this time of year."

He opened the gate and followed her to the porch, wondering how one girl, barely a woman, could disarm him so. He was twenty-eight, for pity's sake, and she was more than a month away from eighteen. He was used to women flirting and seducing; he knew how to handle that. But this . . . friendship, with a girl who stirred his blood as much as his mind, totally unnerved him. She was unlike anyone he'd ever met, with a passion for God and family that offered him a taste of something he'd never known before. For the first time, he understood completely why John was in love with her. He released a shallow breath. He could certainly attest to that. She exuded this sweet femininity that made him want to protect her and take care of her. And she had this knack for making him feel different. Utterly male.

*And almost clean.*

She settled on the swing with the carefree air of a little girl, belying the soft curve of her figure beneath the thick cable sweater she wore. He sat beside her, a bit irritated at the pace of his pulse. When it came to women, he was usually in control. This was uncommon country—wanting a woman who didn't want him—and he wasn't sure he liked it. But if he could get her to fall in love with him—and out of love with his brother—he was fairly certain he'd be back on solid ground.

She clasped slender hands to her knees and took a deep breath, face lifted and eyes closed. "Oh, just smell that air, will you? It smells like wood fires and apple cider and Halloween. I do believe fall is my favorite time of year."

He leaned close to take in the scent of her hair. "Funny, I smell lilacs and Pears soap. And it smells absolutely wonderful."

She opened her eyes and tilted her head. She clasped her hands in her lap. "Michael Brady, I do believe you're trying to embarrass me."

He grinned and reached for her hand, squeezing and then forgetting to let go. He circled her palm with his thumb. "It's not hard to do, Lizzie. You turn pink faster than any girl I've ever seen. But I like it." His voice trailed off to a whisper. "A lot."

She tugged her hand free. "Is it my imagination, or is it getting cool all of a sudden? Maybe we better go in."

He stared at her full lips, ripe with the shimmer of dusk, and swallowed hard. "No, not yet, please. I need to tell you something."

She looked up, and he saw the hesitation in her eyes. Like a doe ready to bolt. He forced himself to go slow and easy, something he wasn't used to. He wasn't going to make the same mistake that Weston character had. She was too important, too special. He couldn't risk scaring her away.

He sat back on the swing and stared out at the street, giving her the chance to relax and escape the intensity that burned in his eyes. "Lizzie, when I came to Boston, I came for one reason. To get John to sign some very important papers. Papers that would release the inheritance our stepmother left to us. But he wouldn't do it."

"Why?"

He glanced at her, gauging how much he should divulge.

"Because he wants nothing to do with his past, and I can't say I blame him."

A frown creased her brow. She rested a hand on his arm. "Michael, what happened to Brady when he was young? I know it was something awful, but he refuses to talk about it. To anyone."

Michael covered her hand with his own. "I can't tell you that, Lizzie. It would destroy my brother if anyone knew. And I love him too much to do that. But suffice it to say it was enough to change him forever. So much so that I don't know who he is anymore. As far as I can tell, he doesn't have any love for me. And certainly there was no love lost between him and our stepmother. To be honest with you, I'm not sure he can love at all."

She backed away, her body suddenly rigid against the corner of the swing. Her voice was soft and pleading. "Don't say that, please. Brady has more love inside of him than anyone I've ever known."

He flinched at the defensive look in her eyes and looked away. "Okay, let me qualify that. I'm not sure he can love . . . a woman."

He heard her harsh intake of breath and looked up. Tears pooled in her eyes, and he reached to caress her face with his hand. "Listen to me, Lizzie. I know you're in love with my brother, but I don't want to see you hurt. You and I both know that he has no intention of returning that love—at least, not the way you want. He can't, Lizzie. Don't you know that?"

She nodded. A silver trail of tears shimmered down her cheek.

He took her hand and held it between both of his. "John can't love you that way, but I can. Will you let me? Will you let me love you like you deserve to be loved?"

She shook her head and looked away. "No, Michael, please . . ."

He lifted her chin with his finger, directing her gaze to his.

"I love you, Lizzie. Never planned on it. Never wanted to. I came to Boston purely to force John to sign. And I came to you because I thought if I could make him jealous, he would do anything to keep me away. It was blackmail, pure and simple. Only it backfired. Instead of making John relent, I fell into my own trap. God help me, Lizzie, I've never been in love before, but I'm in love with you something fierce."

"*No* . . . you can't be . . ." Her voice was a weak moan and her face as pale as the moonlight that spilled across the white-washed porch.

"I'm afraid I am," he whispered. "And I have to know. Will you give me a chance?"

She shook her head. "Michael, I can't. I promised Brady—"

"You want a man who seeks God? I'm seeking God. You want a Brady who will love you, body and soul, then I'm the man you need. My brother is just going to have to understand, because he's not offering that, but I am." He shifted close and took her hand. "Marry me, Lizzie. I can make you happy. Just give me a chance."

He traced her jaw with his thumb. Seconds passed as he stared into her eyes, his pulse pounding in his veins. All at once, need overtook him, and with slow deliberation, he lowered his mouth to hers. The taste of her lips almost undid him. Heat pulsed through him, but he fought it off, caressing her lips with as much gentleness as she deserved. With every shred of willpower he possessed, he pulled away, his ragged breathing all but giving him away.

Lizzie felt as if she were suspended in time, eyes closed and chin elevated from the kiss that had taken her by surprise. The brisk fall air was alive with the sounds of night—a medley of tree frogs and baying dogs and the hooting of a faraway screech owl. But all she could hear was the low sound of her own blood rushing in her ears. For a moment she had been paralyzed, caught off-guard. And then the fantasy had kicked in—Brady kissing her—as she had always dreamed he would . . . tender, reverent, like the man she'd fallen in love with so many years ago.

She opened her eyes and blinked, and Michael's handsome face blurred into view. Her heart clutched. He was so much like Brady with his gentle eyes that darkened to coffee brown whenever he was pensive, like now, as he studied her expression. His hard-chiseled face bore the same late-day shadow of beard as Brady's, and both men possessed a smile that could weaken her knees. But there the similarity ended. Where Brady had a quiet strength that emanated from his relationship with God, Michael seemed to take his newfound faith in stride, his confidence clearly rooted in himself. He was louder and bolder, his lively sense of humor contrasting sharply with Brady's unassuming manner and dry wit. Michael was the older twin, if minutes mattered, but it was Brady who owned the maturity that Lizzie loved.

She drew in a deep breath. But she *had* felt something when he'd kissed her. Something warm and sweet and compelling. Had the feeling been because of Michael? Or because of his brother?

"Will you, Lizzie? Will you give me a chance?" His voice was soft—like his kiss had been—breaking her reverie.

"I don't know, Michael, I . . . I'd have to think about it, pray about it . . ."

He grinned. "That's more than I hoped for."

"And talk to Brady."

His smile faded. He took a deep breath. "I figured as much. But you and I both know what he's going to say. He'll tell you I have no faith in God. But he's wrong, Lizzie. You've changed me—opened my eyes to things I've never seen before. Things like God and family and love. My brother used to be right about me. But not anymore."

His thumb skimmed along the curve of her jaw, causing her stomach to flutter. "So you'll think about it?"

She nodded.

He smiled and feathered a loose curl away from her face. "While you're thinking, Lizzie, do me a favor? Think on this." And in slow motion, he held her face in his hands and kissed her again, as slow and heated as warm wax glazing the side of a steady-burning candle. A soft moan left his lips and merged with one of her own, locked deep in her throat.

With a faint shiver, he rose and pulled her to her feet, then led her to the door. He slowly caressed her cheek, the tips of his fingers heating her skin. He gave her a smile that left her as breathless as his kiss. "Think on it, Lizzie, will you? I know I will."

# 14

Faith couldn't stop blubbering. All it took was the sweet scent of her newborn niece, a glimpse at that tiny, rosebud mouth, and the heady realization that the baby she cradled in her arms bore the name of a twin sister she had loved and lost.

*Hope Dennehy.* The very name infused Faith with some of her own—hope that this little girl would, somehow, someway, possess the sweetness and kindness of an aunt she would never know. Faith swallowed hard, desperate to thwart a sob that threatened at the back of her throat. *Oh, Hope, I wish you were here!*

Vivid blue eyes blinked back, sending Faith into yet another crying jag.

Charity looked up from the clean diapers she was folding. The sunlight streaming in the windows shone around her like a halo of contentment, highlighting golden wisps of hair escaped from the loose chignon at the back of her neck. Behind her, the "modern" kitchen Mitch insisted she should have was light and airy, the latest in Boone white enamel cabinets giving it a clean, open look. Pale yellow curtains fluttered on the windows, infusing the cozy room with an unseasonably warm breeze tinged with the earthy scent of fall. She grinned. "Babies are supposed to be a good thing, Faith. She's going to think you don't like her if you cry every time you hold her."

Faith swiped the wetness from her eyes and pressed a soft

kiss to Hope's perfect little nose. "I can't help it. You were once the baby that Hope and I doted on, and now here you are, with a baby of your own."

Charity hoisted a brow. Her gaze flicked to where Lizzie sat at the table, bouncing Henry Patrick on her knee. Henry smiled and gurgled with every lift of Lizzie's arms.

"Two," Charity muttered with a good-natured smile. "But it's my own fault. I should have known that my husband never does anything halfway."

Faith pressed a cheek to the soft, blond fuzz that feathered her niece's head. The smell of innocence plucked at her heart. Hope's eyes fluttered shut, and Faith tucked her close to her chest. "Yes, that certainly sounds like Mitch Dennehy. But love him or not, I'll have you know he's caused me a lot of grief with Collin, especially where these two babies are concerned."

Charity groaned as she bent to stack the clean, folded diapers into a wooden wash basket. She straightened and pushed a flaxen strand of hair from her eyes. "Don't tell me he's still nursing that grudge over you being engaged to Mitch?"

"Well, I didn't think so . . . until you got pregnant." She glanced at Charity, then at Lizzie. "Remember when I told you about my problem, where he wouldn't leave me alone?" Her cheeks warmed the slightest bit, but she forged on. "You know . . . in the bedroom?"

Charity chuckled. "Oh yes. Your problem . . . my pipedream. Hold that thought for a moment. Anybody want tea?"

"Oooo, yes, please!" Lizzie said, cuddling a sleepy Henry in her arms. "Is it my imagination, or is it chilly in here?"

"Your imagination," Charity muttered. "Everyone knows it's always been a runaway train. I'm stifling." She lowered the window sash to an inch and reached for the teakettle, filling it with water and putting it on to boil. She sighed and looked down at the bulge around her hips and tummy. "Of course, it could be all the extra weight suffocating my figure beneath layers of fat."

"Charity, stop!" Faith said. "For pity's sake, you just had twins barely two months ago. Besides, I don't see Mitch complaining. We all know he's never been an overly demonstrative man, but lately he's been worse than Collin, nuzzling you all the time, mooning over you like some lovesick suitor. Face it, the guy is loopy over you, extra pounds or not."

Charity propped her hands on her hips and stood up straight, thrusting already ample breasts, now engorged with milk, in a show of confidence. An impish grin curved her lips. "Yeah, he is, isn't he? Poor guy. Since I've given him a son and a daughter, and the doctor has given us the go-ahead—" she winked—"he can't seem to keep his hands off me." A sigh parted from her lips as she plopped in her chair. "A dream come true . . . except for the exhaustion and weight."

"It'll come off," Lizzie said with a grin. "Wait till the twins start crawling and walking. You'll run yourself silly trying to keep up. You should be back to your old figure in no time."

"And too tired to flaunt it," Faith quipped with a tease in her tone.

Charity notched her chin in a stubborn stance all too familiar from their youth. "Never!" A playful glint lit her eyes. "But speaking of tired, I believe you were talking about Collin wearing you out?"

It was Lizzie's turn to blush. "Stop! I'm too young to hear this."

Faith shot her a crooked grin. "No, you're not. It's about time you hear about the real world instead of what you read in those books." She shifted Hope to her other shoulder and sank back into the chair. "I hate to say it, but I think Collin is jealous of Mitch. It was bad enough before, while you were pregnant, but since you've had the babies, saints preserve us, he's like a man on a mission."

Lizzie cocked her head. "A mission?"

Faith shot her a sideways glance. "To get me pregnant."

Lizzie blushed. "Well, don't you want a baby?"

"Of course. But it's not happening as quickly as it did for Charity, and frankly, Collin wants it so much that it makes me nervous . . . which, trust me, is not good for the process." She blew a stray hair out of her eyes. "He thinks the problem is me."

"You? Oh, doesn't that sound just like a man?" A singsong whistle squealed from the teakettle, and Charity jumped up to steep the tea. She placed a spoon and steaming cup before each of her sisters, then retrieved her own, along with sugar and cream. The spicy citrus scent of Earl Grey drifted in the air. She blew on her tea, then frowned and took a sip. "What, he thinks you're not fertile?"

"No, he thinks I'm stressed. Wants me to quit the *Herald*."

Lizzie stopped stirring to look up in shock. "He wants you to quit what you love . . . *before* you get pregnant?"

Faith arched her brows and spooned some sugar into her cup. "My point exactly. For some strange reason, Collin thinks my job *is* the problem—claims I focus too much on it."

"And not enough on him, I suppose. Excuse me, but is that not what a good employee is supposed to do?" Charity shifted in the chair and rolled her eyes. "That man needs to relax and let nature take its course. *And* enjoy his sleep. Once his dream comes true, a good night's sleep will be pretty hard to come by, trust me."

Faith scrunched her nose and sipped her tea. "I know, I tell him that all the time. But he's dead set on having a family as soon as possible."

"Well, it has been almost three years since you were married," Lizzie said.

Faith sighed, her gaze suddenly lost in the steamy depths of Earl Grey. "I know."

Lizzie touched her arm. "Are you afraid? That you won't be able to have a baby?"

"No, not really. I know Collin is, but for some reason I'm not. I'm content with our lives right now. I trust that God will make me a mother in his own time. But for now, I don't need a baby to be happy. I love Collin and I love my job. For five years I've been writing feature articles on the side while serving my time in the typing pool, not counting my year of copywriting in Dublin. Now, when Father has been hinting that I may actually be promoted to copywriter—a near-impossible feat for a woman from the typing pool—Collin suddenly wants me to quit."

She cupped her warm teacup in her hands, idly stroking its rim, then exhaled and took a sip. "It's not fair. All my life I've had this dream to be a copywriter, and now my husband thinks my dream stands in the way of his."

"Well, you'd have to quit after you have a baby anyway," Lizzie said.

"I know, and I'm fine with that. When God decides it's time for me to be a mother, I'll embrace it and give it my all. But it hasn't happened yet, and I'm so close to getting that promotion at work, that I find myself . . ." She chewed on her lip and glanced up. "Fighting him."

Charity's eyes circled in shock. "You mean you tell him no when he wants to—?"

Lizzie popped from the chair like one of Katie's tiddledy-winks, her face as pink as the blanket that swaddled little Hope. She quickly handed a slumbering Henry off to his mother. "Cookies, anyone?"

Both Charity and Faith ignored her. "No, of course not. I love Collin way too much, and God knows what a fragile ego the man has. When I say I 'fight' him, I mean—" she swallowed hard, then tapped several fingers to her heart—"in here."

Charity draped Henry on her shoulder like a limp rag. She dipped her head in a nod that took in the whole of Faith's body. "But not . . ."

Warmth surged to Faith's cheeks. "No! As if I could. Telling him no would crush the man."

"Then what's the problem? How can he possibly complain?"

Without a word, Lizzie retrieved a saucer from the cabinet for some sugar cookies she took from a white ceramic crock on the counter. She placed them on the table and settled back in her seat.

Faith reached for a cookie and gave her a grateful smile. "Because from the very beginning, Collin and I have had this special connection, a sixth sense, if you will, where we seem to know what's on the other's mind. I worry about that. I think he knows I don't want a baby right now, and he's blaming my job. And part of it is his stubborn male pride too, wanting control—"

"Sweet mother of Job, what is it with men anyway, always wanting control? Mitch is the same way, and it drives me crazy."

Lizzie blew on her tea. "I know exactly what you mean. I'm not married to Brady, but he certainly tries to run my life as if I were."

Faith sighed deeply, causing little Hope to shudder in her sleep. She gave her sisters a lopsided smile. "I'm afraid they come by it naturally."

"What do you mean, 'naturally'?" Charity huffed. "Unnaturally is more like it. It's not natural to be a bully."

"That's exactly what I thought when Collin bullied me with the submission Scripture the year before we were married."

Charity's left brow cocked a full half inch. "Submission Scripture? Come again?"

Faith drew in a deep breath, preparing for her sisters' reactions. "Ephesians 5:22—'Wives, submit yourselves unto your own husbands, as unto the Lord.'"

Lizzie's eyes widened, accentuating their violet hue. "What does *that* mean?"

"You mean do whatever they say, without a fight?" Charity's tone was a near-shriek, disrupting Henry's sleep. He grunted and groaned, finally settling down when Charity patted his back, none too gently.

Faith chuckled. "I can see you're not thrilled with this particular part of the Bible, so let me tell you what Mrs. Gerson told me." She took a deep breath. " 'Wives, submit yourselves unto your own husbands,' only let's replace 'submit' with 'respect.' "

Charity's eyes narrowed. "And when does this get good?"

"In the Bible, God often underscores the importance of something by order of appearance. For instance, notice that after Ephesians 5:22 comes Ephesians 5:25—'Husbands, love your wives, even as Christ also loved the church.' So, if you boil these two Scriptures down in order of appearance, here's what you have:

"Wives, respect your husbands.

"Husbands, love your wives.

"Mrs. Gerson believes this is cause and effect. When a woman respects her husband, it automatically increases the husband's love for his wife. God addresses the women first because Eve was the one who sinned first, taking control away from Adam and robbing him of his authority and self-respect. If a wife respects her husband, then her respect restores his rightful authority and elevates him to be the man God intended him to be. When that happens, he feels good about himself, and the 'effect' is his love grows for the woman who made him feel that way."

Charity squinted. "So let me get this straight. Mitch will love me more if I submit—"

"Respect," Faith corrected.

"Respect him more?"

Faith nodded. "It's cause and effect, like Mrs. Gerson says. God knew that what women want more than anything is to be cherished by the man they love." Faith's lips curled into a thin smile. "Nobody's proven that more than you, Charity. And that's why Lizzie and other women have been reading romance novels for years. Yet men seldom do. Why? Because what a man needs most is to be 'respected' by the woman he loves. Bottom line? Women crave love and men crave respect. And in Ephesians 5:22–25, God gives us the perfect solution."

Charity rubbed her head. "Goodness, that hurts just thinking about it."

Faith took a sip of tea. "It does, doesn't it?"

Lizzie blinked. "How did we start on this anyway?"

Faith sighed and propped her chin in her hand. "Because deep down inside, a part of me worries that my dream to be a copywriter might be in conflict with my submitting to Collin."

"Oh," Lizzie uttered. "So what are you going to do?"

"Pray about it and wait, I guess. After all, he hasn't actually *told* me to quit."

Charity grinned. "Parsing Scripture, are we, now? Never thought I'd see the day."

Faith notched her chin in the air. "Well, I never said I was perfect."

"Speaking of 'perfect,'" Lizzie said, "and not to change the subject, but did your heart not just burst with pride when Father apologized at dinner the other night?" She spooned more sugar into her cup. "Dear Lord above, I hope I have a marriage like theirs someday."

"You will, Lizzie," Faith said. "I'm just glad they're back to normal. Mother looks like a young girl again with that glow in her face. And Father has been acting almost as spunky as Collin and Mitch these days, the way he's been hovering over her." She sighed. "I hope and pray we all have marriages like them. As a matter of fact, Mother's the perfect example of Ephesians 5:22. I don't know what happened between those two, but trust me, if Collin had been sleeping at his shop for over a month, I would have burned the place down. With him in it."

Charity chuckled. "How did that Irish temper of yours ever hook up with God?"

"I don't know—his mercy, I guess."

Lizzie sighed and sagged back in the chair, jealous of her sisters for the first time she could remember. "You two are so lucky. Both of you have wonderful marriages, just like Mother and Father. I wish I could be sure of having that too. I mean, I was sure when I thought it would be Brady, but apparently that's not meant to be. And now that Michael says he's in love with me—"

"What?" Faith and Charity jerked up in their chairs at the same time, wrenching a faint cry from both of the twins. The sisters commenced patting with a fury while their shocked gazes locked on Lizzie's face. "How? When?"

Lizzie worked her bottom lip, brows sloped over anxious eyes. "He told me the other night, after dinner with the family. Said that Brady couldn't love me the way I wanted, but that he could."

"Sweet saints above," Faith muttered, still patting Hope like a house afire.

"And what did you say?" Charity demanded, her tone as shocked as the look on Faith's face.

Lizzie started to nibble on a nail. "Well, at first I told him no, that I'd promised Brady, but then he . . . well, he . . ."

Both sisters gaped, a hand frozen on the back of each twin.

Lizzie swallowed hard. "He kissed me, and well, now I'm confused."

"You *liked* it?" Charity asked.

Lizzie nodded, peeking over a well-chewed thumbnail.

Faith slumped back in the chair and stared at Charity. "Saints in heaven, what are we going to do? She can't fall for Michael. It will destroy Brady. And besides, he has no faith in God—"

"He's trying, though," Lizzie said.

Charity's lips skewed in thought. "No, she can't fall in love with him. We know nothing about him, but . . ." She sat up with a smile that suggested trouble. "He might just be the ultimate bait to turn his brother's head."

"Oh no you don't," Lizzie cried, spitting a piece of nail out of her mouth. "I'm through using people to turn John Brady's head. And what's more, I will not do that to Michael. He's done nothing but treat me with respect, going to church with us and behaving like a perfect gentleman—"

Charity arched a brow. "Like in Brady's apartment?"

Lizzie blushed. "That was different. He told me he was just trying to light a fire under his brother because he knew I was in love with him. But he hasn't laid a finger on me since, and it's been almost two months." She sucked in a deep breath. "Until the other night."

"So, how did you leave it?" Charity wanted to know.

"I told him I would think about it . . . and pray about it." She gulped more air. "And talk to Brady."

Faith shook her head. "I wouldn't want to be there for that conversation."

"Do you like him?" Charity asked, her eyes searching Lizzie's.

Lizzie thought about Michael—how easy he was to talk to, how attentive he seemed to be, the softness of his kiss—and felt a faint stirring of excitement and trepidation. "I think so," she whispered, staring down at her clenched hands, "but I'm not sure. I haven't allowed myself to think of him that way, because of Brady. But now . . ."

She looked up at her sisters, and a sudden flare of annoyance rose within. "Now I wonder why I should let Brady have any say at all. He certainly doesn't want me—why should he keep me from someone who does?"

Faith leaned forward, the intensity of her gaze making Lizzie squirm. "That's anger talking, Lizzie, and frustration, which is understandable. But the thing that worries me the most, regardless of Brady, is whether Michael is the type of man God wants for you, a man cut from the same cloth as Father, Mitch, and Collin . . . *and* Brady." She paused. "Is he?"

Lizzie closed her eyes, seeing Michael's handsome face in her mind. He had done nothing to show her otherwise. Had, in fact, lavished more kindness and attention on her in the last two months than Brady had in the last six. And his newfound faith was young, certainly, but growing. Because of her.

She sighed and opened her eyes. "I don't know, Faith. I

don't know what God wants for me anymore. I thought I did. I thought it was Brady. Was convinced to the depth of my soul that God intended him for me. But apparently that hope was birthed by nothing more than the delusions of a thirteen-year-old girl. I'm confused and don't know what to make of Michael's attention. But I'll tell you one thing I do know. It's time I grow up and get on with my life. And that means without Brady." A sad smile lingered on her lips. "At least the stubborn one."

Faith reached for her hand and gave it a squeeze. "We're in this with you, Lizzie, all the way. We'll pray you through it, I promise."

Lizzie smiled and blinked back the wetness that seeped into her eyes. She squeezed Faith's hand and reached for Charity's. "I know that," she whispered, grateful for the love and support of her sisters. "I'd be lost if I didn't."

Collin hadn't seen Brady in this good of a mood since Miss Ramona cancelled the spring recital. Not that John Brady rejoiced in two-thirds of the dance troupe contracting chickenpox, but the reprieve from four hours of "culture," as Brady liked to call it, had definitely put a bounce in his step. Over the last week, despite a ridiculous workload, Brady had been smiling and whistling ad nauseam, taking whatever jobs Collin piled on with his usual grace and good humor, and then some.

Collin glanced up from the invoices he was drafting and scowled. Having to work on a Saturday always put him in a bad mood. But Brady was cranking out jobs faster than Collin could bill them, and it was starting to get on his nerves. Not the speed, which enabled them to have the best month on the books ever, but the blasted off-key whistling that went along with it.

"Ya think you can close the coffin on that particular song, ol' buddy? 'Amazing Grace' is starting to wear thin on my patience."

Brady looked up and grinned. Collin could swear he saw undulating ripples of heat rise from the press his partner had been laboring over since six a.m., steaming his face with a sheen of hard-earned sweat. Brady flicked the lever on the machine, and the roar of the press expired, along with Collin's patience.

Ambling into the room where Collin sat, Brady mopped his face with a gray towel that had once been white. "Thin? I'd say you're fresh out. You've been glaring at those invoices like we owe money instead of making it hand over fist. You still fretting over the fact we have to hire a new man . . . or are you back to butting heads with Faith?"

Collin shoved the stack of invoices out of his way and put his feet up on his desk with a grunt. He rubbed an ink-stained hand over his face. "No, I'm resigned to the fact that we can't do everything ourselves anymore, and I think the new guy we hired will work out well. And it's time for us to grow, so that's not a problem."

"So, it's Faith, then." Brady positioned himself on the well-worn corner where so many of their conversations took place. "Still the baby thing?"

Collin peeked up beneath the hand shielding his eyes and gave Brady a halfhearted smile. "No, she's been wonderful, almost as intent as me. Praying with me about it, always ready and willing no matter how tired she may be." The smile broadened on his lips. "She's even been giving me a taste of my own medicine lately, on those rare nights when the only thing I have on my mind is sleep."

Brady laughed. "I always said you were a bad influence."

Collin grinned. "Yeah, I guess I am. No, Faith is amazing. Our marriage is the best thing that ever happened to me."

Brady squinted and folded his arms. "But?"

Collin sighed and reached for a pencil off his desk. He

proceeded to twirl it between his fingers, careful to avoid Brady's eyes. "*But*, it's looking like she'll be promoted to copywriter."

"That's wonderful. She's worked for that over five years now. So, what's the problem?"

"The problem is, I'm not happy about it and I should be, because I love her more than life itself. I feel like a royal jerk. I mean, here she is, accomplishing something few women ever get the chance to do, a lifelong dream of hers, and how do I react? I'm sullen and resentful because I worry it will shift her focus off of me and the baby."

"The baby?"

Collin pursed his lips. "The baby I hope to have and probably would have if my wife stayed home and concentrated on having a family rather than a job." He groaned and tossed the pencil on the desk. "Dear Lord, how much more selfish can I get?"

Brady's lips, pressed in a noncommittal line, suddenly squirmed to the right. "Not much."

Collin's gaze narrowed. "I always appreciate your support, John, especially when it comes to clarifying my faults, but what am I supposed to do about this? I feel like a heel."

"You're not a heel, Collin, you're a human being who, like the rest of the human race, has heel tendencies. Have you prayed about it?"

Collin blinked. "What?"

Brady's lips twisted, as if fighting a smile. "You know, asked God to help you be the supportive husband Faith needs, or asked him to bless her in this situation?"

Collin's jaw dropped. "And why would I do that? I don't *want* her to be a copywriter."

"No, but if it happens, apparently God does. We're going for his agenda, not yours, remember? You've been asking God that if Faith is supposed to quit, she would, right?"

"Yeah."

"Well, if she gets promoted, looks to me like it's where she's supposed to be right now. You're just going to have to trust God for the timing of your family and pray to be the husband Faith needs right now—supportive and proud of her."

Collin expelled all the frustration he was feeling in one draining breath. "I know. And I am proud of her. She's a great writer and a hard worker and she deserves this promotion." He glanced up. "But you gotta help me out here, Brady. What do I do besides pray?"

"Tell her how proud you are, then encourage her, celebrate with a surprise party when she gets the promotion, no matter how you feel inside. Make it a big deal, because it is. She has the rest of her life to be the mother of your children—let her enjoy her dream for however long she can." Brady stood to his feet and held the dirty rag out, his grin stretching ear to ear. "And for pity's sake, pray for God to help you be happy for her and content with it. Then wipe that ink off your face. You're starting to look like me."

Collin grabbed the ink-streaked towel and wiped his cheek. He tossed it aside and opened his top desk drawer to pull out an apple Faith had packed in his lunch. "Thanks, John. But if I wanted to look like you, I'd have to paste a goofy grin on my face and offend your delicate sensitivities with off-key whistling. I don't know what's been driving me crazier the last few weeks—the whistling or the nonstop smiles. What's got you in such a chipper mood these days? Can't be just the new hire."

Ruddy color stained Brady's thick neck, and Collin leaned forward with a grin. "So, what's up? You got a lady you've been hiding from me?"

For all of his six-foot-three height, John Brady looked more like an awkward high schooler with his fists shoved deep in his pockets and his cheeks as red as the apple in Collin's hand. His throat bobbed, but the grin still shone on his face. "I think so, Collin. I'm in love."

Mid-bite, Collin began to choke, prompting Brady to slap him hard on the back. Collin waved him away and gaped. "What?"

Brady sat back on the desk, exposing more teeth than Collin had ever seen. "I'm in love, Collin—for the first time in my life—in every possible way. Spiritually, emotionally, mentally, physically."

Collin shook his head in disbelief, the apple limp in his hand. "Who?"

Brady grinned again, and Collin would have laid money on the table that the man's facial muscles were going to be screaming tonight, given his smile that bordered on delirium.

"Beth," Brady whispered.

Collin sat straight up. "Our Beth? *Lizzie?*"

Brady nodded, his face beaming like a man who had just seen the face of God.

"What? When? Sweet saints, does she even know?"

"Nope, not yet. I'm planning on taking it real slow, getting to know her as a woman, to make sure I can handle it before I let her know. I think the feelings of shame are gone, but I want to make sure so I don't hurt her again. I'm taking her fishing with Katie and Cluny this weekend, kind of like a date, only she doesn't know that."

A dozen questions ricocheted in Collin's mind as he stared, his jaw sagging low. "I don't understand. How? When? Why did this all happen? I thought you couldn't go there."

Brady's grin softened into a smile. "I couldn't, not until Father Mac helped me get past it. I've been counseling with him for the last four months. I finally realized I've been in love with Beth all along, only the shame of my past wouldn't allow me to see it. But I'm free now, and with God's help, I intend to make her my wife."

For several seconds, Collin just stared, certain his mouth would lock in the gaping position as surely as Brady's smile would permanently freeze on his face. And then a mist of joy sprang to his eyes and he bolted from the chair, seizing his friend in a fierce embrace. "Sweet chorus of angels, John, I couldn't be happier. Brothers at last!"

Brady's voice was gruff. "I know, Collin. I never thought I could be this happy."

Collin slapped him on the back and then pumped his hand in a hearty handshake. "It's nothing short of God's blessings, my friend, long, long overdue—" His words suddenly fused to his tongue. The smile faded from his face.

Brady frowned. "What's wrong?"

Collin's chest tightened as he thought of Lizzie and the secret Faith had sworn him to.

"Collin? Something's wrong—what is it?"

Collin looked away and threaded his fingers through his hair. "Yeah, yeah, there is. I don't think it's anything serious yet, but—"

Brady latched a hand to his arm and jerked him around. "You have to tell me—is Lizzie seeing someone?"

Collin studied his friend, measuring his words carefully. "She's been seeing your brother—you know that."

The tension in Brady's face eased a bit as he removed his hand from Collin's arm. "Yeah, I know that. Going to church with her and an occasional dinner at the house. But she promised me, Collin, promised she'd only fall for a man who loves God with all of his heart. And that's not Michael, I can tell you that."

Collin turned and slumped into his chair, eyeing Brady through wary eyes. "No, no, it's not. But I have to tell you, ol' buddy, the dinners have been more than occasional, and the spiritual effort more than convincing. Your brother's a charmer, John, and everybody knows that Lizzie's a romantic. I can't go into it, but I'm telling you now. If you are going to make your move, I suggest you do it sooner rather than later."

Brady stared, the smile completely wiped from his face. "What do you know, Collin? What do you know about Lizzie's feelings for Michael?"

"I can't go into it, Brady, but trust me on this."

Brady hovered over his desk, ink-stained hands pressed white on the marred surface. "I want to know, right now. Is Beth falling for my brother?"

"I can't tell you that, John, but read between the lines."

"Did Faith tell you something I should know?"

"Yeah, she did. But she also made me promise not to tell you."

Brady leaned in, his eyes burning with a fury that Collin had seldom seen. "So help me, Collin, if you don't tell me right now, I will come across this desk . . ."

Collin stared at his friend, indecision roiling in his gut. He'd promised his wife because she'd promised her sister. But Brady had a right to know—Lizzie belonged with him. He took a deep breath and prayed to heaven that Faith would never find out. "He's in love with her, Brady, or at least he told her so."

"He's lying."

"Maybe, but Lizzie doesn't seem to think so. He says he can give her what you can't."

Brady stared, his eyes glazed like a man who'd gone without sleep for days on end. A nerve fluttered in his cheek. "That no-good, lousy—"

"He asked her to think about it, to pray about it."

A swear word hissed from Brady's mouth, the sound strange to Collin's ears. Brady's fist bludgeoned Collin's desk. "He's using her!"

"I don't think so, John," Collin whispered, reluctant to go on. "He wants to marry her."

Brady sucked in a sharp breath, and his face paled. His shoulders sagged as he put a hand to his head. "But she doesn't love him."

"No, but she's confused. And he's not making it easy on her."

Brady glanced up, a razor edge to his voice. "What do you mean?"

Collin shifted in the chair. "So help me, God, if Faith ever finds out I told you this—"

"Spit it out it, Collin . . . *now!*"

Collin weighed his options and decided if he were in Brady's place, he'd want to know. Besides, he'd already said enough to break his promise to Faith; what was one more detail? He locked eyes with his friend. "According to Faith, Michael's kissed Lizzie several times, and it's muddied the waters for her." Collin drew in a deep breath, then exhaled slowly. "Faith seems to think Lizzie's falling for him, John."

Brady tried to breathe, but the air adhered to the walls of his throat. He stared in a daze as Collin's words taunted in his brain. *Lizzie's falling for him, John.*

"John!"

Brady blinked and Collin blurred back into view, his brow wrinkled with worry.

"You have to tell her you love her. Right away. You can't afford to wait."

Brady closed his eyes and willed himself to calm down. He would get through this. God didn't bring him this far to lose Beth to his brother. A cold shiver quivered through him, and he opened his eyes. "I can't, Collin. And you can't tell Faith, either. I need you to swear to me. I'm not going to risk hurting Beth again if I can't handle the intimacy between us. Not until I know I'm totally free. I won't hurt her again. I can't—I love her too much."

Collin stared, his mouth set in a grim line. "Then you may lose her, John."

Brady stood to his feet and rolled the kinks from his neck. Suddenly he felt as tired and worn as the overheated press in the back room. "No, I won't. There's another way." He peered down at Collin, his gaze intense. "Swear to me, Collin, now . . . that you won't tell Faith."

Collin studied him for several seconds before releasing a

heavy sigh. "I swear, but so help me, John, you better have a foolproof plan up your sleeve."

"I do." His mouth settled into a thin line. "I'll just give my brother what he wants."

Collin shot him a narrow gaze. "What do you mean?"

"I mean it's a good thing we hired that pressman when we did. He starts next Monday, right?"

"Yeah, but what's that got to do with your brother?"

Brady swiped the dirty rag from the desk and slung it over his shoulder. He gave Collin a pointed look. "I'm almost caught up, but I suggest you get him in here now—*today*—because come Monday, I'm going to New York."

Collin sat up in the chair. His eyes circled in shock. "New York? What the blazes for?"

"To make a deal with the devil," Brady muttered. He headed toward the back room with resolve stiffening his spine. He tightened his jaw and shot his partner a look intended to end all discussion. "Get the new hire in here today, Collin, and I'll be back in a few hours to help you break him in."

And before Collin could answer, Brady jerked his jacket off the hook and slammed the door behind, leaving his partner little choice but to comply.

❦   ❦

Brady stood on School Street and gazed up at the gleaming white marble front of the fourteen-story Parker House Hotel, wondering which room would be the scene of the crime. A scowl tipped the edges of his clamped lips. The crime his brother had committed in using Beth for his own purposes. *And* the crime he was about to commit in rewarding him for his efforts. Despite the brisk day, Brady shoved the rolled-up sleeves of his starched white shirt farther up his arms and reached for the sculpted bronze doors of one of Boston's luxury hotels, a prestigious landmark since 1855. He entered the oak-paneled lobby with its crystal chandeliers and elegant furnishings, once frequented by the likes of Thoreau, Hawthorne, Longfellow, and Dickens, and felt an immediate surge of anger. It was the perfect place for the upper class. But as far as Brady was concerned, it was no place for his brother, who had no class at all. Even without the inheritance, he didn't need the money, and yet he'd had no qualms about using Beth to force Brady's hand.

Brady ignored the curious looks from various well-to-do guests in the plush lobby, and made his way to the imposing marble front desk. Once Collin had spilled the bad news, Brady had left him in a stupor and gone home to clean up and change. But even with his fresh-scrubbed face, clean shirt, and newly pressed seersucker slacks, he was no match for the fashionably dressed clientele of The Parker, and the look of surprise on the clerk's face indicated as much.

"Why, good morning, Mr. Brady. You're up and about early today. I don't believe the mail has arrived yet, but how may I be of assistance?"

Brady gave the clerk a tight-lipped smile. "I'm John Brady, looking for my brother, Michael. May I have his room number, please?"

Comprehension flooded the man's face, coupled with relief, no doubt, that the modestly dressed gentleman before him was not a guest. "Yes, sir, of course. Suite 315. You may use the elevator across the lobby or the staircase to your right. Good day, Mr. Brady."

Brady mumbled his thanks and took the stairs two at time, barely out of breath when he reached the third landing. His heart was pumping at a fast clip, but not from the steps. Thinly disguised fury simmered beneath his calm exterior, and he flexed his clenched fingers to ease the tension. He saw the glint of a brass-plated room number on a suite at the end of the hall and strode toward the door. With several hard thrusts, he hammered the paneled oak with his fist, totally indifferent to the fact that it was only nine a.m. and his brother was probably still asleep.

Brady waited, his breathing little more than a halting pattern of shallow air as he thought about Michael kissing Beth. With a fresh rush of ire, he pounded on the door until his fist was numb from the effort, ignoring the sound of doors opening behind him down the hall.

"What the devil is going on . . ." Michael's door lashed open in a tirade of expletives, underscoring the unwelcome disruption of his sleep. His glare turned to shock as he stared, obviously caught off guard in rumpled silk pajamas, with bleary eyes and a growth of bristle on his tightly pressed jaw. He blinked. "John! What the devil are you doing here?"

"You win, Michael. Leave her alone and I'll sign the papers."

"What?"

"You heard me. I'll sign the papers. You and Helena can have it all—the printing business, the house, the estate—only give me your word you'll leave Beth alone."

Michael scoured his face with his hand, avoiding Brady's eyes. "It's not that easy anymore, John. I'm in love with her."

The words detonated Brady's anger like the flick of a grenade. He fisted Michael by his silk shoulders and slammed him hard against the oak door. "The devil you are! I know you. To you she's just another pretty face, a means to get to me. Let her go, Michael. I'll give you everything you want."

Michael pushed back, ramming Brady against the doorjamb with a grunt. He readied his stance, fists raised and eyes glinting. "You don't know me, little brother, any more than you know yourself. You could have avoided all of this, but instead you harbored ill feelings from the past despite your oh-so-noble relationship with God. You had her—all to yourself—but your warped pride kept you away—from Lizzie and from me. I wanted you to sign, it's true, but I also wanted to become brothers again, John, but your sick perspective wouldn't allow that."

The painful blast of Michael's words caused Brady to falter

back in shock, his brother's neatly placed barb depleting his fury. *Dear God, he's right.* His own unwillingness to let go of the past had imprisoned him, kept him from Beth's love and restoration with his brother. Even now, he could feel the bitterness roiling in his stomach, in defiance of the God who had called him to forgive.

*Lucille.* He closed his eyes and tasted the hate on his tongue for the woman who had stolen his past. The woman who was trying to steal his future.

*No, my son.*

The sense of the Spirit was so strong that Brady flinched against the door, opening his eyes to his estranged brother, an unlikely bearer of the truth. Cold realization prickled through him like shards of glass, severing the lies he had believed far too long. It wasn't Lucille who had stolen his past, nor Lucille who was trying to steal his future. It was sin that had robbed him of the hope and blessing of God in his life.

Sin, and only sin.

First, Lucille's.

And then his.

Brady listed against the door and put his head in his hands. *God forgive me.*

He'd thought he'd dealt with the hate, on his own and then again with Father Mac, but for the first time, he could clearly see he'd been deceived. Running away had only dulled it, convincing him he no longer bore a grudge. But Lucille still haunted him from the grave, shackled by the tentacles of his own hate. A hate that prevented him from giving his love to Beth . . . and granting the kinship his brother deserved.

Sorrow pricked his eyes. "Forgive me, Michael, you're right. My sick perspective on Lucille . . . my hate for her . . . was my own choice, my own sin. It kept me from loving Beth the way I should and from giving you and Helena the simple courtesy of procuring your rightful inheritance. Please forgive me."

Michael slowly lowered his fists and exhaled. "I forgive you,

John. If Lucille had done to me what she did to you, I don't know that I'd forgive her either." He stepped back and nodded toward the elaborate parlor of his guest suite. "You want to come in?"

Brady shook his head. "No, thanks. If you don't mind, we'll have plenty of time to talk in New York."

Michael's brow jutted high. "You'll come? Even though you know how I feel about Lizzie?"

Brady released a halting breath. "Yeah. On one condition."

Michael folded his arms and cocked against the door. "What?"

"I'm in love with her, Michael. Have been for a long time. And she loves me, too, you know that."

Michael's eyes narrowed. "So?"

"So, I'm asking you to give me time. I'll return to New York and sign anything you want. Only you have to give me your word to stay away from Beth for one month. After that, she's fair game. And we remain on good terms as brothers."

"And what if I don't?"

"Then I don't sign, you never see me again, and I ask Beth to marry me tonight, dealing you a triple loss."

Michael stood to his full height, fists clenched at his sides. "Don't be so sure she'll say yes, little brother. We've gotten very close."

Brady worked at restraining his anger, his jaw tight. "So I've heard. Do we have a deal?"

Michael rested his hands on his hips and lowered his head, studying the paisley carpet as if weighing his chances. He glanced up at Brady, his eyes in a squint. "Why a month? Why not go head-to-head? Afraid you'll lose?"

Brady kneaded the back of his neck, eyeing his brother with cool composure. "Because I want to take it slow. I don't want to hurt her again."

"In case you can't? Love her as a woman, I mean?"

Blood shot straight to Brady's cheeks. His arms stiffened at his sides, and a nerve twitched in his jaw. "You don't make this brother thing easy. Give me your answer—*now*!"

Michael grinned. "Okay, John, you have a deal. When do we leave?"

"I have your word? You'll stay away for a full month, from the day I sign the papers?"

"I'll give you my word I'll try—"

"No, Michael. I want your word you *will* stay away from Beth. For a solid month."

Michael studied him with a curious gaze and then slowly smiled. "Sure, little brother, I'll stay away from *Beth*. For a solid month."

Brady released a shaky breath. "Okay. Then we leave on Monday morning. Pick me up at the shop in that fancy car of yours—nine a.m. sharp." Brady turned to leave.

Michael grabbed his arm. "Wait a minute. This is Saturday, and Lizzie's babysitting for Charity tonight. And she told me she's busy all day tomorrow."

Brady's lips flickered in a near smile. "Yeah, I know. She's going fishing with Cluny and me, then out to dinner. Should be a fairly late night, I think. Goodbye, Michael."

"But when am I supposed to tell her goodbye?"

Brady glanced at his watch. "Well, you can always say good-bye in the vestibule of church on Sunday. Or in about two hours, she has a thirty-minute lunch break at Bookends, then about half that much time before she, Mary, and Millie go to Charity's to babysit." Brady grinned. "Twins can be a lot of trouble, you know."

Michael's smile turned sour. "Yeah, I know—firsthand."

With a scowl and a flick of his silk-sleeved arm, he promptly slammed the door, fanning Brady's face with a most satisfying breeze.

# 15

Brady was a nervous wreck. He paced back and forth from his kitchen to the parlor in clipped, jerky strides sure to make Miss Hercules dizzy as she moped on the floor, eyes tracking his every move.

"Cluny? You about done? For pity's sake, we're going fishing, not to a church social."

"Keep your shirt on, Brady, I'm almost there."

Brady glanced down at his own tan cable-knit sweater. He wondered if it was overkill for a crisp fall afternoon, given the fact that Beth had a warming effect on him lately. He unbuttoned the cuff of the white shirt beneath and thrust the thick sleeves up, revealing muscled arms strained with tension. He blew out a blast of frustration and yanked the sleeves back down, then glanced down the hall. "*Cluny?*"

"Coming! Just one more thing."

"What in sweet blazes are you doing, and why didn't you do it at home?"

"Cain't. Gram would get suspicious if I took a bath, and besides, she doesn't have that sweet-smelling stuff."

Brady halted, midstride. "You're using my aftershave?"

Cluny strutted out of the bathroom dressed in brown knickers and a thick cream sweater that did wonders for his sunken chest. His blond hair was slicked back with brilliantine, revealing a glowing pink face that looked as if he'd tried to scrub his freckles off. He parked his hands on his hips and strolled up to Brady, leaning close to give him a whiff. "So, what do you think? I do believe Katie Rose may just swoon."

Brady took a step back and fanned the air with his hand. "Yeah, from asphyxiation. How much did you use, anyway? The whole bottle?"

Cluny appeared hurt. "Nope, just a few drops." He crossed his arms and scowled. "Besides, it wouldn't hurt for you to slap a little on. It sure beats the fish smell you'll be wearing before we're through."

Brady shot him a narrow look, realizing the kid was probably right. He started toward the bathroom, mumbling under his breath.

"You cussing again, Brady?"

"No. And I don't cuss. Is there any left in the blasted bottle or did you use it all?"

"You're awfully touchy for a guy about to go fishing with his girl and best buddy."

Brady poked his head out of the bathroom, singeing Cluny with a look. "She's not my girl—yet. And if you so much as breathe a word to Katie Rose—"

"My lips are sealed." Cluny crossed his heart and winked. He strode down the hall, patting his cheeks with the aftershave. "You got the worms?"

Cluny hoisted a tin can. "Right here."

"Good." Brady reached for his tackle box and four rods, prompting Miss Hercules to jump up, ready to go. He clutched Cluny by the scruff of the neck and led him to the door, then wrinkled his nose. "Don't know why I bothered to put any aftershave on. All I need to do is rub against you. Come on, you little troublemaker. I can only hope the walk will air you out."

Brady was certain that Cluny had chattered all the way to the O'Connors' front gate, but for the life of him, he couldn't remember one word the kid had said. All he knew for sure was his mouth was dry and his hands were sweating, and the blasted sweater was so hot that he worried even Cluny's aftershave wouldn't save him.

"Brady? You coming?"

Brady snapped out of his fog at the base of the O'Connor steps, realizing his legs were stiff. They refused to budge, two mules with heels dug in. He blinked up at Cluny, poised on the top step with a furrow in his brow and Miss Hercules by his side.

"You okay, Brady?"

A reedy breath escaped through his lips. *Okay?* How in blue blazes could he be okay? He was about to spend an afternoon and evening with a woman who wreaked havoc with his internal thermostat, sent his pulse into overdrive with a bat of her violet eyes. *Okay?* Not even close. Brady licked his lips, wondering when all the moisture had left his mouth.

Sweet God in heaven, he wasn't equipped for this! He had little or no experience with women. A six-week engagement before he'd left for the war didn't even count, it was so long ago. And since then, he hadn't allowed himself to even look at a girl, much less date one. He thought of Beth's sweet face, her graceful, beautiful form with soft curves in all the right places . . .

God help him, he was a goner! Sweat broke out on the back of his neck, and he jerked at the sound of Cluny's voice.

"Brady, are you sick?"

"No, Cluny, I'm fine." He sucked in a deep breath and licked his lips once again. "Just a little dizzy, that's all."

Cluny slacked a hip and flashed some teeth. "Sure you're not scared?"

Brady mounted the steps, blistering Cluny with a glare. "I said I was dizzy."

"Yeah, dizzy for Lizzie and scared of a girl."

Brady forced a grim smile. "It's a good thing you don't live with me anymore, or I'd kick your sorry little butt out. Ring the bell."

Despite Cluny's annoying grin, there had never been a more perfect Sunday afternoon. The sky was a brilliant blue and tufted with thick cotton-ball clouds that rolled across the heavens, playing cat and mouse with a pale sun. A soft breeze feathered his cheek, tickling his senses with the smells of moist autumn leaves, smoky wood fires, and the faint scent of the sea. He inhaled deeply and grinned as he reached the top step, suddenly overpowered by Bay Rum. Brady shook his head as he watched Cluny press the bell for the second time. That little lothario better hope and pray that Katie had a cold.

"Brady! We've missed you." Katie bolted out the door and threw her arms around Brady's waist, ignoring the tackle box and poles clutched in his hands.

Brady chuckled and attempted to hug her back. "Whoa, Katie, there are hooks on these rods. I've missed you too."

Cluny cocked a hip and tucked the can of worms under his arm. "What about me and Miss Hercules? Did you miss us?"

Her nose tipped up considerably. "Miss Hercules, yes. You, I don't know. Who are you again?"

He chuckled, and the sound rumbled lower than Brady remembered. "Only the guy who's gonna catch all the fish today," he declared in a tone that brooked no doubt. He scrubbed Miss Hercules' snout and ambled over to the swing to sit.

She dismissed him with a toss of her hair and turned her attention to Brady. "Lizzie's inside packing the lunch. You want to come in?"

Cluny rose to his feet, and Katie pinned him with a glare. "Not you. The worms and the mutt will miss you."

Brady grinned. "No thanks, Katie, I better stay out here with Cluny. I don't think your mother would appreciate my traipsing through her house with these rods." He hesitated. "Unless Beth needs help with the basket?"

"Who needs help with a basket? I'll have you know I have more muscles from stacking books than either Mary or Millie."

Brady's head jerked up. One of the rods slipped, clattering against the wooden basket in Beth's hand. Heat braised the back of his neck as he bent to retrieve it.

She laughed. "Heavens, Brady, I won't be in danger on this fishing expedition, will I?"

The heat traveled to his cheeks, and his palms began to sweat. His tongue was as dry as the smirk on Cluny's face. He covered with a lopsided grin. "Don't think so, Beth. Only thing biting should be the fish. Here, give me that basket." He handed the tackle box to Katie, then fisted the rods in one hand and the basket in the other. "Thanks for offering to bring a picnic lunch. Do we have everything?"

"I think so . . . no, wait, I forgot the blanket." She disappeared inside and then returned with a well-worn quilt. "Mother said we could use this. Now we just have to lock the door since everyone's still at church for the pancake breakfast." She closed the door and tested the knob, then flashed a smile that spiked Brady's body temperature by several degrees. "Ready?"

Brady nodded dumbly, wondering for the hundredth time when she had grown into such a beauty. He was grateful that O'Reilly Park was close as she chattered alongside, barely noticing that Cluny and Katie had run on ahead, shadowed by Miss Hercules. Brady studied Beth out of the corner of his eye, well aware that his breathing had escalated, but not from the walk. For the first time in his life, the woman he'd once considered a little sister now took his breath away. From the lavender cashmere sweater that brought out her eyes to a startling degree, to the pastel woolen skirt that fell just below the knee, revealing long, perfectly shaped legs—Brady felt as if he were seeing her for the very first time. He trained his focus straight ahead. God help him, he liked what he saw— way, *way* too much.

When they reached the lake, Cluny was teaching Katie how to skip stones across the water while Miss Hercules waded close to the shore, stalking anything that moved. Brady deposited the basket on a bed of freshly fallen leaves beneath a gnarled oak at lake's edge. He squinted at the sunlight that flickered through the last vestige of golden foliage overhead. One gilded leaf fluttered against his cheek on a gentle breeze, almost like a caress from the hand of God.

He scanned the shore of the deep blue lake as it sparkled in the sun, taking in the vignettes of a perfect autumn day. Miniature homemade boats skimmed across the shimmering surface, their tiny sails billowing in the breeze as fathers and sons cheered on. Families skittered in the sun while fathers baited hooks and mothers jostled babies and laughed at toddlers chasing dogs through mountains of leaves. The air echoed with the laughter of children and the chatter of birds, and in the midst of the magical moment, Brady could feel God's peace light on him as gently as the oak leaves drifting from the limbs overhead.

He drew in a deep breath—thick with the loamy scent of the mossy bank, the earthy smell of wet leaves fringing the lake, and the lingering trace of Cluny—and slowly released it again. His anxiety drifted away on a sigh of gratitude. *Thank you, God.* He took the blanket from Beth as she struggled to place it, shook it out and spread it evenly on the ground. She quickly busied herself with unloading the basket, and he suddenly realized her chattering had stopped. But it didn't matter. This was Beth, the little girl he'd mentored, the friend he respected, the woman he loved. And, God willing, the wife he would cherish.

*And make love to.*

The sudden thought caused his heart to catch. No, he would take this slowly, he vowed, prayerfully, until he was sure his past wouldn't stand in the way. There was no way he would hurt her again. She was too important.

"What's for lunch? I'm starved!" Cluny skidded onto the quilt on his knees, bunching the corner.

Brady thumped him on the head. "Hey, bud, keep those

muddy shoes off Beth's blanket. And move over. The rest of us have to share, you know. You're getting way too big."

Cluny winked at Katie. "Hear that, Katie Rose? Brady says I'm getting too big."

Katie scrunched her nose. "Egos don't count."

"Oooo, chocolate cake!" Cluny lifted the lid and peeked in the basket.

Katie slapped the lid closed. "Don't touch. And it's devil's food," she stated in a bored tone. Her lips lifted in a smirk. "In your honor, of course."

Beth laughed. "Be nice, Katie. After all, this is Cluny's day."

Cluny blinked. "Why? It ain't my birthday."

Heat prickled the back of Brady's neck when Beth looked his way. She handed him a piece of fried chicken and smiled. "I know, but Brady felt so badly about sending you back to your gram, that he wanted to have a special day where he focused only on you."

Cluny looked at Brady, and one of his spindly brows spiked high. "Only on me, eh?"

Brady reached for a drumstick and tossed it at the kid. "Here, eat. Things are less complicated when your mouth is full."

They ate until they were ready to burst, at least Cluny and he did, giving the leftovers to Miss Hercules. He and Beth chatted quietly while Katie and Cluny traded good-natured insults and polished off the cake.

"Race ya to the dock," Cluny challenged, and Katie popped up.

"Last one there baits all the hooks," she shrieked. Her blond hair whipped in the breeze as she flew toward a long stretch of wooden planking down the shore. "Don't forget the poles," she called. Her giggles rose in the air, punctuated by Miss Hercules's woofs. Both of them left Cluny in the dust.

"Hey, cheaters bait their own hooks," he yelled. He scrambled up and snatched two poles, then turned and shot them a grin. "I better go show her how it's done." He tore after Katie and the dog with a gleam in his eye.

Brady shook his head and smiled. "He's a cocky little thing. I would have given my eyeteeth for a tenth of his confidence at that age."

Beth began repacking the basket, her eyes trained on the task at hand. "Speaking of his age, Brady, we've been friends for a long time, and I've always wondered—what happened to you back then? You know, when you were Cluny's age? I've always wanted to ask, but I never had the nerve."

Brady's throat tightened as he helped her clean up. "Someday I hope to tell you all about it, Beth, but I'm not there yet. I haven't really allowed myself to think about it until recently, not until Father Mac helped me to face a few things. The healing's begun, but I've got a ways to go."

Her eyes were flecked with concern. "I'm glad, Brady, glad that at least you're able to talk to Father Mac. It's not good to keep all that pain inside."

"I know," he whispered, then jumped to his feet and brushed off his slacks. "Ready to take on a few bass?"

He offered a hand, and she sprang up with a nervous giggle. "Well, I haven't fished in a long time. Not since I was little when Father would bring us here during the summers. We'd have family fishing tournaments, you know, and Charity would nearly always win. Sean and Faith used to get so mad, but nobody had a knack for reeling them in like Charity."

Brady grinned. "Now, why am I not surprised?" Tucking his tackle box under his arm, he grabbed the rods in one hand and took her hand in the other. "Come on. Let's get you set up. Lures or worms? What's it gonna be?"

She wrinkled her nose. "Lures, please."

He chuckled. "Don't tell me you're afraid of a little ol' earthworm, Elizabeth?"

She shivered. "Not in the ground, I'm not, but my stomach gets a bit queasy when I see them squirming on a hook."

"Okay, lures it is." He plopped down on a weathered wooden bench and dropped the tackle box in his lap while Beth perched beside him. In no time, he had a shiny silver minnow dangling from her rod. He stood to his feet. "Okay, you know how to work a reel?"

She shook her head.

"It's real easy. Watch." He cradled the rod in his right hand, pressed the button release, and arced the fishing line up in a clean sweep across the water. Squinting in concentration, he feathered the spool with his right thumb and watched the glimmer of silver splash in the water before nudging the release once again. He turned and gave Beth a smile. "See? It's not too hard. Your turn."

She bit her lip and tentatively took the rod. "Well, okay, but I'm not sure I'll be all that good. Let's see, I hold it like this . . . then I press this . . . and then I do this . . ." In one fierce jerk, she whipped the line high over her head and yanked it back down.

"Whoa, little buddy, the fish are in the lake, not in my trousers," Brady said with a chuckle. He carefully took the rod from her hands and reached back to disengage the hook from the seat of his pants.

Beth's cheeks bloomed bright red. She put a hand to her mouth and tried not to laugh. "Oh, Brady, I'm so sorry! Does it hurt?"

He grinned. "Nope, Collin's given me bigger pains in the behind than this. Here, let me show you how to cast it over your head. But first, I need to get rid of this sweater before I pass out from heat stroke." He shimmied the garment over his head and tossed it on the bench with a breath of relief, then rolled up the sleeves of his shirt. "Whew! Much better. Okay, let's try this again."

He put the rod in her right hand, then circled her from behind. He grasped his hands over hers. All at once, the scent of her hair and the nearness of her body distracted him, sending a jolt of heat searing through him. He fought it off, chewing on his lip as he forced himself to concentrate on the casting. "Okay, you hold the rod here, then release the button, then lift the rod like this . . ." His arm gently guided hers up and out, landing the lure in a perfect cast that rippled across the water.

"I did it!" she cried.

"Yes, you did. Now press the button release again so you don't lose your line."

She notched the button and turned, her face flushed a delicate shade of excitement. With a giggle, she threw herself into his arms, almost gouging his eye with her rod as she hugged.

He closed his eyes and swallowed the lump in his throat.

"Oh, Brady, this is so much fun! Can I do it again?" She pulled away and stared up. Her violet eyes brimmed with excitement.

He smiled, and then his gaze dropped to her full lips, forcing the breath to congeal in his lungs. He cleared his throat and stepped back. "Sure, Beth, you try it this time."

Lizzie blinked, feeling a flutter in her stomach. *What on earth just happened?* One minute Brady was teaching her how to cast, and the next . . .

She spun around to hide the heat that crept in her face and quickly swallowed her shock, desperate to focus on the rod in her hands. But his eyes . . . sweet saints, they'd had the same dreamy quality she'd seen in Michael's, a kind of half-lidded stare that settled on her mouth, causing her heart to stop. She drew in a ragged breath and steeled her jaw. No! It was nothing more than her imagination playing cruel tricks on her. "Focus, Lizzie," she muttered under her breath, squinting at the lake as she swung the rod. The lure plopped into the water with shocking precision. Her lips flattened in grim satisfaction. *Good! Maybe I can hook some fish, if nothing else.*

"Good cast!" Brady said. He seated himself on the bench once again. "Now just relax and wait for the first strong nibble, then jerk the rod and reel her in."

*Relax?* Lizzie sighed and stared at the spot where her line disappeared, her good mood sinking as rapidly as the steel lure plunging to the bottom of O'Reilly Lake. From the moment Brady had picked them up, she'd been as jittery as a school of minnows, chattering like a magpie all the way to the park. She hadn't relished the idea of telling him about Michael, about his proposal and how her feelings for him were changing. And she especially didn't want to ruin this day. But the picnic lunch had calmed her down considerably, easing her back into the same comfortable, wonderful relationship they'd always shared.

But she *had* to tell him, and it needed to be soon. Since Michael had kissed her over a month ago, her heart had resolved to move on and let go of John Brady. He didn't want her, but his brother did. And since she had taken that mental leap, Michael had helped her in taking emotional steps as well. His visits had become more frequent and more intense, until she found herself thinking of him more and more. Her concern over his lack of spiritual depth when compared to Brady was diminishing, replaced instead with a growing pride over having led him to God. Other than an occasional niggling doubt over the level of his true commitment, Lizzie felt confident his spiritual potential, although not likely to rival Brady's, could come close.

*Almost.*

Lizzie sighed. Who was she kidding? No one could come close to John Brady. Not unless they lived in a church or monastery.

Brady stood to his feet and moved farther down the bank, casting his line with all the ease of a skilled angler. She stole a glimpse out of the corner of her eye and felt a tug at her heart. For a man who spent his days smeared with ink and under a press, John Brady was a graceful athlete in every sense of the word. Be it basketball with Father Mac or boxing with Collin, Brady was a natural who seldom lost. With every sail of his line over the water, his well-conditioned muscles would tense and then relax, his gaze fixed like a man whose every hope rested on that blasted lure. Not a care in the world. And totally oblivious that her heart was still his.

*But not for long.* A wasp buzzed her face and she shooed him away with a surge of annoyance. She was through being stung by John Brady. With another thrust of her line, she turned her attention to thoughts of Michael and immediately felt the strain ease in her back. She would tell Brady tonight, after he walked her home. Argument over.

The afternoon flew by as quickly as the geese overhead, winging their way south against a watercolor sky. Miss Hercules was the proud recipient of a steak bone someone had kindly left behind, and Katie was thrilled with her haul of six bluegill, one tiny striped bass, and a tin can sporting a clump of seaweed. Cluny appeared to strut a bit taller with his stringer of decent crappie and bluegill, and even Lizzie couldn't help but be proud of three small bass that Brady insisted were "keepers." Combined with his bounty of good-sized bass, it promised to be a real feast, and Lizzie could feel her mouth watering over the fish fry Brady planned when he returned from his trip.

They washed up at Brady's flat after stashing their fish on ice and feeding Miss Hercules, and Lizzie didn't mind the faint smell of fish in the air. They ate pasta and shrimp by candlelight at Pietro's, where the Italian owner welcomed Brady like a son, eyeing Lizzie with more than a bit of curiosity as he kissed her hand.

The moon hung high in the sky when they finally left the restaurant, dropping Cluny and Miss Hercules off at Gram's before they headed home to Donovan Street. Katie's eyes were drooping when the trio trudged up the steps of the front porch, and her shoulders slumped with fatigue as she turned to give Brady a hug.

"I had a wonderful time, Brady. Thanks for inviting me."

Brady smiled and gave her a squeeze. "Hope Cluny didn't drive you crazy."

She yawned. "He did, but he's not too bad once you get past the smell."

Brady grinned and kissed her on the forehead. "Must be a pretty smart guy, choosing you as a friend."

She sighed and bobbed her head. "Must be. Good night, Brady."

"Good night, Katie."

Lizzie glanced up, stifling a yawn of her own. "Goodness, what time is it?"

Brady held his wristwatch up to the light streaming from the parlor window. "Nine o'clock. It's been a long day for you, I guess."

She smiled. "But a wonderful one. Thank you, Brady, for fishing and dinner, and everything. Would you like to come in for a bit?" She glanced at the window. "Collin and Faith will probably still be here if you want to visit."

*No.* He didn't want to visit with Collin, or Faith, or anyone else. All he wanted to do was stand right here on this porch and stare at Beth for the rest of the night. He pushed a strand of hair from her eyes and forced a smile. "No, better not. I have an early day tomorrow. I promised Collin I'd give him a couple of quality hours before Michael picks me up."

Lizzie hugged her arms to her sides and stared at her feet. "Speaking of Michael," she whispered.

Brady lifted her chin with his finger. "No, Beth. Not tonight, please. I'll be spending the next week with my brother. I don't want to talk about him right now."

He feathered the line of her brow with his thumb, longing to ease the worry he saw etched in her face. "It was a wonderful day. One of the best of my life. I hope to have many more when I come back from New York."

Confusion clouded her eyes. "Brady, I—"

He slowly slid his thumb down the side of her face to rest at the curve of her jaw. He heard her soft intake of breath as he leaned in close, pressing his lips to her cheek. He craved the touch of her mouth against his, but he refused to give in. Not until he was sure. He wanted his desire to be pure, untainted by his past. But God help him, he wanted her—to hold her, to touch her. He stepped away and stood to his full height.

"Good night, Beth," he whispered, "I'll see you later this week." And with everything in him, he forced himself to turn and hurry down the steps like a man with the devil on his heels.

Lizzie closed her eyes, and heat collided with hurt as she touched her face, still branded by the burn of his lips. She listed against the door. He'd done it again. Given her a day of laughter and friendship and joy, and then walked away, taking her heart with him. Tears pooled beneath her closed lids, slowly seeping down a cheek that still quivered from his kiss. A sob erupted from her throat. "Why, God?" she rasped. "Why can't you just take him out of my heart? He doesn't want me. Can't you please set me free?"

A wave of frustration all too familiar engulfed her, followed by a rush of anger. With a painful heave, she squared her shoulders and vowed—*once again*—that John Brady had hurt her for the last time. Her lips settled into a grim line. If it meant the end of their friendship to get over him, then so be it. Someday, perhaps, when she was safely married and long past her childhood fantasies of him, they could be friends once again. But apparently not now, she thought with a jolt of grief. At least not without heartbreak as a constant companion.

She took a deep breath and quietly opened the door, hoping and praying no one in the parlor would even notice she'd come in. She hurried toward the staircase, desperate to get to her room before someone could stop her.

"Lizzie?" Her father's voice boomed from the parlor in a tone that froze her foot to the floor. She sighed and dropped her head. "Come in here this instant, young lady."

She groaned and put her head in her hands, tempted to lie and tell him she had to use the bathroom. She quickly swiped at her eyes and headed to the parlor, girding herself for the inquisition. "Yes, Father?"

Lizzie was sure the blush in her face complemented her tearstains quite nicely, given the looks on her family's faces. The strains of "Amazing Grace" filled the room as the Salvation Army Band rendered its nightly performance on Father's new, state-of-the-art radio.

Patrick peered over his newspaper and immediately frowned. "Lizzie . . . have you been crying?"

"Goodness, are you all right?" Marcy asked, knitting needles halted midair. She quickly removed a ball of yarn and half-knitted sweater from her lap and started to rise from her chair.

"Don't get up, Mother, please. Yes, I'm fine, really. I'm just very, very tired."

"What's wrong?" Faith rose sleepy-eyed from the love seat where she'd apparently been dozing with stockinged feet curled in Collin's lap as he read the paper.

"Nothing's *wrong*," Lizzie insisted. "Mitch and Charity already left, I suppose—" She glanced at the other side of the room and stopped, stunned to see Michael Brady sprawled on the floor with her brother. The two were playing with the magic linking rings in Steven's Mysto Magic set.

Relief flooded through her. "*Michael?* What are you doing here?"

He handed the rings off to Steven and rose to his feet, brushing the wrinkles from his trousers. He smiled, but his eyes registered concern. "I'm sure John told you we're leaving in the morning. I apologize for barging in like this, Lizzie, but I wanted to say goodbye. I won't be back for a while."

"Why are your eyes red?" Patrick asked again. "Have you been crying?"

She tore her gaze from Michael to offer her father a pitiful smile. "Yes, Father, maybe a little, but I promise, nothing's wro—"

"Did something happen with Brady?" Collin demanded. "Why didn't he come in?"

Faith jumped up and tugged at his arm. "Come on, Collin, I'm tired—take me home."

"But I want to know—did you two fight?" He put the paper aside and waited.

"This is between Lizzie and Brady, not us," Faith said, lowering her voice to a whisper.

Lizzie sighed. "No, Collin, we didn't fight. It was a lovely day. I'm just tired, that's all."

"Nobody cries when they're tired," he mumbled, allowing Faith to drag him up from the love seat. "Good night, everyone. Thanks for dinner, Marcy."

"You're welcome, Collin. Faith, come to dinner Tuesday night, and we'll finish sewing that dress, all right?"

Faith kissed her mother on the cheek, then her father. "Sounds great. Thanks, Mother. Good night, everyone. Have a safe trip, Michael."

Collin turned at the door. "Yeah, good night, Michael. It's always nice to go home, isn't it? I bet you miss it."

"Not as much as I did."

Collin's jaw tightened as he glanced at Lizzie, then back at Michael. "Take care of your brother for me, will you? And don't let him dawdle too long. I'm no good at running that temperamental press of his. I swear it gets more ink on me than the blasted paper."

Michael smiled. "He won't be gone long, a week tops. But I am looking forward to spending time with him."

Collin nodded. He ushered Faith out the door.

Marcy rose and gave Lizzie a hug. "I'm glad you had fun today. I've never seen Katie so tuckered out." She bent to give Patrick a good-night kiss. "I'm going up. Are you coming soon?"

"Shortly, darlin'. I want to finish this article."

"All right, my love. Steven—get those magic pieces picked up, please. You've got school tomorrow." She turned and gave Michael a hug. "We enjoyed your company this evening, Michael. Have a safe trip home."

"Thanks, Mrs. O'Connor." He hesitated. "Mr. O'Connor, would you mind if I had a few moments with Lizzie out on the porch?"

Patrick reached for his paper. "No, go right ahead. You've earned it after keeping company with the entire family most of the night. Will we be seeing you again?"

"I hope so, sir."

"Good, then have a safe trip."

"Thank you, sir, I will." Michael moved toward the front door and snatched Lizzie's jacket off the coat rack. He held it while she slipped it on, then opened the door.

Lizzie hurried to kiss her father good night before following Michael outside. She settled on the far side of the swing and turned to face him, suddenly shy. "You certainly shocked me, coming here tonight."

He sat on the other end and studied her, his eyelids weighted with concern. "I had to come, Lizzie. You know I'm in love with you. I couldn't leave without saying goodbye."

She closed her eyes and let his words soothe her ravaged spirit. Oh, Lord, was it wrong that it felt so good to hear? That Michael was in love with her . . . even if Brady wasn't?

She heard him shift closer on the swing and opened her eyes. He took her hand in his, grazing her palm with the pad of his thumb. Her stomach fluttered. "How long will you be gone?" she whispered, afraid to hear his answer. She dreaded facing her heartbreak alone, without Michael as a buffer. Over the last few months, his attention had helped to ease the hurt of Brady's rejection, rekindling hope that one day, maybe, she could be free from the pain.

"A month."

"Oh . . . ," she said, her voice trailing off.

"Trust me, I don't want to stay away, but I have to. I made a promise to John."

She jolted upright. "You what?"

"But only for a month, and then I'll be back, I promise."

"But why would he ask you to do that?"

"You know why. He loves you and wants the best for you. Unfortunately, he doesn't think I'm it."

Anger stiffened her spine. "But, he has no right. Who does he think he is?"

Michael tucked a finger beneath her chin. "Your friend, a big brother, someone who thinks he needs to look out for you."

"Well, he's not! And I resent it. So help me, Michael, if there was something I could do to get that through his thick skull—"

Michael hesitated, then squeezed her hand. "There is," he whispered.

Lizzie turned to study his handsome face. Her pulse quickened. "What?"

He reached into his coat pocket and produced a tiny velvet box. The sight of it effectively trapped the air in her throat. He gently placed it on her lap. "Open it."

She did as he asked, fingers trembling, and promptly caught her breath. Never had she seen a more exquisite diamond, pear-shaped with at least a dozen different facets, in a stone far larger than even Charity's. It glimmered and twinkled in the moonlight, as if pleading Michael's case. "It's so beautiful . . ."

"Enough to keep?"

She looked up, torn by the look of hope in his eyes. "Oh, Michael, I . . . I don't know. This is all so sudden."

"Not for me. It only took a few weeks to realize I'd never met anyone like you before, and I'm pretty sure I never will again. Say it, Lizzie . . . say you'll become my wife."

She stared at the diamond, then back up again, her mind in turmoil. "I'm so confused, I just don't know." She chewed on her lip, reluctant to go on. "I'm not sure that I love you."

He lifted her chin with his finger. "You care about me, don't you?"

"Oh yes, yes I do—more than I ever thought I could, given my feelings for Brady, but I don't know if it's enough."

"It is for me. For now. I can make it grow, I know I can. John loves you as a sister and a friend, but I'm offering something he can't—marriage, children, and a good life. I'm a wealthy man, Lizzie. I can take care of you, love you like you deserve to be loved. Say yes—please."

She hesitated, her heart racing.

He traced a finger over her lips. "You are attracted to me, aren't you? At least a little?"

The heat of his touch converged with the heat of her face. "I think so," she whispered, her voice barely a croak.

A faint smile played on his lips. "You think so? Well, since we're contemplating marriage, don't you think it would be a good idea to make sure?" He leaned in, heating her blood with the gentle tug of his mouth against her ear. His lips roamed to explore her throat, and she closed her eyes, barely aware her head had eased back. All at once she released a soft gasp when his mouth covered hers, coaxing her with a gentle sway before he deepened the kiss. "Marry me," he whispered, his breath hot against her cheek. "We can start planning the wedding in a month, when I come back. I won't take no for an answer." He took the box from her hand and put the ring on her finger, then scooted her close. "Say it, Lizzie, say you'll marry me."

She stared at the ring and then up at his face. "Oh, Michael, there's a part of me that wants to say yes so badly. When I'm with you, I forget all about the hurt over Brady and I feel . . . safe."

He grinned and tilted her back, giving her a look that was anything but "safe." "Then say yes. I guarantee I'll make you forget all about my brother." He followed through with a kiss that convinced her he was more than capable.

She pulled away, her body tingling. "Michael, I—"

"Say yes or I'll . . ." He started for her lips again, his half-lidded look leaving no doubt of his intentions.

"Yes!" she cried in a rush. She held him at bay, palms flat on his chest.

*Yes? Do I really mean that?* Michael's eyes fixated on her lips, and she felt a flutter in her stomach. She blinked up at him, suddenly realizing that the thought of being married to this man—sleeping with this man—made her feel heady. Just like romance was supposed to be. Or so she'd read.

He grinned and stood to his feet, hoisting her up in his arms. "You just made me the happiest guy in Boston, Lizzie O'Connor." He spun her around with a chuckle, then slowly released her, setting her down and pulling her close. He kissed her again, his mouth gentle against hers. "I have to go, but I'll be back in a month, and I'll call you every night. In the meantime, don't let anybody talk you out of this, okay? Especially my brother. He'll get used to the idea in time, I promise."

His mention of Brady darkened her mood. "No one's going to talk me out of this, Michael . . . *especially* your brother."

He kissed her on the nose. "That's a girl. So, I'll see you in a month?"

She nodded and he led her to the door. He took her left hand and kissed it. "Promise you won't take it off?"

She glanced at the ring and thought about what a powerful barrier it would make against her feelings for John Brady. "Not even when I sleep. Good night, Michael." She stood on tiptoe and kissed him lightly on the lips.

"Good night, Lizzie. I hope your dreams will be as sweet as mine." He turned and ambled down the steps, whistling all the way. She closed the door and flicked the lock, then hung her jacket on the hook. She held her left hand up and sighed. The diamond glittered with promise, pledging some semblance of peace from the pain of John Brady, she supposed. She started for the stairs.

"Lizzie?"

She blinked, suddenly aware of the light in the parlor. "Father? What are you still doing up?" She glanced at the clock on the mantel. "It's after ten, and Mother went up ages ago."

Patrick looked up at his daughter and felt his stomach twist. God help him, his sweet little Lizzie was changing. She was once his shy little girl, content with exploring love between the covers of a book. Now she stood before him, a young woman intent on experiencing it for herself. And for some reason he couldn't quite put his finger on, the thought left him more than a bit unsettled. He lowered the paper to his lap and gave her a tired smile. "Waiting for you, darlin'." He tapped the wide arm of his chair. "Mind sitting a while, to talk to your tired, old father?"

A hint of a blush settled in her cheeks. She smiled and ambled over. "Tired maybe, Father, but never old," she said with a laugh, leaning into him as he tucked an arm around her shoulder.

He bundled her close, his heart melancholy over yet another daughter growing up, growing away. He sighed and patted her leg. "So, you had a good time with Brady today?"

She nodded, and the slight movement tickled his chin. He hesitated. "Is that why you were crying? Because the day was good, but the situation is not?"

She nodded again, and he felt her shiver. He rubbed her arm and laid his head on top of hers. "You'll get past it, Lizzie, I promise. God will make a way."

"He already has, Father," she whispered.

His stomach tightened. "Michael?"

She nodded, then slowly sat up, searching his eyes. She quietly held out her left hand.

Patrick blinked, astonishment trapping the words in his throat.

"He loves me, Father, and I think he can help me get past Brady." She stared at the diamond, tracing its shape.

Patrick clasped her other hand in his. "But do you love him, darlin'?"

She continued to gaze at the glimmering stone, lost in a faraway stare.

Patrick shook her hand. "Lizzie, do you love him?"

Her eyes flickered, breaking her reverie. "No, but I think I can. I care about him a great deal. And he's changed, drawn closer to God—because of me." She looked at him then, with the slightest lift of her chin. "And if I can't have the Brady I love, Father, then maybe I can save the Brady who loves me."

"Darlin', marriage isn't for saving people."

She hesitated. "No, but maybe God is using it to save both of us from the pain of our pasts—mine with Brady, and Michael's with his family. A new direction—uniting us as one, to serve him."

He pulled her back with a sigh. "Well, time will tell, I suppose. After all, that's what long engagements are for—to make sure."

She stiffened in his arms. "I don't want a long engagement."

"What?" Patrick turned her to face him. "What do you mean, you don't want a long engagement? Of course you do. You're not even in love with the man. You're in love with his brother, for pity's sake. You need time to get over Brady."

Lizzie pushed away and stood. Her expression reminded him more of Charity than his little Beth. "I need Michael to get over Brady, Father, and no one is going to talk me out of it."

Patrick pushed his ottoman out and slowly rose, his motions hampered by shock. This was his Lizzie? Defiant, strong-willed? Dear Lord, when had he lost his little girl? He stared her down. "Don't take that tone with me, Elizabeth Marie. I'm your father, and you will listen to what I say. I'll not have you going off half-cocked, marrying one man so you can get over another. Have you even prayed about it?"

Wetness shimmered in her eyes as she stood, arms folded and clutched tightly at her waist. "Yes, I've prayed about it . . .

for four, long years I've prayed about it. Prayed that God would free me from the spell of John Brady. But the only answer I've gotten is heartbreak, so I guess it's up to me."

Patrick cinched her arm and pushed her into his chair. He faced her, perched on the edge of his ottoman. "No, it's not up to you. It's up to God. Have you even prayed about *Michael*? Whether he's the man you should marry?"

She bit her lip and shook her head, sending trails of tears down both cheeks.

Patrick sighed and kneaded his forehead with the tips of his fingers. He drew in a deep breath and took Lizzie's hand in his. "Darlin', I love you, and my heart grieves over the pain you've experienced because of Brady, and I like Michael, I really do. But you can't rush into this, not without prayer. Especially when you're not sure if you even love the man."

She sniffed and looked away. "I care about him, Father." She fingered the diamond on her finger, avoiding his gaze. "And he makes me feel . . . warm inside . . . the way I'd always read it would be."

Patrick's jaw tightened. "There's more to marriage, darlin', than a heated kiss."

Color flooded her cheeks. "Father, please—"

"No, Lizzie, you listen to me. You've always had your head buried in a book, certain that falling in love would cure all your ills. Attraction is certainly important, but marriage requires far more. It takes commitment and love and especially respect. I like Michael, I do, but there are two things I demand of you before I'll agree. One, we will pray about this now, whether you like it or not, because I'll not have my daughter say yes to a man when God says no. And two, you will not get married in a rush. You will, instead, get to know Michael over a respectable period of time, allowing your family to get to know him as well."

Lizzie bit her lip. "How long?"

"A year, just like Faith and Collin."

"A year?" Tears started to well all over again. "No, Father, please—six months."

"Absolutely not—"

"But Charity and Mitch got married the day after he arrived—"

"That's because Mitch Dennehy has no patience whatsoever and took it upon himself without letting anyone know."

"Don't force me to elope, Father . . ."

Patrick gave her a narrow gaze, working his jaw back and forth as he contemplated her fate. He released a tired groan. "You've been spending way too much time with Charity, Lizzie. You're starting to pick up some of her bad habits." He sighed. "Six months, then."

"From today."

He jutted a brow. "Don't push it, young lady. I'm still your father."

She grinned and threw herself into his arms, hugging his neck. "Oh, Father, I love you! And you're going to love Michael, I just know it."

"It's not my loving him that has me worried, darlin'. But if he's the man God has in mind, then I'm sure I'll like him just fine." He tapped her on the knee. "Move over."

She scooted up on the arm and waited for him to settle back into his chair before she leaned back once again. He pulled her close, cherishing this moment when he could pray with his daughter, knowing full well that the burden for her well-being would shift from his shoulders to God's. He closed his eyes and began to pray—for God's direction in her life, for wisdom and for peace, and for the grace to get through it all.

When he was done, he squeezed her shoulder and kissed her on the head. He lifted the hand with the diamond and studied it with a wary eye. "It certainly is obscene-looking. Must have cost a small fortune." He hesitated while a shadow of a smile quirked the corners of his mouth. "And to be honest, I feel sorry for Mitch."

Lizzie gave him a quizzical smile. "Mitch? Why?"

Patrick yawned and lumbered to his feet, stretching his arms high over his head. "Because when Charity sees that rock on your finger, darlin', she won't be giving him a moment's peace until she has one as big or bigger."

Lizzie giggled. "Oh, Father, she's not that bad."

Patrick chuckled and doused the light. He curled an arm around Lizzie's shoulder as they headed from the room. "No, darlin', she's worse."

## 16

Sleep. All he wanted was sleep. Mitch brushed his teeth in slow, methodic rhythm, eyes closed because he could barely keep them open. Between the *Herald*, the twins, and Charity, his energy reserve was dangerously low, so much so he doubted if even his wife could stir him tonight.

Two silky arms embraced him from behind, fingers circling on his bare stomach just above the pull tie of his pajama bottoms. His eyes flipped open. He felt the press of Charity's breasts against his back as she feathered his shoulder blade with soft little kisses.

He moaned. "Charity, my body is exhausted, and yours should be too."

"Not yet, darling, but I bet you can manage it."

He gulped a quick drink of water and spit it out, dropping his toothbrush in the sink. He spun around to ward her off, hands pinned to her shoulders. "Come on, little girl, the twins had us both up most of last night and all I want to do is sleep."

"No problem. Sleep it is." She tugged at the silky tie of her satin nightgown and turned toward the door, slipping one strap off a shoulder and then the other.

Mitch grabbed the back of her gown from behind and hiked it back up before it could hit the floor. "What the devil are you doing?" he rasped.

She smiled over her shoulder. "I could ask you the same thing. I thought you were tired."

He jerked the straps back into place and whirled her around, hands locked on her arms. "Look, Charity, I love you to pieces, you know that. But *please*, I need my sleep tonight."

She stroked his cheek and smiled. "I told you it was no problem, darling."

"Then what the devil were you doing?"

"Getting ready for bed."

"By taking your nightgown off?"

She hunched her shoulders. "Just felt like sleeping without it tonight, that's all."

He moaned. "You know I can't sleep like that."

She grinned. "I know." She folded her arms across her chest, blue eyes twinkling. "But maybe we can strike a deal."

Mitch swabbed a hand over bleary eyes. "God help me."

"Now, hear me out. You're tired and so am I. But there is another way you can demonstrate your love for me."

He sighed and folded his arms. "And what might that be?"

She held up her left hand and studied her diamond ring. "You know, we were in such a rush when we got married, that we just grabbed the first ring we saw." She squinted and cocked her head. "Kind of a shame my little sister's ring is bigger than mine, don't you think?"

He scooped her close and groaned. "No! And speaking of rings, when did all of this happen, anyway? I knew Michael was interested, but I thought Lizzie was in all-fire love with Brady, for pity's sake. Now she's engaged to his brother?"

Charity scowled and laid her head against his chest, neatly derailed from her original line of thinking. "I know, but it's Brady's own fault. He's made it pretty clear that Lizzie would never be more than a sister to him, so what do you expect? Michael's here every week, patiently biding his time and slowly winning her heart. I don't blame her a bit for wanting to move on. I certainly would."

It was Mitch's turn to scowl. He tightened his hold. "Yeah, I know. You're just lucky I came after you before you made a real mess of your life."

She sighed against his chest. "I know," she whispered, her tone almost reverent in agreement. "But apparently Lizzie won't be so lucky. Brady's lost her, Mitch, and it really makes me sad."

"Does he even know . . . about the engagement, I mean?"

"No, he's out of town with Michael, but she plans to tell him when he gets back. I suspect he'll take it pretty hard, but he'll have no choice. Lizzie will be his sister-in-law, not his wife, and he alone bears the blame for that." She sighed again. "He's going to need a lot of prayer. I suspect they all will."

He kissed the top of her head. "Trust me, in this family they'll be well covered. Well, he certainly has the means to take care of her. You think they'll live in New York or Boston?"

"Boston, if my prayers have anything to say about it, but I don't think they've discussed any of the details yet." Her head tilted up. "Nice job of changing the subject, Dennehy, but it won't work."

"Come on, Charity, a bigger ring won't make you happy."

She nuzzled his chest with her lips. "It might."

He swept his hands up the sides of her waist, and his energy suddenly rekindled. Tipping her chin up with his finger, he kissed her lightly on the mouth. She wrapped her arms around his neck and kissed him back, drawing a moan from his lips. He picked her up in his arms and carried her to their bed, suddenly wide awake. "No ring, little girl," he whispered in her ear, "but I can certainly honor your first request."

She giggled and stroked his cheek. "But you were tired, remember? And you didn't shave tonight, did you?"

He flipped the covers back and laid her down on the bed. "Nope. I had sleep on my mind, if you recall."

She grinned and bit her lip. "I do. It's okay. A little razor burn won't hurt."

He headed to the bathroom. "Nope, won't take a minute. Don't go anywhere."

She leaned back and extended one arm behind, head in her hand. Stretching to full advantage, she slithered one shoulder strap down for effect. "I'd make it quick, if I were you."

He hurried to the sink and hurled the medicine chest open with a bang, fumbling for his shaving cream. He thought of his wife, posing on their bed, and the blood started pumping in his veins. He grinned in the mirror, skimming the razor across his jaw in record time. She was a vixen through and through, but she was all his, and he thanked God he'd finally come to his senses and married her. He splashed warm water in his face and reached for a towel, drying his face before slapping the bathroom light out. He hurried to their bed . . . and stopped.

She lay deathly still on her back, one strap off her shoulder and one arm limp overhead. Her full lips emitted tiny puffs of air every time she breathed, indicating she was sound asleep. He blinked. Awake or asleep, she was the most beautiful woman he'd ever known. His lips twisted. Although at the moment, he preferred her awake.

He walked over and pulled the cover up to her chin, then reached down to press a soft kiss to her lips. She moaned and turned on her side, the little puffs commencing once again. He turned out her light, then shuffled to his side of the bed and slipped under the sheet with a heavy sigh. Life with Charity was never boring. Even if he didn't get much sleep.

The crash of shattering glass sounded from the open bathroom down the hall, and Faith glanced up, hairbrush halted in hand and still cleaving to her scalp. A hiss that sounded dangerously close to a swear word reached her ears. She chewed on her lip. "Oh, goodness, I didn't leave my lilac water on the back of the commode again, did I?" she called loudly, knowing full well that she had.

She heard another questionable phrase followed by the clinking of glass in the wastebasket before her husband appeared in the door, towel tied at his waist and fisting a soggy rag. The sweet scent of lilacs floated into the room, belying the heat in his eyes. And not the usual heat she saw when he came to their bed.

"Collin, I am sooo sorry! I know it belongs in the closet, but the hot bath seems to rob me of every thought in my head." *Charity, help me,* she thought, gnawing on her lip again. She gave him a half smile, then made a poor attempt at batting her eyes. "Every thought but you, that is."

He stood in an aura of lilacs, muscles tight and slick from his bath while little rivulets of water dribbled from his dark head. The strain in his face was as tight as the towel clenched low on his hips, a sure sign she didn't have Charity's skill.

His eyes narrowed. "Knock it off, Faith. I married you, not Charity. Although I may question that decision if I see that blasted lilac water one more time."

She placed the brush on her vanity and rushed to his side, tugging at the noxious rag in his hand. "I won't do it again, I promise. Let me clean it up, please."

His lips flattened. "Already did. Although God knows it doesn't smell like it. You might want to buy another fragrance. This one is losing its effect . . . fast."

She smiled and scooped an arm around his waist, pressing a soft kiss to his moist chest. "I will, Collin, I promise. Now hurry and get ready for bed so I can make it up to you."

He stroked her cheek, but his tone was flat. "Not tonight, Little Bit, please. I'm not in the mood."

She faltered back. "Not in the mood?" She stared, unable to believe Collin McGuire had even uttered the words. "I didn't think that phrase was in your vocabulary."

No smile, no smirk, no nothing. "Sorry, Faith, but all I want to do is sleep." He kissed her head. "You go to bed, okay? I'll be in shortly." He turned and disappeared into the bathroom once again, this time shutting the door behind him.

Faith shuffled to their bed in a near stupor and turned out the light. He'd told her about moods like this in his past, moods where he'd wrestled with bouts of depression, but she had never seen them in almost three years of marriage. Unless they were embroiled in a rare fight, Collin was always up, always ready to tease, always ready to . . .

She slipped under the covers with a shiver, reflecting on his behavior, wondering when the malaise had set in. She'd noticed he'd been quiet all night, but he'd been fine this morning before he'd left for work, and great over the weekend, especially with the new hire working out so well. Sunday night dinner with the family had been good, although he had seemed a bit edgy on the way home. She rolled on her side and closed her eyes, deep in thought. All at once her lids popped open and she caught her breath. Lizzie and Michael—of course! The engagement. That had to be it. His mood had shifted right after dinner, with Lizzie's visit.

Faith sat up and pushed the hair from her eyes. The news had shocked everyone, of course, although it really shouldn't have been a surprise. Lizzie was tired of pining over Brady, she'd made no bones about that. And Michael's intentions had certainly become clear over the last month, his focus on both God and Lizzie escalated considerably. Faith leaned back against the headboard and chewed on her thumbnail. She just hoped it was for real. She liked Michael well enough, but none of them had known him for more than a few months. She sighed. At least they would have six months to pray about it and get to know him better.

She heard the bathroom door squeal open in a shaft of light that immediately went to black. Collin padded to the bed and got in, ignoring Faith as she sat up in the shadows.

"I thought you were going to sleep," he mumbled. He closed his eyes and stretched the length of the bed.

"Couldn't sleep. Not when I know something is bothering you."

"Go to bed, Faith. I'm fine."

"No, you're not. I've never seen you like this. Depressed. Withdrawn. Talk to me Collin, please."

"Nothing to talk about. I'm just in a mood."

"You're upset about Lizzie, aren't you? About the engagement."

He turned on his side, his back to her as he adjusted his head on the pillow. "I'm tired and I don't want to talk. I love you. Go to bed."

She slithered down under the covers and nestled up against him, circling his waist with her arm. "I love you too, Collin, which is why we need to talk. If not to air your frustration, then at least to pray."

She felt the swell of his chest as he drew in a deep breath and exhaled. "Pray, then."

"Are you worried about Brady?"

"Faith!"

"Sorry! Dear Lord, we come before you tonight to lift up my husband and this upset that he is obviously experiencing. Help him to trust you and find your peace in the midst of whatever is bothering him tonight. Give him sweet sleep, Lord, as you promise in your Word—"

"Pray for Brady." His whisper was harsh in the dark.

She hesitated. "Collin, he'll be fine—"

*"Pray!"* he rasped, the tension of his command tightening his stomach beneath her hand.

"And, God, we pray for Brady. We know this news will come as a shock, but help him to get past it and to be happy for Lizzie and his brother—"

He whirled around, the whites of his eyes expanded in anger. "No! Pray for strength, not to get past it, but to . . ." He stopped. The anger slowly faded from his face. He dropped back on the pillow and closed his eyes.

She grabbed his arm. "Collin, what's wrong? Why are you acting like this? And how are we supposed to pray for Brady? To do what?"

"I can't tell you."

"Why not?"

He mauled his face with the palms of his hands, fingers sweeping up into his wet hair. "I promised."

Faith sat up, flecks of irritation prickling her tone. "You've broken promises before, Collin. It's not your strong suit, you know."

His eyes blazed open, glinting with anger. "I swore to him, all right? Is that good enough for you?"

"Collin, I'm sorry. I didn't mean to push. I'm just worried about you. But whatever this is, I'd like to be specific when I pray. I won't tell Lizzie, if that's what you're worried about—"

"I said *no*! Just pray, Faith—*now*—for strength for Brady to do the right thing. Or I will. Then, please, just let me go to sleep."

She stared for several seconds, then slowly lay down beside him, cradling his chest with her arm. "Lord God, your Word says you have not given us the spirit of fear, but of power, and love and a sound mind. We ask right now that you cast fear out of both my husband and John Brady, and give them peace. Give Brady the power, the love, and the sound mind to do what you want him to do. Strengthen him in this situation, Lord, and see him through. Your Word says all things work together for good for those who love God and are called according to his purpose. That's John Brady to the letter, Lord, so please, work this out for his good. In Jesus' name. Amen."

She felt the tension siphon from her husband's body. She closed her eyes and gently stroked his chest. His heart was pounding beneath the heat of her hand. "Good night, Collin," she whispered. "I love you."

"Good night, Faith. I love you too."

The closer they got to Forest Hills, the farther up his throat his breakfast seemed to climb. Or maybe it was bile. Either way, Brady didn't have a good taste in his mouth, but then shame had always left a bitter bite on his tongue. He stared straight ahead as they drove, stiff and tense as Michael's Packard glided along curving cobblestone streets lined with stately trees, manicured parks, and picture-perfect squares. He remembered all too well the home of his youth, with its lush landscaping and wrought-iron streetlamps resembling old English lanterns. Fancy brick mansions with regal towers and imposing spires, resplendent with ivy that gleamed in the sun. All carefully designed to reflect the elegance and charm of the finest garden communities of England. Beautiful on the outside, deadly on the inside. At least in his case. A shiver traveled his spine. Whited sepulchers, full of dead men's bones.

He stole a glance at Michael out of the corner of his eye. His brother was dressed to the nines in a gray Norfolk suit with belted waist and matching driving cap, one arm draped casually over his door while he steered his cherry-red roadster with the other. Not a strand of his hair, carefully slicked back in the Valentino style of the day, ruffled in the cool breeze. Unlike Brady's longer cut, which flapped in the wind, void of all hair cream.

Brady squinted. Michael was a good-looking man, he supposed, but the thought shocked him in terms of himself, the spitting image of his brother. He had never considered himself handsome, although people had often told him so. But then his mind hadn't focused on what he saw in the mirror. Only what he saw in his soul.

They'd actually spent the first few hours talking about their childhood—summer vacations in the Hamptons and treks to Europe. Idle chitchat that had escalated into a near argument when Michael had broached the forbidden subject. At the time, his glance had been casual but his tone subdued, veering from one conversation to the other as smoothly as the Packard changed lanes.

"Yeah, those were good times," he had said, his gaze flicking to Brady. "Unfortunately overshadowed by bad." He paused. "What happened that night anyway, John? The night you went away. I never really knew."

The question, spoken so quietly, so innocently, had sucked the air from Brady's lungs. Every muscle in his body tensed, sending his heart rate accelerating. He looked away, his eyes riveted on the passing scenery. "I don't remember."

"It altered your life, and you don't remember?"

His hand fisted on the seat. "That's right."

"I always thought lying was a sin."

Brady spun to face him, his eyes itching with fury. "Go to the devil, Michael! I told you I don't remember."

"Don't get riled, I just think you need to get it out, that's all. Talk about it."

Brady glared, his tone less than kind. "With you?"

"Yeah, with me. Who else but your own flesh and blood, the brother who knows your past but loves you anyway."

"I told you. I don't remember."

"Selective memory, I suppose."

Brady stared straight ahead, his tone hard. "No, blind drunk. Are you satisfied?"

Michael gave him a sideways glance. "You were drunk? You really don't remember?"

Brady closed his eyes, remembering certain details with perfect clarity—the scent of Lucille's perfume, the burn of whiskey on his tongue, the sinful touch of rumpled silk sheets. He could remember it all, painful memories cloaked in shame. A boy defiled, a woman scorned, the pelting rain on the roof overhead. Guilt whirling and walls spinning as he'd stumbled to his room. Lightning and thunder . . . and Lucille in a rage. While Helena wept in her arms.

He squeezed his eyes shut, the air thin in his lungs. The memories stopped there, drowned like his innocence in a sea of cheap bourbon and costly regret.

Michael's voice was quiet. "John, I can see you don't want to talk about this now, but sometime soon, we need to—you, me, and Helena. For your sake and for hers. So we can be a family again. Like old times."

Old times. A shiver traveled Brady's spine. They had never been a family. Not since Lucille had come to call. Acid churned in his stomach as he stared out his side window, barely seeing the West Side Tennis Club as it zipped by in a blur.

Lucille had applied for a nanny position the summer of their tenth year, a mere six months after their mother had passed away, but Brady was certain her credentials had been better suited to landing a wealthy husband. Although his parents' marriage had never seemed particularly close, his father had been devastated when he lost his wife, burying himself in the management of his thriving printing companies.

Over the years, he and Michael had had their fair share of nannies, but none had prepared them for Lucille. Barely out of high school, she'd come across much older than she was, with an air of sophistication honed, they learned much later, from a questionable lifestyle rather than a respectable upbringing. She had been a beautiful woman, with hair the color of sunlight gleaming on a field of wheat. Deep blue eyes that always shone with a glint of tease, as if she had a secret she wanted to share. It only took one brief interview for their father to hire her, despite baggage that included a four-year-old daughter. And so they'd become a family—little Helena, Michael, and him—nurtured by a woman who had captured his father's heart. And his. Shame burned in his cheeks.

He closed his eyes. He knew now that he had been little more than a victim of circumstance. But no more so than Lucille. After his father's death, her drinking had escalated, along with her need for comfort. And so the bond they shared had deepened through endless conversations that revealed the tragic little girl behind the lost woman. Orphaned at ten years of age, she had been foisted on an alcoholic aunt with little use for a niece who exuded the strong promise of beauty. Most nights Aunt Lena had passed out long before her husband made his way to Lucille's room. A faint shiver traveled Brady's spine. A commonality he and Lucille had shared—the disruption of innocence at too early an age.

He drew in a deep breath and opened his eyes, totally oblivious to the passing scenery. The only image he saw was Lucille's tragic face, blue eyes washed in tears and chin raised in defiance as she'd confided in her seventeen-year-old stepson. Her confession had sealed his sympathy . . . and his fate. His heart had gone out to her as a thirteen-year-old runaway who'd been desperate to escape. But she'd taken a job as a scullery maid in a mansion where escape was not to be. Nobly robed by day, her magistrate employer would disrobe at night, seeking unholy pleasures in the still of the evening. At the first hint of pregnancy, he had turned her out on the streets, forcing her to seek refuge with her aunt—a perverted refuge that set the course for her life.

The Packard slowed as it veered through open wrought-iron gates hinged to towering stone pillars. Brady jolted from his reverie with air thick in his throat. His gaze slowly traveled up the meticulous lawn with its sculpted gardens and marble terraces flanking a Norman-style stone mansion. His eyes lifted to the second story where his room had once been, and sweat beaded on the back of his neck.

"I spoke to Helena last night. She's nervous as a cat."

Brady whirled to face him with shock glazing his eyes. "What?"

Michael blinked, then eased into an awkward grin. "Naw, John, I just meant she's nervous because she's anxious to see you again. Wonders what you'll think of her all grown up. She's missed you. We both have."

His breath seeped slowly through lips still parted in distress. He nodded dumbly and turned back to the house, girding himself for what lay ahead. *God help me.*

The Packard heaved to a stop—as did his heart—in front of a cascade of marble stairs. The portico was besieged by his stepmother's pillar roses, now wintering and awaiting spring's pruning. In the summer, they coiled and tangled about the columns like a verdant serpent dominating its prey, the dark green canes deeply rooted in the earth. Bloom stems, thick with thorns and purpose, always smothered the lower half of the posts, obscuring them with jagged leaves and blooms so potent, their musky scent invaded the foyer. They had been Lucille's favorite, creamy blossoms with a trace of pink at the heart. The faintest of colors—like the watery stain of sin on a child's soul.

Michael jerked the advance lever up and switched the ignition off. "Home, sweet home." He opened his door and glanced at his watch. "A little past two—not too bad. We made pretty good time, but I'll bet you're starved. Don't worry about the bags, Hugh'll take care of them. Helena's waiting lunch."

Brady didn't move, fused to his seat as firmly as the piping stitched to the red leather cushion. He stared straight ahead, his breathing ragged.

Michael turned on the steps. "John, the sooner you face this, the sooner you'll be free. Helena needs to see you . . . as much as you need to see her. What happened a long time ago is over, done. Put it behind and let's start again."

Brady nodded slowly and grasped the handle with bloodless fingers. He stepped from the vehicle and slammed the door shut, flexing his hand as he drew in a deep breath.

Michael touched his shoulder. "There's healing inside, John. For all of us." He squeezed his shoulder and led him up the stairs.

The entryway wasn't as cavernous as he remembered. As a boy, it had seemed as grand as the ballroom in the east wing of the house. Its gleaming mahogany balustrade curved around two-thirds of the second-floor landing before sweeping down the far side of the room. Color-rich oil paintings graced the walls, staggered as the steps declined, reflecting stern faces from a heritage he'd rather forget. The smell of his past invaded his senses—the fresh scent of lemon oil and flowers no matter the season, all mingling with the faint whiff of a wood fire burning in the parlor. He closed his eyes and could almost detect the sweet aroma of his father's cigars, distinct and robust, like the man who'd enjoyed them.

Michael tossed his cap, and it landed on a burlwood table graced with a crystal vase of fresh flowers. He ran a hand over his head and glanced around. "Helena?"

Brady tensed as marble, wood, and rich-hued Persian rugs blurred before him. Somewhere upstairs he heard a door slam, followed by the faint patter of feet. His hands were sweating, and he rubbed them against his tweed waistcoat, heat radiating from his bulky knitted sweater beneath. He quickly unbuttoned his jacket and took it off.

"Welcome back, Mr. Brady. My apologies for not greeting you at the door, but I didn't hear you arrive." A tall gentleman in a black suit hurried in from the back of the foyer, his expression as starched and crisp as his impeccable white shirt. He stood before Michael with a quiet click of his heels, offering a stiff smile that indicated he didn't relish being caught off guard.

"Not a problem, Hugh, my brother and I just arrived. Is Helena in the kitchen?"

"No, sir. I believe the young miss is upstairs putting the finishing touches on your brother's room."

Michael lifted the coat hanging limp in Brady's hands and handed it to Hugh. "Good, good. Hugh, this is my brother John from Boston. Would you tell Mrs. Briggs we're ready for lunch?"

"Very good, sir." Hugh glanced at Brady and nodded, his eyes guarded. "Good afternoon, Mr. Brady. It's good to make your acquaintance. Your brother has spoken highly of you."

Brady forced a smile. "Thank you, Hugh. I wouldn't believe everything he says."

The corners of the butler's mouth flickered. "Yes, sir."

"Michael!"

All eyes riveted on the second-floor landing where a petite girl hovered over the railing, hands clutched to the banister. A shaft of refracted light from an etched-glass window overhead illuminated soft wisps of her golden hair, and her face was so radiant, she reminded Brady of an angel smiling down from above.

"Helena!"

One word from Michael and she flew down the stairs, cheeks pink with excitement. She was a woman of twenty-one, but seemed little more than a girl of sixteen as she threw herself into her brother's arms with a squeal. "Oh, I've missed you something fierce! I'm so glad you're home."

Michael chuckled and kissed her on the head. He gave her a squeeze, then looped an arm around her waist. "Helena, say hello to your brother, John."

The exuberance in her eyes faded into a shyness he remembered all too well from their youth. She looked up at him beneath a fringe of sooty lashes, her cupid-bow mouth forming the barest of smiles.

"Hello, John," she whispered. "Thank you for coming."

He nodded, his throat working as he extended his hand. "Hello, Helena. It's been a long time." She smiled and gently shook it, her touch searing him like a jolt of electricity. He cleared his throat and shoved his hands in his pockets.

"Too long. Do I look like you expected?"

He studied her, taking in the contour of a face that was more heart-shaped than her mother's, with a chin less defined, and realized the resemblance was actually minimal except for the eyes. They stared back with the same sapphire-blue as Lucille's, sending a chill down his spine. "A little."

She grinned and winked at Michael, dispelling Brady's thoughts. "Well, you look *exactly* like I expected," she said with a chuckle. She squeezed Michael's upper arm with a twinkle in her eyes. "Although a bit more muscular, perhaps."

Michael appeared hurt. "Hey, John does hard labor in a small print shop, what do you expect? And I've been away from my conditioning while in Boston."

She pressed a kiss to his cheek. "Well, you're still two of the most handsome men I know. I'm proud to be your stepsister." She latched an arm through Michael's and shot Brady a shy smile. "Shall we go in to lunch? I want to hear all about what you've been doing these last eleven years, John. We have a lot to catch up on, and I'll bet you're starving too. A little sustenance is just what we need."

"Sounds great," he said, his smile shaky at best. He drew in a deep breath and followed them into the dining room. He needed sustenance, all right. *The spiritual kind.* His eyes fixed on his stepsister from the back, marveling at the woman she'd become. When he had seen her last, she had been a scrawny ten-year-old who had been as shy as her mother had been flirtatious. A gentle child who had dogged his and Michael's every step. He studied her now, noting the teasing tilt of her head as she smiled up at Michael with adoring eyes. He surmised she'd inherited Lucille's skill with men, albeit decidedly more innocent. Without question, his stepsister had grown into a beauty, just like her mother. Brady hoped and prayed the similarities ended there.

A strange sensation came over him as he entered the dining room. It felt odd being here, where so many meals had been shared in happier times. Brady pulled out Helena's chair, then sat across the way, while Michael seated himself at the head where their father once presided.

Unlike the rest of the house, the family's private dining area was an intimate room. It had a stone fireplace on one side and an expansive bay window on the other, offering a peaceful view of rolling terrain edged by gardens. This room had afforded Brady some of the few fond memories in this house. It had been Lucille who'd coaxed their father into buying one of the first homes in the exclusive Forest Hills Gardens community. Its grand scale and lavishness reflected her fondness for pretense. But it had been their father who'd insisted on one room where simplicity and warmth could prevail, choosing to make the dining room one of the few havens in an otherwise cold stone mansion. Upon their father's request, Mrs. Briggs served the meals rather than the butler, the housekeeper's warm and motherly manner a welcome touch in their extravagant lives. Brady glanced at the warm, honey-colored walls hung with gilded oil paintings of pastoral scenes. He could almost hear the excitement in Pop's baritone voice as he'd planned hunting excursions with his sons or a family outing by the sea.

The wonderful smell of pot roast watered his mouth, reminding him he hadn't eaten since breakfast. The kitchen door swung open and their beloved housekeeper, one of the bright spots of his youth, stepped through the door toting a tray of hand-carved beef and roasted potatoes. Her face was moist from the savory steam billowing into the air.

Brady shot to his feet and took the tray from her hands. "Mrs. Briggs! How are you?"

"John Brady, as I live and breathe, where have you been keeping yourself? Don't you know there are people here who missed you?" She pulled at a handkerchief tucked in her sleeve and mopped her round cheeks with a chubby hand that had once shooed him away from her coveted cookie dough. Several strands of snow-white hair fluttered about her face as she patted.

He laughed, the first ease of tension he'd experienced since he'd entered the house. "I live in Boston, Mrs. Briggs, part owner of a small but promising printing business. I landed there because of a buddy from the war."

"Goodness' sakes, John, you were in that dreadful war?"

Her piercing gray eyes perused him head to toe, stubby arms perched on ample hips. "Well, it certainly looks as if the good Lord took care of you."

He smiled, the memory of her not-so-subtle references to "the good Lord" no longer an irritant. "Yes, ma'am, he did. You might say my Bible was the most powerful weapon I had. Thanks for praying for me all those years."

Her face flushed pink against the white lacy collar of her uniform. "My pleasure, John. I always knew you would grow into a fine man. Now you dig into that roast, do you hear? I've got vegetables and biscuits to fetch from the kitchen." She bustled back through the door, allowing a mouthwatering whiff of fresh-baked apple pie to escape into the room.

Brady shook his head and set the platter in front of Helena. "I can't believe she's still working. She must be near seventy."

Michael chuckled. "Seventy-three, but still going strong. Although she did retire a few years back, when Helga took over. But I'll have you know that when Helga told her you were coming home for a visit, Mrs. Briggs insisted on being here today to serve the homecoming lunch." Michael gave him a lazy smile. "She always did like you better, you know. You care to say grace, John?"

Brady paused, a napkin dangling in his hand as he stared at Michael. He glanced at Helena, whose surprise appeared to be equal to his, then back at his brother. "*Grace?*"

Michael's lips quirked. He shook his napkin out and placed it in his lap. "Must I remind you I've been dining at the O'Connors'?"

An uncommon mix of irritation and humor twitched on Brady's lips. "No reminder necessary. Glad to see they've been a good influence on you."

Michael winked at Helena, then grinned at Brady. "They have. But not as good as you're likely to be, little brother. Shall we thank God for our food . . . and our good fortune?"

Brady jerked awake, his mind in a momentary fog as he blinked at the crystal chandelier overhead. Realization struck, and the muscles in his stomach instantly knotted. He sat up on the bed and stared, his breathing shallow and his pulse racing. Despite the fact he'd been here for almost a week, he still awakened with a jolt every time. Only one more night, he thought to himself with relief. The nights had been the worst, full of strange dreams and sick feelings, a stark contrast to the days he shared with his brother and stepsister.

He actually enjoyed spending time with Helena, who had taken him shopping several times, her favorite thing to do, while Michael attended to business. Midweek they had met with Lucille's attorney, finalizing the disbursement of inheritance with a sweep of Brady's hand. Michael had been right. Lucille had left the house to Brady, stipulating that both Helena and Michael could live there as long as they liked. She compensated Michael with the printing company and Helena with an obscene art and jewelry collection. The balance of the estate was divided into equal thirds.

His gaze darted around the room where he'd spent the last years of his youth. Heavy brocade drapes, the same deep green as the plush carpet, trailed to the floor, split by white gossamer sheers that faded to pink as dusk invaded the sky. Dark mahogany bookcases filled with leather-bound books lined the wall by the French doors, where an antiquated telescope stood mounted on a stand. His gaze settled on the intricately carved wardrobe on the far side of the room, and sweat immediately layered the back of his neck.

His hand instinctively touched the open Bible he'd been reading before he'd fallen asleep, desperate for the strength it offered. His throat felt tight. He licked his dry lips as his breathing accelerated, eyes trained on the mahogany wardrobe—the one he'd avoided all week. The one with the secret drawer.

All at once the memory of that final night in this room tainted his mind and he shot up off the bed as if scalded, his body trembling. He stood for several seconds, his breathing coming in rasps, then slowly moved toward the wardrobe. Would they still be there? The gifts from his father? Favors meant to make a man out of a boy?

His fingers felt thick as he opened the wardrobe, bending to unlatch the lock hidden far in the back. He heard it click and carefully pried it open. His gasp violated the stillness of the room.

*Empty!*

His legs buckled and he fell to his knees, relief washing through him like a tide. *Gone!* All the vile poison, the alcohol that had fed his desires, primed him for Lucille, all gone, gone. *Thank you, God!*

He drew in a deep breath, still shaking from the sickening pull of his father's liquid vice. Livingston Brady had been a decent man, but a godless one, hell-bent on having boys just like him—virile, powerful, insatiable. Thirsting, just like him, after all that life offered.

His mother had never known about her boys' wicked little habit, and his father would have never guessed the damage it would do. He'd died and left a legacy to his son—a young widow who needed a shoulder to cry on. And much, much more.

Brady closed his eyes, his heart rate slowly returning to normal. God had been with him, even then. He knew now that the prayers of Mrs. Briggs had factored into his salvation. How much had she known? Had she guessed he'd shared the sins of his father . . . as well as his wife?

*Had Michael?*

"God forgive me," he whispered, even though he knew that God had long since done so. But being in this house again, seeing Michael and Helena, bombarded his brain with doubts. Would he ever be free from the perversion of his past? Really and truly free?

*And ye shall know the truth, and the truth shall make you free.*

*The truth.* Brady hung his head. "God help me to find it," he whispered, wetness pricking his eyes. He thought of Helena and shivered. "And give me the strength to hear it."

❧ ❧

"I can't believe you're leaving tomorrow. It seems like you just got here." Helena propped her chin in her hand and gave him a pretty pout.

He smiled, more relaxed than he ever thought he'd be in this house. But it had been a good week. He'd finally gotten to know his brother and stepsister better, and the three of them had attained a harmony of sorts, laughing, joking, almost becoming family again. That is, when he didn't let the past get in the way. He leaned back in the chair and stretched his legs, raising a toast with a crystal goblet of Helena's homemade ginger ale punch.

"I'll be back from time to time. And you can always visit me in Boston, you know." He downed his fifth glass.

She scrunched her nose. "It won't be the same, and you know it."

Michael stood to his feet and swooped all three goblets up from the table. He took them to the sideboard and ladled more punch. "Once he goes back to work, Helena, you'd never see him anyway. He works day and night." He placed her glass on the table, then handed Brady his.

"Thank you, Michael," she said, sipping her punch with a dreamy look in her eyes. She hiccupped, and her hand flew to her mouth. "Ooops! Excuse me."

"Yeah, thanks, Michael, although the more I drink, the thirstier I seem to get." He reached for his glass and paused, the rim halfway to his lips. A crease furrowed his brow. "Helena, are you sure there's no alcohol in this?"

Michael laughed. "Our sister is not a lawbreaker, John. She wouldn't put alcohol in her punch."

Brady sniffed his drink and lowered the glass. "I don't smell any, but I've got this warm, relaxed glow spreading through my limbs, like I've just soaked in a hot bath." He draped one arm on the table and leaned in, giving her a half smile. "Helena, did you put alcohol in this punch?"

Her eyes flicked to Michael, then back to Brady. She giggled and X'd a finger over the front of her pretty pink dress. "No, John, I didn't. Cross my heart and hope to die."

He gave Michael a woozy stare and arched a brow. "Did you?"

Michael grinned and cuffed him on the shoulder before swiping Brady's glass from the table. "Shall we continue this farewell party in the parlor?"

Brady stood to his feet, and the room began to rotate. He clutched the back of his chair to steady himself. "Michael! Are you trying to get me drunk?"

Michael chuckled at the door, goblets in hand. "Didn't have to try very hard, little brother. You're a lightweight. When's the last time you had alcohol anyway, before prohibition?"

Brady moaned and pressed a hand to his head to try and stop the spinning. "Seventeen," he mumbled.

Michael gaped. "The year nineteen seventeen? Or the *age* seventeen?"

Brady grabbed his water glass and chugged. He took a deep breath and anchored his hand to the chair as he began to weave. "The age."

Helena took his arm with a giggle. "Easy does it, John. I'm a bit lightheaded too, but I do believe you're drunk as a skunk."

She ushered him into the parlor where he tumbled into the comfortable armchair he'd monopolized all week. Of course, anything would feel comfortable as limp and relaxed as he was right now. He knew he should be angry, but he hadn't felt this free in a long time.

He shot them a stupid grin. "Remind me to slap you silly when I sober up. Why'd you do this anyway?"

Michael handed him his drink, then plopped down in a leather wing chair the color of his eyes—glossy brown. He hoisted his feet up on the ottoman and sipped his punch. "Had to, John. This is your last night here, and we needed to celebrate." He glanced at Helena, curled up on a blue flame-stitch love seat. His grin faded to a faint smile. "Besides, we have some air to clear."

Brady rested his head on the back of the couch and studied his brother with slitted eyes. A flick of alarm curled in his stomach. He stretched his legs out on the ottoman and took a quick drink. "What kind of air?"

"You know what kind, John," Michael said quietly. "You and Helena need to talk. About that night. About what happened. It's the only way the two of you will get past this."

Brady swallowed another drink and closed his eyes. The room began to whirl, and he quickly opened them again, fighting off the nausea rising in his gut. Perhaps Michael was right. He needed to hear the truth, and he wasn't sure he could have done it sober. It had taken months of prayer and therapy for Matt to convince him he even had a right to love someone as pure and innocent as Beth. He braced himself for the facts as seen through the eyes of a ten-year-old girl. Helena held the key to setting him free or destroying months of healing. He shut his eyes, and felt his world spin out of control.

*God help me.*

"John."

Her whisper jolted him and he stared at her with eyes open wide. She knelt on the floor beside him and took his hand, her face earnest.

"Michael says you don't remember what happened that night. But I want you to be free from this. You're my brother, John, and I love you."

*Then tell me nothing happened.*

"That night—the night of the storm—I was frightened, so I ran to Mother's room, but she wasn't there." Tears shimmered in her eyes, and she brushed them away with the side of her hand. "I knew Michael wasn't home yet, so I came to your room."

The air in Brady's lungs stilled. He stared at his stepsister, his body paralyzed with fear.

She looked away. "You weren't alone, John, and I didn't understand." With a quiver in her lip, she returned her gaze to his. "Mother was sleeping in your bed."

Numbness buzzed in his brain. He tried to stagger up. "No, she wasn't! I left her in her room, I swear."

She clung to his hand. "It's okay, John. I forgive you because I love you. I just want to know why."

A sick feeling roiled in his gut, threatening to rise. He jerked his hand free and stood, unsteady on his legs. His voice was a hoarse rasp. "God help me, Helena, we'd been drinking, it's true, and your mother was lonely, but I . . . I couldn't . . . wouldn't give her the comfort she wanted. I fled to my room, I swear, and I was alone."

She jumped to her feet, her eyes glints of amethyst in a pale face. "No, John, you weren't. Just admit it and let it go." She put a hand on his arm and lifted her chin. "My mother said you seduced her."

Bile soured his tongue, threatening the contents of his stomach. "No!"

"She said you told her you loved her, that you needed her . . ."

He moved to steady his hand on the back of the chair, the memory of his feelings and desire for his father's wife making him dizzy.

"Did you, John? Did you tell her you wanted her?"

He never blinked as shock glazed in his eyes. "I . . . did, but I . . . I never acted on it, I swear."

Helena's voice was but a faint whisper. "My mother said you did . . . and even though I didn't understand it at the time, I saw you, John . . . I saw you both."

Her words, spoken in the gentlest of tones, shattered any peace he ever hoped to have. He had no recall of that night in his room, not since he'd staggered from Lucille's bed, but he had hoped—*prayed*—that his fears had been totally wrong.

He sagged against the back of the chair with a low groan, despair suffocating him like the darkest of tombs. *God help me, I'm a monster.*

With trembling hands, he released her hold and gently pushed her away. Her face was a blur as tears streamed his own, and his voice broke with pain. "Helena, I'm sorry, sorry you had to witness that. I didn't remember. Please believe me—I never meant to hurt you or your mother. And God forgive me, that's why I left."

She drew in a deep breath and stood on tiptoe, cradling his face in her hands. "I forgive you, John, because I love you. Then and now."

He nodded and staggered toward the door, perversion leeching the life from his soul like a slow-bleeding death. *I forgive you, John*, she had whispered. But it didn't matter.

He could never forgive himself.

## 17

Mary tugged her jacket closer and hunched her shoulders. "As much as I hate to admit it, I really needed tonight—Millie, Frank, and the whole questionable dance-marathon atmosphere." She clutched her overnight bag close to her chest as if bracing against the frigid November night.

Lizzie squinted at her out of the corner of her eye, then unlatched the gate to her yard despite fingers stiff with the cold. Her chuckle billowed into the air. "Well, anything to do with Millie is usually questionable, that's for sure. But it was fun, wasn't it? I think Frank may be on the verge of making an honest woman of her."

Mary followed her to the front porch. "'Honest' might be a stretch, since it is Millie we're talking about, but I've certainly been praying he would. I think it would do Millie good to settle down, even if it is with Frank."

Lizzie unlocked the door and butted it open, peering into the dimly lit parlor. She glanced at the clock on the mantel. "Ten thirty on a Saturday night, and nobody's up?" She winked at Mary as she flung her coat on the rack by the door. "Mother and Father must have gone to bed early since Katie's spending the night at Charity's."

Mary smiled and hung up her coat. "You're so lucky, Lizzie. Your parents have everything in a marriage I've ever wanted. They act more like newlyweds than people married for a quarter of a century." She sighed. "I sure hope I have that someday."

"I know, me too," Lizzie whispered. She thought of Michael's diamond ring, safely tucked in her drawer until she could muster the courage to tell Mary the truth. She hoped she and Michael would have the depth of love for God and each other that her parents shared. At least someday, God willing.

They tiptoed upstairs to Lizzie's room and quietly shut the door. Lizzie kicked off her shoes and flopped on her bed while Mary did the same on Katie's.

"Speaking of wonderful relationships, I've been dying to ask—how's it been going with Harold? Has he asked you out for any more sodas after Adult Catechism Class?"

Mary blushed. "As a matter of fact, he has. Twice now. And he actually hinted at asking me out to dinner."

"No! Shy Harold? I'd say that's progress. And you think there's potential?"

"Oh yes," Mary breathed. She plopped her chin in her hand and grinned. "I mean, when it comes to loving God, he's no John Brady, but he sure knows his Catechism." Her blue eyes brimmed with excitement. "And he sure is cute."

"Oh, Mary, I'm so excited for you. Wouldn't it be wonderful if both you and Millie ended up getting married in the next year or so?"

Mary rolled on her back and stared at the ceiling, a dreamy look in her eyes. "More than wonderful. I never dreamed my life could be like this—a good job, good friends, and the interest of a good man." She sighed. "None of it would have happened if it hadn't been for John Brady, you know. He saved my life."

*Yeah, well, he's ruining mine.* The mention of Brady's name spoiled Lizzie's good mood. She jumped up from the bed and traipsed to her closet, unhooking her nightgown from the back of the door. She quickly undressed, then shimmied the gown over her head. She thought about Michael, and relief flooded through her. Her eyes flicked to the nightstand drawer where she'd put the ring. She needed to tell Mary. *Tonight*—whether Mary liked it or not.

Lizzie scowled as she hung up her clothes. For some reason, her best friend and her fiancé did not get along, and it bothered Lizzie a great deal. Their one and only meeting at the bookstore had been less than cordial, but Lizzie blamed that on John Brady too. To Mary, Brady was one rung below the Pope, and anyone Brady didn't like, Mary didn't either. Her lips flattened as she closed the closet door. And one thing was for dead certain—papal tendencies or no—Brady didn't like his brother.

"Why the frown? Does Brady still bother you that much?" Mary reached for her overnight bag. Her brow puckered as she unbuttoned her blouse.

Lizzie exhaled and dropped down on the bed. She scooted up against the headboard and bunched a pillow between her chest and tented knees. "Yeah, I guess he does. I thought I could get used to the idea of just being friends, but after the day at the lake, I don't think it's possible. At least, not until I'm safely married to someone else."

"Oh, Lizzie, I'm so sorry. I thought you had fun with Brady last week—did something happen to stir things up?"

"No, nothing out of the ordinary. Just Brady being Brady, and me loving him that way." Her lips skewed into a sad smile. "It was a wonderful day, as usual, talking, laughing, teaching me to use his rod and reel. And then all of sudden he just looked at me, and I swear, Mary, my stomach did a flip right on the spot. I felt so foolish that I'm sure I turned seven shades of red." She sighed and laid her head against the pillow. "Somehow I managed to get through dinner, which was wonderful, of course, all the way up until the moment he kissed me on the porch."

Mary's arms grappled wildly inside her nightgown before her head popped through in shock. *"Brady kissed you?"*

Lizzie pursed her lips. "On the cheek. But that's just it, Mary.

For one heart-stopping moment, I actually thought he was going to kiss me—Lizzie O'Connor—right on the lips, even though I *know* it's the last thing he would ever do." She closed her eyes to ward off the tears that stung beneath her lids. "I was so heartbroken that I broke down and cried after he left. *Again.*"

"Oh, Lizzie . . ."

"I'm through, Mary, through with heartbreak over John Brady. There's only one way to get over him, apparently, and that's by falling in love with someone else."

Mary sat down next to Lizzie and gave her a hug. "I totally agree. When I arrived in Boston, I was running away from heartbreak too. And then I met Harold, and suddenly everything made sense. You'll meet someone too, Lizzie. I'll bet the right guy will come along any day now and sweep you off your feet—probably way before Harold even works up the courage to ask me for a second date."

Lizzie turned and took Mary's hands in hers. "Someone already has."

Mary's lips parted. "What?"

Lizzie reached over and opened her nightstand drawer, tugging the diamond ring from its velvet box. Her heart pounded as she slipped it on her finger.

Mary gasped, her gaze locked on Lizzie's hand. "What? Who?"

"Michael."

Mary blinked and took Lizzie's hand in hers, the shock evident in the tightening of her fingers. "But how? When?"

"Last week, after Brady walked me to the door. Oh, Mary, I was so devastated and so depressed and then all of a sudden, there he was, sprawled on the floor playing Magic Mysto with Steven like he belonged there. Talking to Mother and Father like one of their own—"

"But he's not!"

"No, but he could be. Don't you see? I've prayed and prayed

all this time to get over Brady when the answer has been right under my nose the last three months. Michael loves me, Mary, and he wants to make me his wife."

Mary jerked her hand away. "But he's no good, Lizzie, at least not according to Brady."

Lizzie bristled. "I'm done living my life according to Brady. Besides, when it comes to forgiving his brother, I've learned that John Brady is no saint. Michael has changed a lot, and no thanks to John. If I can be a positive influence on him, then why not?"

"Because you don't love him!"

Lizzie drew in a deep breath and exhaled slowly. "You're wrong, Mary, I do love him. Maybe not in the starry-eyed, fairy-tale way that I love Brady, but then that's nothing more than a little girl's fantasy. Well, I'm all grown up now, and so are my needs. And unlike Brady, Michael has offered to fulfill them. He loves me."

"But he doesn't love God—not like his brother."

Exasperation puffed from Lizzie's lips. "Nobody loves God like his brother. I'm beginning to realize that he's the exception rather than the rule, and it's not fair to judge Michael—or any other man—according to Brady's standards. Michael is a man with an unfortunate past who's looking to be a good man. I think I can help him."

"Do you even know his past? Or why Brady doesn't trust him?"

Lizzie studied the worry in her friend's face and touched a hand to her cheek. "A little. I know that he was jealous of John because he was their stepmother's favorite, and that it caused a terrible rift between them. And I know something awful happened to John, but neither Brady nor Michael will tell me what it was." She hesitated, her voice lowering to a whisper. "Mary, you're my best friend and I need you to be happy for me."

"But, Lizzie, I—"

Lizzie gently stilled her lips. "*Please.*"

The blue of Mary's eyes glistened. She nodded and looked away. "Okay, if that's what you want."

"It is."

"Have you told Brady yet?"

Lizzie moistened her lips. "No, not yet. He left with Michael the next day to sign inheritance papers in New York, but he's due back tomorrow. I was planning on telling him right after church."

Mary nodded.

"It's going to be okay, Mary, I promise. Father is making us wait six long months, so we have plenty of time to pray about it."

Mary's chin elevated the slightest degree. "Don't think I won't."

Lizzie smiled and squeezed her in a tight hug. "No, Mary, I would never think that. Not in a million years."

ᕲᏚ ᏸᕲ

A third thunderous boom sounded at the door as Collin stumbled down the hall of his flat in a daze. He scrubbed one hand across his bare chest and stifled a yawn with the other, hurrying as quickly as his comatose body would allow. He glanced at the clock on the parlor mantel and groaned. Six a.m.! The hinges of the front door rattled with another frantic pounding.

"I'm coming," he screamed, irritated at the loss of precious Sunday-morning sleep. He unlatched the lock and flung the door open, ready to take the intruder on.

"H-he's dead! B-Brady's dead!" Cluny trembled on the threshold, his freckled face bloated and red from a crying jag still in progress.

Fear constricted Collin's throat. He grabbed him by the shoulders. "What are you talking about? Where is he?"

"In h-his b-bed. H-he won't w-wake up."

Collin tightened his grip. "Calm down, Cluny. Did you shake him? You know what a sound sleeper he is."

Cluny's throat bobbed as he shook his head. "N-no, I was afraid because h-he wouldn't answer. We were supposed to work out at the gym last night, you know, after he got home? But he didn't show, so I got scared and came over this morning. I yelled his name over and over, but h-he w-wouldn't answer!"

"Collin? What's going on?"

Collin glanced over his shoulder at Faith, barefoot and sleepy-eyed. "It's Brady. He might be sick. Would you mind getting Cluny something to eat while I go check on him?"

"No! I'm going with you."

Collin turned back to study the boy. His chin, although quivering, had a stubborn bent. "Okay, little buddy, we'll go together. Wait here while I put on some clothes."

Collin didn't waste any time. His fingers trembled as he buttoned the fly of his trousers, not even bothering to tuck in his shirt. Faith handed him his shoes and clean socks, and he yanked them on before grazing her cheek with a quick kiss. "Start praying, will you, Faith? Hopefully I'll be right back, but if not, I'll meet you at church."

She nodded and he flew down the hall, snatching his coat on the way out. They sprinted to Brady's apartment, six blocks north, Cluny huffing on his heels all the way. At Brady's building, Collin took the steps three at a time. His blood throbbed in his veins as he heaved the glass door open. Cluny shot through, his spindly legs pumping up the steps like his shoes were on fire.

"The door's open," he rasped. "Brady gave me a key."

They were both out of breath when they reached Brady's room. He lay facedown on the bed, clothes rumpled and shoes still on. His arms and legs were sprawled at odd angles in a sea of covers, and the side of his jaw was shadowed with at least two days' growth of stubble. No movement whatsoever, not even the faintest rise or fall of his breathing.

Collin shook him. "John, wake up!"

Nothing.

He shook harder. "John! Do you hear me? Wake up!" His heart hammered in his chest. He grabbed Brady's wrist and checked for a pulse. Still nothing.

Cluny started crying.

Frantic, Collin lunged for his other wrist beneath a mound of covers. His hand hit something hard and he blinked, feeling a bottle still clutched in Brady's hand. *Alcohol?* Collin rechecked his pulse. Relief flooded his veins. *There!* A beat—slow and irregular—but there all the same.

He glanced up at Cluny, careful to keep the bottle hidden. "Bud, I need you to go get Father Mac, will you? He's got time before Mass, so tell him Brady needs him right away."

Cluny nodded and darted down the hall, slamming the front door behind him.

Collin snatched the unmarked bottle from beneath the covers and sniffed. He detected the faintest odor of alcohol from what looked like a quarter bottle of water. The bed linens were soaked where the bottle had lain, still clutched in Brady's hand.

*Vodka?* Where the devil had he gotten it? Collin hurried down the hall and threw the bottle in the trash. He clattered through several cabinets until he found the coffee, and the smell of ground beans made him hungry. He poured water into Brady's antiquated percolator and added the coffee to the steel basket before flipping the switch. He rolled his sleeves and rattled around in the drawer under the stove to grab a good-sized pot, then ducked into the bathroom to turn on the light. When he returned to Brady's room, he laid the pot on the bed.

"Come on, John, in my former drunks, I always felt better when I threw up, so we need to empty your stomach." He rolled Brady over and dragged him toward the headboard. He managed to sit him up, breathing hard from the effort, then pushed the pot in his lap.

"This wouldn't have happened if you'd learned to drink during the war," he muttered, still in shock that alcohol had crossed John Brady's lips. In all the years he'd known him and all the times he'd tried to get him to drink on their leaves, he had never seen him tip more than a ginger ale. His jaw hardened. *Which meant something in New York had pushed him way over the edge.*

"Come on, ol' buddy, I've got payback to do after all those times you cleaned up after me." He held John's scruffy chin with one hand and opened his mouth with the other, jabbing a finger to the back of his throat.

Brady's body jerked as he gagged, but his eyes remained cemented closed. Collin tried it two more times. It finally paid off like a slot machine in Virginia City. A foul-smelling curtain of liquid gushed from his lips, spraying Brady, the bedding, and Collin with a nauseating slime. Collin gagged as he held Brady's head over the pot. He looked away and tried not to breathe.

He heard Brady moan and was so relieved, he took a deep gulp of air. *Wrong move.* He fought back a heave and leaned forward to search Brady's pale face. "Hey, buddy, you got this all backwards. You're supposed to be holding my head, re-member?"

Brady's eyes opened to slits. "Collin?"

"Yeah, John, it's me. How ya doing?"

Brady licked his lips and scowled. "What's that smell?"

Collin chuckled. "The contents of your stomach . . . I assume after a partial bottle of vodka."

Brady groaned and fell back against the headboard, head banging the wall.

"Brady?"

No answer.

"John! Wake up!"

One eyelid flickered, then stilled. Drool snaked its way down the side of his mouth.

"Okay, ol' buddy, I don't want to do this, but we need to wake you up." Collin put the pot aside and heaved him up and over his shoulder with a grunt. He staggered under his weight before steadying himself, then wrinkled his nose. "Besides, you stink."

He hauled him into the bathroom and laid him in the tub. He took his shoes off and dropped them on the floor. With a flick of his wrist, he turned the cold water on and flipped the shower lever.

Cold spray pelted Brady's chest and face like a hailstorm, causing him to jerk like a drunken marionette. A curse word gurgled in his mouth. "What the devil are you doing?"

Collin's smile was grim. "Cleaning ya up. You smell like a sewer."

"Turn it off, you no-good—" A colorful string of words burned Collin's ears.

He fought a grin as he turned the water off. "Drinking and swearing. Tell me, John, what other bad habits did you pick up in New York?"

Brady groaned, eyes still pasted shut. "Shut up, Collin."

"That any way to talk to a buddy who got out of bed at six a.m. on a Sunday morning to brew you coffee? Now, do you want to take your own shower, or do you want me to give you one?"

"I don't want coffee, and I don't want a shower. Leave me alone."

Collin reached for the faucet handle. "Fine, a shower it is—"

Brady's eyelids peeled open faster than a tightly rolled window shade. He glared, and the whites of his eyes were so spidered with blood vessels that they complemented the red vomit stains on his shirt. "So help me, God, if you touch that faucet one more time . . ."

Collin cocked a hip. "Don't get testy with me, buster. I'm

the one Cluny hauled out of bed at the crack of dawn 'cause he thought you were dead. I'm short on sleep, so don't push me. It wouldn't take a whole lot to turn this water on and let your sorry butt drown."

Brady closed his eyes and moaned. "Cluny found me?"

Collin exhaled his frustration. "Yeah, but he doesn't know you were drunk. I kept the bottle out of sight 'til I sent him to get Father Mac."

Brady jolted up too quickly. He groaned and put a hand to his head. "You sent for Matt? Are you crazy?"

"No, John, just worried sick. What the devil happened in New York, anyway? I've never seen you drink a drop of liquor, much less pass out stinking drunk."

"I don't want to talk about it." Brady tried to wobble to his feet and failed.

"Well, too bloomin' bad, John, because you need to talk to somebody." Collin hefted him under his arms until Brady teetered on his feet in the tub, water sluicing off him like a fountain. "I suggest you strip down and take a shower, ol' buddy. The way you smell right now is a real sin—one that even Father Mac can't absolve."

"Collin . . ."

He turned at the door.

"Did you make the coffee strong?"

"You bet. Stronger than that poison you poured down your gullet."

Brady pressed a hand to the wall and nodded. "Will you send Cluny home when Matt gets here?"

"Yeah."

"And get me clean clothes from the drawer?"

"Sure. Anything else?"

"I could really use two aspirins from the kitchen cabinet, if you don't mind."

"Will do." He started to close the door.

"And, Collin . . ."

"Yeah, John?"

"Will you pray for me?"

Collin's jaw twitched with emotion. He attempted a smile. "Haven't stopped since you left for New York. Now get cleaned up. You can't afford to offend the clergy."

Brady nodded.

Collin closed the door and sagged against it. *Please, God, help him.*

He took a deep breath and headed into the bedroom to clean up the mess. The sound of the shower sent him to the bureau drawers, where neatly folded stacks of T-shirts and underwear reminded him what an orderly man John Brady was. Too orderly to be thrown into chaos by a bout with the bottle. He slipped into the bathroom and put the clean underwear on the back of the commode, then returned to the bedroom to peel the offensive cover off the bed. He wadded it into a ball before tossing it into the empty hamper. He held his breath while he emptied the vomit into the toilet and flushed, then trekked to the kitchen to scour the pot within an inch of its life. He palmed a couple of aspirin, poured two cups of coffee, and carried one to the bathroom.

Steam billowed into the air, misting Collin's face with a fine sheen of moisture. He paused, head cocked. "You still alive in there?"

"No."

Collin grinned. Brady's voice sounded like a rusty tin can. "Coffee and aspirin on the commode." He stooped to pick up the dirty clothing and closed the door. He hurled them toward the hamper and headed to the kitchen.

The nutty smell of fresh-brewed coffee sharpened his appetite, and he peered into the near-empty icebox. *Bingo!* No meat, but a dozen eggs. Better than nothing, he thought as he began cracking them into a fry pan. He lit the stove and doused the soupy mixture with a heavy dose of salt and pepper. Week-old bread lay in the breadbox. The cut side of the loaf sported an unhealthy tinge of green, but Collin grabbed a knife from the drawer and cut the questionable piece off. He sliced two more, finally popping them into the newfangled toaster he and Faith had given Brady for Christmas. He heard the shower stop and looked up at the clock on the wall. Six forty-five. Not bad. From the ranks of the dead to the land of the living in under an hour.

The front door flew open just as he scraped the last of the eggs onto a plate and slid them in the oven to keep warm.

"Is he still alive?" Cluny croaked, face as white as the collar around Father Mac's neck.

Collin smiled and reached for another cup. "Yeah, bud, he's alive. May not feel like it, but he is. Acts a lot like he's got a touch of the flu. Threw up." He nodded at Father Mac. "Thanks for coming, Father. Coffee?"

"Bless you, my son. Cluny caught me before I got my first sip."

"I'll have some too. And do I smell toast?" Cluny dropped into a chair at the table, his fears apparently alleviated by hunger.

"Sorry, bud, but I'm afraid you need to hightail it home."

"I ain't leaving."

Collin set a steaming mug in front of Father Mac. "Have to. You can't risk getting sick."

Cluny's lower lip protruded considerably. "I'm not leaving Brady."

"Sorry, but he specifically told me to send you home. You want to upset him when he's sick?"

"No, but—"

Collin tugged him to his feet. "Come on, he's sicker than the time Miss Hercules ate your gram's whole roasted turkey. Remember how she puked all over and slept for days? That's what Brady needs—rest. He'll see you tomorrow, I promise."

"Tell him I missed him, will ya?"

"Will do." Collin pushed him toward the door.

Cluny turned, the freckles on his face stark against his pale skin. "And, Collin?"

"Yeah, bud?"

"Tell him I'm praying."

Collin blinked, astounded for the hundredth time at the healing effect John Brady had on people's lives. "He's lucky to have you as a friend, Cluny."

"Shoot, no, Collin. I'm the lucky one." He turned to go, and Collin shut the door, determined to fight the emotion in his eyes.

"What happened?" Father Mac asked quietly, his coffee untouched.

Collin turned and exhaled. He was suddenly exhausted. He grabbed his cup from the counter and sank into a chair across from Matt. "I don't know, Father, but whatever it was, it was enough to put away a half bottle of vodka."

"I didn't know he even drank anymore."

Collin took a sip of his coffee. His eyes locked with Matt's over the rim. "He doesn't, not since he was seventeen. Couldn't even get him to go off the wagon during the war when we took leaves in Paris." Fear sifted through him. "If the hell of war couldn't get him to drink, I shudder to think what happened in New York."

Father Mac frowned. "He would have seen his stepsister in New York, right?"

"Yeah, I think so. Helena. She and Michael still live in the house where they all grew up, which is where he stayed, I assume."

Matt nodded, his eyes distracted and far away as he sipped his coffee.

The bathroom door creaked open, and their heads jerked up. They stared, still as stone, as Brady walked into the kitchen, coffee cup limp in his hand. His hygiene considerably improved, he was clean-shaven and hair slicked back, but his eyes were still red and glassy.

Dead and lifeless, Collin thought, and his stomach twisted. He jumped to his feet. "I have eggs and toast in the oven. More coffee?"

"No," Brady muttered and dropped into a chair. His eyes trained on the empty cup in his hand.

Collin ignored him and filled his cup before topping both his and Father Mac's. He plunked a plate of eggs and toast onto the table, along with plates and utensils. "Eat," he said.

Brady continued to stare, his bleary gaze lost in a sea of bitter coffee. "I'm not hungry."

"Yeah, well, you need a little something other than vodka to sustain that thick head of yours."

That woke him up. His head shot up, and the red in his eyes singed like fire. "Go to the devil, Collin. As if I didn't pull your head out of the latrine more times than I can count."

Collin eased back into his chair, all humor depleted. "That's right, John, you did. Which makes this all the more upsetting. What's going on?"

Brady closed his eyes and ran a shaky hand over his face. "I can't tell you."

"Why? From the very beginning, you've known everything about me—my past, my present, what I think, what I feel. The best of friends, closer than brothers. Don't you think I deserve the same?"

Brady lowered his head. "You do, but I can't tell you."

Collin's jaw tightened. "Why?"

"Because I'm not ready."

Collin slammed his fist on the table. "Not ready for what? To be a friend?"

Brady's head lunged up, his eyes swimming with pain. "No, Collin, not ready to lose one."

Collin blinked. He swallowed the emotion lumped in his throat and nodded. "If I leave, will you promise to talk to Father Mac?"

Brady nodded slowly, his eyes dull.

Collin stood. He glanced at Father Mac. "Can you try to get him to eat? I want him healthy at work tomorrow." Collin gave Brady's shoulder a quick squeeze. "I'm tired of carrying him." He started for the door.

"Collin?"

"Yeah?"

"I'll have half of the day's work done before you even shadow the door."

Collin turned, hand poised on the knob. His throat tightened. "I want you to know, John, whatever you did, no matter how bad you think it may be, I will stand by you. I'm proud to call you my friend, because I know who you are—a man of integrity, honor, and passion for God. And nothing—*nothing*—you can say will ever change that for me. I love you like a brother and always will. See you tomorrow." The door clicked softly behind him.

Brady drew in a deep breath and avoided Matt's gaze. Tears filled his eyes. "Like a brother," he whispered. "That doesn't sound so good right about now."

Father Mac leveled beefy arms on the table and leaned in. His tone was quiet. "Worse than you thought?"

Brady's laughter held no mirth. "Yeah. Not only was I a child drunk, but apparently I was depraved enough to sleep with my father's wife."

He heard Father Mac flinch, the faint intake of breath piercing Brady's consciousness anew. He was an infidel. A lost soul. A man who committed incest and adultery to gratify his own flesh.

He staggered to his feet, suddenly craving the numbing effect of the bottles he'd stolen from Michael's stash. "I'd rather you leave, Matt. I feel sick and need to lie down."

A firm grip fisted his arm. "No, John, we need to deal with this now. Once and for all."

Brady jerked away, his eyes itching with tension. "And

how do you propose to do that, Matt? What exactly do you have? A potion or magic formula that will make it all go away?"

Father Mac stared. The brown of his eyes deepened with intensity in a face that radiated pure peace and calm. "No potion, John, and no formula. Just the saving blood of Jesus Christ."

The impact of Matt's words pierced his heart. He looked away. "Maybe that's not enough this time."

"It's always enough, John." Father Mac pulled out a chair. "Sit. Please?"

Brady hesitated, then did as he was asked, slowly sinking into the chair. He leaned his elbows on the table and put his face in his hands. "How can God forgive something like this? Adultery, incest?"

Father Mac exhaled and sat down beside him. He placed a hand on his shoulder. "He does it all the time. I know a man who committed adultery and then murdered his lover's husband, but God forgave him."

Brady looked up with shock in his eyes.

A faint smile shadowed Matt's lips. "In fact, he called him a man after his own heart."

"King David?"

Father Mac nodded. He removed his hand from Brady's shoulder and took a drink of his coffee. He wrinkled his nose. "Cold. Want me to warm it up?"

Father Mac didn't wait for his answer, but dumped both cups and replaced them with hot. He set them on the table and sat back down. "King David was an unusual character. Loved God with all of his heart, but had this unfortunate flaw." Father Mac paused to taste his coffee, then quirked his lips. "He was human. For instance, one day he's dancing before the Lord in a linen ephod, not giving a whit that his wife thinks he's making a fool of himself. Then down the road a bit, he's lusting after a married woman he sees taking a bath on the roof of her house. And what does he do, this man who loves God with all of his heart? He takes her to his bed, then has her husband sent to the battlefront to be killed."

Father Mac leaned in, his gaze intent. "He committed adultery and murder, yet he's *still* the only man in the Bible God refers to as 'a man after his own heart.' Now why is that, I wonder? I'll tell you why. Because David was a man who had a love affair with God. Imagine that—emotionally involved with the God of the universe. Trusted him, worshiped him, sought after him—and all without restraint. Did he mess up? You bet. Did he repent? With all of his heart, aching inside whenever he offended his God. Why? Because he had a Father-son relationship with him, loved him, and wanted to please him." Father Mac hesitated, slowly tracing his finger along the rim of his cup. He finally raised his eyes to capture Brady with a fixed stare. "Just like you, John."

Brady looked away, swallowing the emotion trapped in his throat. "'Cursed be he that lieth with his father's wife.' Deuteronomy 27:20." His voice was flat. "How do you respond to that?"

"'If we confess our sins, he is faithful and just to forgive us . . . and to cleanse us from all unrighteousness.' 1 John 1:9."

Brady peered through slitted lids. "And you believe that? For something as vile as this?"

"'God is not a man, that he should lie.' Numbers 23:19."

A ghost of a smile flickered on Brady's lips. "Since when do you have Scripture down cold?"

Father Mac pushed up the sleeves of his cassock. A hint of a smile appeared. "Since I began butting heads with you."

"I know the Scriptures, Matt. It's just that when it comes to me, I have trouble believing they could apply." He expelled a slow, jagged breath. "But you're saying that if I confess right now . . . my sins with Lucille . . . they're over with? Gone?"

"'Cast into the depths of the sea.' Micah 7:19."

Brady closed his eyes, feeling the first glimmer of hope he'd felt in a long, long while. Over with. Gone. Miles away from guilty. *As far as the east is from the west, so far hath he removed our transgressions from us.*

He looked up at the touch of Father Mac's hand on his arm.

"You ready?" Father Mac asked.

Brady nodded, exhaling softly. He gripped Father Mac's hand like a lifeline, a man desperate for absolution. "More than ready," he whispered. He drew in a deep breath and made the sign of the cross, then bowed his head.

"Bless me, Father, for I have sinned . . ."

## 18

Sweet saints in heaven, she hadn't been this nervous since the night Collin had first brought him home to dinner. Lizzie chewed on her lip, purposely dragging her feet as she made her way down Rumpole Street to Brady's apartment. Despite the cold weather, her palms were moist. She rubbed them hard against her long woolen coat and loosened the red plaid scarf tied around her neck so she could breathe.

John Morrison Brady—Collin's war buddy, business partner, and all-around best friend—had captured her heart the moment he'd asked about her favorite books, making her feel special for the first time in her life. Since then, he had held her heart in the palm of his hand and never let go.

Lizzie touched the ring hidden deep in her pocket and picked up her pace. *Until now.*

She hesitated at the steps of his building to take a deep breath. This would probably be the last time she would see him for a long, long time, other than Thanksgiving and Christmas. *And the wedding.*

The clash of feelings inside unnerved her: intense sadness steeled with resolve, merging with anticipation for her future. A future with Michael rather than John.

But deep down inside, hope collided with regret. Michael was special to her, he really was. She fingered the ring in her pocket. But she *loved* Brady. She mounted the last step and stopped, hand clutched on the knob of the glass-paned door. She squeezed her eyes shut and willed her mind to let go of John and think only of Michael—the way he made her laugh, the low timbre of his voice when he told her he loved her, his gentleness, his boldness . . . *his kisses*. Her stomach fluttered, and she opened her eyes. This could work. She could love this man, and she knew it. She pressed a shaky hand to her stomach to quell the memory of his kiss, then exhaled slowly. Sweet saints, wasn't she already well on her way?

Her confidence was reasonably strong when she knocked on Brady's door, although she wished she could have told him after Mass. It would have been the perfect place, cocooned in the sacred strength of St. Stephen's Church. She'd seen him, head bowed, in his favorite pew clear at the back of the church. She'd had it all planned—pulling him aside after the service when the building was empty, sitting in the alcove to the right of the sanctuary. They could have privacy there, she thought, and yet she could still draw on the strength of Jesus, sprawled on the bench in the balcony. But unfortunately, Brady ducked out right after Mass, and so here she was, standing at his door. She knocked again—harder this time, as if to dispel any lingering doubts.

The door swung open, and suddenly all doubts crashed to her feet. He stood before her, the man she knew she would love till the day she died. He was dressed in the same gray dress slacks he'd worn to church, but his white, starched shirt was unbuttoned almost halfway down, providing a glimpse of a hard-muscled chest matted with hair.

Heat braised her cheeks, and she quickly averted her gaze to his bare feet. "Brady, I'm sorry to barge in like this . . ."

He pulled her inside. "Don't apologize, Beth, I'm glad you're here." He closed the door and leaned against it. "I've missed you."

A painful longing kindled inside of her, and her eyelids fluttered closed. *Me too—for the rest of my life.* She stepped back and slipped her hand into her pocket, squeezing the diamond in her palm to draw from its strength.

"Are you all right?" He was by her side in a heartbeat. He led her to the table and pulled a chair out, then reached for her coat. "Here, let me hang that up, and then I'll finish changing. You want some coffee?"

She sat down and hugged her arms to her waist. "No, I can't stay. If you don't mind, I just need to tell you something."

He hesitated, then scraped out a chair to sit beside her.

She stopped him with a hand to his arm, avoiding his eyes. "No, John, not so close, please. This will be hard enough as it is."

His pause was longer this time before he moved to sit on the other side of the table. He cleared his throat. "What's on your mind, Beth?"

She looked up then . . . and wished she hadn't. His eyes were dark pools of worry shadowed by a sunkenness that suggested more than a few sleepless nights. Hard-chiseled features seemed all the more gaunt, given the pallor of his skin and the sag of his shoulders. She suddenly realized he didn't look well and shot to her feet. "Oh, Brady, are you sick? You look awful!"

The edge of his lips quirked. "Thanks, Beth, but I'll be fine. Talk to me."

She lost her nerve and headed for the door. "No, no, it can wait, really. You look short on sleep and probably need to go right to bed—"

He gripped her arm, and the hard line of his jaw was a clear indication he wasn't long on patience either. He sat her down with a firm hand. "Out with it, Beth, *now*. I can sleep later." He loomed over her with that quiet energy he possessed, hip cocked and arms propped loose on his hips. The picture of calm except for the intensity of his eyes. She didn't want to hurt him, but she knew she would, and the thought crushed her. *Oh, Brady, why does it have to be this way?*

"Beth?"

She blinked, suddenly aware they were face-to-face as he squatted beside her. She could see the darkening of his jaw from the emergence of stubble, and those tiny flecks of gold in the brown of his eyes.

He took her hand in his, warming her with his gaze. "Is this about Michael?"

She caught her breath and nodded.

"He wants to marry you, doesn't he?"

She nodded again, not daring to believe it could be this easy.

He stood to his feet. "Well, you can't marry him, and that's all there is to it."

Her reverie popped like a soap bubble. She shot to her feet. "What? And who are *you* to tell me what I can or cannot do? For the last four and a half years, you have tried to bully me into whatever you want. Well, not anymore!" She groped in her pocket and shoved the ring on her trembling finger. She thrust her left hand in his face and lifted her chin. "You've always seen me as a sister, John. Well, congratulations, you've gotten your wish!"

She may as well have gouged him, letting the diamond draw blood across his paralyzed cheek. *Same effect.* All feeling left his body for a split second except for a faraway buzzing, as if he had just polished off another half bottle of Michael's vodka. He couldn't feel his heart pumping and realized it had stopped, along with the air locked in his throat. And then in a painful squeeze of his heart, both pulse and air rushed back, surging on a tidal wave of pain so strong, he felt as if he were bleeding. *God, no! She belongs to me!*

She shoved him out of her way and started to leave, but he was too fast. When she opened the door, he slammed it shut and pushed her against it. "You can't marry my brother. Not when you're in love with me."

Her eyes flared wide, then narrowed to slits. "Was in love with you!" she screamed. She twisted away. "For all the good it did. Well, now I'm in love with Michael, and there's nothing you can do about it."

*Nothing?* He stared at her face, her full lips pursed in defiance and her violet eyes bright with anger, and all resolve to take it slow melted into a pool of warmth at the bottom of his stomach. Father Mac had convinced him. Assured him he was free of the perversion of his past. Free enough, at least, to marry Beth—if she would have him.

He studied her now and knew that she would . . .

At least if it were the John Brady she knew and loved.

A flicker of fear feathered his stomach. Tell her, Matt had warned, and Brady promised he would . . . once his ring was on her finger. But for now, his focus needed to be on getting it there.

The rhythm of his pulse quickened and he swallowed hard, like a child about to taste his first candy after a long season of Lent. His lips parted as his gaze fixed on her mouth, and a heat he'd denied far too long radiated through him like an August sun on a mile of blacktop. In slow motion, he reeled her into his arms, ignoring the stiffness of her body. He bent his head until his mouth hovered over hers.

"Nothing? Oh, but there is, Beth," he whispered, studying her lips through hooded eyes.

Her mouth parted in shock when his lips grazed hers, and he could smell the sweet scent of mint on her breath. An aching moan rumbled low in his throat, and he took her again, molding his mouth with a need that shook him.

He felt her tension melt beneath his touch and he deepened the kiss, heady with the taste of her. His lips wandered to explore the curve of her jaw and then the softness of her throat, losing himself in the scent of lilacs and innocence and *Beth*. A soft moan left her lips, and it undid him, luring him back with a fervor that consumed him.

All at once she lurched away, her tender mouth pink and swollen with desire. She thrust a trembling hand to his chest and stared with wild eyes, chest heaving. "*No!* How could you? You don't want me—you're just trying to stop me from marrying Michael."

He gripped her in his arms, his breathing ragged and shallow. "No, Beth, I'm not trying to *stop* you from marrying Michael . . . I'm trying to *make* you marry me."

The blood stilled in her veins. Had she heard him right? He wanted to marry her? Was it for real . . . or a last resort to prevent her from marrying his brother? She wavered, dizzy at the prospect that it could be true. Her pulse was still racing from the heat of his kiss, but her hopes had been dashed so many times before . . .

"Beth?" He cupped her face in his hands. "Forgive me, I've been a fool. Because of my past . . . I just couldn't see . . . how much I needed you, wanted you. I love you, Elizabeth, with all of my heart. Don't marry Michael, *please*. Marry me."

She pressed a hand to her mouth, and tears filled her eyes. "Oh, Brady, do you mean it?"

He caressed the side of her face with his palm, then feathered the corner of her lip with his thumb. Heating her with a stare, he leaned in and closed his eyes, nuzzling her mouth in a gentle mating that fluttered through her like a warm, gentle breeze.

"Oh, Brady, I love you. I've always loved you."

She felt the tug of his smile beneath the heat of his lips. "Say it, Elizabeth, say you'll marry me."

A joyous giggle bubbled in her chest. "Oh yes, yes, John, I will. Mrs. Brady . . . oh, I like the sound of that."

He pulled away. "Mrs. *John* Brady," he said in a gruff tone. He lifted her left hand. "Take the ring off, Beth."

She stared at the diamond and felt a stab of sadness. She had come here to tell Brady goodbye. Now she'd be telling Michael instead. With a soft sigh, she tugged it off and slipped it back into her pocket.

He lifted her chin with his finger, and she saw worry clouding his eyes. "Are you in love with him?"

She hesitated, not sure how to answer. Michael had been there when Brady had turned her away. Before she had known it, he'd stolen a piece of her heart. Did she love him? Maybe a little, but nothing like the torch she carried for his brother—her soul mate, her mentor, her friend.

She laid her head against his chest and breathed in the clean scent of him with his starched shirt and musk soap. "Not like I love you. Never like I've loved you."

His arms enclosed her in a fierce hug, and the sweetness of the moment would be with her forever. "You need to tell him," he whispered.

She sighed against his chest. "I'll call—tonight—I promise." She clutched him tightly and pressed a gentle kiss to his bare chest. All at once, his hands fanned the length of her, from shoulder to hips in one hungry sweep. She lifted her head, and he gave her a half-lidded gaze that quivered her stomach. Slowly, he bent to kiss her, possessing her mouth with a fierce gentleness.

His breathing was uneven when he finally pulled away, hands trembling as he gripped her at arm's length. "We need to get you out of here, Beth. *Now.*" He released her to fumble with the buttons of his shirt, eyes heating hers as he tucked it in his waistband. He gave her a quick kiss on the lips, then retrieved shoes and socks from the bedroom. He put them on and grabbed his coat from the hook by the door.

"I'll tell you one thing right now, Elizabeth O'Connor," he said in a tone that brooked no argument. He snatched his keys from the table and led her out the door, locking it on the way. "This will *not* be a long engagement."

God preserve her, it was like walking on air! Lizzie closed the front door and leaned back, propped against it with a silly smile on her face. She closed her eyes and sighed, wondering how long this floating effect would last. She replayed Brady's proposal in her mind and smiled at the shiver of delight that raced through her. She opened her eyes and immediately lost herself in a faraway stare, chewing on the tip of her finger as she thought of his kisses. Heat instantly surged to her cheeks and traveled south. She pressed a hand to her waist and bit her lip. Oh my, but the man could do funny things to her stomach—wonderful, warm, quivering things that she'd only dreamed about. She closed her eyes again and sagged against the door, breathless at the thought of sharing a life—and a bed—with John Morrison Brady. A husband, a lover . . . the man of her dreams!

"Lizzie, are you all right? Your face is red as that scarf around your neck."

*Redder*, she imagined as she glanced up at her mother, whose scrutiny now braised her cheeks as much as her illicit thoughts of Brady. She masked her humiliation with a bright smile. "No, Mother, I'm not 'all right.' I'm better than all right. In fact, at this very moment, I would say I'm happier than I've ever been in my life." She pressed a hand to her mouth and giggled, fresh awareness hitting her full force. "Oh, Mother, I'm getting married!"

Marcy blinked, pausing on the last step with a laundry basket cocked on her hip. She gave Lizzie a patient smile. "Yes, dear, I know."

Lizzie giggled again and rushed to take the basket from Marcy's hand, then set it on the floor. "No, I can see it in your face—you think I've lost my mind, but I haven't. Only my heart—to John Morrison Brady!"

"What?"

"Brady finally did it! He asked me to marry him."

Marcy's jaw dropped. "W-what?" she repeated with a stutter.

Lizzie grabbed her hands and shook them. "He did it, Mother. Don't you see? He loves me—has all along—and he's asked me to be his wife!"

Marcy faltered back and put a hand to her chest. "Oh, dear

Lord, I do believe I need to sit." She dropped to the bottom step and started fanning her face with one of Patrick's underwear shorts from the laundry basket. "Sweet saints, I thought the drama was over and done once Charity got married. When did this all happen?"

"After church this morning. I was going to tell him about the engagement after Mass, but I didn't catch him in time, so I went to his apartment. I told him we needed to talk, and he guessed it was about his brother. He told me in no uncertain terms that I couldn't marry Michael."

Marcy's brow angled a half inch. "And that ruffled your feathers?"

Lizzie pursed her lips, remembering her reaction. "That's putting it mildly. I said I was through with his bullying and flaunted the ring right in his face. I told him flat out that I was going to marry Michael, and there was nothing he could do about it."

Marcy put a hand to her mouth. "Oh my."

"But he did—he kissed the daylights out of me, Mother, and as God is my witness, I was pure putty in his hands." She sighed. "Neither of us wants a long engagement."

Marcy bit her lip. "Oh my. Yes, well, I can certainly see why. I'll have to talk to your father, of course. You know how he feels about that. But since we've all known Brady for years, I think it's best if you two got married sooner rather than later. Is that . . . um . . . where you were all afternoon . . . at Brady's apartment?"

Lizzie blushed. "No, Brady hurried us out right after he proposed. Trust me, Mother, both of us are intent on doing things God's way no matter the rush of emotions we're feeling right now. So we got a bite to eat downtown, then spent the day planning. He brought me home because he promised Cluny he'd take him to the gym tonight." She sighed. "Mrs. John Brady. It has a nice ring, don't you think?"

Marcy's brow furrowed. "Speaking of 'rings,' when are you going to tell Michael?"

Lizzie moaned and hunkered down next to her mother on the step, less giddy at the mention of Michael's name. "As soon as possible. He needs to be the first to know, I suppose, before I tell the family tonight at dinner." She sucked in a deep breath to dispel the sick feeling over hurting Michael, then chewed on her lip. "But he'll be fine, I hope. After all, he's known all along how I felt about his brother." She glanced at her mother. "Oh, Mother, won't Collin be ecstatic?"

Marcy appeared to be coming out of her stupor. She hugged Lizzie with a deep groan and then brushed the moisture from her eyes. "Not only Collin, my love, but every single person in this family. Brady's like one of our own—you know that."

Lizzie sighed. "Yes, Mother, I do. I've always known. Unfortunately that stubborn man didn't." She grinned. "But he's in luck—I'm in a forgiving mood."

Marcy chuckled. "Better learn to cultivate that, Lizzie. He is a man, after all."

Lizzie smiled and rested her head against her mother's. "I don't expect to need it, Mother. John Brady is the most perfect and amazing man I have ever met."

Marcy stroked her daughter's hair and smiled. "They all are, darling . . . in the beginning. And then God uses them to make us grow . . . into most 'amazing' women."

❧ ☙

"What a day! My partner is back to help carry the load, my best friend is getting married, and I just beat Patrick O'Connor at chess. It just doesn't get any better than this." Collin stood and stretched, then leaned to nibble the back of Faith's neck as she chatted with Charity on the sofa. He lowered his voice and teased the tip of her earlobe with his teeth. "Or maybe it does," he whispered.

Faith made a pretense of shooing him away, but quickly

rose with a blush staining her cheeks. "Well, we better go then, before he wants a rematch. I'm tired."

"Nothing but a fluke," Patrick groused. He winked at Faith, then grinned at Collin. "Kind of like my daughter marrying the likes of you."

Mitch glanced up from his paper. "I'll go along with that."

Collin chuckled and bent to kiss Marcy's cheek. "A fluke for me, but the hand of God for you, Dennehy. Good night, Marcy. Dinner was wonderful. Thanks for the game, Patrick."

Charity snuggled close to her husband's side despite a sleeping Henry on her lap. She twirled a curl at the back of his head. "Did you hear that? The hand of God. Kind of makes me sound like an angel, doesn't it?"

His lips quirked while he ignored her, newspaper in hand. "No, and blasphemy is a sin, little girl."

Charity nuzzled his neck. "So is ignoring your wife."

Lizzie jumped up from the love seat and stretched her arms in a wide yawn. "Well, while you lovebirds head home, I'm going upstairs to dream of Brady."

"Oh, Lizzie, I am so happy for you," Faith said.

She gave her a tight hug while Collin ambled into the foyer to get their coats, whistling several bars from "Yes, We Have No Bananas." He grinned at the thought of Brady becoming family and deftly snatched their coats from the rack. The doorbell rang, and he draped the wraps over his arm. "I'll get it," he called. He opened the door, and his smile instantly went stale.

"I need to see Lizzie—*now!*" Michael's tone matched the scowl on his face.

"Michael! Look, I'm sorry about you and Lizzie—"

"Save it, Collin. We both know where your sympathies lie."

"Come on, Michael. You had to know she's been in love with Brady for years."

"Yeah, I knew, but that didn't stop John from breaking her heart over and over again, now did it? Well, I'm the one who picked up the pieces, Collin, and I'm not about to let them go. Where is she?"

Collin glanced over his shoulder where Lizzie and her sisters were huddled in conversation. He turned back to Michael with a press of his jaw. "Leave her alone, Michael. She's happier than I've ever seen her. If you love her, let it go."

"Yeah? Well, it's because I love her that I won't let it go. My brother will end up hurting her again, and I can't let him do that." Michael shoved Collin out of the way and pushed his way into the hall. "Lizzie? I need to talk to you."

Collin tossed the coats on the floor and gripped Michael's shoulder. He pinned his head with an arm to his throat. "I said, leave her alone!"

"Collin! Stop it—now!" Lizzie ran to Michael's side. She glared at her brother-in-law. "What on earth is wrong with you?"

"He pushed me," Collin muttered.

"Well, for pity's sake, you're a grown man. Act like it." Lizzie touched a finger to Michael's red throat. "Are you all right?"

"No, Lizzie, I'm not. We need to talk. Now."

"Come on, Collin, I'm tired. Take me home." Faith squeezed Lizzie's arm and smiled at Michael. She picked their coats up and pushed Collin through the front door. "Good night, everyone."

"Right behind you," Charity said. She nodded at Michael and unlatched their coats from the rack, then bounded back into the parlor to bundle the twins in their blankets. She handed Henry off to Mitch, who stood ready and armed with a heavy tote filled to the brim with baby paraphernalia. "Good night, everyone. See you next week." She kissed her father and mother, then lifted Hope from Marcy's shoulder. With a pat on Lizzie's arm and a sympathetic smile at Michael, she rushed out the door with Mitch close behind.

Patrick rose. "Marcy, Sean, let's give these two some privacy. Steven, Katie, upstairs. It's time for bed."

"But it's only nine fif—"

Patrick silenced her with a look before entering the foyer. He extended his hand. "Hello, Michael. Give me your coat. You sure know how to clear a room, son."

Michael slipped his jacket off and handed it to Patrick. "Yes, sir. I hope to clear the air with Lizzie as effectively. Thank you for allowing me to speak with her. You understand, this came as quite a shock."

Patrick squeezed Lizzie's shoulder, then hung the coat on the rack. "Yes, well, that's an understatement all the way around. Good night, Lizzie, Michael."

Patrick herded the family up the stairs, leaving Lizzie and Michael alone. Michael silently took her hand and drew her into the parlor to the sofa, where he sat beside her. Her heart ached the moment she faced him. Heavy lids and faint shadows reflected his fatigue despite eyes dark with intensity. Apparently he'd driven straight from New York the moment she'd called, and the thought weighted her with guilt. She touched his hand. "Michael, I'm so sorry . . ."

He clutched her hands in his. "No, Lizzie, I know you've been in love with John for years, so don't apologize for that. But I thought—or hoped—you also had feelings for me."

She looked away, feeling the blush in her cheeks at the warm stroke of his thumb on her palm. She bit her lip and slowly removed her hands from his. "I do have feelings for you, Michael. I . . . care about you very much."

"But you don't love me."

She forced her gaze to his. "I don't know. I think I do a little, or at least I was on my way. But whatever's there, Michael, it can't compete with the love I have for Brady. Since I was a little girl, I've known he was the perfect man for me."

His tone was hard. "Yeah, 'perfect.'"

She blinked. "What is that supposed to mean?"

He drew in a deep breath and studied her for several seconds as if weighing his words. He exhaled slowly. "Look, Lizzie, you asked me once what happened to my brother years ago, but I wouldn't tell you. Because despite the fact that we are obviously not close, John and I are blood, and I don't want to hurt him. But . . ."

Everything within her stilled—her heart, her mind, the air in her throat—all of it, teetering.

"I love you too, enough to stop you from making a mistake. It's true—I want you to marry me more than anything, but even if you won't, I want you to be happy. And after a week in New York with John, I'm scared to death that not only will he *not* make you happy, but I think he's going to end up hurting you again."

She jerked away, but he gripped her arms. "Not on purpose, Lizzie, because he loves you, he really does. But the problems of his past are so deep, so damaging, that I worry he can never be the husband you need him to be."

Tears burned her eyes. "Let me go!" He released her, and she stood to her feet. "I'll get your ring and then you can go."

She slipped out of the parlor and up to her room, tiptoeing in the dark to her nightstand drawer. She closed the ring in her hand.

"Lizzie? Are you still gonna marry Brady, even though Michael is here?" Katie's voice floated from across the room.

"Yes, darling, I am. I'm just giving Michael his ring back." She pressed a kiss to Katie's forehead. "You go to sleep now. I'll be up soon, okay?"

Katie nodded and turned over.

Lizzie moved to the window where moonlight streamed across her face. She held the ring up to the light and released a heavy sigh. Michael was just angry, she thought. And she didn't blame him. She had no right to treat him harshly. When he'd left, she'd been engaged to him. Now she was engaged to his brother, and the absurdity of the situation made her feel a little foolish. Ring tightly in hand, she ran downstairs where Michael remained seated on the sofa, his head in his hands.

She moved across the room to sit beside him, and he looked

up, breaking her heart with the soulful look in his eyes. She gently took his hand and pressed the diamond in his palm, closing his fingers over it.

He stood still for several seconds, his eyes never straying from hers, then slowly pocketed the ring. "I love you, Lizzie. I always will. John's a lucky man, which I suppose he deserves given his unlucky past. I just hope and pray he doesn't break your heart." He rose and started for the door.

"Michael . . ."

He paused.

"I just love him. You understand that, don't you?"

His back rose and fell with a heavy breath. "Yes."

"Whatever's in his past, it can't change that."

He turned. "It's not his past I'm concerned about, Lizzie. It's your future. And yes, it could. Good night."

Fear clawed at her throat. She ran after him. "Nothing could be that bad . . ."

He turned at the door, his coat draped over his arm. "Then why are you afraid?"

Dread skittered in her stomach like scorpions waiting to sting. A fragile thread of air seeped from her lips. "Tell me, then," she whispered.

Regret shadowed his features. "Do you really want to know?"

"Yes." Her voice was a hoarse whisper.

"It's going to hurt. Are you sure?"

Her pulse pounded in her brain. "Yes."

He observed her with sorrowful eyes, obviously wrestling with the weight of his decision. He finally nodded and took her hand to lead her back to the parlor.

When he spoke, he sounded quiet and low, and far more like his brother than himself. "All right, Lizzie," he whispered, "I'll tell you what I know."

❧ ❧

Marcy heard it first. Guttural sobs rising on the stairs. She shot up in the bed just as Lizzie staggered into their room, her body heaving with soul-wrenching sorrow. She fell into her mother's arms, and Patrick seized up in the bed, his eyes wide in the dark. "Lizzie? Is that you? What's wrong?"

She was weeping too hard to speak, and the words were so muddled that all Marcy could make out was Brady's name.

Patrick pulled her from Marcy's arms into his lap like when she'd been small, a little girl so afraid of storms. He rocked her gently against his chest and stroked her hair. "Nothing can be this bad, darlin', nothing. Not as long as we have God to turn to."

Marcy rubbed Lizzie's back while her eyes locked with Patrick's, reflecting the worry she saw in his. "Lizzie, you have to calm down and tell us what happened," she said.

Lizzie nodded, and her body shook with heaves that slowly tapered off. She sniffed and wiped a sleeve against her face, and Patrick reached for his handkerchief on the nightstand. He pressed it into her hand and kissed her cheek. With a final quiver, she settled back against his chest. Her face was a mask of tragedy in the moonlit room.

"It's Brady," she whispered, her eyes lost in a cold stare.

"What about Brady, darlin'?" Patrick said.

"He . . . slept with his father's wife."

Marcy's body went numb at the shock of her words, robbing her of all ability to speak. She heard Patrick's harsh intake of breath, a violent hissing in a silent room. Seconds hung in the air like minutes, riddled with the ragged beat of her pulse. *No! Please, God, no.*

"Tell us everything," Patrick whispered. His voice sounded like a stranger's, cold, unfamiliar, and as tight as the fist clenched around his daughter's shoulder.

"He was s-seventeen and she was twenty-five. Michael says he was drunk and seduced her . . ." A sob choked and she started to heave.

Marcy gasped and Patrick swore under his breath.

"H-his ten-year-old stepsister f-found them." Lizzie began to weep, keening against her father's side. "M-Michael s-said Brady left home that night, and stole his stepmother's jewels before he ran away."

"Oh, God help us." Marcy made the sign of the cross.

"A-and t-then . . ."

Marcy's voice rose with alarm. "There's more?"

Lizzie nodded as a broken sob heaved from her lips. "M-Michael is w-worried b-because he says Brady h-has a temper and g-gets violent when he drinks."

Patrick gripped her arms. "Brady drinks?"

Lizzie stared as if in a stupor. "Since he was fourteen," she whispered. A spasm shuddered through her. "Michael says that Brady . . . that he . . . lived on skid row for almost a y-year after he left. And t-this l-last week, when he w-was in N-New York, he got b-blind drunk and tried to kill Michael."

Patrick exhaled slowly. "Lizzie, have you ever seen any indication of this before? Brady's temper, his drinking, his past?"

She shook her head. "No, I-I just knew he had a checkered past. That he never wanted to talk about it."

Patrick grunted. "I can certainly see why. I'll wager even Collin doesn't know."

"He doesn't. Michael says nobody does."

Marcy stroked her daughter's hair. "Maybe it's not true, then. Maybe Michael is making it up . . . or exaggerating."

Fresh tears swam in Lizzie's eyes. "Oh, Mother, I pray you're right. When Michael told me tonight, I felt like a part of me died inside. I love Brady, but if this were true . . . I just don't know what I would do."

"You'll forgive him, Lizzie, just like God has," Marcy said quietly.

Patrick shifted in the bed and punched his pillow several times before stuffing it behind his back. "No, Marcy, she'll forget him. Any man who could do that to his own family, I don't want for my daughter."

A sob erupted from Lizzie's throat.

"Patrick, we don't even know if it's true. Brady deserves the right to defend himself."

Lizzie lurched from Patrick's hold and jumped up from the bed. "God help me, I can't handle this. I need to know—right now!"

"Lizzie!" Patrick rose up in the bed, his tone paralyzing her where she stood.

She put her hands to her face and started to sob.

"You are not going anywhere tonight. We are going to pray about this, and then you are going to bed. You can talk to him in the morning."

She shook her head and took several steps toward the door. "No, Father, I won't be able to sleep—"

"Lizzie!" Patrick's tone was sharp with warning.

Marcy rushed to her side. "Your father's right. We'll pray about it, sleep on it, then you can talk to him in the morning." She ushered her back to the bed, and Lizzie started to cry. "Patrick, will you pray?" she whispered.

He put his arms around them both and bowed his head. "Lord God, our hearts are heavy, but we trust in your Word which says 'weeping may endure for a night, but joy cometh in the morning.' Be in this situation, Lord, work it out for Lizzie and Brady's good, bringing joy in the morning. Reveal the truth, no matter what it may be, and give each of us the strength to receive it. And help all of us to sleep, Lord, especially Lizzie. Give her a peaceful night. Amen."

Patrick squeezed Lizzie's shoulders and pressed a kiss to her head. His voice was low and rough. "Lizzie, whether truth or not, we are bound by God to silence. Exposing Brady's past edifies no one and hurts everyone. Do you understand what I'm saying?"

She nodded and rose to her feet, her tear-streaked face iridescent in the milky moonlight.

"Good night, darlin'. Get some sleep. This will all work out. Trust me."

"Lizzie, do you want me to lie with you for a while?" Marcy asked.

She nodded.

Marcy kissed Patrick's cheek. "I'll snuggle in as soon as she falls asleep."

He watched the two of them leave and slowly laid his head back on the pillow, staring at the ceiling, a father in shock. God have mercy, he didn't want to feel this way toward Brady, he didn't! But if it were true . . . how could he ever accept the man?

*Trust me*, he had told his daughter. Patrick shivered with a cold, sinking fear. God help him—he couldn't even trust himself.

❧ ❧

She supposed the prayer had worked—at least half. She had slept, but it had been anything but peaceful. Her dreams had been a bizarre kaleidoscope of Michael and Brady in a surreal tug-of-war. Mother had stayed with her most of the night, sneaking out in the early hours of the morning when Father rose to get ready for work.

Lizzie's eyelids felt too heavy to open, no doubt Michael's revelations weighting them closed. That and a restless night that did little more than paste her eyes shut. She managed to open one eye and blink at the clock, then jolted up in bed at the late hour. Nine o'clock! She threw her covers aside and lumbered to her feet, her face still numb from hours of weeping. She thought of Brady, and a sharp pain seared through her. *No, God, please!*

She dressed slowly as her thoughts rambled, and she was glad Katie and Steven had already left for school. Father and Sean would both be at work by now, so only Mother would be downstairs to wish her well in her quest for the truth.

*The truth.* Lizzie wavered on her feet while a sickening

dizziness whirled in her brain. Her Brady—always so decent, so kind, so perfect. Her knight in shining armor—tarnished by sins too painful to ponder. She reached for the bureau to steady herself, praying for God to give her strength. *And ye shall know the truth, and the truth shall make you free.* Oh, God, let it be so!

Her mother looked up when she entered the kitchen, and her tired eyes mirrored Lizzie's. "Were you able to sleep?" Marcy asked.

"Some. Thank you for staying with me, Mother. I couldn't have gotten through the night without you."

"Are you going to see him this morning?"

Lizzie drew in a deep breath. "Yes, right now."

Marcy's smile was weary. She squeezed her hand. "Trust God, Lizzie."

Lizzie nodded. But even so, she pushed through the swinging door with a growing sense of dread. She slipped her coat on and headed outside, so lost in fragmented thoughts that she jolted when she finally reached the window of McGuire and Brady Printing Company. She peered inside and saw Collin hunched over his desk and Brady in the back. Tears stung her eyes, and she turned away. *God, help me, please.* She rubbed at the wetness with the edge of her scarf and straightened her shoulders. She could do this. She could.

She opened the door, and the bell jangled overhead. Collin looked up and started to smile. He sat up in his chair. "Lizzie? What's wrong?"

That's all it took. Tears started to flow, and Collin jumped up and rounded the desk. He pulled her to him, and she collapsed in his arms with a sob. "Oh, Collin . . ."

He glanced over his shoulder and put two fingers to his mouth. A shrill whistle carried over the droning noise of Brady's press before it ground to a halt.

She heard his swift stride as he entered the room. "Beth? What's wrong?"

Collin handed her over, and Brady swallowed her up in a

tight hug. The smell of ink and solvent, Bay Rum, and soap filled her senses with painful longing, and she wept all the harder. He gripped her arms and held her away, his eyes dark with worry as he scanned her face. "Beth, tell me what's wrong!"

He stroked her cheek with a gentle touch, and she suddenly realized those same hands may have violated his stepmother and God knows how many others. She lunged away, her hand quivering as she warded him off.

"No! Don't touch me, please. Not yet. Not until I know . . ."

He flinched as if she had struck him.

"Lizzie, you're acting crazy. Until you know what?" Collin demanded.

Brady stared, lips parted in shock.

Water pooled in her eyes, and his handsome face blurred before her, distorting into an image of a man she loved and one she hated. Her father had told her to keep the silence, to tell no one, but anger told her she didn't care. The man of her dreams could very well be nothing more than a lie, destroying years of trust and faith.

Her fingers balled into fists at her sides. "The truth! I want the truth," she whispered harshly, her voice strained and foreign to her own ears.

Collin grabbed Brady's arm. "John, what's she talking about?"

Brady's face was calm and resigned, a pale backdrop for dark eyes steeped in pain. "She's talking about my brother," he whispered. "He told her—"

"Told her what?" Collin demanded.

"Is it true?" Lizzie shouted. Thoughts of his depravity flashed in her mind, and she felt sick to her stomach.

He turned and walked to the back of the shop.

Lizzie followed, her heart hammering in her chest. "I want to know, Brady. *Is it true?*"

He kept his back to her and lowered his head, his tension obvious from the muscles straining his shirt.

She had always had too vivid an imagination. Now it conjured thoughts of that same muscled back lying prone over his father's wife. Her fury rose and she flew at him from behind, pummeling him hard with her fists.

He spun around to fend her off, and Collin restrained her from behind. "Lizzie, stop!"

She wrenched against Collin's hold, her chest heaving as revulsion rose in her throat like vomit. "It's true, isn't it? You slept with your own stepmother!"

There was a faint whirring in his brain, as if reality had given way to madness. His blood slowed to a crawl and he stared, first at the woman he cherished and then at the friend he loved, and knew his life would never be the same again. He could feel the hope bleed from his soul as shame slithered in. A shame hard-fought and beaten. Until now. All gone in the blink of an eye . . . or a cold stare of shock. He looked away, unable to bear the loathing of the two people he loved the most.

"Answer me!" Beth's voice rose to a shriek, unnatural as it slashed through his numbness. He slowly looked up, meeting her gaze without wavering.

She shivered and took a deep breath. "Is it true?" she repeated, her voice an octave calmer, edging toward hopeful.

His eyes shifted from her pale face to Collin's, taking in his friend's parted lips and eyes glazed with shock. He could lie and save his life. Or tell the truth and save his soul. He shifted, his limbs and fingers dead at his sides. He looked back at Beth, and a nerve quivered in his cheek. "Yes."

Her hand flew to her mouth.

"Dear God, John, why?" Collin's voice cracked with emotion.

Brady's eyes never strayed from Beth's. "I was seventeen and very drunk."

Her face looked so fragile, so young—bone china, easily shattered.

Like their love.

Her voice quivered. "Michael said . . ." She paused, emotion bobbing in her throat. "He s-said you have a drinking problem, since the age of fourteen, and that when you ran away at seventeen, you lived on skid row as a drunk."

Collin turned away.

Heat braised the back of Brady's neck. "Yes. For eight months."

Her voice was so low, so broken, he had to strain to hear it. "And that you robbed your stepmother, stole her jewelry before you left."

His eyes flicked to Collin's back, bent and weighted. He clenched his jaw. "Not robbed, Beth. I only took what was mine—my mother's diamond ring, a gold watch fob, and brass bookends from my father."

Her eyelids fluttered closed, and she swayed on her feet. He shifted to catch her, but she jerked away to grasp at a nearby press. Her cheeks glistened with tears as she pierced him with a look of disbelief.

"Dear God, Brady, what kind of man *are* you?"

Conviction stiffened his chin. "A forgiven one, Beth. By God, if not by you."

"Forgiven?" She rose up, fingers clenched. He had never heard her voice so shrill. "Forgiveness requires the truth."

"You have the truth, Beth. You know what kind of man I am."

"Do I?" Fresh tears spilled, and she wiped her eyes with the sleeve of her coat.

Brady reached for his handkerchief, but Collin handed his first, his look guarded as he glanced at Brady. She wiped her eyes with a trembling hand and lifted her chin.

"Michael s-says you have a v-vile temper and that l-last week in N-New York, you . . . you got drunk and tried to k-kill him."

Collin stared, open-mouthed.

Heat traveled Brady's neck. He focused on an ink stain on

the wall. "It's true I had a drinking problem in the past, Beth, but I don't drink anymore."

She looked up, eyes puffy and raw. "So he's lying about New York, then?"

Heat gorged his cheeks, and he forced himself to meet her gaze. "No."

She listed against the press, the handkerchief to her mouth. A heave shivered her slight frame. "Is there anything else I need to know?"

"Only that I love you."

She shook her head, her tone lifeless, dead. "I don't know, John. I don't know if that's enough anymore. You've broken my trust, and I worry that . . . I'll never get it back." Her voice broke on a sob.

"Beth, please—"

"No!" Her once-gentle eyes darkened with anger he'd never seen before, deepening to a cold, dark blue. "You were the one man I looked up to more than any other—the perfect man. But you're not. Now every time you touch me, hold me, I'll always wonder . . . how many others have you defiled . . . and how many lies have you told?"

Her words drained the blood from his face. All at once he felt vile and dirty and unworthy of love, much less forgiveness. He closed his eyes, and a cold shaft of realization pierced his heart. It was over. Life as he knew it was over. He had lost the love of Beth and the respect of Collin. And nothing was left.

Nothing but rage.

In sobriety, he had never been a man of temper, but he felt it now, burning in his gut with murderous intent. He wanted to lash out, to hurt, to destroy . . . just like he'd been destroyed. He thought of Michael, and a spasm of violence jerked through his body like an electric shock. Dear God, he would kill him!

He ripped the apron from his waist, shredding the ties, and slammed it into the press with a curse. He heard Beth crying, but he no longer cared. Nothing mattered. Not Beth, not Collin, not God. In a blind rage, he strode to the back door and flung it open, shattering a pane of glass.

"John! Where are you going?" Collin gripped his arm.

He shoved it away. "To do what I should have done all along."

Collin blocked him. "Hurting Michael is only going to make things worse."

"Get out of my way, Collin, or I'll hurt you too."

"John, none of it matters, not to me." He shot a frantic look over Brady's shoulder. "Lizzie, tell him—now! Tell him it doesn't matter!"

"I'm telling you for the last time, Collin—get out of my way!"

"Lizzie!" Collin shouted. "Tell him now!"

Brady slammed Collin hard against the door, buckling him at the knees. He heard Beth scream, but it didn't matter. Nothing mattered.

At least not anymore.

❧ ❧

Brady slumped at his kitchen table, eyes glazed with alcohol and his conscience glazed with remorse. He tipped the last of the vodka from the bottle he'd stolen from Michael's hotel room—right after he had stormed in and vented his fury with a well-placed fist. He cursed as the final drops dribbled into his glass and hurled the bottle at the wall. It struck the pane of his favorite nautical picture and shattered it, raining a million tiny pieces over the sofa.

He rubbed his sore jaw with the side of his hand and grimaced. The ache of Michael's return punch throbbed far less than Brady's guilt over bloodying his brother. Michael would be a pitiful sight in the morning—black and blue, Brady thought. Not unlike his own conscience at the moment. He gulped the dregs of the alcohol and stared in a daze at the open Bible on the seat, littered with shards of glass. Splintered, just like his hope, over the broken promises of God.

The empty glass dropped from his hand. He closed his eyes and reeled. A painful sob rose in his chest. No. Not God's broken promises—*his*. He'd prided himself on being a man of God, honest and true. But he had never been completely honest with himself or those he loved. Instead, he'd presented an image of the man he wanted them to see rather than the man that he was. Not perfect, not holy, but fractured and broken. Like the nautical picture on the wall—an earthen vessel, not fit for holy things.

*But we have this treasure in earthen vessels, that the excellency of the power may be of God, and not of us.*

Brady groaned and put his face in his hands. He thought of his brother as he'd left him—battered and stunned. Michael bleeding on the floor, Lizzie bleeding in her heart. And Collin—a friendship betrayed by a man too proud to admit he was human. A wrenching sob broke forth, and he collapsed on the table, a man of sorrows, void of all hope.

*We are troubled on every side, yet not distressed . . . perplexed, but not in despair . . .*

His shoulders heaved as he wept.

*Persecuted, but not forsaken; cast down, but not destroyed . . .*

His ragged breathing slowed.

*For our light affliction, which is but for a moment, worketh for us a far more exceeding and eternal weight of glory.*

*Glory.* He raised his head, and through the fog in his mind, a flicker of hope . . .

*My grace is sufficient for thee: for my strength is made perfect in weakness. Most gladly therefore will I rather glory in my infirmities, that the power of Christ may rest upon me.*

Tears spilled from his eyes at the sudden realization. *Glory*— God's, not his.

He staggered to his feet, and revelation overtook him like a flood tide. Through the haze and sway of the liquor, God's Word pierced his consciousness with startling clarity. His weakness

. . . God's strength. With renewed purpose, he made his way to the door. He reached for the phone in the hall and dialed a number, grateful that his neighbors were at work and their children were at school. His fingers trembled, but his resolve was as steady as it had ever been.

"Mrs. Clary? Good morning, it's Brady. Is Father Mac in?"

He waited, and the stillness overflowed with the pounding of his pulse. A voice finally answered, and emotion flooded his eyes, choking the words on his lips. He paused to draw in a ragged breath and cleared his throat.

"Father Mac? It's John. Can we talk?"

Collin unlocked the door to his apartment and trudged inside, not even bothering to turn on the light. It was well past midnight, and his bones ached, not to mention his heart. He had spent the day with Brady, packing up his apartment before he left Boston forever. For Collin, this day ranked up there with the worst of his life: the day his father died, the day he went to war, the day he learned Faith was going to marry another man. He slung his coat on the hook by the door and paused, feeling as depleted as when he'd wakened from one of those mind-numbing drunks Brady had always nursed him through. He closed his eyes and swallowed the grief in his throat. *Why, God?*

He had lost a friend today. A brother, a partner, a man he would respect until the day he died, and the despair was more than he could handle. A silent heave shook him, and he put his head in his hands, desperate to fight the emotion lodged in his throat. *Why, John?*

But he knew why. What man could stay knowing he repulsed the woman he loved? Lizzie was young and naïve and ill-prepared to deal with a man chained to a past like Brady's. Forgiveness would come, Collin knew, but it would be slow. Too slow, and too late for John Morrison Brady.

A light flicked on at the end of the hall and Collin saw Faith standing, silhouetted in their bedroom door. She hurried to him then, bare feet padding on the wooden floor and nightgown flaring in the breeze. The moment she touched him, the dam of emotion broke and he wept in her arms. They stood huddled in the hall, the silence filled with his agony as he clung to her small frame.

She stroked his wet cheek. "Come to bed, Collin," she whispered. "You need your sleep, and we need to pray."

He nodded and allowed her to lead him down the hall, her hand in his. He sat down on the bed and kicked off his shoes. His eyes trailed into a hard stare.

The touch of her hand on his shoulder brought him back to the present. "Did you get everything packed?"

He sat, dirty socks balled in his hands. "Yeah, took us until after six to box everything up. The man had enough books to open his own library." He tossed the socks at the hamper. "He's giving them all away. A box to Esther, one to Cluny, one for us . . . and two for Lizzie. When she's ready."

"She'll appreciate that."

"Yeah." Collin said, his tone bitter. He stood and stripped off his shirt, then stepped out of his trousers. He hurled both in the direction of the socks.

"Was Cluny there?" Faith asked, obviously hoping to steer his thoughts away from the sister he blamed for Brady's departure.

Collin kneaded the bridge of his nose and sighed. "Yeah. Cried like a baby when Brady finally sent him home."

"He'll be devastated without him," she whispered.

"Won't we all," he muttered. He pulled a clean pair of pajama bottoms out of his drawer and headed for the bathroom. "I need to shower. I smell like Clancy's on a bad day."

A bad day. The worst in two long weeks of bad days. He closed the door behind him and turned on the shower, rotating the lever all the way to scalding. He brushed his teeth unaware, his mind too absorbed in the events of the last sixteen hours—the day his life would change forever. He swished water in his mouth and took a drink, spitting it out like he wished he could do to the sick taste in his throat. He discarded his underwear and stepped into the shower. The billows of steam flushed tears from his eyes.

They had prayed tonight. For the last time. And after a day of moving and an evening of reminiscing, John Morrison Brady had once again proven himself to be the man of honor that Collin knew him to be. John had wanted to pray for Lizzie and Michael, but Collin had balked. "I can't," he had said.

But he did, because John had taught him how. How to forgive and how to let go, lessons John had learned well, in far harder ways than Collin had ever known. He was a man of principle with an unprincipled past, bent on a path in which God would use both for his glory.

He would be a priest. The revelation stung all over again, as biting and searing as the hot water that pelted his body. A mentor to many instead of just a few, and a mighty force in the hand of God.

"Father Mac has connections," he'd said, "even for a late bloomer like me." There had been a smile on his face at the time, but Collin hadn't missed the grief in his eyes. Or maybe it had been a reflection of his own. The weeks had passed in a blur, moments filled with the necessities of leaving. He'd trained a new man on his press and spent precious time with Cluny. Shot hoops with Matt and made amends with Michael. Apologized to Lizzie and said his goodbyes to the O'Connors. But at the end of the day, most evenings had been devoted to the gym, a place where two men could talk and sweat and vent their frustrations. And be friends . . . for the very last time.

He turned the water off and reached for a towel, hoping Faith had fallen asleep. She would want to talk . . . and pray. And he wasn't ready. He exhaled a weary breath. *Please, God, maybe tomorrow.*

He turned out the light and opened the door, grateful for the darkness of the room. He moved to the bed and slipped under the covers, aware she was still awake. She nestled close to his side, and he braced himself for the questions. *How was Brady? How was he? Did they blame Lizzie?*

Her arm encircled him in a protective hold, and he felt her breath, warm against his chest. "You need your sleep," she whispered. "We can pray tomorrow. I love you, Collin."

Tears stung and he clasped her tightly, wetness spilling from his eyes as he absorbed her warmth, her love, her understanding. "I love you, Faith . . . with everything in me," he whispered, his words rough with emotion.

She snuggled closer, and he shut his eyes. Relaxation stole over him with the heat of her body and the scent of her hair, and he knew before long he would drift into a healing slumber. Not because he was physically spent. Not because he was emotionally drained. But because he knew—as sure as the steady beat of her pulse against his own—his wife's prayers would not wait until morning.

19

"Lizzie, look! Michael sent flowers." Katie's face was as flushed as her pink satin dress as she ran into the Bride's Room of St. Stephen's Church.

Lizzie turned at the mirror, effectively wrinkling the silk tulle veil flowing from her lace cloche headpiece. She smiled at Katie who held up a bouquet of red and white roses. "Now, why would he do that?" Lizzie asked. "With bouquets every-where, and flowers all over the altar?"

Charity arched a brow and swatted at the veil. "Because it's romantic, you goose." She stuck a pin between her teeth. "Now turn around. I can't pin this cap if you keep moving."

Faith eyed the lush bouquet, then glanced at Lizzie's modest nosegay of white and lavender daisies resting on the vanity. "I don't know, Lizzie, you may want to consider carrying Mi-chael's instead—it's gorgeous."

"But, why red and white?" Katie demanded. "Isn't he sup-posed to send all red for love?"

Lizzie took the bouquet from her sister, trying hard not to move as she read the card. *Can't wait to spend the rest of my life with you. All my love, Michael.* She smiled and sniffed the roses. "Well, red stands for love, and white stands for purity."

Katie slacked a hip. "Why? Because you're pure and he's in love?"

"I'm in love too, Katie Rose," Lizzie scolded playfully, tugging a curly strand of Katie's hair.

Charity groaned. "Lizzie, if you move one more time, so help me, I'm going to poke you with this pin."

"Well, you don't act like it," Katie complained, ignoring Charity. "At least not like you did with Brady."

Lizzie sighed and handed the flowers back to Katie, not anxious to discuss Michael's brother. She'd spent the last six months trying to forget that John Brady even existed, and this was the day she would finally turn that corner. "Katie, would you see if you can find some water to put these in? And then would you go get Mother?"

Katie shoved the tissue-wrapped bouquet under her arm with little or no regard for romantic sentiments. "Okay, but I'll sure be glad when this whole wedding thing is over. This stupid dress itches."

"Lizzie, I'm so sorry—your father had trouble with his tie." Marcy rushed in, looking more like an older sister than a mother. She had finally shingled her hair, much to the angst of her husband, and her lemon organdy dress complemented her blue eyes perfectly. Flaxen waves shimmered with glimmers of silver, framing a delicate face that now sported a dewy glow of excitement. She stopped halfway, her eyes flaring wide. "Oh, Lizzie, you look absolutely stunning!"

Lizzie turned to look in the mirror and caught her breath, really seeing herself for the very first time. The lacy cap covered all of her hair in the style of the day, with only glimpses of chestnut curls peeking out at the side. A pouf of tulle mounded at the back of her neck before it cascaded over her shoulders and pooled at her feet. With a feeling of awe, she touched the tiny seed pearls trimming her scooped-necked dress, a perfect complement to a single strand of pearls Michael had given her. Her white satin shift shimmered with a hint of lavender, accentuating the violet shade of her almond-shaped eyes, which now misted at the realization she was finally a bride. And then, for no particular reason, she thought of Brady, and suddenly her image swam in the mirror.

Marcy touched her arm. "Are you all right?"

Lizzie smiled and squeezed her hand. "Just a little nervous, that's all."

"Here, you don't want to look like a raccoon, do you?" Charity pushed one of Mitch's clean handkerchiefs into Lizzie's hand. She pulled three more from her purse and dispensed them to Faith and her mother, then kept one for herself. "Don't tell Mitch where you got these. I swear he hoards them."

Faith chuckled and dabbed at her eyes. "Probably because you have a habit of reducing him to tears."

Charity looked in the mirror and adjusted her elbow-length gloves. "Nothing wrong with a little emotion, Faith. You should know that being married to Collin. It's the mark of a sensitive man."

"Sensitive? Are we still talking about Mitch here?"

Charity's lips squirmed as she shifted the bustline of her dress. "Sister dear, you have no idea." She eyed the straight lines of her satin gown and groaned. "These shift-style dresses make me look fat."

"Stop it, Charity. You all look gorgeous, especially Lizzie," Marcy said with a proud smile. She glanced up at the clock on the wall. "Oh my, look at the time. We best move into the vestibule. I think I hear Mrs. Curry at the organ."

"Lizzie?"

All four women looked up with a start. Mary stood in the door, her face as white and fragile as the lace on Lizzie's dress. Lizzie rushed to her side and took her hand.

"Mary, you look sick. Are you all right?"

She shook her head. "No . . . no, I'm not."

Lizzie pulled her into the room and sat her down. She glanced up at her mother and sisters. "Go on ahead, and I'll be right out. Charity, will you grab my bouquet, and Mother, you may want to ask Mrs. Curry to wait on the wedding march."

Marcy nodded, her face etched with concern. "Don't be too long, Lizzie."

"Mary, can I get you anything, a glass of water, aspirin?" Faith asked.

"No—thank you. I'll be fine. I just need to speak with Lizzie privately."

"Come on, girls. Lizzie, we'll be right outside." Marcy ushered Faith and Charity out, then closed the door.

"What's wrong? Is it Harold?"

"No, Lizzie, not Harold."

"Then what?"

Mary looked away, her hands trembling in her lap. Her voice was barely a whisper. "I had a dream last night. A nightmare, really." She looked up then, her eyes desperate and full of pain. She grabbed Lizzie's hand. "Don't marry Michael, Lizzie, I'm begging you!"

"What?" Lizzie pulled away, her heart pounding in her chest. "Mary, why?"

She lowered her head, avoiding Lizzie's gaze. "I can't tell you the dream, it was too awful—but it's a warning, I just know it."

Lizzie bent to peer in Mary's face. "Mary, it was only a dream. Everything will be all right, you'll see. I know you're not fond of Michael, but he loves me, and in my own way, I love him. Sometimes, I just think it boils down to faith. I've prayed for this day since I was a little girl, asked God over and over to bring me the right man to marry. And I trust that he has." She suddenly rose and smoothed her dress. Her tone was quiet. "At one time I'd hoped it would be Brady." A faint smile shadowed her lips. "But a girl can't go up against God and a vocation, now can she?"

A knock sounded at the door. Charity popped her head in. "The natives are getting restless. Are you coming?"

Mary grabbed her hand. "Lizzie, please . . ."

Lizzie pulled her to her feet. Her voice was gentle but firm.

"Go . . . and find a seat. Everyone's waiting, and so is Michael. I'll see you after." She kissed her cheek. "I love you, Mary—like a sister."

"No!" Mary's cry paralyzed her at the door. Lizzie turned, shocked to see tears streaming her best friend's face. Mary's lips parted with a tremble. "If you marry Michael, I *will* be your sister."

Lizzie blinked. "What? Mary, what are you trying to say?"

Mary stumbled forward. Her eyes pled for mercy. "Forgive me, Lizzie, *please*. My name isn't Mary. It's Helena Brady."

❧ ❧

She was little more than a zombie slumped in a chair, barely aware of the turmoil going on around her. Somewhere in her mind she knew her mother was crying and her father was pacing and her sisters were hovering about, worried sick. She had never heard Mitch curse before . . . or maybe it had been Collin—but some low-hissed obscenity filtered through the fog nonetheless. And together, along with the sickening drone in her brain, the muffled sounds created a surreal nightmare from which she could not wake up.

Brady had deceived her. Mary had lied. And Michael had deluded her to the point of fraud. She closed her eyes, still reeling from the shock of it all. A family trait, no doubt, compliments of a heritage so steeped in shame, it was a wonder Brady had survived at all.

But he had, and no thanks to Michael, who had misled her and his own flesh and blood in the name of love. *Mrs. Michael Brady.* Lizzie shivered as if she'd had a near-death experience, then realized she'd had. Her future had teetered on the precipice of hell, mere seconds away from destroying her life. But God had delivered her. From a man who walked with God when people were watching . . . and danced with the devil when they were not.

"Let me in—*now*! She's going to be my wife!" Michael screamed and pushed through the door. He rammed so hard, Collin tumbled into a freestanding sanctuary light that sent both crashing to the floor. "Lizzie, let me explain!"

Mitch had him in a choke hold before Collin could right himself and the candle. "Not in this lifetime, you two-faced bucket of scum."

Michael tried to lunge forward, but Mitch jerked him back, twisting his arm behind his back. Michael groaned. "Lizzie, listen to me, please. I'm sorry I didn't tell you Mary was my stepsister, but I had my reasons."

Lizzie slowly rose to her feet and pried the diamond ring from her finger. With trembling hands she moved to slip it into his vest pocket. "Please don't waste your breath, Michael, I already know your reasons."

The blood siphoned from his face. He looked at Helena with eyes unnaturally bright. "What did you tell her?"

"Everything," Lizzie whispered. She moved to where Helena sat hunched in a chair, hand to her eyes and body quivering with silent weeping. Lizzie put a protective arm around her shoulder and looked up, a hint of defiance in her violet eyes. "Every vile secret you have."

He wrenched against Mitch's hold. "You lousy whore—I'm going to break your neck."

Mitch jerked a rock-solid arm against Michael's throat, stealing his wind. "Not if I break yours first. Just give me the word, Lizzie, and I'll take him out. I swear, I never liked the guy."

"Mitch, no!" Marcy cried.

Collin stepped forward with wild eyes. "Yeah, let me, instead." He raised his fist and struck like a rattler. "This one's for Brady, you lowlife." The punch clipped Michael in the gut, and he doubled over in pain. Marcy and Faith screamed.

"Collin! For the love of God, control yourself!" Father Mac stood in the door, garbed in white vestments trimmed in gold.

His voice rang with authority and shock. "Mitch, unhand him this instant. This is not the time for heated emotions. We need restraint and rational thinking."

Mitch grunted and shoved him away.

Michael staggered, then rebounded and tried to take a pot-shot at Collin. A ragged breath hissed from Michael's lips as Mitch choked him again with another muscled arm to his throat. "Tell *him* that, Father," Mitch said.

Father Mac strode up to Michael with all the cold deliberation of a gunslinger at high noon. He prodded a menacing finger into the pleated dress shirt of Michael's double-breasted tuxedo and glared into his scarlet face, unnaturally elevated from the press of Mitch's arm. He fairly spat his words. "You know, on second thought, Michael, maybe you don't need to be here right now. I think I may just ask Mitch and Collin to keep you company outside for a while."

Michael managed to gargle a curse before Mitch cut off his air.

Father Mac arched a brow. "Oh, that will cost you penance, I'm afraid. Say, twenty minutes in the back room with your ex-future brothers-in-law?" Father Mac glanced at Mitch and nodded toward the door. "You can keep him quiet in the usher's room. We won't be long." His lips twitched the slightest bit. "And remember, we're to turn the other cheek—and I don't mean his. Keep in mind it's a sin to bloody a man." He glanced at Patrick, the two exchanging looks of bridled anger. "Or in cases like this, maybe it's a sin not to," he muttered. "I always get the two confused."

Mitch and Collin took him outside. Michael's ranting faded as they closed the door. Father Mac set up two wooden folding chairs next to Helena's and offered one to Lizzie. She sat down and took Helena's hand, avoiding his penetrating gaze.

He sat and leaned forward, arms propped on his knees and head resting on clasped hands. "How are you, Lizzie?" he asked, his voice suddenly quiet.

His gentle tone immediately produced tears in her eyes. "Devastated, Father. Not just over Michael, but what he did to Mar—to Helena, to me, and to—" Her voice broke on a sob.

Marcy rushed to her side and put a protective hand on her shoulder.

Father Mac pulled a handkerchief from beneath his vestments. He handed it to her, then lifted her chin with a gentle prod of his fingers. "Lizzie, Brady has chosen to forgive all. You can do no less. But before we talk about John, I'd like to talk to you and Helena about why you called the wedding off." He looked up at Faith and Charity. "Would one of you mind getting your mother a chair, please, and perhaps for yourselves as well? Both of you can stay to support your sister if you like, but given the delicate nature of this discussion, perhaps Sean should take Katie and Steven outside for a while." Father Mac glanced up at Sean. "Is that all right with you, Sean?"

"But, I want to stay," Katie insisted.

Patrick grilled her with a look. "Defying your parents is one thing, Katie Rose, but defying a priest borders on sacrilege. I suggest you go quietly—*now*."

"Come on, Katie, I'll buy you and Steven a soda at Robinson's," Sean said.

She stalked to the door, lips pursed tight. "Bribery. That's a sin too, isn't it, Father?"

The door closed, and Father Mac turned his focus on Helena. "Mary—or Helena, I should say." He paused to run a hand over his face. "That's going to take some getting used to, I'm afraid." He drew in a deep breath. "Let's start at the beginning, shall we? Why did you lie about who you were?"

Helena peeked up with eyes as raw as Lizzie's, her face flushed with shame. "I . . . didn't intend to lie, Father, I promise. Michael needed Brady to sign the will before the inheritance could be distributed, and he didn't think John would do it for him. So he sent me."

She looked down and fidgeted with the tips of her polished

nails. "When I walked into John's shop that first day, it was obvious he didn't recognize me. I mean, why should he? I hadn't seen him since I was ten. And I wanted to tell him who I was so badly, really I did, but I was afraid. He was so warm and kind that I . . . I thought he would hate me if he knew who I really was." She bit the edge of her lip and looked up with timid eyes. "So I lied," she whispered, "and things went from bad to worse."

"How's that?" Father Mac asked, settling back into his chair.

"I not only lied to Brady, but to Lizzie and to everyone at Bookends. I never intended to stay in Boston for longer than a day or two, but when I saw John, I . . . I wanted to get to know him again. He'd been my favorite growing up, as well as my mother's. He was the quiet brother, but the kind one too, always letting me tag along when he went fishing, reading me stories, even playing hopscotch if I asked. Michael would make fun of him, calling him a mama's boy because John always preferred being home rather than out with Michael." She drew in a deep breath. It quivered out again in a shaky sigh. "I just wanted to see if he had changed, that's all. And he had—he was even kinder and gentler than I remembered."

"So you fabricated this life of Mary Carpenter. When you became close to Lizzie, why didn't you tell her the truth?"

She glanced at Lizzie. "I wanted to more than anything because Lizzie was the best friend I've ever had. The only real friend I've ever had," she whispered. "Except for John."

Father Mac studied her with a furrowed brow. "Then why didn't you?"

Helena put a hand to her eyes, obviously uneasy with what she was about to say. "Because I was afraid . . . afraid she would hate me."

"For lying about your identity?"

She lowered her head, one palm still obscuring her eyes. "Yes, and for not telling her the truth . . . about the kind of man that Michael is." She drew in a deep breath and suddenly straightened in the chair, her back rigid and her lips resolute. "Back when I first came to Boston and didn't return home after several days, Michael called me at the Parker House Hotel. When I told him I wasn't coming back, he flew into a rage, not only because I failed to bring John back, but because . . . I wouldn't be in New York anymore." Her shoulders cringed in a painful heave. "You see, I was convenient."

"Convenient?" Father Mac asked.

Helena looked up and nodded. Her eyes, glossy with tears, were steeped in shame. "I was his charge, his slave, if you will, to do his bidding." She shivered. "You might say he was blackmailing me."

Father Mac leaned forward. "Blackmailing you?"

Her chin began to quiver and tears streamed down her face. "You s-see, a-after John left home, Mother's drinking escalated until she was little more than a zombie, day in and day out." A hardness settled over Helena's features. "And Michael took full advantage. John had always been my defender, my buffer against Michael's cruelty, but then he left, and suddenly I was at Michael's mercy." A bitter laugh rasped from her throat. "Mercy. As if that's a word Michael knows anything about. I felt so alone, so lost. No desire to fight or even to live. I was little more than a shell, too afraid of Michael to stand up to him." She shielded her eyes once again. "So I did whatever he told me to do—whether it was right or wrong." Her body convulsed with a tearful heave.

"Helena, you don't have to go on—"

She looked up, her eyes almost wild. "Yes, Father, I do! Lizzie needs to know what kind of man she almost married . . . and I need to be free."

Father Mac exhaled slowly. "I see. So Michael was blackmailing you. Why?"

"He didn't want me to tell Lizzie who I was. He was afraid I would tell her about his sordid past and his countless . . . indiscretions with women. I tried to dissuade her without divulging the truth, but Lizzie always defended him, saying I didn't know Michael. And I began to believe that maybe I didn't. That perhaps he had changed. For the first time ever, I could tell he was in love, really in love. And I hoped . . . that maybe Lizzie had changed him . . . just like John had changed me. After all, I was no longer Helena Brady. I was Mary Carpenter, a woman who, according to John, was 'a new creature in Christ Jesus.' So I decided to keep quiet. Until last night."

"What happened last night, Helena?" Father Mac asked quietly.

Helena peered beyond him, lost in a vacant stare. "Michael was drunk when he came to my apartment. He seemed a bit melancholy and started rambling . . . about how he'd only started seeing Lizzie as a means to force John to sign. But he'd gotten caught in his own trap, he said, and fallen in love. Said Lizzie made him feel whole and clean . . . for the first time in his life. When he first started seeing her, he knew I wasn't happy about it, but he threatened me. Told me if I tried to stop it, he would reveal everything—to Lizzie and to Brady—tell them that I was a liar and a fraud."

She shivered. "I couldn't let him do that. I couldn't risk losing the respect and trust of the two people I loved most in this world. So I lied to myself, forced myself to believe that it would be all right if Michael married Lizzie. After all, she had changed him so much already, softened him almost, that I thought she would be good for him. I hoped she could reform him, eradicate his past . . . just like Brady had done for me." She closed her eyes. "But I was wrong."

Father Mac worked to appear calm. He rested his head on clasped hands, but his eyes burned with silent fury. "What do you mean, Helena?" he whispered.

Helena drew in a cleansing breath. "Michael is a man of strong appetites, Father. I know he loves Lizzie, but he's not good at being faithful, celibate. But I thought Lizzie had changed all that. I told him I was proud of him for turning over a new leaf. That's when he laughed and said a bachelor at the Parker House was never lonely. It was then I realized Michael had no intention of being faithful to Lizzie. Not only has he been . . . entertaining other women at the Parker all along, but he made it abundantly clear he had no intention of changing after they were married."

Patrick put his head in his hands, while Father Mac waited for Helena to go on.

"I told him I would tell Lizzie, but he laughed. Said that he didn't think I would, that I had too much to lose." She shivered and her eyes swam with tears of regret as she searched her friend's face. "But after last night, I realized that you had so much more to lose . . . and I . . . I couldn't allow that. Please forgive me, Lizzie, for letting it get this far."

"Helena," Father Mac leaned forward. The intensity of his tone captured their attention. "As far as the details of your past . . . have you received the Sacrament of Penance?"

Helena nodded.

He drew in a deep breath. "Good, good. Then as John said, you are indeed a new creature in Christ Jesus." He rested a firm hand on her arm and exhaled slowly. "And speaking of John, I'd like to ask a few more questions, if I may." He glanced at Lizzie. "Who in this room knows about John's past?"

Lizzie met her father's gaze across the room, while her mother took her hand. "Only my parents," she whispered.

He nodded and glanced up, first at Charity, and then back at Faith. "Girls, if you would be kind enough to step outside, I would appreciate it."

Charity squeezed Lizzie's shoulder and followed Faith from the room. When the door closed behind them, Father Mac turned back to Helena. "When Brady went to New York to sign the papers, he told me he met his stepsister—"

Helena caught her breath. "What?"

"He said he met 'Helena,' and that she confirmed the fears he had about his past."

Helena's lips parted as comprehension flickered in her eyes. "No, Michael wouldn't . . ."

Father Mac's eyes narrowed. "Yes, apparently he did. I have a hunch that Michael was well aware of John's inner struggles over his love for Lizzie and knew that his brother's deep-seated shame kept him from pursuing it. I think he wanted to keep them apart and used John's shame and guilt over his past to do just that."

Father Mac leveled a sober gaze on Lizzie. "But John and I had counseled for months before the trip to New York, and again the day after he returned. He had reconciled with God over his attraction to his stepmother at the age of seventeen and his affinity for alcohol at the age of fourteen . . ." Father Mac hesitated and turned back to Helena. "But he never could tell me for sure what happened that night with your mother. He said he remembered the two of them talking and drinking in your mother's room, and he admitted thinking—feeling things . . . he knew he shouldn't. They were both drunk and apparently intimacies took place, but he swears he told her no and fled for his room. He remembers nothing from that moment on . . . until your mother's screams woke him in the night and you stood there crying. He said she accused him of . . . seducing her . . . using her, and he simply didn't know the truth. That is, not until New York, when his supposed stepsister told him that he slept with your mother."

Helena gasped.

Father Mac shifted his gaze from Helena to Lizzie. "But even then, although he was bruised and battered from what he believed to be true, after a lot of prayer and soul-searching, he was finally ready to pursue the love he longed to have with you, Lizzie."

A hand flew to Lizzie's mouth, and fresh tears welled in her eyes.

Father Mac returned his gaze to Helena. "So, we need to know, Helena . . . Lizzie, me, and especially John . . . what happened that night?" His voice lowered to barely audible. "Did John have relations with your mother?"

Helena's eyes widened in shock. "Oh no, Father, never! And I swear I thought he knew that. My mother woke me with her screaming that night, and I ran to John's room, sobbing when I saw their terrible row. And, yes, she accused him of that, but I thought he knew the truth! Years later—before she died—she told me she regretted that night because it ruined everything that she and John had had. They had been so close, the best of friends, but in a moment of weakness, she had tried to become more, and his rejection had enraged her. It all happened so fast—one moment they were screaming, and then the next, John was gone."

"Did you believe your mother's story—that John had seduced her?"

Helena put her head in her hands. When she spoke, her tone was thick with shame. "Yes—until I learned the truth before she died."

Father Mac stood and pulled Helena to her feet. He enfolded her in a protective embrace, his jaw taut with tension. "It's all right, Helena. It's over. You've done the right thing, and now you're free from your past."

Her body shuddered as she wept against his chest. "But John . . . I thought he knew . . . knew it was all a lie. That the only demon he wrestled with was bitterness."

Father Mac sighed. "No, the devil wasn't about to let him off that easily. Not a man like John." His eyes flicked to Lizzie as she sat in a daze, shoulders slumped and eyes lost in a vacant stare. He sat Helena back in her chair, then squatted in front of Lizzie. He took her limp hand in his. "Don't blame yourself, please. John doesn't blame you."

She shook her head, and the motion dislodged rivulets of tears from her eyes. "No, John wouldn't. But I do. I've known from the age of thirteen the caliber of man he was, Father, but I blamed him anyway, for a past I was all too willing to believe." She squeezed her eyes shut. "How could I do that?"

Father Mac gently took her face in the palm of his hand. His heart twisted at the guilt he saw when she opened her eyes. "It's called humanity, Lizzie," he whispered, "and by its very nature, we are drawn close to the breast of a forgiving God."

Her chin trembled. "But I love him, Father, and yet I condemned him."

"As he condemned himself, Elizabeth. Consider yourself in good company."

She sniffed and pushed a tear from her eye. "In good company. Oh, Father, how I wish that were true—now and in the future."

He stood to his feet and smiled. "Then I suggest you stop wishing and start praying, young lady. Has John Brady taught you nothing?"

Her eyes misted as she rose to give him a hug. "No, Father, he's taught me everything."

❧ ❧

Lizzie went through the motions of getting ready for bed, but her heart wasn't in it. What was the use, she wondered? She wouldn't sleep anyway. At least not well, if the last month had been any indication. She finished brushing her teeth and spit in the sink, wishing she could expel the malaise inside as easily. But apparently it was here to stay, lodged in her chest along with the guilt that, lately, made her rib cage feel two sizes too small. She took a deep breath and exhaled, hoping to release some of the tension inside, but the motion only made her feel more depleted—not only of air, but of the will to breathe it.

She blinked at her reflection in the mirror, momentarily shocked by what she saw: a woman instead of a little girl. She took note of the subtle changes that indicated as much—the fullness of her heart-shaped face, now thinned and matured, and violet eyes, once so wide and wondering, now tapered into those of a woman in pain. After years of pining to grow up and leave her youth behind, she had finally arrived. Her eighteenth birthday had long since come and gone, and now, along with it, any chance of happiness she'd ever hoped to have.

She turned out the bathroom light and lumbered down the hall, praying that Katie had fallen asleep. Her little sister would want to chat, no doubt, and Lizzie had little to say these days. Not since she'd called the wedding off. No, since then, she'd existed in a fog of self-doubt and condemnation, wondering why anyone would want to talk to her, much less love her. She didn't deserve it. Not after what she'd done to Brady.

She tiptoed into their dark room, grateful to hear the even rhythm of Katie's breathing that indicated she was fast asleep. The sound was raspy and nasal, and Lizzie's lips softened into a tired smile. The poor thing, all stopped up by a nasty cold. She bent to tuck her sister in, then leaned to kiss her cheek.

"Give her a restful sleep, dear God," she whispered, "and help her to get well." She crawled into her own bed and blinked at the ceiling, fighting the usual prick of tears in her eyes. "And I'll take the same, if you're so inclined, Lord, although I would certainly understand if you're not."

She turned on her side, and then the other, but as usual these nights, all positions of comfort evaded her. Her body felt heavy, but her eyelids were not, and so she stared, her gaze lost in a wide shaft of moonlight. The hands on the clock slowly ticked by, and she considered trudging downstairs to read one of her books in the parlor, but even that held no appeal. How could she lose herself in the fantasy of romance now, after it had deluded her so completely? She had staked everything—her heart, her hopes—on happily ever after with the man of her dreams. Only her dreams had become a nightmare that was obviously here to stay. Now, she not only had to live with the pain of loving a man she could never have, but also the guilt of wounding him to the core.

And for what? Childhood fantasies that bore little resemblance to the truth. A critical lesson learned too little, too late.

She shivered and closed her eyes. There was no such thing as a fairy-tale romance, she had discovered, no such thing as a fairy-tale prince. Not when humanity stood in the way, with its inevitable failings and flaws.

With a heavy sigh, she rose from her bed and traipsed to the window, drawn by the solace of an inky sky studded with stars and a ribbon of moonlight. She donned her robe and slippers, then tiptoed from the room and down the stairs, grimacing as they squeaked on her descent. Unwilling to evoke painful memories, she avoided the front porch altogether and made her way through the kitchen and out the back door. She sank into the porch swing with a broken sob, overcome with one single thought: *I've ruined my life forever.*

The sounds of night with its crooning crickets and hooting owls was suddenly disrupted by the creak of the back door. "Trouble sleeping again, darlin'?"

Lizzie's head jolted up. "Father, did I waken you?"

He quietly shut the screen door and settled down beside her. He hooked an arm around her shoulder and tucked her close. "No, Lizzie, I was up. Couldn't sleep, either." He rested his head against hers and released a weary breath. "Because of you."

She burrowed into his hold and swiped at the tears in her eyes. "I'm sorry, Father, but I'm trying to be happy, really I am."

"I know, darlin', but I guess it seems pretty impossible right about now, doesn't it?"

With a nod of her head, she sighed against his shoulder. She felt the rise and fall of his chest as he drew in a deep breath and exhaled again. When he finally spoke, his voice was tender and low. "Believe it or not, darlin', that's how it was for me when I cut myself off from your mother last year. It was like a slow death, Lizzie. Everything was a struggle—living, breathing, sleeping."

"I know, I remember how awful it was for all of us, especially you and Mother." She hesitated for several seconds. "What changed, Father . . . to turn it all around?"

His deep chuckle vibrated against her cheek. "Your mother's bulldog tenacity in loving me and forgiving me in the face of my anger. Despite the fact that I treated her horribly, she never stopped trusting God nor applying his precepts, not once. If she had given in to her own anger and bitterness, I shudder to think what might have happened. But she knew she couldn't, that she had to be strong, because I couldn't be. I was too steeped in sin."

Lizzie pulled away to study his face. "Sin?"

He nodded and exhaled. "Anger and bitterness. I tried my best to forgive her, to let it go, but I couldn't seem to do it, no matter how much I prayed."

Her sigh was heavy. "I know the feeling. I've been praying for a month now that God would heal my broken heart and give me joy again, but I can't seem to shake this gloom."

He kissed the top of her head. "And you've forgiven Brady and Michael and Helena, correct?"

"Completely. I'll admit, it took some time to let my anger toward Michael go, but I honestly feel that I have."

"So your heart is free of sin, then?"

"I think so."

"That's good, darlin', because the Bible says that if we regard iniquity in our hearts, the Lord will not hear our prayers." He paused. "Are you feeling sorry for yourself, then?"

Lizzie blinked. Her cheek twitched against the smooth cotton of her father's robe. She didn't answer.

"Because if you are," he continued in a quiet tone, "that could be your culprit. I learned that the hard way with your mother. No matter how hard I prayed to forgive her and let go, I couldn't seem to do it. Finally realized I was weighted down under a mountain of self-pity. Trouble is, it's one of those sins nobody thinks about. Insidious, but it will take you down, Lizzie, trust me."

She sighed. "I guess I've been mired in it for the last month, haven't I?"

He chuckled. "Keep in mind that I still hold the record, little girl. Almost two months before I saw the light. Don't wait that long, Lizzie. Exchange that poor-me attitude for a heart of gratitude. You have good friends and a family who love you more than you can imagine. And someday, you'll have a good man too." He kissed her head again and rose to his feet. "Now we best be getting some sleep, I think, or we'll both be feeling a wee bit sorry for ourselves come morning. You coming?"

Lizzie looked up. "In a bit, Father. But first, I think I need some time alone."

"Don't be too late. You don't want to be dragging in the morning."

He turned to go, and all at once, the sight of his tall, sturdy frame flooded her with a profound sense of peace and gratitude. He was her father, faithful and true, loving her, protecting her . . . no matter what.

*Just like God.*

Her heart swelled with love for the tired man before her. "Daddy, wait!" She jumped to her feet and clutched him tightly about the waist, tears of joy stinging her eyes. "Oh, Daddy, I love you so much."

His strong arms swallowed her up in a voracious hug, and the waver in his voice matched hers to a quiver. "And I you, darlin', and I you. Now you say your prayers, Lizzie, then hustle yourself upstairs and get some sleep, eh?" He tweaked her chin. "And while you're at it, say a few for me, darlin'. Morning's looking awfully close."

# 20

"Father! Troll Face is cheating again."

Brady hesitated, arms extended midair and fingers poised on the basketball, trying to decide what was more important at the moment—correcting Leroy for the twentieth time or making the shot. His jaw shifted to the right and he let the ball go, allowing it to arc into the net with a satisfying swoosh. A chorus of groans echoed throughout the weedy blacktop parking lot of St. Mary's Seminary, and Brady hung his head, his satisfaction short-lived. *Good job, "Father,"* he thought to himself, *you just trounced a group of ten-year-olds.*

Brady palmed the ball and tucked it under his arm, wondering if it was unseasonably warm for late May or if he was just out of shape from lack of Clancy's gym the past seven months. He squinted up at the sweltering sun and silently bemoaned the ill-fitting black cassock he wore, longing for the cool comfort of one of his old, ragged T-shirts. It was one of the few things he disliked about this place—this dismal one-piece garb, too tight and too hot to suit him.

A cool breeze ruffled the back of his head and he closed his eyes, taking in the sounds of Baltimore. He was grateful for the diversion of a city street littered with wild weeds and even wilder children. The blare of horns and laughter merged with the fresh smell of bread and asphalt, creating an atmosphere that took him far away from the pain of printer's ink, lilac water, and Pears soap.

Most of the time.

A thundercloud edged over the sun, and he opened his eyes to shadows that matched those in his mind. He took a deep breath and proceeded to roll the sleeves of his cassock, biting back a grin as he studied the tragic face of Leroy Davis. "Leroy, if I hear the name Troll Face one more time, you're off the court for a week. Understood?"

"But, Father—" The whites of Leroy's eyes went wide, contrasting sharply with the deep ebony of his skin, which now glistened with a sheen of sweat.

"Understood?" Brady repeated. He latched a palm to the back of Leroy's neck in playful coercion, tickling until Leroy squirmed with giggles.

"Yes, Father," Leroy croaked.

Brady let go, shaking his head. It did no good to remind these street urchins that he hadn't earned that title just yet. To them, he was Father Brady, basketball hero in priestly garb, and there was little he could say to change that. He glanced at his watch. "Good, then we have time for another game before I have to go in."

"I'm on Father's team this time." Timothy "Troll Face" Troller started to hop in the air with considerable agility given a pudgy body that sported more freckles than pounds. "I'm sick of losing."

"Yeah, ten years is a long time to be a loser." Jerome "Geronimo" Blackwell flicked the back of Timothy's sweat-soaked head.

"Ow! Father, he hit me—"

Brady leveled a stern gaze in Jerome's direction, causing the lanky boy to shoot a sheepish grin. "Sorry, Father."

Brady cocked a hip. "I'm not the one you flicked, Jerome."

"Yeah, I am!" Timothy folded balloon-size arms across a barrel chest and waited, his freckles bunched in a frown.

With a roll of his eyes, Jerome puffed out a sigh. "Sorry, Troll Fa—"

Brady angled a brow.

"Sorry, Tim."

Brady handed the ball to Timothy and winked. "Okay, Tim, you and Murphy are captains . . . and you pick first."

"No fair, Father, he'll pick you!" Murphy wailed.

"Yeah, and Murphy'll pick me," Jerome moaned.

Brady rolled his neck and laughed. "It's just a game, boys, not life and death. We'll go easy on you, I promise."

"Speak for yourself, Father, I plan to crush them like a—"

"John!"

Brady glanced up to see Father Hannifin waving from the second-story window of the brick seminary on the other side of Paca Street. The priest leaned out the window and put a hand to his mouth.

"You have a visitor. You can take it in my study."

Brady blinked, then waved his acknowledgment. *Had to be Father Mac. No one else even knew he was here.* His jaw tightened. He had wanted a clean break. No letters, no contact, no memories. Father Mac had argued with him, but Brady had insisted. A frown puckered his brow. *Then why was Matt here?*

Brady tapped Timothy on the head. "Okay, bud, I gotta go, so it's all yours. You still get first pick." He gave Jerome the evil eye. "And I want the names of anybody who gives you any trouble, okay?"

"You coming back, Father?" Timothy asked with hopeful eyes.

"Not today, bud, but I'll see you all tomorrow, same time, same place." He ruffled Tim's hair. "Make sure you return the ball to Father Lopez before you head home, you hear?"

"Yes, sir."

Brady sprinted toward the door, shooting a grin over his shoulder. "And practice hard. I expect someone to take me on one of these days."

Brady waited for a Model T to putter by before crossing the street, his thoughts in a jumble as he shot in the back door and vaulted the steps two at a time. He was huffing when he finally reached Father Hannifin's study. He paused, hands on his knees to catch his breath, then knocked on the door.

"Come on in, John."

Father Hannifin stood at his desk with a smile on his face that didn't quite match the concern in his eyes or the serious slope of his brows. Brady's eyes flicked from the elderly chancellor to Father Mac, who sat on a divan across the room.

Matt stood to his feet and walked over. He pumped Brady's hand with a solid grip. "John, it's good to see you." A twinkle lit his eyes. "And good to see you're sharpening your basketball skills with such keen competition."

Brady's lips quirked into a wry smile. "Hate to tell you, Father, but the competition here is actually a step up."

Father Mac laughed and slapped him on the shoulder. "You look good, John. Seminary life must agree with you."

Brady glanced at Father Hannifin with a smile. "Well, it's not easy by a long shot, but I think I'm holding my own."

"Well, if you two don't mind, I have a class to attend to." Father Hannifin picked up a portfolio and rounded his desk to shake Matt's hand. "It's been good to visit with you again, Matt. Are you sure you can't stay the night?"

"I wish I could, but I need to get back. It's a long drive to Boston, so I'll leave right after I speak with John."

Father Hannifin nodded, then glanced at John as he headed for the door. "Take your time. I'll let Father Lyons know you won't make class this afternoon." He slipped out a side door and closed it with a somber click.

Father Mac sat down on one of two wooden chairs in front of the chancellor's desk and angled toward Brady.

Brady followed suit and drew in a deep breath. "I'm glad to see you, Matt, but why are you here?"

Father Mac ignored the question. He pursed his lips and

studied Brady's face for a moment. "Are you happy here, John?"

Happy? Brady sank back and forced a smile, forearms flat on the arms of the chair. "As happy as I can be, given what's happened. I think a better word to describe how I feel is peace. I can honestly say I'm at peace for the first time in my life."

"No grudges, then?"

Brady closed his eyes and began to massage the bridge of his nose. Grudges? Toward Michael for betraying him? Toward Lizzie for not loving him? Hurt that felt the size of a basketball bobbed in his throat. He opened his eyes and managed a smile. "I'm working on it . . . and praying like a fiend."

The corners of Father Mac's mouth flickered.

"So! Since you're here, how is Boston?"

Father Mac propped elbows on the arms of the chair, hands tented. He assessed Brady through hooded eyes. "You mean, how's Beth?"

Brady flinched. Just the sound of her name produced a slash of sadness that unnerved him completely. He stood to his feet and wandered to the window, struggling to keep his voice light. "And Collin, and Cluny and all the rest."

Father Mac chuckled. "Well, Collin and Cluny are fine, of course. Collin's taken Cluny under his wing since you left, which is a good thing because now Cluny actually wins at basketball."

Brady grinned out the window.

"But Beth . . . Lizzie . . . well, she's fine too, I suppose . . ."

Brady stared, his heart slowing to the pace of the watery wisps of clouds easing across the pewter sky. "So, marriage agrees with her then."

Matt's tone was hesitant. "Well, not marriage so much as . . . the escape of it."

The words moved in Brady's brain in slow motion, like the clouds drifting before him. He turned. His eyes locked on Matt's. "The escape of it? What's that supposed to mean?"

"It means she didn't marry Michael."

Brady blinked. Relief flooded him against his will. "Why not?"

Father Mac's gaze never wavered from his. "Because the day of the wedding, your stepsister Helena told Lizzie that Michael's been cheating on her all along and had no intention of stopping after they were married."

He felt the blood leach from his face. "Dear God, no . . ."

"So Lizzie called the wedding off while Collin and Mitch sent Michael packing." Father Mac's lips twisted. "And none too gently, I understand."

Brady sagged into the chair with a sick feeling in his gut. He dropped his head into his hand. "God help her, she must hate us. Deceived by both Bradys."

Father Mac cleared his throat. "I'm afraid it's all three."

Brady looked up. "What?"

Father Mac turned in the chair to stare at Brady dead on. The concern in his eyes tightened Brady's throat. "You see, Helena deceived Lizzie too. She allowed her to believe she was someone else."

Brady squinted, trying to make sense of Matt's words. "What are you saying?"

Father Mac spoke slowly, deliberately, his voice just above a whisper. "I'm saying that Mary Carpenter is Helena Brady."

Brady's mind reeled. Mary? *His stepsister?* But how could that be? His thoughts flashed back to the day she first walked into the shop, and the truth of it hit him full force. *Helena.* The same golden hair, gentle spirit, and haunted eyes he'd seen in her as a child seemed all too obvious now. He closed his eyes, seeing her thirst for God and her kinship with him. The image of their hug on the couch the night Cluny had found them suddenly burned in his mind. Heat surged up his neck. *Lord, no!*

He felt Father Mac's touch, gentle on his arm. "John, you didn't know. And you didn't act on it."

He swallowed and nodded. "Then who . . . was the woman in New York?"

"A girlfriend of Michael's, apparently. He set the whole thing up to play on your guilt in an effort to keep you away from Lizzie. But Helena's here with me now. She wants to see you—to ask forgiveness—and to give you a precious gift."

Brady looked up, his eyes moist with shock. "A gift?"

Father Mac rose and gripped Brady's shoulder. "The truth, my friend." He moved to the side door and opened it, nodding to someone in the next room.

Brady stood to his feet.

Mary stepped through the door, and he struggled to fight the emotion welling in his chest. She came and stood before him, hands pinched in a tight clasp. Her chin seemed to quiver as she looked up at him. "Oh, John . . ."

His heart squeezed in his chest, and he heaved her up in his arms with little regard for the tears streaming his own face. "Oh, Helena, I've missed you!"

"John, all those years, I've never stopped thinking about you." They clung for several moments while Helena's weeping filled the room.

Father Mac gently tugged on her arm, indicating the chair next to Brady. He pulled a handkerchief from his pocket and handed it to Helena as she sat down, then quirked a brow at Brady. "You have your own, I trust?"

Brady produced his from the pocket of his cassock, feeling pretty foolish as he wiped his eyes. "This thing lacks comfort and is as hot as the devil, but at least it has deep pockets."

Father Mac grinned. "You're not here for the wardrobe, John."

"No, I'm not. It's not exactly a selling point, Father." He took Helena's hand and smiled. "You're beautiful, Helena. I always knew you would be."

She blushed. "Not on the inside. Not until you."

It was his turn to blush.

She laid her hand on top of his. "I'm sorry, John. Sorry it took me so long to confirm to you what I already know. You're a man of principle. Something I knew nothing about until I met you for the second time. If only . . . if only I hadn't deceived you, maybe all of this could have been avoided. Forgive me, John, please."

He lifted her chin with his finger. "Helena, we share the same past. You don't have to explain yourself to me. All that matters now is that the blood of Christ has set us both free."

A smile quivered on her lips. "No, John, that's not all that matters. The truth matters, and I want you to know it." She paused and drew in a deep breath, her eyes finally meeting his. "That night that I found you and Mother fighting in your room . . . I want you to know that what she accused you of didn't happen. She confessed it to me before she died. Said she wanted to hurt you as badly as you had hurt her, and when she found you passed out, she took a gamble that you wouldn't remember much of what went on. So she lied." Mary leaned forward and put a gentle hand on Brady's arm. "Nothing happened, John, I swear."

Brady stared, the meaning in her words soothing his tortured soul like the balm of Gilead.

"It wasn't until she became sick and accepted the Lord that she confessed and asked my forgiveness. She said she loved you, John, and had hoped the guilt would drive you back to her. But you left instead, and it crushed her. Because you see, she may have married your father, but it was you she fell in love with, no matter the age difference." Helena's eyes welled with tears. "She was a twenty-five-year-old woman who had lost her soul. A little girl with a strong penchant for bourbon . . . and her seventeen-year-old stepson. When you told her no, you destroyed her world."

Brady blinked to diffuse the wetness in his eyes. "No, Helena," he whispered, "sin destroyed her world, just like it did mine. But our God delivered us. I'm glad Lucille found the truth before she died."

Helena shuddered. "But Michael hasn't, John, and my heart grieves for him."

Brady stroked her cheek, her tears wet against his palm. "Not yet, Helena, but I have hope. Prayer is a powerful thing."

She nodded and dabbed her eyes with the handkerchief.

Father Mac rose from the sofa. "Helena, we need to be on our way soon. Would you mind if I had a few words with John alone before we leave? I'm sure he'll walk us out to the car, and you can say your goodbyes then."

Brady stood and helped her to her feet. She sniffed, and her smile was shaky. "Thank you for understanding, John, and for being such a wonderful brother and friend." She perched on tiptoe to brush a kiss to his cheek and then gave him a tight hug. "I love you, Johnny."

He closed his eyes and squeezed her tightly. "I love you too, Helena. Always have."

She nodded and hurried from the room, leaving Brady to stare after her with a full heart. He turned to Father Mac. "Thanks, Matt. That was the most precious gift you could have given me."

A ghost of a smile flitted at the edge of Matt's lips. "Maybe not, John."

Brady slowly sat down on the corner of Father Hannifin's desk and folded his arms. He studied Matt with a narrow gaze. "Okay, what's up the sleeve of your cassock, Matt?"

Father Mac laughed and strolled back to the sofa. He sat down and lounged back with a faint smile on his lips, a telling contrast to his eyes, which were deadly serious. "Lizzie's free, John."

Brady's body stiffened, along with the smile on his face. "It's too late, Matt."

"Why?"

"*Why?*" Brady's brows shifted a full inch above his eyes, which were wide with disbelief. "Because I'm going to be a priest, or have you forgotten the strings you pulled to get me in here?"

"No, nor the reason you asked me to."

Brady glared. "I asked because I have a calling."

Father Mac never blinked. "No, you asked because you were running away."

Brady gouged the back of his neck in frustration. "Then why the devil did you do it?"

"Because at the time, it seemed like the right thing to do. And you would have made a great priest."

Brady slammed a fist on the desk. "*Will* make a great priest, Matt! Nothing's changed."

"No, nothing's changed. You still love Lizzie, and you're still running away."

Brady swore under his breath and strode to the window.

"That may be a first, John—swearing in the Chancellor's office."

There was a note of levity in his tone that Brady didn't appreciate. He stared out the window, eyes fixed hard on the boys shooting baskets in the empty lot across the street. He was forging relationships with those boys, making a difference in their lives, drawing them to God. Just like he'd done with Cluny. He closed his eyes and saw Gram's freckle-faced boy, and a pang of homesickness hit him so strong that he bent over at the window, hands white on the sill. *No, God, why now?*

He forced his eyes open to clear his thoughts, only to spot a man toting boxes out of a small shop across the way. A rush of longing suddenly overwhelmed him to see Collin again, to feel the rumble of his favorite press, to smell the ink and the solvent, and, yes, even to attend one of Miss Ramona's blasted recitals.

"What's stopping you, John? Lizzie is all you ever wanted."

He spun around. "Not anymore."

Father Mac eyed him from the couch, his gaze penetrating. "You haven't forgiven her."

"I have, Matt, I swear it."

"Then you're afraid . . . because she hurt you once, and you don't trust her. And you'd rather run away than risk that again."

Brady stared, the truth of Matt's words piercing him to the core. He moved away from the window and slumped into the chair. He exhaled a weary breath. "You know me too well, Matt. I can't go back there."

"Never figured you for a coward, John."

Brady glanced at him out of the corner of his eye. "Well, maybe you *don't* know me so well."

Father Mac rose to his feet and stretched his arms high overhead. "I know you, John. Too well. Which is why I brought Lizzie here." He moved toward the side door.

Brady jumped up, his body going numb. "You're lying!"

Father Mac grinned at the look on his face. He rested a hand on the knob. "Nope, priests aren't supposed to do that, or haven't they covered that yet?" He turned the knob and opened the door, shooting Brady a stern look over his shoulder. "Don't give her any trouble. I got you into this place, I can get you thrown out." He disappeared into the next room, and Brady felt the floor shift beneath his feet.

"Hello, Brady."

His pulse took off the moment she stepped through the door. It had been over seven months since he'd seen her, and he wasn't prepared for the shock of it. No semblance of the little girl he'd once mentored remained in the woman standing before him. She seemed taller and more willowy than he remembered, lips fuller and eyes more violet. Her face had a dewy glow that was uniquely Beth, and her lilac scent carried across the room like a hypnotic drug. He took a step back, for once grateful for the clerical protection of his priestly garb.

"Hello, Beth," he whispered.

She took a timid step forward and pressed a delicate hand to the scalloped neckline of her blue silk dress. She inclined her head to his cassock and gave him a shy smile. "You look like a priest."

He sucked in a deep breath and took another step back, resting a hand on top of the wooden chair. "Not yet."

She nodded and moved forward, closing the distance between them until she hovered behind the chair next to his. Her tone was low, soft. "I've missed you."

He gripped the back of the chair, his hands slick with sweat. "Yeah, I've missed . . . Boston."

She hesitated. Graceful fingers lighted on the back of her chair. "Only Boston?"

He wasn't sure if it was the seclusion of this hallowed place or the fact that he hadn't been close to a female in over seven months, but the woman standing two chairs away put the fear of God in him like no seminary ever could. He knew then that Matt had been right. He was running away. And at the moment, he couldn't do it fast enough. He opted for safety and slowly eased around the desk to sit in Father Hannifin's chair, fortified by the heavy oak barrier that now stood between them. He drew in a calming breath and forged a bright smile.

"No, of course not. I miss Collin, Cluny, you, and your family."

His gut tightened when he saw the disappointment in her face. Suddenly she was his Beth again—eyes wide and vulnerable and that full lower lip shifting to the right as if fighting the urge to chew on it. His heart softened and he wanted to vault over that desk and pull her into his arms, stroke her hair, and make the worry go away. But he couldn't. Not this time. That would only lead her on, and his mind was made up. He'd made a commitment to God.

He cleared his throat. "I'm sorry about Michael."

She blinked. He was sorry? That she hadn't married Michael?

Her lips parted in hurt while her mind swayed at the gamut

of emotions swirling through her. After a month of prayer, she believed she'd done the right thing asking Father Mac to bring her here. And when he'd agreed without batting an eye, she felt it confirmed. And yes, she had been nervous, chattering like a magpie on the long drive down, certain that Father Mac would have liked to put her out at the next stop. The wait in the next room had been torturous, just knowing Brady was with Father Mac on the other side of the wall.

Her stomach had fluttered at first sight of him, bonded with a longing so powerful, it weakened her knees. He was far too tall and handsome for a priest to be, his sculpted features tanned and weathered as if he spent hours outside. Or maybe he was just flushed. The cinnamon-colored hair was considerably shorter now, accentuating the clean line of a stubborn jaw. And his dark hazel eyes, usually melting with warmth, seemed more than a bit wary. He was nervous, she knew, judging from the death grip he'd had on the chair, and the realization had infused her with the strength she needed—until he'd distanced himself behind that ridiculous desk. This was the man who had claimed to love her with all his heart? The man who hadn't wanted a long engagement? And all he could say was . . . he was sorry she hadn't married Michael?

A mix of embarrassment and anger heated her cheeks and she plopped into the chair, determined to have her say. She drew in a cleansing breath, forcing her emotions to calm. "Don't be sorry, John, I'm not. I cared for Michael—or the man I thought he was—but I realize now I was just running away."

He leaned back against the imposing leather wing chair with all the authority of an archbishop. His face was a mask as he studied her, giving nothing away save the slightest shift of a lump in his throat. He positioned his elbows on the armrest and angled his hands like she'd seen Father Mac do, fingers laced teepee-style, as if in a counseling session. Her mouth twitched. Something they obviously taught in the seminary, she thought, quite certain Brady's "counseling" would not be to her liking. He remained silent.

She scooted to the edge of her chair and folded her hands, garnering the courage to go on. "You see, I was running away from you, John. I think I've loved you from the moment we met, and whether it was the infatuation of a little girl or the deeper yearnings of a grown woman . . . my heart was in your hands." Her gaze dropped to her fingers, clenched tight on the desk. "A dangerous place to be," she whispered. She heard him shift in his chair and glanced up, heartened at least to see regret in his eyes.

She drew in a deep breath and exhaled, once more avoiding his gaze. "You turned me away more times than I can count, and although I understand why now, I can't deny that it cut me to the quick, each and every time." Her eyelids flickered closed, and she felt the emotion working in her throat. "Enough to make me wary . . . and enough to make me vulnerable—to Michael."

His chair squeaked as he leaned forward. "Beth, please—"

She put a hand up and lowered her head, her closed lids twitching with resolve. "No, John, let me finish . . . please. This is . . . hard enough as it is."

The chair squealed once again as he eased back, and she inhaled as if sucking in strength. "When you returned from New York and asked me to marry you, I was overjoyed . . . but I was also afraid. My trust was fragile, John, shattered too many times by my own foolish hopes and dreams. But I loved you so much, I thought . . . I hoped . . . that my trust in you would be restored." She hesitated, then placed a hand to her eyes to shield her face. "When Michael told me about your past, I was devastated, stunned that in all the years I'd opened my heart to you, you never once trusted me with yours. Suddenly all I could think of was that the man I revered and loved since the age of thirteen was not the man I knew at all. In one fell swoop, all my fairy-tale dreams came crashing down, and I hated you for that—for what Michael said you did, for hiding the depravity of your past, for always touting the truth and then keeping it from me." She shuddered involuntarily, resting a trembling hand on the desk. "But most of all, I hated you for breaking my trust and wounding my soul."

She felt the warmth of his fingers as he reached for her hand, and his whisper was as taut as the arm he extended across the desk. "I never meant to hurt you, Beth."

She looked up into his eyes then, and the grief she saw mingled with her own. "I know. And I never meant to hurt you, either. To turn on you like I did." Her thumb circled tightly around his. "It taught me a lot about myself . . . and a lot about you. About who both of us are." A faint smile touched her lips. "We're nothing more than Christians, John—human beings with clay feet and a strong God. You asked for my forgiveness before you left, and now I'm asking for yours."

Moisture glinted in his eyes. "You're a woman after God's own heart, Elizabeth. I'm proud of you."

She gave him a feeble grin. "Does that mean I'm forgiven?"

He pulled his hands from hers and leaned back in his chair. "Forgiven, yes, but never forgotten. Ever."

Her pulse skipped a beat. *Ever?* She searched his face for some sign of promise, the faintest glimmer of hope that he would not turn her away again.

She realized she'd stopped breathing and quickly drew in some air. She exhaled. "Good, because I don't intend to forget you or even try. I'm in love with you, John, and I don't want to live without you."

His body went rigid, if possible, even more than before, seated ramrod straight against the spine of the chair. His color faded, and she saw the same press of his jaw she'd witnessed a thousand times, a John Brady trademark that a battle would be waged. He clasped his hands in clerical mode.

"Beth, you know I love you too, but things are different now. I've committed my life to God . . ."

An uncommon anger lifted her to her feet, slow and smoldering, like molten lava rising within. "So you're doing it again . . . turning me away—"

"Beth, please—"

"Even though you love me and we were meant for each other."

"No, Beth, I was meant to be here. God is the only thing I want."

She flinched. So he wasn't going to make this easy? *Fine.* Neither would she. She pressed both palms flat on the desk and leaned in, her eyes scorching his. "That's a barefaced lie, and in a Chancellor's office too. God is not the only thing you want, and we both know it."

He rose. "I don't want to have this conversation, Beth. My mind's made up."

"Good. Then let's set conversation aside." She shoved a chair out of the way and rounded the desk, too miffed to smile at the look of disbelief on his face.

He stumbled against the chair. "What are you doing?"

"Proving a point," she said with heat in her tone.

Charity was right. A kiss was the only thing this man would understand, the only thing that would remind him that he loved her, wanted her. And as sure as the shock on his face, she knew his desires were not just limited to God. And once she got her hands on him, he was going to know it too. When it came to seduction, she may not be Charity, but she did have one advantage over John Morrison Brady. She knew his weakness, his Achilles' heel. Her lips pressed tight as she focused on his mouth. She lunged, and the mouth in question parted in surprise.

He grunted and wedged the swivel chair between them, jowls clamped tighter than a mule's. "For God's sake, woman, think what you're doing! I'm wearing the garb of a priest."

"And the mantle of a coward, but that's not going to stop me, either." She hunched over the chair, fingers gripped tight on the arms. "One kiss, John, that's all it will take to send me home."

She tried to jerk the chair to the side, but he only clutched it to him, his breathing keeping pace with hers. "Stop it, Elizabeth! I don't want this."

"Then prove it. If that's true, one kiss will tell me."

He stared, fingers pinched hard on the leather and knuckles strained white as his face.

He paused too long and she sprang. She hurled the chair from her path and clutched him. He staggered against the windowsill with a hiss of his breath, and she fell against him, welded to his waist. His scent teased her—peppermint and soap and the hint of a basketball game—and the warmth of longing replaced the heat of her anger. He tried to pry her away, but she pressed in, melding her body to his.

"I love you, John, and you love me."

"Beth, *stop*!" She heard the fury in his voice and felt it in his grip. His fingers dug in as he forced her to arm's length. She blinked several times, and cold reality wrung hot tears from her eyes. In one depleted breath, she sagged in his grasp. A sob wrenched from her throat and she listed to the side.

She had lost.

He relaxed his hold. "Beth, you'll get over this, you will." His voice, soft and low, only caused her to cry harder.

She started to turn away and he tugged her to him in one feather-light motion. He wrapped his arms around her and soothed her with gentle rocking, like he had done in all the tragedies of her life. She closed her eyes and allowed the pain of loss to finally have its way.

"I love you, little buddy, and always will. But God has someone better for you than me."

"There . . . is . . . n-no one better than y-you," she heaved.

He reached in his pocket and handed her his handkerchief, lifting her chin with his thumb. His lips quirked, but there was pain in his gaze. "It's time for you to go," he said softly. He pushed the hair back from her eyes.

Lizzie's lip quivered. He bent to kiss her forehead, and a blur of black cotton swam before her. She closed her eyes and felt his lips against her brow, just like that night on the porch so long ago. Her breath stilled. *One kiss, Charity had said . . . that's all it would take.*

He slowly pulled away, and with little left to lose and everything to gain, she clung to his neck and yanked him down. He jerked when she took his parted lips by surprise, but she held firm, cleaving despite the stiffness of his body. A gentle moan escaped her, and she burrowed in, the taste of him sweet in her mouth. His body was rigid and his lips hard, but his lack of response only fueled her resolve. Anger and desire raged through her, and with one hand locked to his neck, she swept his powerful back with the other and pulled him closer. His lips parted in a gasp and she deepened the kiss, the heat of his body merging with hers.

*God help me, I can't do this!* His blood pounded through his veins like heat stroke, making him dizzy with every demand of her mouth. His body felt like putty, but his will was pure steel, and by God, he'd bend it to breaking if need be. To prove, once and for all, that he was right. That he belonged here, and she in Boston, married to someone else who would taste her like this.

But God help him, his rapid-fire pulse wouldn't comply, nor the dangerous heat searing all intent. He didn't want to be rough, but he had no choice. He shoved her away, and she reeled and staggered against the chair. He reached to steady her, but she pushed him away, tears of shock spilling from her eyes. She turned to go.

He caught her arm. "Beth, I'm sorry—"

She spun around, eyes flashing. "No, you're not!"

"Elizabeth, please, let's not end it this way—"

"Not 'us,' John, you. You and your pride. You're a matched pair." She lifted her chin, and a spark of determined fire glittered in her eyes despite the wetness sheening her cheeks. "It always seems to be the last thing you hold on to, isn't it? Too proud to confess your past, too proud to stay in Boston, and too proud to love me. Well, she's your mistress, John, so go ahead and put your arms around her and hold on tight." She pushed the chair out of the way and circled the desk, giving him a withering glare. "But I guarantee, she will never keep you warm."

"Beth, wait, that's not fair. The seminary is my life now, and I'm not a man who quits."

She paused, her hand suddenly limp on the back of a chair. Her head bowed. "No . . . only with me."

He watched her move toward the door and felt a stab of grief so sharp, it locked the breath in his throat. He *was* quitting . . . *her* . . . forever. The comprehension suddenly crippled his mind. Her heart was *his* . . . a gift from God . . . and he was letting her go. He stared down at the black cassock he wore, and felt the heat of it stifle both his body and his hope. And in one ragged beat of his heart he knew—knew this life he'd chosen would never fit.

*Just like the cassock.*

She touched the knob, and his mouth went dry. "Beth, wait . . ."

Her back tensed at the door, and in four desperate strides, he was there. His hand covered hers on the knob, and he turned her around, blood pumping through his veins like adrenaline.

"You didn't hear me," he whispered, "I said let's not end it this way."

With a deep groan that rose from the depths, he swallowed her up in his arms and crushed her to his chest while his body quivered at what he'd almost lost. "Oh, Beth, forgive me for being the most stubborn man alive." He set her back down and took her face in his hands, his eyes stinging with wetness. "I love you, and I've been so stupid and so blind with pride. Let me make it up to you, please."

She started to cry, and he bent to kiss the tears away. His lips caressed her wet face, her eyes, her lips. Her weeping grew, and he silenced it with his mouth, devouring her like a man with a craving no one could satisfy.

No one but her.

A dangerous heat engulfed him. He drew in a cleansing breath and held her away, arms tight with restraint. He glanced down at the cassock, then back up before giving her a crooked smile.

"I'm getting warm, little girl, and for once I can't blame the garb."

She laughed and wiped her face with her sleeve, her eyes glowing. "I love you, John, with all of my heart."

He tucked a finger under her chin and gave her a gentle kiss. "Good, I'm gonna need it, Elizabeth. I've got this thing with pride, you know."

She burrowed into his arms with a giggle that rumbled his chest. "Oh, really? Well, if there's one thing I have as much as love, it's patience—thanks to you."

He grinned and kissed the top of her head. "Mmm . . . your patience, my pride. Should be interesting." He pulled back and studied her with sober eyes, still shaken that his pride had almost cost him the most precious thing in his life. "Promise me, Beth, that you'll always let me know when my pride gets in the way."

It was her turn to grin. "No problem, Brady, and we can start right now, if you like." She stood on tiptoe and gave him a sweet peck on the lips, followed by a pretty jag of her brow. "The name is Lizzie, and I suggest you get used to it."

# 21

"What do you mean, something's missing?" Brady ducked low to glance into the small, cracked mirror over the washstand of the usher's room. He hefted his chin and ran a calloused hand over his jaw to make sure there were no stray whiskers before adjusting the knot of his tie. With a tug at the sleeves of his tuxedo, he frowned in the mirror. "What could be missing?"

Collin slacked a hip against the wall and folded his arms, his expression puckered in thought. "Mmm . . . let's see, vest buttoned, boutonnière in place, shoes shined, and tie looks good." He reached over and adjusted the handkerchief peeking out of Brady's upper pocket. He clicked his tongue. "Nope, something's missing, I can feel it."

Brady turned and huffed out a sigh, nerves strung as tight as the cords on Mrs. Leary's harp, its melody filtering in from the vestibule. "Don't do this to me, Collin, I'm a nervous wreck as it is. What the devil is missing?"

Collin exchanged a glance with Mitch, who was fiddling with Patrick's tie. "Wait! I know what it is." A slow grin made its way across his lips, a perfect match for the twinkle in his eye. He patted Brady's cheek. "Ink, ol' buddy. You just don't look the same without it."

Brady smacked him away. "My stomach's in knots, my hands are sweating, and my voice is two octaves higher. And you choose *this* moment to give me grief?"

Collin chuckled and squinted in the mirror to adjust his tie. "Just getting you primed, my friend. There's lots of grief in marriage, you know."

Brady cocked a brow. "For Faith, you mean."

Collin grinned. "Yeah, she's one lucky girl."

"Father Mac says fifteen minutes." Sean popped his head in the door. "Say, you boys look almost as pretty as the ladies."

"Except I can't get this blasted tie right." Patrick scowled at Mitch. "I thought you knew how to do this. This looks like a goiter, not a four-in-hand knot. Why can't you just tie it like yours?"

Mitch's jaw shifted back and forth, a clear signal his patience was in jeopardy. "Because I didn't tie it. Charity did."

Patrick gaped. "Saints alive, you're thirty-nine years old and you don't know how to tie a four-in-one?"

Mitch's eyes narrowed. A nerve flickered in his cheek, just above the noticeably forced smile. "Sean, mind telling Marcy her *forty-five-year-old* husband needs help with his tie?"

Collin chuckled and sauntered to the door. "Don't bother, Sean, I'm headed that way." He winked at Brady. "The air's a *litttttle* too thick in here for me."

Collin strolled across the vestibule with hands in his pockets and a whistle on his lips. He nodded at Mrs. Leary as she plucked away at her harp, then knocked on the door of the Bride's Room.

"Who is it?"

Collin leaned close to the door. "Open up, it's your husband."

The door inched open and Faith peeked out. "What do you want, Collin, we're less than thirteen minutes away."

He arched a brow and flattened a palm to the door, carefully pushing it open. "Then I suggest you let me in, Little Bit, because I've got two messages to deliver." He scanned the room and found Marcy futzing with Lizzie's veil. "Marcy, Patrick needs you now, before he and Mitch come to blows.

Apparently his assistant editor can't tie a four-in-one to save his soul."

Charity's mouth twitched. "I swear, sometimes that man is so helpless . . ." She winked at Lizzie. "And sometimes he's not."

Marcy spun around. "Thanks, Collin." She gave Lizzie a quick squeeze and darted out the door. "I'll hurry, I promise."

Collin saluted as she passed and then turned to give Lizzie a low whistle. He shoved his hands in his pockets. "Wow, Lizzie, you look absolutely gorgeous. Hard to believe it took this long to get that mule to commit."

Lizzie's giggle was nervous. "Well, he hasn't committed yet. He still has . . . ," she glanced at the clock on the wall, "a little over eleven minutes to back out." She bit her lip. "How is he?"

Collin wandered over to scoop an arm around Faith's waist. He gave her a quick peck on the cheek. "Haven't seen him this nervous since Miss Ramona cornered him at bingo."

"Good," Charity said with an evil grin. "He deserves to sweat a little after the palpitations he's given this family over the last year."

"Well, he's sweating all right, with palpitations right along with it. I swear, Lizzie, that man is plain goofy over you. He's been near worthless at the shop this last week. I'll be glad to see you put him out of his misery."

Lizzie checked her face in the mirror one last time, then shot him a grin. "Not as glad as me. John Brady has put me through more mood swings than Charity did Mitch, pregnant with twins."

"Speaking of the love of my life, how is he holding up?" Charity asked, giving Collin a wry smile. "Weddings, babies, or funerals—the man just doesn't do well."

Collin chuckled. "Another thing he and Patrick have in common, I think. Yep, I'd say he and Brady are pretty neck and neck as far as frayed nerves this morning. Only Mitch looks a shade more dangerous, kind of like it could go from a wedding to a funeral real fast."

Charity crossed her hands over her heart and pretended to swoon, punctuating it with a roll of her eyes. "Oh, be still my heart, he's such a romantic."

Marcy rushed back in, her face flushed with excitement. "I swear your father gets better looking with age, inability to tie knots notwithstanding. He looks so handsome in his tuxedo!" She sighed. "Eight minutes, ladies. Collin, the knot is tied and the war is over. I suggest you rejoin the ranks."

He turned to go, and Faith grabbed his arm. "Wait! You said you had two messages to deliver. What's the other?"

"Oh, yeah. One for Marcy . . ." The slow smile reappeared. "And one for my wife." In one sweep of his arm, he dipped her low and kissed her thoroughly. Then with a smoky look in his eyes, he tugged her back up and grazed her chin with his thumb. "That's just to let you know," he said, his voice warm and slow as heated honey, "I'd marry you all over again."

Her throat bobbed, and her cheeks turned a soft shade of pink. "Me too, Collin," she whispered.

Charity rolled her eyes and shot Lizzie a lopsided smile. "Explain to me how you and I are the romantic ones, and she gets *that* . . . while all we get is a mule and a grouch."

"Just lucky, I guess," Collin quipped on his way out the door.

The organ started to play, and Lizzie felt her breakfast rise in her stomach. She put a hand to her mouth and squelched a tiny belch. "Please, God, don't let me throw up."

Charity rubbed her sister's back. "That's normal, Lizzie. Not attractive, mind you, but very, very normal. Pregnancy and weddings . . . does it every time. Right, Mother?"

"Oh my, yes," Marcy said with a laugh.

Lizzie dabbed a handkerchief to her throat. "And hot . . . is anyone else hot?"

"Yes, it's close in here," Marcy said. She pressed a hand to her own cheek. "But hopefully the vestibule will be cool—"

The door flew open, and Mitch barreled through like a bull on the run. He made a beeline for Marcy and shoved Patrick's wallet into her hand. "This is bulging in his pocket. Says to carry it in your purse." He turned to go and stopped, staring hard at the bride. "You look beautiful, Lizzie." His gaze shifted to his wife and traveled from her face, down her body, and back up again. Movement flickered in his jaw, and the heat in his eyes took on a smoldering quality. "You know, little girl, it's downright criminal how you take my breath away."

He left as quickly as he'd come. Charity stood, jaw sagging and cheeks braised. She snatched a hymnal off the bookshelf and began to fan herself. "I stand corrected. The grouch does have his moments. And yes, Lizzie, it *is* hot in here."

Faith handed Lizzie her bouquet. "Come on, sis, you can't let him wait at the altar too long. He might pass out."

Lizzie sucked in a deep breath and nodded. She followed her sisters and mother out the door. One slippered foot in the vestibule, and her throat immediately swelled with emotion. Sean stood at the front of the line with Marcy on his arm, ready to escort her down the aisle. He turned and winked at her. Faith and Charity stood behind them, blond and auburn heads bent close as they whispered, and Lizzie felt the prick of wetness in her eyes. Two sisters—so different and so dear. She closed her eyes to stave off the tears, but the gratitude in her heart wouldn't allow it. *Thank you, God, for your hand in my life.*

She felt a gentle touch and opened her eyes. Her father smiled down at her, his eyes as misty as hers.

"I'd offer you my handkerchief, darlin', but I suspect I'll be needing it too. I'm not sure I want to give you away."

She grinned and pressed a hand to her heart, love welling in her chest faster than tears in her eyes. "You'll never get rid of me, Daddy, because you'll always be right here."

He nodded, and his lips pressed tight as if not trusting himself to speak.

The first chords of the wedding march vibrated through the vestibule, and Lizzie took her father's arm. She closed her eyes to seal the moment with the strong touch of his hand on her wrist, the scent of his musk soap, and the hint of pipe tobacco. She watched as Faith and Charity each made their way down the aisle, pinned by the gazes of their husbands who stood beside Brady at the altar.

Her moment came, and joy overtook her like a tide too long from the shore. She breathed in the sweet scent of lilacs and incense, and her eyes suddenly flitted to the bench in the balcony, expecting to see a flutter of white. "I love you, Jesus," she whispered, quite certain he was already well aware.

She blinked to clear the blur from her eyes, and Brady came into view, unleashing all her emotion. He stood, a half head taller than Collin, and his handsome face was chiseled with calm and shadowed with a ghost of a smile. A weak sob broke free from her throat, and he grinned, lighting his eyes with such love that her heart swelled with joy.

"I love you," he mouthed, and she nodded, never taking her eyes from his.

Her father stopped at the foot of the altar and turned to kiss her cheek. "I love my girl," he whispered.

Lizzie closed her eyes and hugged him tightly. "I love you too, Daddy. Thank you for everything." She felt his pat on her back and opened her eyes to see Helena, sitting with Harold in the first pew of the groom's side. Helena blew her a kiss, and Lizzie grinned.

And then it came—the bittersweet moment she'd waited a lifetime for. Her father let go . . . and Brady took over.

Patrick relinquished her arm, but not his hold. He watched Brady's arm sweep his daughter's waist, and a wave of melancholy threatened. He tightened his jaw and slipped into the first pew, unwilling to meet Marcy's eyes for fear he would break. She sidled close and he gripped her fiercely, wondering how grief and joy could share the same heart. She squeezed his hand and he swallowed some air, then released it in one calming breath. He bent close to her ear.

"Three down, one to go," he whispered, the levity of his tone a welcome relief.

She turned and smiled, and his boundless gratitude for this woman weakened him all over again.

"I love you, Marcy," he whispered, then took her by surprise with a sound kiss on the lips.

The haunting strains of *Ave Maria* drifted through the church, and Patrick settled in to listen, his heart full and his peace restored. A faint smile curved on his lips. With three daughters married and settled, life could only get easier, he thought to himself. The pew jolted as Katie shifted beside them. Out of the corner of his eye he saw her, looking like an angel in blue chiffon and ribbons. Until her elbow flashed, gouging Cluny in the side. Patrick groaned and closed his eyes. *God help me.*

Father Mac's voice rang out from the pulpit, and Brady's heart pumped with pure joy. "And the Lord God said, it is not good that the man should be alone; I will make him a helpmate for him . . ."

Brady stole a glimpse at his bride and swallowed hard. He could barely believe that within the hour, Beth would be his wife. He squeezed her hand, and his lips tilted into a smile. *Lizzie,* he corrected, and felt her gentle squeeze back.

*"And Adam said, This is now bone of my bones, and flesh of my flesh . . . therefore shall a man leave his father and his mother, and shall cleave unto his wife: and they shall be one flesh."*

Brady closed his eyes. *One flesh.* Joined together in God. Tears stung his lids, and gratitude overtook him. How did someone like him deserve this? The love of a good woman . . . and the love of God?

His eyes lifted to the cross over the altar, and he had his answer. *The love of God.* Real and true and so alive that the reality made him tremble . . .

He felt the flicker of Lizzie's hand in his and glanced down. She smiled up, and his heart turned over. Speaking of love that made him tremble! He gave her a crooked smile, enjoying the glorious warmth that flooded within. *Thank you, God,* he thought with a bob of his throat, and his smile made way for a grin.

# Acknowledgments

To my agent Natasha Kern and my editor Lonnie Hull Dupont—truly my "divine connections"—I'm still in awe that I get to work with both of you.

To the great team at Revell, thank you for your patience and support! Especially Cheryl Van Andel, and Dan Thornberg, for their great covers and inexhaustible patience, and to Barb Barnes, whose keen eye and kind heart has made editing an absolute joy for me—thank you, my friend!

To the Seekers, whose humor, talent and prayers have added so much to my life and kept me afloat more times than I can count.

To "Club D"—Judy, Linda, Charlotte, and Ruth—your input has enriched my books as your friendship has enriched my life.

To my dear friends and former coworkers Carol Ann, Tammy, Cynthia, Sandy, Anna, Betty, and Jenny—thank you for all of your support and help. Just as books come to an end, so do seasons of friends being together. But thank God our friendship will live on forever.

To my lifelong friends, Joyce, Charlotte, and Rusceilla—thank you for a lifetime of love and support.

To my precious prayer partners and best friends, Joy, Karen,

Pat, and Diane—you cover me with prayer and love, day in and day out. What a gift from God you are in my life!

To my aunt Julie, my mother-in-law Leona, and my sisters, Dee Dee, Mary, Pat, Rosie, Susie, and especially Ellie and Katie, for your continued love and support, and to my dear sisters-in-law, Diana, Mary, and Lisa. I am blessed to call you family.

To my daughter Amy, who shaped and molded the ending of this book—you are brilliant and beautiful, and I am so proud to be your mom. To my son Matt and daughter-in-law Katie—separately, you are amazing people, but together, you are God's definition of what a new marriage in Christ should be. I love you all so much!

To the love of my life, Keith Lessman, the best thing that has ever happened to me, aside from Jesus—life with you is the best romance of all.

And to the God of Israel for sending his Son to pull me from the pit—you are the air that I breathe and the joy of my soul, and I will worship you forever.

# Coming Summer 2010
# A SNEAK PEEK

*An excerpt from Julie's next series . . .*

Jack chuckled and massaged Katie's shoulder. "Hear that, doll?
You're a bad influence—both on Gen's figure and my wallet.
Anybody else want anything? I'm buying." His gaze flitted to
the soda jerk who was bent over the chrome and leather stools
with a rag in his hand. Jack put two fingers to his teeth and
let loose with a deafening whistle. "Hey, kid, shake a leg—we
have an order over here."

The "kid's" back tightened as he rose to his full height, revealing both a broad, muscled back and the fact that he was
anything but a kid. In a slow, deliberate motion he turned, eyeing the clock before facing them dead-on. A nerve flickered in
his angular jaw while his blue eyes glittered. He forced a smile
as tight as the short sleeves of his white button-down shirt,
which—Katie hadn't noticed before—strained with biceps as
intimidating as the man's penetrating gaze. "Sure thing, but
we close in ten minutes. Sorry, sodas and ice cream only." He
strolled to their booth with a casual gait as steady and slow as
the Southern drawl of his voice. "What'll it be?"

Katie felt the tension in Jack's manner as he cradled an arm around her shoulder. He lounged back against the booth, eyes locked on the soda jerk. "I know it's late, but the lady here says she's hungry. She wants a hamburger and fries."

The man's blue eyes flicked to Katie and held, his cool smile braising her cheeks with a rare blush. He nodded a head of white blond thatch toward a large sign over the jukebox. "I apologize, miss, but as you can plainly see, we don't serve entrees after nine."

Katie blinked. *And the world would end if he cooked a hamburger after nine?* Her stomach rumbled, and she straightened her shoulders with willful resolve. Suddenly, the thought of a thick, juicy hamburger taunted her—just like the annoyingly calm look on the soda jerk's face. Tilting her chin in a coy manner, she gave him the half-lidded smile that always worked wonders on Jack. For good measure, she propped her chin in her hand and resorted to a slow sweep of lashes. "Aw, come on now, mister, you can make one teeny, tiny exception, can't you? Just for me? We'll make it worth your while, I promise."

His gaze shifted to the clock and back, and then he disarmed her with a smile that made her forget she was hungry for food. "I really wish I could, miss, but a rule is a rule. But if I say so myself, my true talent lies in making one of the best chocolate malts in all of Boston."

She stared, openmouthed at his polite refusal. Despite the faint smile on his lips, his eyes seemed to pierce right through her. A second rush of heat invaded her cheeks. *The nerve!* She jutted her chin in the air and matched his gaze with a searing one of her own. "Yes, well, it's nice to know you have *some* talent, but no thank you. Not even if they're the best on the Eastern seaboard. Let's go, Jack."

Jack drew her close while his thumb glazed the side of her arm. "Come on, Katydid, settle down. I know you're hungry, but this guy is obviously new and doesn't realize who we are."

He cocked his head and flashed a patronizing smile. "We're some of Mr. Robinson's best customers, kid. So, tell me, what's your name?"

Drawing in a deep breath, the "kid" shifted his stance and exhaled. "The name is Luke." He shot a glance at the clock, then looked back. His gaze softened. "Look, I'm sorry, I really am, but Pop Robinson sets the rules, not me. The grills take forever to cool down, so we do them at nine. Hate to tell ya, but they're already clean as a whistle and shut down for the night. Now, I have to be somewhere at ten thirty, but if you give me your drink or ice cream orders, I'll get them as fast as I can."

Katie started to rise, but Jack yanked her back down. "That would be great, Luke, just great. Give us six of your best chocolate malts and six glasses of water, and then we'll be on our way, okay?"

"But I don't want his stupid ma—"

"Hush, Katydid, I do, and if Luke here is nice enough to make them for us, everything is jake." He smiled again, all the while fondling a golden tress of Katie's smooth Dutch Boy bob as it curved against her jaw. "Besides, you need something in your stomach. I don't want you cranky on the way home." As if to underscore his romantic hopes, his hand absently dropped to caress the long, glass-beaded necklace that draped the front of her silk dress. His fingers lingered along her collarbone with a familiarity that deepened the already uncomfortable blush on her cheeks.

"Sure thing," Luke said, his eyes taking in the intimate gesture with cool disregard. His gaze met and held hers for several seconds, unsettling her with apparent disapproval. He turned away.

Her ire soared. "Extra whipped cream and chocolate sprinkles," Katie said in a clipped tone.

He turned and nodded, his large, full lips pressed tight. "You bet, miss." He started toward the counter.

"And don't skimp on the cherries," she called after him.

He kept walking, but the stiff muscles cording his neck and back told her he'd more than heard. She forced a smile to deflect her embarrassment and took a deep breath. "Well, he's a sunny individual, isn't he? Night help must be hard to come by."

"At least he's nice to look at," Lilly said with a sigh.

"He's a two-bit soda jerk, Lil, with more attitude than brains," Roger Hampton muttered. "We oughta complain to Robinson."

"Humph . . . he's not that special." Katie's eyes narrowed while she watched him scoop ice cream into the mixer.

"Come on, Katie, you're just miffed because you didn't get your hamburger. The man is a real sheik and you know it." Gen shot a look of longing across the room, then gloated with a grin. "But it is nice to know all men don't wrap around your finger as easily as Jack."

Jack honed in for a kiss. "That's not all I'd like to be wrapped around," he said in a husky tone.

Katie squirmed and pushed him away. "Behave, Worthington, or I'll make your life miserable."

He chuckled. "You already do, doll, but I love every minute."

Katie ignored him. She observed the soda jerk laboring over six chocolate shakes and wrinkled her nose. "Get your specs out, Gen, he's more of a hick than a sheik."

Her frown stayed in place until the soda jerk returned, toting a tray of milkshakes to their booth. "Six Robinson's specials," he said, depositing a tall, frosty glass with a single cherry on top to each at the table. He set Katie's down last with a considerable thud. One maraschino from the mountain of cherries obscuring her malt rolled off, landing on the table with a plop. "Enjoy," he said with a stiff smile. "And let me know if you need more. I wouldn't want you to go hungry."

She swallowed hard, completely unsettled by his direct gaze. "I will. Thank you."

He laid the ticket in front of Jack, then returned to the back to finish cleaning up. She stared at her shake and sighed. Suddenly she'd lost her appetite. With a frown puckering her brow, she pretended to sip, all the while watching farm boy wipe down the counter out of the corner of her eye. Her mood darkened. Okay, all right—she'd give him "good-looking," but she'd bet he was dumb as a post.

"Hey, Katydid, wake up! You haven't even touched your malt."

The others were staring and half done with their shakes. "Sorry, Jack. Guess I'm not as hungry as I thought."

"Did that bozo upset you? Because if he did, I'll tell Pop he needs new help."

"No, no, please. I'm fine, really." She watched as Luke disappeared into the kitchen and ignored the warm shiver that traveled her spine. "Just a bit tired, I guess."

Jack shot a glance at the empty counter and grinned. "Well, we got something that just might wake you up, don't we, boys?" He reached for the laminated menu and set it on top of his untouched glass of water, then gave her a wink. With a quick flick of his wrist, he reversed it on the table and slowly eased the menu out from beneath the upside-down glass. The water sealed perfectly, a flood waiting to gush as soon as the "kid" picked up the glass.

Katie, Lilly, and Gen gasped in unison. "Wow, how did you do that?" Gen sputtered. "Ol' Luke'll be madder than a wet hen when he cleans this table."

"That's not the only thing that'll be wet." Lilly giggled.

Warren and Roger grinned and followed suit, careful to keep an eye on the back room. Jack thumped Roger on the shoulder. "Move over, we're leaving. Gotta get my best girl home." He tugged Katie out of the booth and pulled her toward the front door.

Katie skidded to a stop, heels digging in. "Wait a minute, Jack—aren't you going to pay for the check?"

"Nope, let Jerk Boy pay for it. That'll teach him to be rude to my girl. Come on, guys, hurry." He opened the door with a loud jangle of bells, and when Katie wouldn't budge, he hoisted her up in his arms and sprinted to his Franklin Sports Coupe parked down the street.

"Jack Worthington, you stop this very instant!" Her voice rose to a shriek as she fought his hold to no avail. She could hear her pulse pounding in her ears over the laughter of the group as they bolted for the car and jumped in.

"Come on, Katydid," Jack said with a broad grin. "It's no big deal. We're just having a little fun. Look, I even got you a souvenir." He plopped her in the front seat of his car and pulled her empty Coca Cola glass out of his pocket.

Her jaw dropped. She snatched the glass and shook it in his face. "Jack Worthington, you are nothing more than a brazen thief, and I will not be a party to this! Now, I am marching back there right now and—"

She darted out of the car, but he was too fast. He picked her up with a chuckle and silenced her with a sound kiss, tightening his grip when she started to scream and kick. "Aw, come on, Katydid, don't be such a bearcat. Jerk Boy had it coming, and you know it. Now get in the car like a good girl—we gotta scram."

"How about you scram *after* you pay the bill?" An icy tone confirmed that Jerk Boy was in the vicinity. His voice, deadly calm and barely above a whisper, packed as much heat as a threat from the lips of Al Capone.

Katie froze in Jack's arms, which went as stiff as his pale face. With a slow turn, they faced an apron-clad Colossus of Rhodes, legs straddled and face chiseled in granite. *"Put her down,"* he whispered in a tone as stony as his stance.

Jack lowered her to the ground and eased her behind him. "Says who?" he said with a sneer.

The soda jerk moved in close, towering over Jack by more than half a head. His rock-hard jaw, barely inches from Jack's face, looked intimidating with a full day's growth of blond bristle. His wide lips curved in a near smile, but the blue eyes were pure slits of ice. "Says me, you little piker."

Jack leaned forward and jabbed a finger in the soda jerk's chest. "Piker? Who you calling a coward, Jerk Boy? I'm not paying for anything, especially shoddy service."

The wide smile broadened to a cocky grin. "My service may be shoddy, rich boy, but I guarantee you my thrashing won't be. Trust me, your little girlfriend won't like it if I mess with your face, so I suggest you pay the bill . . ." He fisted Jack's Oxford shirt and jerked him up. "*Now.*"

Genevieve screamed and Warren and Roger jumped from the car. They circled Luke with fists raised, and suddenly it was Jack's turn to grin. "So, how's your confidence now, eh, Jerk Boy? Think you can handle three to one?"

Katie shot from the car and shoved Jack hard in the chest. "Stop it now, or so help me—"

He pushed her aside. "Stay out of this, Katydid."

Warren darted in with a quick swipe, and the soda jerk dodged with the grace of an athlete. His wide grin gleamed white in the lamplight as he egged them on with a wave of his fingers. "Come on, boys, I've lived on the streets all my life, so have at it."

Roger lunged, and Jerk Boy felled him like a tree with a right hook to his jaw. Out of nowhere, Warren rushed from behind, leg poised in a kick. Latching onto his shoe, Jerk Boy yanked him to the pavement with a sickening thud. Katie screeched in horror. She charged forward, only to be looped at the waist by Jack, who tossed her back in the car, flailing and screaming. He turned with a loud roar and rammed his body straight for the soda jerk, head tucked like a raging bull. In a deft move of his foot, Jerk Boy tripped him and sent him skidding into the street.

"Jack!" Katie bolted out of the car and ran to his side. "Are you okay?" She helped him as he lumbered to his feet, the right trouser leg of his gray Oxford bags torn and streaked with dirt.

"Yeah, yeah, I'm okay, doll. Just let me at that slimeball—"

"No!" She planted two petite hands on his chest and shoved him back with more force than her small size warranted. "You're done, Jack! Do you hear me? Or we're through."

He staggered back, a bloody hand to his head. "Come on, Katydid, don't talk like that—"

"I mean it, Jack, I swear."

She whirled around, her eyes singeing all of them within an inch of their lives. "Warren, Roger—get in the car. *Now!*"

"Come on, Jack, are you gonna listen to her? We can take this guy."

Fury pumped in Katie's veins as she spun around and glared. "So what's it going to be, Jack—them or me?"

He glanced from Katie to his friends and then back again, a nerve pulsing in his jaw. His tone was tight as he exhaled his frustration. "Get in the car, we're leaving."

Muttered curses rumbled as the boys stumbled toward the coupe.

Katie darted toward Jack. With a lightning thrust of her hand, she lifted his wallet from the pocket of his trousers as neatly as a veteran pickpocket.

"Katydid, what the devil are you doing—"

She ignored him and marched up to the soda jerk with fire in her eyes. At five foot two, she barely measured to the middle of his chest, but she didn't give a fig if he was seven foot five. No hayseed soda jerk was going to intimidate her! She glared up, annoyance surging at having to crane her neck. "How much do we owe, you roughhouse bully?"

He met her glare with cool confidence, sizing her up with that same probing gaze that had riled her before. "Two-forty-eight total, *miss*. Forty-five cents for three Coca Colas, a dollar fifty for six chocolate shakes"—a shadow of a smile edged the corners of his mouth—"three cents for *extra* cherries—and fifty cents for the glass your boyfriend stole."

She peeled off two crisp dollar bills from Jack's stash and

threw them at his feet, then spun around and snatched the glass from the front seat of the car. She turned and shoved it hard against his rock-solid chest. "Here, keep the change. Not that the service was worth it."

A massive palm locked onto her wrist before she could snatch it away. "Nice girls don't run with riffraff," he breathed.

**Julie Lessman** is a new author who has garnered much writing acclaim, including ten Romance Writers of America awards. She resides in Missouri with her husband and their golden retriever, and has two grown children and a daughter-in-law. She is the author of the Daughters of Boston series, which includes *A Passion Most Pure*, *A Passion Redeemed*, and *A Passion Denied*.

You can contact Julie through her website at www.julie lessman.com.

## Dear Readers,

I hope that reading my books has given you just a touch of the joy I have experienced in writing them. To pour my heart and faith out in a novel on behalf of the Savior of my soul has been a privilege beyond my wildest dreams, and I am truly grateful for your support. It is my prayer that in some small way, the words of these novels will infuse your own dreams with renewed hope, a deepened faith, and greater passion for the true "Author of romance."

Please visit www.revellbooks.com for discussion questions and more information about this book and the others in the series. Check out my website at www.julielessman.com, too.

Here's to a passion most pure . . . may ours ever grow for the Lover of our souls.

## Hugs,
## Julie

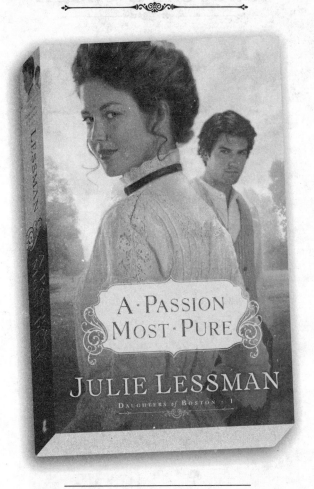